Lizard in the Grass

Lizard in the Grass

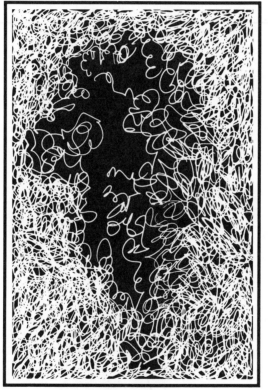

John Mills

ECW PRESS
Downsview Ontario
1980

The publication of this book was made possible by a grant from the Dean of Arts's office, Simon Fraser University. I would like to thank Dean Bob Brown for his assistance and encouragement, and Jack David and Robert Lecker of ECW PRESS for theirs.

Published with the assistance of The Canada Council

These essays were originally published in:

CBC "Audience"
The Fiddlehead
Georgia Straight
Queen's Quarterly
West Coast Review

Canadian Cataloguing in Publication Data

Mills, John, 1930-
Lizard in the grass
ISBN 0-920802-26-5
I. Title.
PS8576.I64A6 1980   C814'.54   C80-094662-6
PR9199.3.M54A6 1980

Printed in Canada by the University of Toronto Press and typeset by Erin Graphics Inc.

ECW PRESS
356 Stong College, York University
Downsview, Ontario M3J 1P3

To Sheila and to Paul

Contents

Part IV: Contemporaries

Introduction

The title of this book comes from a poem by John Skelton:

> Though ye suppose all jeopardies are passed,
> And all is done that ye lookéd for before,
> Ware yet, I rede you, of Fortune's double cast,
> For one false point she is wont to keep in store,
> And under the fell oft fester'd is the sore:
> That when ye think all danger for to pass
> Ware of the lizard lieth lurking in the grass.

This image of a lizard, or snake, lurking in the grass is relevant to me for two reasons: first, it serves as a reminder that nobody ever reaches a haven until the Grim Reaper takes him there and I can therefore use the lizard as a corrective to the smugness I now sense at the end of the essay entitled "Festival at S.F.U." Secondly, most of the pieces in this book were commissioned as extended book-reviews by the editors of *Queen's Quarterly*, *The Fiddlehead*, and *West Coast Review* and the lizard also serves as a good image for the literary critic since he lurks, or should lurk, with his aggressions quiescent and the saurian equivalent of a smile on his face in the presence of good writing but ought, when confronted with bad, flick the perpetrator with his satire. I have tried to meet this ideal as a reviewer and, as a novelist, have frequently been on the receiving end of such treatment. I have always found it salutory.

Like everybody else who has ever lifted a pen in Canada I have felt the urge to write autobiography. Unlike most of my compatriots, however, I can boast that I have succeeded in keeping it out of my fiction but the price the reader must pay for this benison is that he risks encountering it here in a form unmediated by the spirit of invention. I have also included, for their period flavour, certain essays I wrote in the sixties for the so-called underground press.

I would like to thank Kerry McSweeney, Fred Candelaria, Barry Cameron, and Dan MacLeod, not only for their permission to reprint this material but also for their encouragement and criticism.

Part I
Jeopardies

Arms and the Poltroon

I might never have returned to England as early as 1966 had it not been for Californians and my mother's fatal illness. My memories of the country where I was born and which I left with an oath, hurling my ration-book into the River Mersey, thirteen years before were almost entirely negative. But during the period I lived as a graduate student in California I met many people who not only swore by the place but who went there every year almost as though they were pilgrims of some sort. I was so busy agreeing with them, since they were on my Fuller Brush route, that I talked myself into a condition of nostalgia. Thirteen years is a long time, this was the kind of thing I said to people, and things have probably changed. The Brush buyers agreed. They were all of them rich and anglophiliac — the first explains their freedom of movement, the second our success in flogging them expensive rubbish. Their love of English institutions often transcended the borders of absurdity — men and women in black, coal-scuttle hats, scarlet jackets, and shit-catcher trousers used to prance on horseback in the field near our house chasing foxes they'd probably imported for the purpose over the brown, dusty hills of Palo Alto. They rode with packs of beagles and were led by a Kiwani or Shriner disguised as an M.F.H. But their enthusiasm for England was genuine and contagious and I spent half my time around Atherton and Menlo Park encouraging a reluctant population to support the Boston Tea Party and to vilify George the Third.

Paranoia had kept me out of the country for thirteen years. I'd always supposed that somebody would "get" me if I ever set foot there. An income tax official, perhaps, or a recruiting sergeant who'd press gang me into the army for a second time. These fears are not as mad as they sound for though my father died in 1945 we received a dunning letter in 1952 warning him that he owed thirty-two-pound-eight-and-threepence in taxes for the year 1941 and that he should govern himself accordingly. Very much against my mother's wishes I wrote a self-indulgent letter back informing them of the old man's death and suggesting that if they wanted the money they should Burke-and-Hare his corpse out of its resting place in the Battersea cemetery and see if we'd left anything in his pockets. As for the army, I was once sent a rail ticket from London to Crowborough, Sussex, with instructions to report for two weeks with the reserve. At the time I was working on the railroad near Franz, Ontario, and could once again afford to send officialdom a brisk, not to say peremptory, reply. *They* had undoubtedly filed these letters and the possibility of repercussions caused me a twinge of anxiety. Basically, however, I felt unwilling to face England as I remembered it — a land of mean streets, sodden skies, scowling, class-obsessed populace, queues, shortages, Sunday boredom, and rain. Ah, but you should see it now, my friends said. Things are *happening* there . . . Carnaby Street, Mary Quant, mini-skirts, the Beatles, the Stones, explosions of pop-culture . . . new energies have been released. The dreariness, the quiet desperation, had vanished. "The land of virtuous gloom," as Arthur Koestler once called it, had become unzippered and euphoric. This is Tir-nan-Og, they said, the country of the young.

Within a few months of my leaving California I heard that my mother had been taken to hospital and operated on for cancer. I had last seen her six years before when she had spent a year in Montreal during a period when nobody I knew was in very good spiritual condition, so that we had parted on bad terms. Since I believe it important to arrive at some rapprochement with one's parents where possible and where the latter allow it, I was glad I had the time and the means to visit her. It was as well I did so for six months later and two months after my return to Canada she died in a Brighton nursing home.

A man travelling to England in 1966, and sailing up Southampton Water, would have seen, to the east, a huge, red-brick Victorian eyesore a quarter of a mile long, topped and bookended by gothic minarets. It lies some two or three hundred yards back from the shore and was used, in my day, as a military convalescent depot. I was once sent here in order, as the MO put it, "to rest up a few weeks." This phrase made me think of deck-chairs, *A Farewell to Arms*, lawns, and sun-decks where I would spend the hours between chota-peg and burra-peg sipping lemon-barley water brought to me on trays by starched and sexy nursing sisters. I'll recover there, I thought, get my strength back sufficiently to grapple with the army to some purpose. This'll be a sanctuary—nobody kicks sick men around, not in England—I'll read, laze, and smoke myself back into shape.

Instead I came upon Netley first in the way one always confronts new things in England—under drizzling skies and after a train journey of many changes. Six weeks in bed had not improved my stamina so that after lugging a heavy kit bag over a mile from the station I was shaking with exhaustion and self-pity. A Welsh sergeant in the Hussars met me at the entrance and immediately put me on fatigues for being improperly dressed. I got signed in, issued blankets, and released into the bowels of the hospital which was less of a hospital than an unheated greenhouse, for one's first impression is that this is a house of glass. Tall glass partitions separate the rooms from the corridors which, stretching the entire quarter-mile length of the hospital, open out to Southampton Water through huge windows. Biting winds swept the corridors and a damp cold nuzzled its way into the rooms to lurk there despite the fires one was allowed to build under certain conditions, and the conditions were these:

1. No fire will be built before 4:30 p.m.
2. All fires will be out by 7:30 a.m., the grates cleared, dusted, and brought to a high state of polish.
3. No coal, wood, paper nor any other combustible material will be kept in the rooms at any time.

If you could resolve the contradiction between the building of a fire and condition 3 then you were in clover.

There lay fifteen not always comfortable years between the paranoid convalescent and my sleeker, thirty-five-year-old-self—running to fat, short in wind, comparatively affluent—now cruising into Southampton on the *United States* under conditions of luxury which a lean malingerer would have found hard to visualize. I watched the hospital slide past the ship and picked out the line of shingle where we used to go beachcombing—scouring it three abreast in the hope the seas would wash us up something we could flog — but all we ever found was a menu from the *Queen Mary*.

There was another man on deck staring over the rail. I borrowed his binoculars and focused them on Netley's facade. I began telling him how grossly I once hated this building and started to describe that first day at Netley, fifteen years before — the bleakness, the cold, the voices — whining, disgusted, very English. But I quickly bored him and found myself alone.

Fer fuck's sake less get this bleedin fire goin....
Oo's that on the bed?
Git olda some dry wood, Dogsbody....
Soddin road walks... musta done abaht fifteen soddin mile....
Ay, a Yorkshire voice bawled in my ear. It's uhff puhst foh-uh.

So what? I answered sleepily. I'd found my assigned room, dumped my kit-bag, lain on the one vacant bed, shivered violently for a few minutes, then dropped off into a nightmare-ridden doze.

Well, dorntcha want no sooper?

I could see men in overcoats, breaths steaming, trying to light a fire with slivers of driftwood and wet slag. The cold penetrated two shirts, an army sweater, a thick serge tunic, two pairs of trousers, one civilian and one issue, both made of stout, bulky wool, an overcoat, and three available blankets. My teeth began to chatter.

Eddie! The Yorkshireman bawled. Coom on... it's sooper time.

A heavily built man lumbered over as I got to my feet. His back was very straight yet he walked with a lurch and seemed to have difficulty moving his neck.

It's not me military training wot's given me a nice straight back, he said as we walked up the stairs and joined a noisy queue fighting at the dining hall entrance. It's a fuckin great plaster cast stretchin from me ip to me shoulders.

What's that for, I asked. Slipped disc, he said. Or some other fuckin thing. Ow the fuck would *they* know?

Might get your fuckin ticket.

Fuckin ope so.

We got our issue of supper. That *Queen Mary* menu was to put us all in touch with a life one might have supposed would be going on on another planet. Dover Sole, Lobster Thermidor, *Entrecote à la Sauce Bearnaise*... whereas in the cookhouse at Netley they used to empty cans of pilchards-in-tomato-sauce into a long wooden horse-trough and mash them to a red paste to be served with potatoes and cabbage

17

they'd boiled in brine and under pressure for twenty-four hours. Once I saw one of the cooks lift his white smock and piss into the pilchard-brimming trough, stirring it well in.

Daft booncha boogers, he said, cackling with laughter, *fancy eatin that* . . . .

As for me, I dined in the NAFFI that night — eggs, beans, and chips.

It's all over now. All gone. There's no longer any conscription in Britain which is in some ways a pity since, as I shall try to show later, the British Army represented a nadir of experience from which one could only ascend. I point this out to my wife who claims that her life as a student nurse in Britain functioned in the same way. I think she's wrong. You can always stop being a nurse . . . you cannot, without risking a lagging or a stretch, get out of the army. Or at least it seems that you can't. At this point I can hear the reader's angry voice raised against me; you should think yourself lucky, I hear him say, you were in during peace-time. What if you'd had to grapple with trench feet, gas gangrene, lice, frostbite, and chaps running towards you with bayonets? I answer that disease is a natural enemy, like aging and death itself, that the bayoneteer is a hireling who doesn't necessarily hate you, and that the true enemy is to be found among the officers and NCOs on your own side and that nothing I've read in the history and fiction of the great wars has convinced me that I'm wrong.

At any rate, for a few years after World War II, Britain retained its large army — thin red line or end of wedge — by means of the Conscription Act. Most young men of my age accepted, though many of them gloomily, the fact that they would have to spend eighteen months as guests of His Majesty. I did not accept it and, as soon as I reached the critical age, took off for Europe (as we call it in England) with my eyes darting from side to side. Things did not always go too well on the Continent and now and again I would return to my austerity-ridden, ration-booked, coal-shortaged, army-threatening homeland for recuperation. I could not, without exercising more caution than lay within my talent, work there legally so, when an understanding developed between myself and a young lady from Liverpool, I left for Scandinavia hoping to make money either in the Swedish bush as a logger or on the Norwegian whaling fleet. I promised this girl that I would send for her as soon as I'd made our fortunes but nothing worked out in Scandinavia either and I was back, penniless, vowing that I would, for her sake, allow myself to be conscripted. The reader may be inclined to forgive my stupidity when he understands that I was only twenty years of age. In any case, I found myself one morning, in May 1950, being lectured by a very young officer with a cherubic face, Eton accent, and buck teeth: "In the King's Royal Rifles," he said, "we think fahst, we ect fahst, and we *shoot*-damn-straight."

There followed ten weeks of rather pleasant boy-scouting, cops-and-robbers, cowboys-and-Indians work around Winchester with bren guns, grenades, and an extraordinary device called a PIAT cocked, if one were strong enough, by an enormous spring. I was thrown out of the KRRs after ten weeks and into the Royal Army Education Corps from which I got turfed, mainly for lack of High Seriousness, in late October of that year — a disaster which coincided with the seeding, budding, and final blossoming of a misunderstanding between myself and the young lady.

Thus I found myself, by November, a lowly clerk in the Service Corps, the most despised and underdog branch of the army, with prospects neither of promotion nor of access to graft, locked into National Service on behalf of a woman who would no longer speak to me, for a period of service increased to two years because of the Korean War. A classic, but nevertheless dismal, A. E. Housman situation to which I responded by contracting meningitis and going into a coma. On my survival I was sent to this convalescent depot at Netley.

Cruising now into Southampton, I saw that the hospital was deserted. At this time of day there should've been knots of convalescent soldiers outside the building, waiting for supper, scraping their feet in the gravel. I should've been able to hear them bitching, even at this distance. It was a ghost building, that was what it was, and I could imagine the corridors, once clamorous with army boots, the bawling of NCOs, the thumping of hand-drawn polishers, now empty and silent, beginning to silt up. I saw the windows smashed and vacant to admit the full force of the wind which would streak down the quarter-mile corridors tumbling in front of it fag-ends, part-one orders dating fifteen years, carbon paper, shit-house roll, and documents relating to the Korean War. I could see it now as a sanctuary of the genuine sort, as a doss house for bums, pad for kids on LSD, and as a stoating ground for the young lovers of southern Hampshire.

After supper that first night we breathed life into the fire, shoved some

19

of the wet slag we used for fuel over it, and waited, crouching, until it began to generate some heat. We spoke of the no-man's land we occupied between the status of patients, who were kept in warm hospitals, fed amply, and issued a pint of beer a day, and that of soldiers who lived in frigid barracks, ate pigswill and not much of that, and whose access to beer and skittles was as limited as our pay. We discussed the inhabitants of our limbo — appendectomies, pneumonias, underweights, busted legs, spinals, ricketts, and vitamin deficiencies. We spoke with morbid relish of disease and of the miraculous door it opened — the possibility of working our tickets.

You was lucky, Eddie said. You might've ad to spend Christmas in ospital. Down ere you'll get leave wiv us in a few days time.

How long does one stay here?

A mumf, somebody answered. Supposed to be. But box clever and you can stay ere as long as yer like. Bin ere six mumfs, me.

But you adta box clever.

Ho yus . . . I adta box clever.

The fire grew brighter and we watched flames spring up and grow so that they became reflected brilliantly in the panes of the glass partition. I asked them why they tried to stay on here. They pointed out that it was not hard to dodge authority in limbo.

It's fuckin cold, that's the only bleedin drawback.

Not in E-block it ain't, Eddie said, referring to the new building at the back. They got central fuckin eatin.

The food's fuckin rotten, someone warned.

It is everywhere.

We all nodded wisely. A very tall, hoarse-voiced corporal crept into our circle, saying:

Wot you ad wrong wiv you, cock?

I told him. Jabs! he whispered in horror.

Dintyer get no bleedin lumbar punkchah?

I've ad *them* fuckin things, Eddie said. As a matter of fact I've ad three. You lie on yer side wiv yer knees drawn up an they shove a soddin great needle up yer spine.

Worse than that, the man known as Dogsbody said, is an enema. Know what I mean? Enemas, see? Tube goes up yer arse, in goes the Persil, and fer three weeks arter you can shit froo the eye of a needle.

Ow long yer bin in the Kate? somebody asked.

I got eighteen months of it to get through yet, I answered.

I dunno what's up wiv you National Service blokes, a private in the Ox and Bucks Light Infantry said. Bitchin abaht eighteen bleedin

20

months . . . I signed on, I did . . . pissed as a soddin newt. Five with the colours and seven with the reserve. And ere's you whinin about eighteen months. Are you man or mouse?

I thought about it. *I'm a mouse*, I said.

Bloke last week got is ticket wiv meningitis, Eddie said.

Yus, yer wanna try fer yer ticket.

Tell em yer got pains in the fuckin ead.

Black-ahts is favourite. Geezer I know got is ticket wiv black-ahts. E was always blackin-aht, see?

You wanna try it, cock, the corporal advised hoarsely. They discharge a dozen a week ere. Discharge on medical grahnds, know wot I mean? Yer ticket.

My ticket, I affirmed.

An hour later I walked down to the beach, fully dressed plus overcoat and layers of newspapers I'd wrapped between skin and shirt. I shivered in the light, insistent drizzle. I pottered down to the sea's edge, my feet dragging through a mixture of mud and fine gravel. The water was a suicide's black. Across the inlet I could see the lights of Beaulieu competing with the yellowish smog that began to roll up the estuary. I was surprised to find myself weeping uncontrollably. They were tears of self-pity but, thank God, also of rage. From now on, I swore to myself, I'm their enemy. I saw myself as the Free Human Spirit engaged in the eternal conflict with the forces of Oppression and Regimentation though to put it like that is to mock myself as I was then. You'll notice, for instance, that I have given those abstractions capital letters. This is supposed to distance the writer from what he writes — to inform the reader that the author is a sophisticate who has achieved an ironic view, and that he is inviting the reader to share in the joke at the expense of all the insufficiently motivated passions of the young.

Utterly diabolical, in my opinion, since my enemies were certainly real enough — fat, beer-drenched sergeants; shaven-headed and bull-necked corporals; rabbit-chinned and treacherous subalterns and remote, "justice" dispensing colonels who were waiting desperately for a war to start to give their lives meaning. But a man's enemies are not exclusively figures of authority but also those in his own group who lose their nerve and incorporate themselves into the system and thus perpetuate it. I'd watched them change from ordinary, decent civilians into insane supporters of the army's power structure — they had become, in other words, Eichmanns, lick-spittlers, time-servers, and garotteers. I swore on that beach an oath to escape them all and I warmed to my room-mates, huddled over their fire and saw them as Nyms, Pistols, Bardolphs. I began to love every inch of their cunning, malingering heads. Like them, I'd concentrate on working a medical discharge, preferably with a pension, and if I failed, and the War Office wanted me that badly then, by God, let it watch out, I said — I'd be an asp in its basket, a fifth-columnist dedicated to its overthrow by means of passive resistance, rebellion, and sabotage.

Having shouted all this into the wind and greatly relieved by its expression, I returned, purged, to my room.

We were queuing, for this was England again, to get off the ship. The longshoremen were the cause of the queue — they ambled with dignity, refusing to be hurried, through the chaotic piles of trunks and packing cases. Customs men were too few in number to adequately badger the thousand or so passengers. It was raining quietly, of course, and there were groups of bedraggled and badly dressed people on the quay. I scanned the pale faces rapidly for any that resembled the photos I'd seen of my wife's parents and, drawing a blank, sidled with relief to my place in the line. Outside, my feet on land, the cold, knowing it was supposed to be in England, suddenly became intense. With laughable ease it penetrated three sweaters, a jacket, my Arctic parka, and two pairs of trousers. My wife, who had caught the grippe in Montreal, suddenly began to cough uncontrollably. The sky darkened, lights were switched on, night fell. What we want, I said, is a centrally heated hotel. By means of porters and heavy tipping we transferred our baggage to a cab and drove to the Dolphin, a fine, Georgian pub towards the centre of town.

The Dolphin was carpeted and bow-windowed. A huge fire blazed in the lounge. Tweedy ex-public school boys turned salesmen sat around it drinking vodka and lime. The management robbed us of five pounds and led us to a room "with central heating." What this meant was that a towel rack in the bathroom was at a slightly higher temperature than its surrounding air. We ate quickly and my wife took to bed with her bottles of ascorbic acid, Contac-C, and cough mixture. As for me, I walked out into the street to discover whether or not the pub life had changed.

The fine drizzle that had accompanied us from the pier had frozen on the sidewalks producing a thin layer of treacherous *verglass*. Street lamps lit the deserted city with a ghastly sodium yellow. There was no one about so that the pedestrian, journeying to his lukewarm beer, felt alien and furtive — a Jack-the-Ripper. I slunk into a Public Bar and, after a double-scotch with which I silently toasted myself, my wife, central heating, gourmet cooking, survival from virulent disease, demobilization, and the Canadian citizenship which rendered me immune to governmental attack, I asked about Netley.

It's all coming down, somebody said. It's finished.

Finished?

Ah. They used it as an ospital ferr a woil. Did you know it were desoined ferr India?

I knew it, but I thought I'd let him tell it.

They wanted two ospitals, he went on. One ferr India, t'other ferr England. Well, the Croimean war were on at the toim . . .

Arr, Zulu war, Jack . . . .

Zulu war were it? One a they wars — anyhow there were a lot of argument and the plans they got mixed up, loik, and the one desoined ferr India they built over ere.

I could imagine what they built in India. A yellow brick stables with windows carefully pre-smashed, floors designed for polishing with tooth-brushes, grey-veined and shattered porcelain toilets with rusting fixtures, rooms tested for the production of low temperatures, no provision for fire places or stoves.

It's the end of an era, I said.

It was at Netley that I gave some thought to the problems of escape. Desertion was the simplest, most obvious method but this would involve leaving England forever — a step I was at that time reluctant to take. The second possibility was the "mature" one of staying out my time and "making the best of it." On the face of it, however, this was absurd since the army was the proverbial sow's ear notoriously hard to craft into a silk purse. The third and most adventurous option was to "work my ticket" on medical grounds. I had a head start, so to speak, on this course of action since I was still weak from my illness, prone to headaches, very depressed, and unmilitary enough, in a conformist society, to pass as mad. There was another factor. Across the fields from the depot was the new building called E-Block which contained, apart from conventional hospital departments, a psycho-neurotic ward. If I were to play mad I would not have far to go. I was already "on the doorstep." Apart from anything else the place enjoyed central-heating — a consideration, in this bleakest of army winters, of the greatest decisiveness. Each malingerer coveted a stay in E-Block. We would sit huddled over our meager fires plotting means of egress. A room-mate of mine, suffering from a very mild case of 'flu, pretended, at my suggestion, that he had meningitis. I knew the symptoms. One of them is an inability to straighten a bent leg. Accordingly, he reported sick with fever and added this matter of the leg. He was whisked instantly to E-Block from which he returned about a week later, cured and somewhat chagrined. I had forgotten to warn him that they would probably test his spinal fluid by means of a lumbar puncture. He had thawed out, over there in E-Block, but he was, on the whole, disinclined to be grateful to me.

The rest of us got on with the job of malingering quietly and without fuss. Some were fortunate enough to be permanently disabled. Eddie, for example, whose torso was encased in plaster, was given his ticket and went marionetting out into the Free World with an army pension for the rest of his life. Another man, pretending to be anemic, stayed in E-Block for nearly three months. Dogsbody, a regular soldier who'd undergone a late conversion to the concept of liberty, convinced Them he was allergic to khaki then disappeared into some research centre where, for all I know, he malingers still. But it was by no means so easy for everyone: a man reporting sick with headaches, depression, or just plain dottiness, ran a discouraging gamut of shock-treatment, insulin, lumbar-puncture, straight-jacket, pentathol, and long, psychiatric examination. You had to watch your step, all right. You had to box clever.

In the early evenings the reading-room of the Southampton library was filled with soldiery engaged in learning by rote the symptoms of his choice. I for one spent over a week there pouring through well-thumbed medical treatises acquiring a knowledge of allergies, megrims, back ailments, blood conditions, kidney malfunction, brain tumours, paranoia, manic depression, and hebephrenia along with a taste for medical literature I have not yet lost. Few novelists can invent such dead-pan, wildly funny (except, of course, for the patient) narratives as exist in medical journals. Consider, for example, the following case history:

One afternoon in February, 1956, he suddenly experienced a sensation as if he had received a blow in the stomach, and soon afterwards there was a pulling sensation in the jaws, followed by an impulse to dress in female clothes. On the way home from work, he bought some female underwear and secretly put it on when he reached home. He then felt "completely calm" for a few minutes, then he experienced a feeling of revulsion and later that night burnt the clothes.... On all such similar occasions this

24

desire was ushered in by epigastric and jaw sensations. . . . It was now impossible for him to hide the transvestite activity from his wife and though he worked efficiently at the bank all day, he would spend his evenings at home completely dressed in female clothes, using cosmetics and adopting female mannerisms. . . . On examination there was no physcial abnormality except for a subcutaneous nodule behind the left ear. (Davies and Morgenstern, "A Case of Cysticercosis, Temporal Lobe Epilepsy, and Transvestism," *Neurosurg. Psychiat.*, 23 [1960], 247-49)

I doubt if even Nabokov could cap that subcutaneous nodule — it is a *masterstroke.*

In the juvenescence of that year I was ready to act. I overstayed a weekend pass by one day and got a chit from a civilian doctor to the effect that I was too scared to face the journey back to Netley. He'd also written me a prescription for a sedative. The chit was accepted and the MO called me in for an interview. What's all this? he said. I remained silent, withdrawn.

It says here you were frightened to come back by train. Why?
Sir.
Whaddyer mean, "sir"?
I shrugged. What is it about trains that upsets you? he asked in a friendlier tone.

I don't know, I said after a long pause. The noise . . . the way they sway from side to side . . . the compartments are so small . . . .

You could've come back by bus, he said, with what he may have thought was devastating logic.

It . . . it was the thought of coming back here, I suppose . . . what with everything else . . . just one damned thing on top of another . . . .

Nobody in his right mind, he said testily, wants to come back here after going home on leave. What's the matter with you? You think *I* like coming back to this place? But I don't get the better of some poor, innocent, civilian quack and go around flourishing a chit.

Oh well, he said finally. You've got the chit and I suppose I'll have to respect it . . . get any headaches? he asked suddenly.

I nodded. So did he. He scribbled something on his pad . . . with any luck "this man is a possible Bedlamite" . . . then he kicked me out.

You done wrong, one of the malingerers said, back in my room. When e arst you abaht them eadaches you shoulda give im the fuckin works.

Not *im,* another critic said. E done juss wot e should a

25

done . . . don't overdo it, thass my motter . . . keep the fuckin bastards guessin . . . .

Yuss, I'm in fiver a *that* . . . *corse* yer gotta keep the bastards guessin . . . but now, see, what is gotta do, see, is ter get ter see the bleedin doctor again . . . .

That's under control, I boasted. Tomorrow morning.

The morning room inspections were carried out by the fat Welsh sergeant who'd greeted me on arrival and taken such a dislike to me. That morning he strode into the billet, little pig eyes darting from side to side, sharp creases in his trousers, gaiters nicely blancoed, and his boots in a high state of polish, as they say. Two corporals marched in behind him. *Shun!* he squeaked. We tottered to attention. He caught sight of my unmade bed and blenched. Voss diss? he shrieked. Voss diss, you? I fixed him with a stony glare then bent down, picked up a boot, and threw it at the partition. It sailed across the room, smashed its way through a pane of glass, and landed in the corridor and slid on its side amid its shards along the floor's highly polished surface until it came to rest against the far wall. As soon as the Welshman was able to regain his breath he did the correct military thing and ordered the corporal behind him to fall in two men and march me to the guard house.

This lay three-quarters of a mile down the long approach drive. The progress of escort and prisoner was by no means as regimental as it should have been since one of my guardians was anaemic, the other limped from a recent cartilege operation, and the corporal himself was convalescing from pneumonia and had to abandon us after a hundred yards or so and I could see him, as I looked back, sitting by the side of the road with his head in his hands.

The charge against me was dismissed, I was forced to pay for the window, and sent to the cookhouse where, it was thought, I would be kept out of trouble. It was clear that my presence there, after a day or two, was an embarrassment to the head cook and I was sent to the boiler room. This was warm, silent, and deserted. For over a week I stoked my furnace gently every half an hour and occupied the spare time in trying to learn Spanish from a book. After I've worked my ticket, I fantasized, I'll go to Spain . . . somewhere where there's sun, warm seas, and lovely towns. Somewhere where a man could live off the land away from this drizzling sky and from the sights and sounds of industrial civilization in which a man can acquire dignity only through learning to malinger. I made a reclining chair out of a pile of coke and thumbed through my irregular verbs . . . the present disappeared and daydreams took its place.

E-Block to us was what the Grail was to Arthur's knights. I achieved it shortly after my relegation to the boiler-room and for two days felt lulled by its warmth, food, and lack of pressure. I lay silently on my bed trying to hide an elation inconsistent with my reputation as a depressive and observed the other inmates. They were a mixed bunch. One of them imagined he was the skipper of an ocean liner and would pace the long, well-buffed floor with his hands behind his back peering keenly always through the same window as he guided the course of his vessel over the ice and snow of a Hampshire field. Mostly he was silent and intense though once in a while he would bark an appropriate command such as Midships! or, Steady as she goes, Number One! Another feigned religious melancholy and, like myself, would lie for most of the day on his bed uttering the occasional hollow groan and sometimes he would anathematize "the bloody City of Lichfield" in the manner of George Fox. I suspected that he, like the skipper and the man we all called "the sex-maniac," was an imposter and this turned out to be correct for they were all of them kicked out of the P.-N. ward about a week after my arrival. Their behaviour contrasted rather sharply with those, a majority, who were genuinely ill. These men seemed superficially normal and it was only by means of small signals—the flickering away of eyes, an over-excited shout at a card game, a sob caught in the throat—that one knew there was something wrong. If I want to survive here, I thought, I must practice subtlety.

Let me put it this way. Suppose you were asked at a party to perform in a charade and that the role you were assigned was that of "madman." You would have immediate access to a number of largely comic stereotypes—the man who sits on a piece of toast and claims he's a poached egg, the zany with lolling tongue and uncontrolled eyeballs, the imitator of Napoleon, or Christ, or Alexander the Great, etc. These are *conceptions* of what madmen are like and they do not correspond very much to reality. Nevertheless I think you would choose one of them because the conception is shared by the audience. Thus, however you played your role, you would be playing it for laughs—you would render your madman as a *grotesque* and the audience, appreciating your skill, nevertheless recognizes that you are a man playing a role. Thus the skipper and his friends were Brechtian actors *demonstrating* madmen whilst themselves preserving an alienating distance from their outward behaviour.

It occurred to me that if I could sense this alienation within my

27

malingering friends then so, on a good day, could a psychiatrist.

Accordingly, I sought for what I later discovered was called "the method." It was not simply a question of imitating the less spectacular forms of psychic disturbance — catatonia, radiator clutching, total withdrawal — but of concentrating my mind on those recent experiences that had depressed me in the first place. These were many and included loss of freedom, the break-up with the girl in Liverpool, the weather, the army *mise en scène*, and the series of humiliations dealt me by authority many of which, as I was now starting to realize, were due to my own stupidity. Whilst deliberately increasing the bleakness of my inner life, I thought it important to participate fully in the social life, such as it was, of the ward and in other ways act normally in the hope that I would create the impression of a man trying hopelessly, though rather gamely, to cope with the external world against considerable odds.

This course of action met with some success but there was a complicating factor. I found it increasingly difficult to ignore certain more positive manifestations: the first sunlight of Spring gleamed on the grey waters of the Solent and daffodils began to thrust their way out of the soil around the elm trees now filling with rooks. The air grew warmer, blowing in from the sea. There was that Spring flavour of things to be done, of journeys to be made. I had recovered completely from the disease that had originally brought me to Netley and, like any other moderately healthy youth, I was beginning to react against uselessness and inactivity. Besides, They were treating me as though I were genuinely sick and this, perversely enough, I began to resent. As February of that year turned into March, I became increasingly uneasy.

March came in like a lion and went out the same way.

My wife and I had been in England for four months and our boat was due to sail back to Canada on the eighteenth of April. We found that there had indeed been some changes in the tone of English life but that these changes affected only the young and comparatively affluent. The poor stayed poor and conditions for people like my mother, whose life was visibly coming to an end, remained abysmal. Our time in England had been dramatic and emotionally harrowing, but I had re-established some rapport with my mother so that, though this trip was to haunt me in many ways for years to come, I had to consider it successful. My wife and I were utterly exhausted by it, however, and, as early as February, we had begun to count the days much as one counts them in jail or in the army.

I failed to work my ticket. The psychiatrist assigned to me maintained the position that depression was a healthy reaction to army life. It *makes* you depressed, he said, it causes *me* to wake up at night screaming in nightmare. He went on to describe his nightmares and to provide me with interpretations, Jungian in tendency, for some of the more extravagant ones. Though his facial tics and over-reactions to any unexpected noise made me at times suspect him of malingering for the purposes of stealing patients' thunder, I felt that here was a man whose burdens were even heavier than mine. I liked him and came clean with him so that one afternoon in early April I found myself dumping my kit-bag in my old room and walking out once more along the deserted beach. I'll get posted abroad, I thought: Trieste, Gibraltar, the Sudan . . . what did the army deprive me of? Nothing. Nothing, since a man who values his freedom is everywhere on the run . . . the army made very little difference. I had just over a year left to do and had I jibed at that. I'd been a self-pitying child and victory, had there been one, would've been hollow.

I gazed across Southampton Water, this time with approval. On the other shore lay the New Forest through which I had cycled when still at school. I had found it good — the thatch of old roofs, the inns encircled by clumps of trees, the grass-grown dockyard of Buckler's Hard where Nelson built his ships — and I should certainly visit it again. I faced the future with optimism.

My unit was in Germany and, though I spent a tolerable year there, it took a long time for me to develop a detached attitude with regard to the army. On one level it is perfectly iniquitous that two years should be carved from the life of a free man; on the other, that same man is taught valuable lessons which stand him in good stead in the capitalist Land of Jobs. The army teaches a man to lie, cheat, steal, and look after Number One. He learns the inner meaning of the French verb *se debrouiller*. At first sight the private soldier is a victim — pushed around by cringing lance-jacks, sadistic corporals, fell and bloated sergeants, thuggish warrant officers, commissioned baboons. But it transpires that since he is *lumpen* and lowly the private soldier has nothing to lose. He is blithely unconcerned with promotion since he knows it is out of his reach. He enjoys security, if you can so describe three ill-planned and poisonously prepared meals a day, and the ulcers and heightened blood-pressure of responsibility trouble him not. He is as a child — feckless and pampered. *Queen's Rules and*

29

Regulations protect him and enfold him like a nurse's arms. He is not supposed to know this, of course — *QRRs* are supposed to be available only to officers — but he quickly finds it out as soon as he has legitimate access to the Company Office and then he becomes a barrack room lawyer. He grows needle-sharp protective spicula from which potential enemies, with rank to maintain, tend to recoil.

The British Army provided one other major service to its temporary victims. It created an environment which *can never be made worse*. So long as he had the intelligence to keep himself out of military prisons, the private soldier knew that whatever happened to him in later life could only be an improvement on his present position. Outside of Buchenwald I defy anybody to show me anything worse than life in Salamanca Barracks, Aldershot. As I have already said, each of us needs a nadir: the underprivileged aristocrat can look back with loathing on Eton or Harrow, the middle classes on their family life, but what about the sons of the sly and undeserving poor? No. I am on the whole grateful to the army for giving me if not an image of hell then at least a sense of anti-paradise. What can ever take its place? I suppose the present generation has to make do with prisons and approved schools but these are not quite the same thing. A young offender has to work quite hard to get into prison these days and, once in, he is soothed by social workers, idealistic chaplains, issue-mongering members of parliament, enlightened screws, book-struck education officers, and governors with humanistic values. Those of my students who have been lagged on drug charges complain of the *blandness* of Canadian jails. Once in a while they will come across a screw of the Old School who will obligingly work them over with his truncheon but on the whole the accent is on what liberals call *rehabilitation*. There are even agencies who will look after them when they've finished their time. I put it to the reader that this presents a totally different picture to that of the army. The prisoner is quite often a man caught committing an offence; the private soldier is plucked from his environment without a by-your-leave and is innocent. There are no agencies or half-way houses for the army man; he is kicked back into civilian life as though to the knacker's yard. The prisoner often enjoys a feeling of solidarity with other prisoners or at least with those convicted of similar offences; the soldier stands alone and every man is his enemy.

I learned to live with this situation by treating it as a game. One day I found myself given the task of pasting in amendments to *Queen's Rules and Regulations*. These amendments were endless, issued almost daily, and incomprehensible. One was supposed to cut each from its sheet and paste it into the appropriate section of the manual. I found that fertile, evocative conundrums, non-sequiturs, *poèmes trouvés*, witticisms, and obscenities could be created by pasting a given amendment to the wrong paragraph. If caught out at this harmless sport one had the cast-iron defence that one was a lowly private soldier and, therefore, a being of negligible intelligence.

Soon I discovered other clerks and skivvies engaged in similar activities. Some of us got together and formed a group. Together we read Kafka, sometimes aloud, and tried to master the art of perpetrating bureaucracy. One of my colleagues did extraordinary things with a kit-bag full of army clothing left in the barracks after the owner had been taken into hospital with appendicitis. My friend surrounded the incident with the appropriate paper work and then deliberately lost a memo. He wrote himself another memo which ordered the kit-bag to be forwarded to central stores in Bielefeldt under the "Y-List" regulations, then got it transferred to England under the forged signature of some fictitious supply officer. From England he moved it to Cairo, then back to Germany en route to Singapore. The paper-work grew exponentially like a "red-tide" and suddenly there was a mess which no one could straighten out, though two courts of inquiry were held. An inextricable, bureaucratic knot had been created which was still ramifying cancerously when I was demobilized a year later. It was out of small, arcane pleasures such as this that we made our lives tolerable.

Two days before we were due to sail, we took a boat out on the Serpentine. The agonies and problems of this particular journey were over with — unresolved but temporarily at an end. Perhaps, I thought, one endured them just as one endured the army, for the sake of the condition of euphoria I was just now, rather tentatively, starting to feel. Many times, over the last few weeks, I had occasion to remind myself that at least I was no longer a member of Her Majesty's Armed Forces. The stratagem had been effective. But at the same time the joy I was experiencing was as nothing compared to that wild elation I felt that first morning the army was behind me when I awoke, like the narrator of a Chaucer poem, with the mid-May sun brilliant in the panes of a lattice window. Nevertheless, the sky above the Serpentine was utterly cloudless and the wind, our implacable enemy throughout the winter, blew now from the Channel and across the Downs — it had dropped and mellowed and felt faintly warm against the skin.

31

Primroses bloomed on the banks of the artificial lake and above the budding trees you could see the old, greyish white buildings of London basking in the sun.

1977

How the Poor Die

It had been seven years since I'd seen my mother and that was in Montreal under circumstances neither of us wanted to remember. Here she was now, though, tiny and very frail, silvery hair a wispy cloud round her head, sunken and very piercing blue eyes, jutting nose sharp as an arrete, and the skin of her temples brownish and flaky. Her energy had begun to return to her, enough at any rate to spark a number of feuds; and her laughter, loud and breathless and entirely without humour, was as I'd remembered it. Her room, up two flights of stairs, was like a skid-row itinerant's—full of knick-knacks carried about in trunks, unpacked from one battered caravanserai to the next. She lived in what in England is called a "bed-sitter" and in Canada "a housekeeping room." A woman named Mrs. Swain presided over the rest of the building: short, white-haired, bland-faced, soft voice, and ingratiating manner—decayed gentlewoman, perhaps, or one who would like to be taken for such. Downstairs she kept a neat, highly polished, well-carpeted hallway, but once behind my mother's door you were in the world of the old, poor, and unwanted. There was a boarded-up fireplace and in front of it an electric fire, a "two-bar," whose meter ticked menacingly and expensively to the left. Two ancient and tattered chairs huddled over this fire and beyond them was a long shelf on which she kept her two battered suitcases containing, one supposed, the few remaining things, the last possessions cherished and retained against long odds. For my mother was at the end of it and these were the last fragments of a lifetime—all that she had to show for those years as a young woman, newlywed, homemaker, mother, widow with property—for all those years which preceded the day the jettisoning began.

Perhaps the life of the poor can be represented by a graph—a line which rises slowly like a scarp slope, reaches a peak, falls rapidly like a scarp face. And this line represents property and reaches the peak at sixty-five. After retirement the pensioner begins to jettison—he sells a table to buy a warm coat, unloads a chesterfield to pay for some coal. If he owns a house, it becomes too large, for his children are abroad, too expensive to heat, and he doesn't want to rent to strangers. So he closes off first one room, then another, then the whole of the "upstairs." He sells off the furniture, for the money comes in useful, and keeps only the smallest of those things which remind him of past times. The pensioner is lucky if he retains his health and if there are enough of his own generation around to visit him and whom he can get out to visit. He may, under these circumstances, finish his life in peace and dignity. But if he has owned no houses then objects must be cast out at a much faster rate. My mother had sold our house twenty years before and spent the money. She'd got rid of the furniture bit by bit as she found it increasingly tiresome to move and now her property consisted of a few old coats and dresses, woollen cardigans, photographs, and miscellaneous gew-gaws. One of them is before me on my desk as I write, a cylindrical wooden jewel box, decorated on the outside with hand-carved flowers and leaves. On the lid is a carving of a young couple dressed in Norwegian national costume. They seem about to be married for the man is carrying a Bible. No, I'm wrong about that. If you look closely you see that it's a beer-stein. At any rate the carving is executed with a naïve playfulness, and the figures were painted in colours once bright, now faded to pastel shades.

The stuff that had passed through her hands! I thought, and now there was nothing . . . collecting things, making a living, building a home, raising children . . . these are diversions and this, what my mother was facing, is the reality. Materially I could not help her, though I had financed her disastrous trip to Montreal, since I had just finished four years as a student and was consequently in debt, but there were, perhaps, more important things I could do for her.

There were photographs along the mantleshelf—several of myself, several of my sister and her son. There was a photograph of Jocelyn and me as a newly married couple and the most recent was one taken in my last year of undergraduate work at U.B.C., a "commencement" photograph in which I wore the gown, hood, short back and sides, and supercilious smirk encouraged by photographers on these occasions. There was a cupboard filled with stuff I remembered from my childhood—photograph albums, *The Ringdove Story Book* she'd given my sister one early Christmas, letters in my nephew's childish scrawl. And in this same cupboard was her latest more sinister possession—the plastic bags and bandages required for her colostomy. And the first thing I'd noticed coming into her room was the smell—it was very familiar for my wife had sold aerosol sprays as part of our Fuller Brush racket—a sweet, herbal odour designed to cover the slight, but persistent, smell of faeces.

We greeted her affectionately, of course. I wasn't sure how much she knew about her condition despite the fact that this was the second thing she began to talk about. The first, and this seemed to me to be a sure sign she was getting better, was her landlady. We rearranged the few old blankets against the crack between floor and door, sat down, and started off.

You saw her, didn't you, my dear? Oh yes. Oh yes, you saw her all right, in spite of her little efforts to hide behind that door... just wanted to get a look at you, that's all it is, just wants to know everybody's business... the sly, rapacious bitch... you'd think butter wouldn't melt in her mouth, wouldn't you?... sweet little smile and a knife in the ribs, that's her... that's her style... don't let her take you in, my dear... you're too good-natured... you don't know the world like I do... it didn't take *me* long to get her measure, the crafty, ravenous, low-class, slattern... nice, well-polished hallway... *but you should get a look of her kitchen*... landladies... they're all the same... suck the life's blood out of you... go behind your back... like that woman did to me... even went to the almoner, the *almoner*, if you please of the *hospital*... wanted to find out if she was going to be stuck with an invalid on her hands... wanted to know if she'd have to carry me up and down the stairs....

Maybe she just wanted to help.

Help? Help? Not *her*, not Mrs. Swain... not by a long shot... artful as a wagonload of monkeys, that one... help? Help *me*? After she's gone behind my back and fixed the electric meter so's I have to sit crouched over it at night dropping one shilling in after the other? She gets a cut you know... ah, they're on to everything these old widows with a bit of property... I'll tell you what else she did... but keep your voice down... she's not very far away, you can be sure of *that*, my dear . . . she went to the Assistance Board and told them she was raising my rent . . . fifteen shillings . . . what's all this? I said to her. What's all what, says she, bold as brass. This extra fifteen bob, I said, Well, she said, why not? She said, it isn't you who pays, she said, and flounced out . . . *She's a vampire* . . . she's in the bathroom now, listening to every word we say. I've had enough of her my dear . . . I'm moving . . . to a cheaper place on Freshfield Road . . . at the end of the month.

In a hoarse whisper she embarked on a discursive analysis of the way of the world and proferred wisdom we should all take through life with us — never leave letters lying around since "people get to know your business that way"; never tell people anything because they'll listen sympathetically then use the information in "evidence against you."

I found this feud with the landlady, these snippets of wisdom, very encouraging. She seemed to be gaining each day both in malice and weight. She switched, after winding up her tirade against her landlady, to a discussion, more reasoned in nature but no less acerbic in manner, of relatives. One aunt was jealous because a mutual friend of theirs had spent a lot of time visiting my mother in the hospital (and what did she expect to gain from *that*, my dear, that's what I'd like to know, though I suppose some would say it was nice of her to take the trouble); another was superficially pleasant but basically two-faced; a third was a back-biter; a niece wasn't to be trusted. It wasn't long before we were back to Mrs. Swain.

I went up to her and told her straight. Mrs. Swain, I said, there are two sides to your nature . . . one is very pleasant, very charming. The other is a devil incarnate . . . you're nothing better than a common black-mailer. And what's more, I said, I'm *leaving*. That's right, *leaving*. And at the end of the month.

The illness had been an ordeal for her, of course. About a year before this she had been getting pains in her stomach, or in what seemed like her stomach. She went to a doctor, an old, doddering man about to retire, who told her there was nothing to worry about and gave her some pills. The pains got slightly worse. She vomited from time to time and started to lose weight. You've got a touch of colitis, he said, and gave her some drops. Her sole thought was whether these pains, this loss of energy, would persist into late summer when my sister was due to pay her a visit. The doctor gave her more drops and told her not to be a *malade imaginaire*. I asked her why she hadn't changed her doctor.

36

You can't do that, she said. For one thing they won't hear criticism of each other . . . it gets their backs up . . . they can make it hot for you in other ways . . . they've got the whole of the government behind them . . . there's nothing you can do about them . . . they've got you completely at their mercy.

Just before my sister arrived she began to pass blood. It's colitis the doctor said. Very typical. Nothing to worry about . . . specialist? What do you mean, specialist? Go to a specialist if you like, of course, I suppose it's your right. Go ahead . . . see what *he* says . . . .

So he gave her an appointment to see a specialist. My mother saved it until after my sister had returned to Canada. She visited this office, was stripped by minions and readied on a table. The specialist entered without a word, examined her wordlessly, shot a few brisk orders to the nurses, then told a nurse to tell her to come back next day for a barium enema. The next day she was filled with a barium compound, ordered to walk over to another table where she was X-rayed. The specialist strode in later while she was getting dressed. There's a growth in your rectum, he said briskly. The whole lot's got to come out. And, with these cryptic words, he strode off. A nurse ordered her to report to the hospital in a week's time whilst another nurse, somewhat more humane, explained that what the specialist meant was that he'd have to perform a colostomy. Is it cancer, my mother asked, but at this the nurse immediately balked and said my mother must not ask questions and must, as a patient, learn to mind her own business.

During her story I was on my feet, pacing the room, uttering cries of horror. That she should have been treated first with such incompetence, then with such contempt, then, finally, as a will-less object, to be knifed and manipulated like a piece of stone did not shock me so much as my mother's calm acceptance of it, the assumption that people are always like this and that nothing more is to be expected from them — that one is lucky if one escapes from an encounter with a fellow human being with one's pockets, reputation, life, still intact. What I found disgusting was her surprise that I should be angered by it, what terrified *her* was the thought that I should be tempted to get the ancient incompetent who'd treated her for colitis struck off the register, to approach her specialist and emend his behaviour. "They can always get you in other ways." These grapplings with the medical profession were nothing more nor less than a demonstration of her world-view's validity. Any show of my hand would merely make things worse for her. And how could I tell her that

37

her doctor's incompetence was not only inexcusable but criminal? That he had, in fact, endangered her life? To have said so would be to have told her that the operation, her suffering, was not to prolong her life at all, and that the surgery had come too late. *All's well, that ends well,* I said. What happened then?

Then she'd had the operation and very nearly died through it. She drifted in and out of unconsciousness and was only fully aware of pain, discomfort, and one particular unpleasantness which made her shudder even now. This was what she called "the drip," the system of bottles and thin rubber tubes which fed into her arm. This was particularly bestial because the spiggot kept falling out. It was during this stage that she received a visit from my in-laws who had driven down one Sunday. We were to hear more about this journey. It had begun when we had wired Jocelyn's parents that my mother was in the hospital and asked them to phone down to find out how she was doing. It was late November, no weather to be out in a frozen call box grappling with the hopelessly inefficient British telephone system. Jocelyn's mother had to do it since Stan, her husband, was incapacitated with what *his* doctor had diagnosed as sciatica, but which turned out to be a critically slipped disc — *his* bout under the knife coincided with our arrival. Anyhow the news, when they'd got through to the hospital finally, after two hours in the call box and some thirty shillings or so later, was not encouraging. They felt they had to see her, they drove down in wind, sleet, and hail, through traffic-blocked suburbs, icy streets, with Stan's sciatica tearing at him, and to the tune of Sybil's nagging, screaming, fearful hysteria and what with all of this they got to Brighton three or four minutes before the visiting hours finished and the hospital staff began booting the visitors out. They found my mother with screens round her bed, blue in colour, liquids dripping into her veins, semi-conscious, and unable to talk. Oh, *no,* Sybil said in exasperation, just before the nurse guided them to the door. My mother, barely conscious, took this for an expression of anger while Sybil later explained it as one of dismay. The truth, like all truth, very probably lies in between.

And afterwards, my mother said, when I became stronger they sent me to a convalescent home at Hastings . . . they were a *dreadful* bunch . . . manners like pigs most of them . . . I couldn't even bear to watch some of them *eat* . . . where they'd been brought up heaven only knows . . . I had to sit next to one old man who crammed his food into his mouth with a spoon, dribbling it out again at the corner of his mouth . . . that's human nature, my dears, in the *raw* . . . IN THE

RAW . . . that's where you see it, in places like that convalescent home . . . and the nurses were dreadful, pert little baggages, most of them, sleeping with Tom, Dick, and Harry if the truth were known . . . but in the medical profession, of course, they always know who to go to . . . they fed us well, I *will* say that for them . . . .

Did you make any friends there?

Friends? Among *that* lot? I should think *not* indeed . . . they are *coarse* . . . you know what I mean? . . . *coarse* . . . dregs of humanity, I should think. These national health places are all the same . . . anybody *decent* has the money to go private . . . snobbish, la-di-da bunch they are, too, my dears. I've worked in private nursing homes myself . . . I could tell you a tale about those places.

The supper, which she insisted on feeding us, was cooked by now and she put a cloth on the little card table she used to eat from and set three places. My mother's cooking was very English — meat pie, greens boiled to a pulp, and watery mashed potatoes — all made edible, provided one were hungry enough, with a bottle of HP sauce. I got up, put a shilling in the meter, and a blanket over my shoulders. The room was damp and cold as a grave but my mother didn't appear to notice it. English people, it is often said, are born chilled and it takes them a lifetime to thaw out. In the interim, of course, low temperatures don't seem to bother them. My own blood had thinned from many years in centrally heated buildings.

I sat toying with doleful pie and lugubrious sprout while the cold of the room ceased being merely noticeable and became malignant. My mother did not appear to be aware of it and had embarked on a tirade against someone I didn't know, apparently an old friend of hers. I could see we were all in for an exhausting three months, though I understood perfectly well that our presence enabled her to release much of her hostility with salutary effect. I wondered whether it bothered me to play lance to her pustule and decided that it didn't. Had my sister been here, however, the anger might, quite quickly, have taken on a personal tinge.

When my sister became pregnant she tried, as they say, "to bring it off." She took pills, hot baths, liberal doses of gin, motorcycle rides, and bad advice. An abortion cost a lot of money in England and neither my sister nor her boy friend could raise it. She decided to have the baby and the boy friend offered "to make an honest woman of her." This she declined on the grounds that neither of them would, under normal circumstances, choose the other as a lifetime com-

39

panion. There remained the business of keeping the facts from my mother. Normally, of course, this wouldn't have mattered very much had my mother been the type of woman one could confide in. But this she certainly was not. Ever since my sister had been a baby my mother would fill her ear with wisdom of the following sort: all men are sex monsters; sex is the only thing they think about; once a man has "enjoyed your body" he has no further use for you; the world is full of "funny customers" (male) who rape you and afterwards bash your head in; that women are divided into the virtuous (very few) and dirty little sluts (the vast majority); that the sole point of a maidenhead is that it can be bartered for a wedding ring; that loss of this maidenhead reduces one's chances of marriage to zero; that the world is full of old maids who've "made fools of themselves" so it's best to keep one's ears open and one's wits about one, sell one's virginity to the highest bidder and, once it's sold, give in. Giving in (or sex) is distasteful but one has to submit to it because your husband will neglect you and seek solace in other women. This means a ruined home and loss of security. The world is full of abandoned women, etc. Never trust other women, particularly sluts, since they'll lure your husband away from you. Her specific advice to my sister consisted of the following: you are too tall for most men, and read too much. You're at a natural disadvantage, since you've got a good brain, and men don't like women to have brains. You're too tall and you have an aquiline nose. Men prefer snub noses and stupidity. Your other, and chief disadvantage, is that you're a natural slut . . . not, perhaps, out of malice, but out of good nature, eagerness to please combined with a lack of wisdom.

My mother then took it upon herself to correct these flaws of character, by lectures, all conducted at a loud, semi-hysterical pitch, curtailments of freedom, a constant watch, a refusal to allow her to mix with boys, and an automatic assumption, loudly and vigorously expressed, that on the occasions my sister did happen to go out on a date then the two of them would have "had sex" out of my sister's easy-going lack of discrimination and wisdom and out of the boy's rapacity — natural in all men. Her morality was a cross between that of Samuel Richardson and the *News of the World*. One other, highly important, factor was the opinion of neighbours. What, for example, would the neighbours think *and go around saying* about a girl, a girl of fifteen, coming home alone after dark . . . what would they say about *her* as *the mother in the case*? (She thought of life in terms of scabrous court scenes.) And if this boy were to see her home, why this was even worse, for what would people, *being what they are*, think about a mother who lets her young daughter prowl around with men who were obviously out for what they could get? What are you trying to prove, anyway, she'd say? Don't you know that the only thing a man would want from you, with your hook nose and good intelligence, is your body? And that once you've given it to him he'll throw you aside like a squeezed lemon?

I used to watch all this — the scenes, fights, tests of will as my sister fought, throughout her childhood and adolescence, towards independence and a view of life emancipated from my mother's. At the age of eighteen she would occasionally come home, after a night out, an hour or so late. My mother, who normally went to bed after the nine o'clock news, would wait up in a state of terrible anxiety, making herself innumerable cups of tea.

Where in the name of God is she? Oh, my God, what's happened to her? Perhaps she's been run over . . . ten-thirty, I told her . . . ten-thirty at the latest . . . *look at the time* . . . after eleven and still no sign . . . John, go down the road and look for her . . . she's been raped and had her throat cut . . . out in the bushes, that's where she is, doing God-knows-what . . . .

It will be obvious to the reader, that at the core of my mother's personality was a horror at the possibility that someone else might be experiencing pleasure — particularly sexual. When she got home, my mother would then set about her: I've been so worried about you . . . why do you do this to me? . . . I thought you'd met with some terrible accident . . . where have you been at *this* hour . . . who've you been with, that's more to the point . . . oh my God as though I hadn't troubles enough what with paying the bills and keeping the home together . . . and all you do is add to my troubles . . . where have you been, *hey*? . . . I demand to know . . . you're no better than a common prostitute, that's what you are, a street-walker . . . haven't you any pride? . . . let them make an absolute fool of you, you dirty slut . . . don't you realize whoever this man is he's back home *laughing* at you . . . what happens if you get pregnant? . . . who'll want you then, I'd like to know? . . . *I* won't have anything to do with you . . . you'd be out on the streets, on your own . . . how would you live, have you ever thought about that? . . . 'cause nobody would give you a job . . . *nobody* . . . nobody wants an unmarried mother . . . social workers, that's what would happen, those social workers would be all over you . . . prying . . . wanting to know all about *me* . . . busybodies, they are . . . *spies* . . . discover all your business and *use it in evidence against you* . . . .

And so on, into the night. Words can hardly describe what pleasure my mother got from this kind of tirade. Her voice, loud normally, would rise to shrieking pitch; she'd stomp rapidly from room to room in her delivery; switching the kettle on, then switching it off, making and unmaking beds in her excitement which, on a word full of sibilants such as "spies" caused her bright blue eyes to flash, dart from side to side, and her lips to curl. My sister would try to shout back at first but would gradually subside into tears and despair. People would go to bed, my mother would thrash for two minutes and sleep soundly, to be up again, bright-eyed, as they say, and bushy-tailed at six a.m. which was her best time and everybody else's worst. She would wake my sister and stand at the foot of the bed while its occupant's eyes were still half-closed:

There'll be no repetition of last night's affair, my lady . . . we'll have the juvenile court on to you if it ever happens again . . . you'll be in by half-past nine, in future . . . having *you* prowling about the streets with funny customers at all hours of the night . . . half-past nine, do you hear? Now get up or you'll be late for work . . . .

One may ask why my sister chose to put up with this treatment — why she didn't pack her bags and take off. But to where? To a bed-sitting room huddled over a gas fire, at the mercy of landladies who, by and large, are just as bastorial as my mother and demand to be paid for it too. But there was another, profounder reason, and that was her sense that my mother, despite her evil mind, her dramatic scenes, her authoritarianism which extended to my sister and not to me (a man can take care of himself), had had a hard and pathetic life. The only man she'd cared for, a man named Harold Warner, had been killed in the First World War just as she was about to marry him . . . on the rebound from this she married a man, a good deal older than herself who turned out to be a drunkard, for whose job security she was forced to plead before unsympathetic employers. When he died, she married my father who was sadistic and ill-tempered and who kept her chronically short of money. At his death she was left with a small amount of money, just enough to enable her to move all of us over to a suburb away from old and unpleasant memories. She was unskilled and took a variety of dirty and underpaid jobs. My sister felt sorry for her and figured life had dealt my mother a bust hand so that my sister's desire to live an emancipated life conflicted with a strong desire to be a comfort to my mother and to do her duty by her, a sense of which my mother had been careful to instil.

When I left for Norway in 1949, however, my sister took the

opportunity of leaving home and of encouraging my mother to sell up and take a job as a housekeeper in pleasant surroundings in Buckinghamshire. It was my mother's Waterloo. From this point on she moved slowly towards the end, sloughing remnants of the "home" she had tried to preserve for so long. It is not surprising then, that my sister gravitated towards those men that she thought would best exemplify all my mother's prejudices — bums, twisters, gamblers, lushes, together with innocent Irishmen and Jews — all the people and all the races that my mother was so terrified of. Just before I left for Norway she started going out with a man named Irish Jim, who played the dogs. He was so Irish as to seem like a stage imitation done by an incompetent and ham actor of Irish parentage and interests, but who was sophisticated enough to know the camp quality of Irishness and who could nonetheless not resist it.

My sister was drawn to him as surely and as irresistably as a masochist is to a whip. If you believe, or if others have made you believe, that the world is full of creeps, shysters, spies, sadists, criminals, rapists, murderers, deceivers, lechers, panders, saboteurs, whore masters, and so on, if you see the average person as a Nazi surgeon in disguise, only too willing to carve you up without benefit of anaesthetic, then you will dismiss all evidence to the contrary as a delusion and all apparent goodness in people as a snare. This was certainly my mother's attitude; it almost, through my mother's hard work as educator, became my sister's. But she possessed a faith in people, an innocence in dealing with them, which my mother was never able to destroy.

The cheap alarm clock ticked noisily on the mantelshelf. My mother was getting tired. We had finished the meal and were sitting over the two-bar, the cold creeping up the stairs and whining outside the door to be let in. She had talked about her operation, but I did not know how much she knew about her own condition. What chances did she have of living longer? If she knew she had less than a year to live, did she want me to share this knowledge? Did she want us to reach some sort of emotional plateau where we could discuss her life, its meaning, and her children's feelings towards her? You've had a lousy time, I said. But you've never had much luck, have you?

Oh, I don't know, dear, she said. I can't complain. I've had good innings, and I'm in my seventieth year. Not many people of my generation have been so lucky. And I've had you children... and a grandchild... what more could I have wanted?

More grandchildren, I suppose, I answered. It's a pity Jocelyn and I haven't got any.

No, she said quite vehemently, no, it's not. You're far better off without them . . . they're a terrible responsibility . . . neither you nor Jocelyn are the type . . . you both value your freedom too much . . . besides, you're too used to not having them now . . . no, my dears, be thankful you don't have them.

And I took this to mean that my mother knew if we were to have children she'd never live to see them. She found such a thought intolerable and all she could pray for now, poor woman, was our sterility.

It was on a day of false spring that we hired a car and took my mother for a drive. It turned out to be her last glimpse of her native Sussex, for two weeks after we got her back to Brighton she told us she had to be readmitted into hospital.

They're making me go back in. *That* place . . . such a nuisance while you're here. You will come and visit me, won't you dear? Of course, I know how *busy* you are . . . so *busy* . . . hardly the time, have you? Still, I know you'll find the time to visit me . . . of course, they'll only allow you an hour a day . . . and it's so far for you to come, isn't it? But just for an hour, dear, that won't kill you, will it? Not since you're going back to Canada so soon and you may not see me again . . . it can't be helped, can it? If they tell you to go back in, *back you go* . . . two little lumps, that's what they told me, two little lumps . . . on the opening, dear. (A mad little chuckle, a baring of the teeth.) Two little lumps, that's all it is . . . *on the opening* . . . .

These lumps she mentioned were what are known as "secondaries." They are growths that manifest the fact that the cancer cells had escaped into her system when they did the major operation. The surgeon would remove them. Then they'd grow again—either on the colostomy opening or elsewhere. He would treat the new ones, but by that time it would be purely a question of prolonging her life for a matter of days. Perhaps they'd give her up, though, and let her die in peace. Let her waft into oblivion on a bier of drugs.

Oh God, she said less guardedly, all I hope is that they don't give me the Drip.

It's just a minor affair, we said. You won't get any Drip.

I couldn't stand that all over again, she said. However, she said, looking on the bright side, there's one consolation. I'll see all my friends on the staff. Thought the world of me, most of them did ... bitches and sluts, the lot of them of course ... Irish, some of them, and *Jamaicans* ....

Blacks, we said, feigning a shudder or two. What about Pakis? we asked. And Yids?

Yids, dear, that's right, that's what your father used to call them. *Tin lids*, he used to say. No there's no Jews there. Catch *them* working in a hospital ... getting *their* lily white hands dirty. No Jew-boys there, thank God.

Then we must all of us count our blessings, we said.

I drove down and ferried her into hospital. The operation was what passes for successful and the next time I visited her I decided to stay in Brighton overnight to save the journey down the following day.

Give me the key, I said. I'll stay at your place.

She glared at me from her bed and bared her teeth.

Well, she hissed, keeping her voice low and out of earshot from the rest of the crowded ward. I don't know what to do, she said. I *suppose* it'll be all right. The landlady doesn't live on the premises ... but I'm so terrified that you'll *smoke* ....

I won't smoke.

What happens if you lose the key?

I won't lose the key, I said, trying not to snarl but at the same time thinking "sod the key."

Well, it's fire I'm worried about. Fire. Whatever you do don't strike any matches ... make sure the electric kettle is switched off. Otherwise it'll boil away and blow a *fuse*.

I won't blow any fuses.

And for God's sake make sure the window's shut before you sleep ... if a wind gets up in the night it'll close with a bang.

I'll remember.

I'm worried about that kettle.

Don't worry about *anything*. Get some rest.

I held her hand until she slept. Her breathing grew regular, though it remained shallow, and despite the paraphernalia of illness surrounding her I sensed her acrimonious vitality. Under the mauve and slender lids her eyes, I felt, were watching me with my mother's own blend of terror, pride, concern, and detestation. My son, she was clearly thinking: professor, firebug, traveller, kettle-fuser, prodigal, scoundrel, married man, traitor, and window-banger.

Then I walked from the hospital up to Freshfield Road. The days were growing longer and, though great flakes of soggy snow stretched down from a lowering sky, it was still light when I let myself into my mother's bed-sitter. It smelt of must, decay, and faintly of turds. Part of the latter smell inhered in the room itself and was a function of her disease, but most crept down fetidly from the upstairs toilet. It put me in mind of an epigraph from an old horror movie called *Cat People*: *As fog gathers in the valleys*, it read, *so evil stays in the low places of the world.*

But it's the only one in the house, my mother had complained. It's used by ten or twelve people. Dirty, filthy bunch they are too, my dear. Old men missing the bowl and *wetting the floor*; young chits who never pull the chain. *The things I've found there ...* my dear, I couldn't *begin* to tell you. It only gets cleaned once a week ... I've been up there a dozen times if I've been there once with one of my sprays ... trying to get rid of the smell ... *What on earth are you doing?* one of those dirty people said ... I'm spraying, I said ... spraying away the odour some of the filthy tenants leave behind them when they come in here, I said . . . Oh, she said, I hope you're not referring to me, she said . . . . So I turned round and said well, I said, if the cap fits, I said, you'll have to wear it, won't you? I said. That put *her* in her place, I can tell you that, my dear. And you know what that little hussy had the impertinence to say to me? Listen, she said, why don't you drop dead, you old bag? That's right ... that's exactly what she said ... *why don't you drop dead, you old bag?* I won't go on before my time, I said, not to please you or anyone else, I said ... she flounced out after that, I can assure you.

I stood for a moment in the barren room working out ways I could make it habitable. There was a heap of old, threadbare carpets and dishcloths lying in an oblique straight line which the door had pushed aside. I replaced them in their rightful position against the draft. I closed the heavy curtain and sat down in the easy chair by the two-bar. I switched the latter on. It glowed for a few moments then darkened rapidly as the meter clicked off. I shoved in a shilling with haste.

The room grew colder, damper.

On the card table was a book from the Brighton Public Library. A. G. Street's *Farmer's Glory*. I tried to read it but, half an hour later, I pushed it aside. I could not concentrate on it. What had my mother found attractive about it? It was the expression of a temperament radically opposed to hers — positive, optimistic, life-affirming. To her the simple account of farming a stretch of country would be heroic ... a terrible battle waged against a long-drawn-out but inevitable failure. She would see Street as Beowulf to Nature's

Grendel. But with Beowulf cast as loser. Street farmed a portion of Saskatchewan and I could almost hear my mother's voice: what about those wild *animals*, my dear, grizzlies and the like prowling round while you sleep? And those dreadful storms . . . not sheet lightning, either, but *forked . . . forked* lighting streaking all round you. And disease . . . what if you were to become ill . . . all those miles from a doctor? And prairie fires . . . burn to a cinder. And the neighbours? Ukrainians, I wouldn't mind betting. In a place like that you'd have to rely on them . . . people like that. No, my dear, no . . . it wouldn't do for me, she'd say.

If there was any central theme to her life it was fear — fear of the dark, of heights, of thunder, of her neighbours' opinions, of employers, of other people "getting to know your business." More generally fear of the social classes above hers, and below it, of foreigners, strangers, Catholics, Jews. These, together with nature, humankind, disease, and death, were some of the forces drawn up against her.

I put the book down and stared at the greasy wall above the suspect and fuseable kettle. What if she were right, I thought. Ah, not about trivia like thunder, heights, or the weather, but about people. Call hers a "bad faith" model of the world. Is it so unreasonable? One would think, listening to her talk, that human beings were utterly depraved — like characters out of *Death on the Installment Plan*. Indeed, she was something like a Céline figure herself. But what if hers were an accurate description of human life? It is true that everywhere man is attuned to joy — he senses it, yearns for it, plans for it, but always, or nearly always, he finds ways to frustrate himself from achieving it. A built-in "dislocation," as someone once put it. And if the phrase "original sin" means anything then that is what it means.

I considered the old lady as sinner. She rejected the joyous aspects of life because fundamentally she did not believe in them. She was scared of neither hardship nor solitude, as though these were the very terms of human existence. I began to wonder what death meant to her — perhaps no more than a drifting back into a welcome unconsciousness. Did she see life like the pagan in the Anglo-Saxon story who saw it as a bird that appears in a lighted mead-hall; it flies in through one window, across the hall, then out another window into the moonless night? Or did she see it as certain types of Christian see it — as a Vale of Tears through which one labours upwards towards the light and an everlasting view? I could not imagine either of these concepts appealing to my mother except in a sort of combination. Life was not a Vale of Tears but an affliction—a series of irritations and discomforts which the outer world tries its best to intensify, from which death as an emptiness, a total obliterating of being, is welcome enough. The slightest divergence from any routine must have been a terrible ordeal for her imagination. She was sustained by no belief except in the Powers of Evil and the forces of chance.

Her enemies were people, relatives, and ordinary physical objects such as a knife, a match, a shard of glass, six inches of water. She was embattled by the male sex, beseiged by her fellow, predatory females; and her foes were her own animal terror and suspicion of her surroundings.

No, her view of life was that it was a narrow ship bouncing on yeasty seas and crashing waves, in shrieking winds and hail—that it was a journey through the darkness, against the cold, the wind, the raging sleet.

There was a newspaper she'd been reading, folded over at an incomplete crossword puzzle. I picked up a ballpoint pen . . . she'd got stuck on a word of eight letters meaning "kind of boat" --ho--e-. I stared at it, mouth agape. It was too much for me—too *hard*.

I shoved the paper aside and found a pack of cards. My mother played a lot of solitaire. What was it like, I thought, to sit in this room over the two-bar, playing solitaire? I dealt the cards into the seven piles of Klondike patience . . . black two on red three, turn . . . red jack on black queen, turn . . . ace of hearts on the top, turn . . . finish . . . turn over the stock, card by card.

Ten grim minutes later I reached the end of it. I stared at the cards in front of me . . . five spades, three hearts, three diamonds . . . and the ace of clubs.

I'd seen the two of clubs, buried, buried well down in the stock. I picked up the pack again and started to shuffle. The room seemed even colder. I put a blanket around my shoulders—some thin scalpel of cold air had crept in through the window frames and had begun dissecting my neck. The two-bar clicked and blackened suddenly, like an ember plunged in water. There were vague noises, then a thudding sound from upstairs. I dealt the cards again, then got up to put a couple of shillings in the meter. They were the last. Nobody near here to change money into the rare, highly prized shillings at *this time of night* . . . and when those are used up, I thought, I'll have to go to bed.

Some bastard flushed the toilet.

Let's make a cup of tea, I thought, staring at the electric and *verboten* kettle. It seemed, from where I sat, like a copper toy. Behind it was my staring wall — stained and greasy from the cooking ring and, possibly, from the deleterious action of being stared at by generations of indigent tenants. Two ancient layers of paper peeled at the top, by the ceiling. The kettle came with the room, so did the cooking ring, the curtains, and the bed.

In fact the only things that were hers were the card table, this chair of little ease, and the piles of near rubbish in the cupboard. I thought of our home in Battersea . . . years ago . . . before the war. An odd place. We had our own toilet, unusual on that street, but of course it was outside the house. Yet, inside, the place was furnished like a palace with a corner cupboard that had belonged to Lord Nelson, fine hunting prints, a wooden plaque of the Iron Duke, a Chippendale or two. A curious, even incongruous, decor for a slum house. The explanation is that all this stuff had been given to my father, or stolen by him, in his capacity as French Polisher who specialized in country seats. And much of it had been left to him by *his* father, also a French Polisher, who had stolen it in *his* day. Where was this invaluable nest-egg now? Sold, flogged off, the lot of it, by my mother and for a song as soon as he was safely in the ground . . . as though anything that recalled her married life was anathema. Thus this card table.

I opened the cupboard and rummaged until I found the photograph album. Picture of my father encumbered by two kids, self and sister, one on each knee, Chanctonbury Ring in background: old man in pork pie hat, open-necked shirt, no collar, *braces*; he was smiling cynically. He was crude, tough, and sadistic (just the man, of course, for my mother, for he represented everything that terrified her). Apart from his French polishing he took an interest in slum youth clubs and worked in one in Battersea night after night, arriving home at midnight. On weekends he would dig in the garden, avoiding my mother, and whistling to himself. Thinking, probably, about World War I. What do I owe him? I hope nothing. A compulsion to make jokes, maybe. The habit of singing gently in cockney while working round the house. His old songs, culled from music-hall and Edwardian ballad, are still on my lips as I paint a wall or sand a cupboard. I catch myself crooning:

> It's a great big shime
> An if she belongta me
> I'd let er knaow oo's oo;
> A-puttin on a feller wot is six foot four

49

An er aonly five foot two.
They adn't bin married not a mumf nor more
When underneef the thumb gaoes *Jim* —
Isn't it a pity that the likes of *er*
Should put upon the likes o-o-o-f *im*?

Voice or no voice, jokes or no jokes, cruelty, war memories, ballads,
toughness, the lot — all dead — all gone. He died in 1945, at the age of
fifty, much, I suspect, to my mother's relief.

Photographs of self and sister when tots — Oh little lamb who
made thee?

A sheaf of older photographs — sepia great aunts, all of them
bombazined and whaleboned and now defunct — the over-fleshed
skeletons you find in everybody's closet.

Lahst
        night
Dahn our alley came a toff.
Right
        old
Geezer wiv a nahsty cough,
Sees
        my
                missus tikes is katey off.
In a very gentlemanly way.

No more photographs. Time to hit the sack. But no, I was wrong. It
was only eight-thirty.

Aha! She'd kept one of my books: *My Picture Book of Soldiers.*
All right. Remembrance of things past. We appear to be into it
tonight. I thumbed the pages nostalgically though even at the age of
seven I was never much taken with the military life. By that age I had
already envisioned my future as a malingerer. But here were
illustrations of men in field caps and puttees polishing tanks left over
from the Battle of Cambrai. In 1937! No wonder, three years later, the
British got kicked out of France. At the end of the book, on the flyleaf,
was an appallingly talentless drawing done by myself. What looked
like a man with the face of a fox, the ears of a cat, the tail of a skunk
stood upright entwined with barbed wire.

It was not barbed wire. I remember drawing this picture and what
it was supposed to represent. There used to be a program on the BBC

50

called "Children's Hour" which ran a serial called "Toy Town." It was M.C.'d by an invert named Uncle Mac who also played one of the characters in the serial—rather an irritating lamb who bleated in a Home Counties BBC regional dialect. (It was said of Uncle Mac, by the way, that his voice carried over the air one afternoon before the engineers had had a chance to fade him out and the message "that should hold the little bastards for a while" entered the homes of millions of his juvenile fans.) I was expected to listen to this program, probably because the stuff was romantically supposed by my mother to appeal to a child. An uneasiness crept over me as I remembered that this drawing was meant to be Larry-the-Lamb but it was an unhappy, put-upon lamb for he was tied to a stake being flagellated by the dim, androgynous figures in the background, intended probably as women. Possibly the image was generated by the contents of the book itself with its tale of military life which featured, as I must have known even then, discipline, court-martial, and Field Punishment Number One. All I know is that I had repressed this picture, and perhaps the fantasies leading to its creation, for at least a quarter of a century. I stared at my own artwork with mounting horror.

> Says,
> ai, gal,
> Eres some noos that I've to tell,
> Yer
> right
> old
> Uncle Fred a Camberwell
> Lahst
> night,
> Croaked is lahst wivvaht a light,
> Leavin you is donkey and a cart.

The black bats of Freshfield Road began to cluster. I must have been about eleven and in the "headmaster's class" at Cheam, Surrey, Church of England School for Boys. A small, frigid classroom with a tiny grate and gas lamps, lit by a flint at the end of a long pole, to illuminate, though dimly, the gloomy winter afternoons. Boys from other classes were sent in frequently to be caned by the headmaster—a tall, powerful man with icy grey eyes and a huge jaw. He was *cool*, for if he experienced any pleasure from these canings he hid it well. About twice a week a terrified child named Bowman would be sent in for a beating — a born loser, as they say. Most of us would undergo this punishment with a sort of bored resignation, but Bowman would resist, not with defiance, but with screams, blubberings, and attempts to escape, running round the room, and hopping over desks . . . the grim-jawed, tight-lipped head after him, quite slowly, confident of final victory, his great hand finally scooping Bowman by the collar. Then he lay the shrieking, threshing boy across the desk and whacked him savagely. The whole scene reminds me now of the rabbit flayed alive in Kosinski's *The Painted Bird*. It would take perhaps twenty minutes, this process, from Bowman's entry to climax across the desk — the same period of time, perhaps, occupied by the faster sexual encounter that might take place during a busy day. Our pleasure, as voyeurs, was almost certainly sexual, of course, but mixed with delight in the breaking of classroom monotony. The Roman holiday . . . .

I stood up and paced the narrow room puffing at an illicit cigarette. Bowman and flagellated lambs! It was enough. The room seemed suddenly filled with my mother's presence.

Stop it, I said aloud. That's enough.

It's the way things are, I could almost hear the presence answer.

I put on my greatcoat and stumbled out into Freshfield Road to find the nearest pub. I would not, if I could find a half-decent hotel, stay the night in that haunted house.

With the aid of a double scotch and a pint of beer at the half-deserted pub down the road I attempted to drown out the messages from my mother's dark, negating soul.

1978

Memoirs of a Laundering Man

Whenever I visit Montreal now I see it as the tourist sees it — as an area bounded north to south by the mountain and the old town, and west to east by Atwater and Pine. Though there is very little left of the once noble Sherbrooke Street and, though strenuous efforts have been made by the municipal government to appease the frantic hunger of local real estate developers by throwing them large scraps of the city to devour, Montreal managed to retain some fraction of its graciousness and individuality and it is difficult for me to believe I once saw it as a sub-arctic slave camp — an embodiment of our civilization at its very worst.

I acquired this perhaps irrational perspective over a bitter period of about eighteen months which began rather ambivalently with my return to southern civilization from the Arctic. In fact it was on New Year's Day, 1959, that I flew from the DEW Line en route to Montreal trading, at Edmonton, a DC4 for what seemed a highly unstable Viscount. This plane lumbered gamely through tempest, crosswind, air-pocket, and down-draught though not without taking its emotional toll on its passengers. I tried to calm my nerves by recalculating, for the thousandth time in eighteen months, my bank account. By the standards of those days the ten thousand dollars or so I had saved in that period formed the beginnings of a private income and it seemed to me that I had solved the chief problem that confronts a writer which is this: how, having sworn dreadful oaths, is he to shun the demon Work? By incarcerating myself in the Arctic I had become the possessor of capital, though it did not look as though I would live to enjoy it. I promised myself to take care of this money despite the fact that even if I were to invest it at ten percent it would only fetch me about eighty dollars a month—hardly enough, as a friend of mine put it, to keep a man in contraceptives. No, if I were ever to get out of this aircraft in one piece I would parlay my money into a small fortune by subtle but, I hoped, honest means—*get me out of this, O Lord, and I shall sin no more*—a judicious real estate venture here, a penny stock there—*Yea though I walk through the valley of the shadow of death I shall fear no evil*—or perhaps a second mortgage or two, a blue chip just for comfort . . . I shall smile at my bank manager . . . put the fellow at his ease . . . get him to cough up a loan as down payment . . . on what? Perhaps an oil tanker, or an ICBM, or a travelling brothel to serve my onanistic brethren up in the Arctic—*and forgive us our trespasses as we forgive them that trespass against us . . . .*

The Viscount, to everybody's relief, ground to a halt at Toronto and refused to go any further. Not even a grizzled bush-pilot flying by the seat of his pants to get the mail through would've put finger to control-column that night. I continued my journey by train. There was much to greet me in Montreal. I owed myself, for instance, several months of gracious living but there was also a complex situation developing which involved my family and which would require gentle, precise injections of hard cash for its resolution. Nevertheless, I experienced that same euphoria a man knows on the day he is sprung from jail or from the army—a feeling of the openness of the world with its roads, fields, and cities; as though each day were a crisp and cloudless morning in early spring—a rising of the sap. Even as my train jolted into Montreal which lay under its protective pall of smog, my mood lasted. It lasted as my taxi slithered along icy streets bordered by sidewalks covered with a snow ground to a filthy, greyish powder by the scurrying, frantic feet of a million pedestrians trying to beat the Big Clock. It lasted even though I felt I had never been away and it was, of course, reinforced by greetings and renewals of friendships and liaisons.

Let me, for a moment, speak of these liaisons. People often ask me what I did for sex on the DEW Line. It is a question easily answered, as is the more pertinent question—*what did you do for women?* The answer is, there *were* no women. Yet I saw no evidence of homosexuality on the DEW Line; it may have been there but I was not

54

moved in that direction myself and neither was my immediate circle. Each of us knew exactly what he was giving up when he signed the contract and it was as though we had resolved, for the duration of that money-making period, to turn ourselves into celibates. I can assure you that this is not as difficult as many people like to make out and the remark, often made to me by both men and women, to the effect that *they* couldn't do without sex for longer than a month at the outside is a self-serving one designed to present the speaker as virile, lusty, multi-orgasmic, and Rabelaisian as to sexual appetites. I can also assure you that I, and everybody I knew in the Arctic, was quite normally sexed, whatever that may mean. But when I returned to Montreal, of course, I was eager to embark on as many sexual adventures as were possible and thus became involved, as could have been predicted, rather too hastily with a number of entirely unsuitable women.

The more positive encounters occurred while my joy at being sprung back into civilization lasted. I seemed to be meeting mostly cheerful girls of the kind who wished eventually to become married women and to own plastic gnomes scattered on a suburban lawn in Hampstead or Outremont and who wished, before they thus imprisoned themselves, to sow their wild oats with men like me too pleasure-seeking to be taken seriously as marriageable propositions. But as the city began to pall on me, and as my responsibilities grew heavier, I became aware that my attentions were diverting themselves to women of a more philosophical, even ponderous, disposition. The first of these was an employee of one of the local newspapers — a girl, some ten years older than myself, who specialized in fashions. She was deeply involved in a strange, half-religion called "Ontology" and her side interests included Zen Bhuddism and Yoga, a discipline she would practise anywhere and at any time; for example, in a crowded restaurant where she might suddenly lift her hand close to her shoulders, stretch her fingers so that her palms were horizontal, then go rigid. When she had precipitated enough uneasiness in the growing number of spectators, she would begin rotating her head, moving it backwards and forwards then, for variation, from side to side like, she may have supposed, a Balinese dancer but, in my opinion, more exactly recalling a badly executed hieroglyphic off the Rosetta stone. I knew, of course, that these attention-catching antics were Josette's method of dealing with an unsatisfactory distribution of component parts of the Soul, but it was an imbalance to which I was beginning to respond as though it were also my own. During the same period I complicated my life by becoming fascinated with a woman called Edna

55

who lacked Josette's resources of eccentricity and exhibitionism and who would spend most of her off-duty time, she was a nurse, staring at a tank of ornamental fish in her otherwise barren apartment. Since those days the name Edna has always, with its leaden syllables, suggested to me a heaviness of spirit and a sluggishness of response to the concept of pleasure — though I agree that this association is totally irrational. I thought, mistakenly as it turned out, that it was my lot, duty, and within my competence to cheer her up. The cheerful girls began to strike me as shallow and frivolous in comparison with Edna and I began to lose my physical interest in them almost as rapidly as they in me.

But the second and ultimately more pressing issue was money. Like other returning DEW Liners, loggers, and lottery winners, I found that normal life had suddenly become much more expensive and my day filled with people who felt very strongly that I had no right to let them struggle on through life without assistance; that any attempt to restrict outflow of money would be regarded as tight-fistedness. The problem is that one agrees with this verdict only too readily. There is only one way out: to make more money. As Bertolt Brecht once put it with magnificent simplicity,

> A jingling pocket
> Makes easy life.

Accordingly, I found myself one morning in early spring in the chalet on the top of Mount Royal drinking coffee, a newspaper before me, advertisements ringed in pencil. Another DEW Liner sat with me, a good friend, a budding laundryman as it turned out. He chose one of the advertisements at random and smart-alecked over to a phone.

Half an hour later we were talking to a seedy, dapper little man with a maquereau moustache, belted raincoat, and soft hat. He claimed to be an executive in some factory or other but he also ran, as a side line, this semi-automatic laundry on Burnside, not far from McGill. There was a short counter in the laundry presided over by a fat, elderly woman whose name was Madame Fourchette. Behind her three girls ironed underwear, whilst against the wall were lined ten fuming washing machines and a huge gas-operated dryer. There was also a small, rattling centrifuge fed by a very fat teen-age girl. Further back a flight of steps made of unistrut led onto a plywood mezzanine. The executive, whose name was Chabot, took us onto his mezzanine and showed us a rusty agglomeration of pipes, struts, valves, U-joints, vats, siphons, tubes, retorts, all covered with thick briny sediment and held together with ancient planks of two-by-four.

"It's the Water Softener," Chabot explained. "Every two weeks you have to Soften The Water."

Also on the mezzanine was a rackful of obviously broken and useless tools, sacks of salt, jam jars full of rusting assorted washers. left-handed screws, bolts, and rings. Against one wall lay an indescribable heap of passé machinery made of cast iron, rather like a turn-of-the-century steam-engine except that it was fitted with hoops and things that looked like weight lifters' dumbbells. Downstairs again I blew my nose and was interested to find the Kleenex had turned jet-black, like some kind of mad litmus paper.

"What's that heap of junk by the wall upstairs?" I asked.

He told me I needn't worry about it. "It's the spring-drop-operated-crucible-blower-mechanism," he said. Then he showed us the water heater, an immense, asbestos covered tub with a gas furnace roaring beneath it. On top, an enormous pipe snaked and elbow-jointed off through a hole that had been cut in the mezzanine floor by a blunt saw. A door led to a washroom then to a passage full of garbage cans, finally to a wicked little slype between the laundry and a Chinese-American restaurant next door. We got back inside with haste. We told Chabot we'd wait around to see how many customers came during the afternoon. Also that we'd study the books, then call him. He left, and so, after an hour, did my friend and I was left to take up my position by the counter. As soon as Chabot disappeared Madame Fourchette said, in a whisper that rattled the windows:

"Ah dat son of a bitch . . . 'ow much you pay, uh? . . . you gib 'im a 'alf what 'e says, uh? Ah don't trust de dirty liddle crook . . . four years I work for 'im . . . four years an' 'e pay me no more dan 'e did de day I started . . . cochon . . . excrement . . . maudit voleur . . . crook, dass what 'e is, Misser Mill'."

"Funny you should take him for a crook," I said. "I think he's something softer and more fancy than a crook. A Kotex salesman for example."

For some reason this remark seemed to turn the old girl on.

"Ah tabernacle! . . . you t'ought so 'uh? Ah my God dat's good . . . Kotex salesman! . . . eh. La . . . Rose Aimée! Rose Aimée! ya dit stung vendeur d'Kotex! Ah mon Dieu! Ah Jésus Christ! Ah maudit sacrilage d'un bordel!"

She screamed with laughter, tears running down her face; the fat teenager cackled and pounded too many sodden sheets into the centrifuge which attacked her with a dreadful snarl. She translated my comment several times into her vile Pointe Aux Trembles argot for the benefit of the three drabs behind her who could not, among them, muster so much as a smile. Shortly after this a customer entered and the old lady transferred her noisy attentions to him. Then she became quite busy. I studied the books: according to Chabot's accountant, after salaries were deducted, expenses paid, bills met, we should be left with about a hundred and fifty a week. It seemed a good deal, for those days, and this is what I told my friend when he arrived, somewhat out of breath from his lunch-hour visit to his girl-friend's apartment. Straightway he phoned Chabot, was quoted ten thousand dollars which he refused, offering fifteen hundred. Chabot riposted, with a sarcastic laugh, that he wasn't going to drop a penny below nine thousand. My friend bashed down the phone then dialled again with an offer of four thousand and, finally, they brought one another down to a price of five thousand five hundred, whereof quit. Just before six o'clock we took the deeds and a cheque to a notary with fat jowls and a receding chin and made the transfer. And this is how one buys a laundry.

That night I phoned Josette with the news that I had finally grown responsible as to the disposition of my DEW-Line money. She was glad I had invested in an honest business but expressed some doubts as to whether it would assist in my spiritual development. Edna, on the other hand, and as befitted the daughter of a Toronto stock-broker, took the view that I had done the right, free-enterprising thing and grew quite positive about it.

"What tremendous news!" she said. "It's magnificent! What an investment! Nearly 14%! And a laundry! Such wonderful opportunities! You must be terribly pleased! How lucky that you saw that ad! You'll never regret it! etc., etc."

Perhaps the first indication that this laundry might prove less of an asset than it first appeared took place shortly after my friend returned to the DEW Line for his third contract, leaving me in sole charge. I had brought a small, used, Morris Minor since I had conceived a loathing of cabs and buses, and that morning drove it over to Burnside Street to supervise the sudsing of Montreal's dirty linen. The day was blithe, with a fresh wind and tiny, high-flying clouds; paper rustled along Sherbrooke Street; man, grinning, scampers for elusive hat; students amble towards McGill and I to the laundry where Mme Fourchette awaited me — a basilisk, perhaps, but this day a eupeptic one.

"Ah, Misser Mill', my 'usban' 'elp you tonight."

"What's this, Madame?"

"My 'usban' Romeo, 'e 'elp you wid my machine. It's no good. It's sinking."

Puzzled, I inspected the line of washers. One of them did, indeed, appear to be sinking. The wooden supports were rotting and the machine had a decided list. One would have to get underneath it whilst another grabbed it, to remove and replace two boards. I examined the slimy treacherous looking wood with some displeasure.

"An' dat odder machine is licking."

"Licking, hey? Well I can fix that right now."

I stumbled up to the mezzanine and unjunked a wrench. It was one of the adjustable sort, that is to say, its lower jaw was supposed to move upwards on a rack by means of a knurled cylinder. This cylinder was rusted, almost welded, to the rest of the tool. I found a pair of pliers and some oil and sat on the floor, assuming a lotus position. My experience of machinery, in the Arctic, told me I was in for a *mauvaise quart d'heure*. I oiled the wrench and tapped it gently with a hammer. I applied the jaws of the pliers to the cylinder at a strategic point. I had a short rest, then, with great concentration, grabbed the handles, squeezing hard, turning at the same time. I let out an involuntary scream. The jaws had slipped wildly, catching the skin between thumb and forefinger a savage bite. I turned tail and went downstairs, licking my wound.

"Ah my God you 'urt yasel' . . . ah maudit Saint ciboire de Christ I 'ear you scream out from down 'ere. Huguette! Huguette! Porte le band-aid-lo."

Huguette brought a first-aid kit and the old party bandaged my hand. I turned my attention to the leaking machine, flexing my pliers. Each machine was raised on a long platform. Underneath there was a sliding plank which would, when operated, expose a system of verdigrised, brazen intestines. Water was dripping from one end of a U-joint. I lay on the floor and got the pliers on a large hexagonal nut. Contorted like a Japanese wrestler I applied terrible pressure. The jaws slid round the nut bringing off a fine shaving of brass. A washing machine to my right burst into life with a shattering, earth-quaking roar . . . I tried again with the pliers, then went upstairs to get the now functioning wrench.

Down on the floor again I reached into the bowels, grabbed the handle, and managed to tighten the nut by a fraction. I examined the bead of water on the joint. It grew slowly, dangled like a prolapsed rectum, then dropped with a light plash onto the blotting paper wood to be converted to a dark stain. But that was all. No other moisture passed that way. I stood up, half crippled, with a feeling of achievement.

"None but the brave deserve the fair, Madame Fourchette," I pointed out.

"Chabot, 'e never work wid 'is 'ands like you, de dirty-son-of-a-bitch. You see 'im wid 'is gloves on all de time? Get a man in, 'e used to say."

My own hands were covered with black slime and verdigris. Another hour and I was due to meet my banker to borrow some money as a down-payment on a triplex. I bent stiffly to close the panel. To my horror water dripped from the *near* end of the U-joint. It was enough to make a man's copy of *The Prophet* slip from his nerveless fingers. I closed the panel with haste and slunk off to the washroom at the back. I looked at my face in the mirror above the stained and rotting basin. It was just a face.

"Don' forget you come back, eh? My 'usban', 'e gonna be 'ere at six."

The afternoon appointment went well. I got my loan. Three sharks, a vendor, a notary, an agent, robbed a fourth and would-be shark, played by myself, of a down-payment for a building in the Hochelaga District—the same area into which my friend Irving Layton, the poet, was pouring royalty and Canada Council money. I felt enlarged and confident as, the sun beginning to set, I drove to the laundry again.

Romeo Fourchette was a small, febrile man with dyed hair and an enormous, frog-like mouth, only one corner of which seemed to function. He worked in a beer parlour and concern over a personality clash with the manager had given him a slight touch of Bell's Palsy which had caused this mouth oddity. Also, one eye refused to blink properly so that it appeared to be weeping. The other eye, however, was red, fiery, and malevolent.

"My 'usban' 'elp you," explained the old lady. Romeo nodded and smiled horribly. We walked over to the listing machine. Romeo said:

"Goddam' it's bad. You 'ole it Misser Mill', and I'll get some wood."

"Wood? Wood? What you mean, wood? It's blocks, you need. Blocks. Unnerstan'? Blocks, *chalice.*"

He turned on his wife with surprising savagery.

"An' what you t'ink we use for blocks, you stupid ol' bag. Hey? Gold? Ah, mange ta merde what you t'ink we use? Misser Mill', I got de blocks already down 'ere."

"O.K., take it easy you two." I went out and got a gallon of white wine from the trunk of my car. "Look, I bought you this."

"Don't gib 'im nottin' to drink de p'tit cochon, till 'es done some work."

Romeo ignored her. "You 'old her, Misser Mill', an' I'll rip out de ol' planks."

I embraced the washing machine with my arms and Romeo knelt down with a claw hammer. My back started to creak—the greasy, slippery sides of the machine became elusive. Slowly, when Romeo had removed a supporting plank, the machine began to slip down through my encircling arms like a yielding debutante. Suddenly I lost control of it. I cried out. "Elle a tire sur moi!" I yelled, "elle a tire sur moi! Vite! Vite!" Romeo ducked aside, nimble as a dwarf acrobat in a circus as the machine eased itself down on its old copper pipes and settled to the floor. There was a sudden smell of marsh gas and a strong rivulet of dirty water gushed across the room.

"Madame . . . ah Jesus . . . the main . . . turn the water off at the main!"

"De main, de main, de main, de main, quick!" screamed Romeo. "Wassa madder wid you?"

She wobbled swiftly to a rusty valve in a pipe near the wall and failed to turn it. With enviable presence of mind she grabbed Romeo's hammer and bashed the valve until it closed. Rust flew up into the air like sparks from a forge. But the rivulet became a trickle, then it stopped. The pool of water on the floor became stagnant and thin, greasy little rainbows glinted at its edges.

"I need a drink," I said, "before we go any further."

I poured three drinks into paper cups as they argued bitterly in French.

"My fault," I said. "Let's try again."

I got the jack out of the car, eased it under the machine with great care and difficulty, cranked until the washer began to list. Romeo blocked it up and finally, after three-quarters of an hour of harrowing toil, the machine was upright again, at its correct height, level, standing over a tangle of bent and squashed tubing.

"Job for the plumber now," I said, evasively. I heard a tapping at the window. It was Josette, come to fetch me. We had planned to eat out to celebrate my new purchase in Hochelaga but since Josette had

61

recently accepted a theory ascribing all disease to constipation, and all constipation to an entity she called mucous, and mucous itself to certain foods taken in combination (for example, fish and potatoes) and since she was now in the habit of confronting *maitre d*'s with her charts and lists of these combinations which she also wished to take in to the chef, a date to eat out with her was not one I looked forward to with as much enthusiasm as might otherwise be expected. At any rate I unlocked the door for her and she stood, classically elegant, surveying the floor of the laundry which suggested more the aftermath of the Dieppe raid than it did a money-making concern. We drank white wine with the Fourchettes, parted from them with many expressions of mutual regard, then walked out to confront the evening on St. Catherine's Street.

One night, months later, as I walked home from God knows where, snow began to fall. It fell hesitantly, without a wind behind it, from a black nimbus cloud six hundred feet above my head. The cloud glowed a sullen yellow where it crossed the downtown ribbons of neon signs; snow furred the outlines of buildings — it lay thin on the streets like a white bile into which one's feet squelched leaving black asphalt footprints. Ridges of snow balanced themselves on the grids of iron steps leading, habitant style, up to my apartment. It snowed all that night and the next day; cars and buses slithering wildly up Côte des Neiges — the slightest, insignificant gradient became a terrible obstacle. The sky was as sullen as a bus queue. Blue overalled men in backs of trucks shovelled chloride and sand onto the patent leather roadway; snow piled on trees and slithered down one's neck in long, shimmering spears; working people crept home in rush hours, overcoats collared high, torsos thrust forward — the Montreal Fandango. Drunkards left the wretched purlieus of the Windsor Station for the less hearty but warmer comforts of the Salvation Army; snow stopped falling, thawed slightly, froze, became palimpested with fresher, hard-packing snow, to be cleared away by great roaring machines with lower jaws grating on the ground, scooping, spewing into trucks a bouillaibaise of yellow sludge, unmelted, car-rotting chloride, pedestrian overshoes, and rusted, discarded car-mufflers. Christmas day dawned yellowly.

During this period I continued to live in the Pine Street-St Denis area driving my thwarted Morris Minor from triplex, to loan-shark, to laundry, to Proctor and Gamble for soap, to City Hall, to Police Court to pay parking fines. Winter brought discontent to customers who would, it seemed, rather wallow at home, gawking, unshaven and beer-canned, at television in a litter of filthy underwear than bring it, like Magi, through the winter evenings, to Madame Fourchette. Profits disappeared—the books glowed red. One week, angered at continuous expenses incurred by never-ending faults in the washers, I replaced the entire ten, borrowing money from the bank against my rapidly falling stocks and shares; a few days later a fire inspector, refusing to be bribed, condemned the water heater and, in order to operate at all, I was forced to buy entirely new equipment. I became the slave of Madame Fourchette. Money vanished. I was engaged in a point-to-point, all over the city, from morning till evening. I had the usual middle-class nightmares in which I was imprisoned in a gigantic, rotating drum, with a hundred others, fighting for a hold on the drum's wall.

Josette had gone: left her job to explore the hinterland of Guatemala where, she had heard, there was an esoteric sect of great religiosity. (She surfaced a year later, totally unenlightened, so far as I could tell.) Other lovers deserted me as I grew more and more morose—worn down by business worries, as they say. My ties to Edna, now under psycho-analysis and busy with, among other things, trying to convince me I was a repressed homosexual, grew stronger. It is a measure of my desperation that I proposed marriage to her. I was, fortunately for all concerned, rejected as, of course, subconsciously I knew I would be. I found it impossible to be alone. Without company I would read, write letters, attack crossword puzzles, write poems, listen to the radio, smoke heavily, make plans, or think about the past. Time yawned and gaped; it became an enemy, something you kill with frenzied action.

One bright morning I stood staring at the telephone. I had left it off the hook, of course, to discourage Madame Fourchette's hysterical early morning calls of which "Misser Mill', Misser Mill', my shimminy, my shimminy, you get down 'ere quick, my shimminy smoking" might be a typical example. But she would, every morning, get the phone company to send a signal down the line. I stared at the instrument and listened to its high-pitched, ullullating whine with considerable displeasure. Something snapped within. I reached down and tore the phone out of the wall by its roots. I got into my car, drove to a gas station, and bought three gallons of white gas. I would wait until nightfall, enter the deserted laundry, sprinkle this gas over floor, walls, plywood mezzanine, water softener, chimney, centrifuge, and crapped-out machine then throw a match to it. It then occurred to me that an old lady lived in an apartment behind the laundry. I would have to warn her: "Madame, you'll have to leave right away—there's going to be a fire." Or I could burn her to a crisp. Why not? I was a business man, wasn't I? Then let's do it right. This is the big time, lady, and somebody's got to lose.

But I rejected the arson possibility. Instead I went back home, packed a bag, and pointed the car to the Victoria Bridge. If I couldn't burn my laundry at least I could leave this maddened, industrial slum behind, head for Mexico, and never come back. The freeway ran south and Montreal's concrete towers lay safely miniaturized in my rear-view mirror. I pressed down the accelerator. The towers disappeared and my heart began to leap for joy. I was free! Feckless! No money! No plans! Just the open road! A recrudescence of my youth! The Wind on the Heath, brother, if only I could feel that I would gladly live forever! But my heart was leaping too soon. The towers had left my mirror because they were now appearing, fully grown and monstrous in my right hand window. The freeway's treachery had been subtle for it had looped me, without my realizing it, round and away from Mexico, back to its tainted and malevolent source.

A man must take such signs seriously. I escaped eventually, but not before much blood had flowed under the bridge and the laundry, with all its debts, sold for a dollar. By that time the rest of my DEW-Line money had vanished, some whittled by my own heavy spending, most by losses on property and stocks, and by the activities of lawyers, notaries, real estate agents, policemen, fire-marshals, health-inspectors, etc., all of whom cluster like gannets round the small business-man in Montreal, and all of whom need paying off.

I am, I need hardly say, no longer a laundering man. I live quietly and carry no big stick. There may be clean, well-functioning, and profitable laundries, but the Burnside laundry was not one of them. It is good to respect laundering men, even to admire them, for attention must be paid to them—but I am glad I am no longer to be counted among their number. The word "laundry" may have pleasurable connotations for many people but when *I* hear it I reach, as Herman Goering used to say about the word "culture," for my revolver.

1980

Festival at Simon Fraser

I.   S.F.U. — The Early Days

The first public appearance of Simon Fraser's new President, Pauline Jewett, took place on a warm September afternoon last year. Our spurious Scottish connection was acknowledged by a trio of bagpipers and Ms. Jewett's oddly unheckled speech was followed by a low-keyed sort of festival which included the distribution of free doughnuts and Pepsi-Cola, the presence of a not-too-obviously talented juggler, a clown or two, and the mingling together in the Mall of a couple of thousand students, staff, and faculty in a rare spirit of community. One of the chief glories of the University, the resident Purcell String Quartet, played Haydn in one corner of the Mall but its performance was heeded only by a small group of students and about half-a-dozen tiny children from the day-care centre who gawked at these well-tempered musicians at a range of two feet.

Occasions of this sort at Simon Fraser have either been totally disastrous or entirely bland. This was neither. In fact I was quite warmed by it and inclined to grow sentimental. I retain a certain affection for S.F.U. even though, as a writer, I am somewhat outside the main flow of its history. Nevertheless it was a part of my life and if there are seven ages of man then the Simon Fraser Age was one of mine—a curiously paradigmatic age since it encompassed birth, growth, maturity, decay, and what may turn out to be an illusory renewal. I was there when S.F.U. was built, when it began to expand, when it stood in danger of being torn apart by internecine warfare, when its hardly audible death rattles, like those of most North American universities, seemed to sigh across the land, and I am there now as what looks like a recrudescence is taking place. I am prompted by this nostalgia to write down my version of the university's early history, and to try to make some generalizations about the academic life and my own stance within it.

Simon Fraser was built in great haste so that what in 1964 was a stretch of bushland on top of a hillock consisting of Eocene sandstone, shale, and conglomerate, about a thousand feet high and dipping fifteen degrees to the south, became by the fall of 1965 a few acres of Passchaendale-consistency mud, concrete bunkers, hard-hatted workmen, cranes, architect's sidemen bearing blueprints, a botch of carpenters, a catamite of interior decorators, security guards dressed in what the first president called "university green," the President himself accompanied by his flotilla of cronies, axemen, succubi, oligarchs, "plumbers," apologists, publicists, dragomen, skivvies, foreswearers, faculty, opportunists, turnkeys, con-men, sycophants, and perjurers. Destined to play Brutus to this man's Caesar was the first chancellor, Gordon Shrum, a tall, overpowering presence with a wide and savage grin redolent of gold-rimmed teeth and whose bustling, autocratic air was that of a Renaissance prince—a Borgia, let us say—and indeed, when togged-up in his academic regalia, scarlet cloak and velvet cushion hat, he put me in mind of Pope Alexander VI plotting his next poisoning or rapier thrust through some arras. I liked Shrum and still like him. There are many good stories about him but, libel laws being what they are, I cannot repeat them. He was also co-chairman of B.C. Hydro and I remember a photograph that appeared in the local paper of Shrum drinking a glass of water labelled "defoliant" intended to show environmentalists that the chemicals used to strip the ground from under the hydro lines were harmless to human life. I believe though, that the glass *did* contain defoliant and that the point of the photograph was that only the superhuman Shrum could drink the stuff without instantly keeling over.

Shrum built Simon Fraser University almost single-handedly. Its construction was precipitated by an educational report delivered to the provincial Government emphasizing the need for immediate creation of higher educational facilities. The Government implemented the report from a variety of motives, many of them, I have no doubt, recessed deep in the unconscious but connected with the anal need to create monuments to Social Credit. The premier in those days was W. A. C. Bennett whose favourite boast, hard to refute, was that he was "plugged into God." S.F.U., then, was either directly or indirectly an Act of God.

It was Shrum, playing Moses to Bennett's Jehovah, who hired the first President—a meteorologist named Patrick McTaggart-Cowan whose reputation had been made at the Department of Transport where he was known as "McFog." As is the case with any other man or woman involved in the pseudo-science of weather prediction, McFog's grasp of phenomenological data was tenuous. The boundaries between fact and fiction remained hazy to him so that though by no means a conscious liar he was not good at picking out the truth and was always liable to occlude the latter with a warm-front of verbiage and misleading information producing obstructions to vision, haze, and layers of alto-stratus through which, according to the DOT manual, "the sun appears as though through ground glass." Nevertheless he was a jovial figure, always willing to while away a few hours with anybody who wanted to see him, a sheep, as Churchill said of Atlee, in sheep's clothing whose main fault was that he surrounded himself with wolves, ferrets, jackals, stoats, and vultures.

The charter faculty was a mixed lot. I remember the strong feeling of depression with which I came away from our first department meeting. "What were they like?" my wife asked. "Two maniacs, two snobs, four losers, and one clown," I answered, "apart from myself and three other nondescript people." My depression sprang from the fear that since I had been hired by the same man who'd hired the rest then I must be subsumed under one of those categories. At the second meeting the department head was forced to leave half-way through, leaving the only full professor in the chair. As soon as the head had left, the department began to tear one another to shreds, guzzling each other's entrails in the most hysterical fashion. I was both fascinated and appalled—fascinated because, like any other writer, I thrive on scabrous confrontations, and appalled because of the implied threat to a security upon which I also thrive.

When the university opened its doors, though, most of the festerings and splinterings, already making themselves apparent, were for the most part hidden. There was one other bad omen. The registrar had for some weeks been corresponding with prospective students, advising them about their courses and working out their programs. He

67

went so far as to tailor-make their timetables — pencilling in their schedules on a form which showed days of the week and hours of the day. This is a laudable idea, of course, but what was not known at the time was that the poor fellow was undergoing a nervous breakdown so that the students were confronted by these perfectly maniacal timetables on which they'd been scheduled for three different classes commencing at the same hour, forcing each of them to be in three places at once, a feat only possible for the Chancellor. On the first day of Simon Fraser's operation, then, the registration concourse was filled with a milling, anxious, paranoid, highly confused mob of students. An augury, as I say. There were to be many such scenes in the years to come.

Nevertheless, the first ceremony went well. The university was opened by Lord Lovat, Chief of the Clan Fraser, who had winged in from Scotland bearing a claymore as a gift, and an honorary degree was thrown at Bennett himself, an action symbolizing the Neoplatonic two-way relationship between the One and the Angelic Mind. The event was marred only by an underground assertion that some dental technician or car salesman from Wichita, Kansas, was the rightful Chief of the Clan but that, though he was present at the ceremony, he had been ignored by the administration because of his obscurity. It was the university's first Class Issue but little was made of it at the time partly, I suppose, because Lovat himself, a lofty aristocrat with an upper-class accent and a noble head of silver hair, stole the show. "Don't you just *hate* that man?" one of my colleagues, a small, splenetic fellow, asked me, clenching and unclenching his fists and trembling all over like an advanced case of Parkinson's Disease. "Don't you just hate that man? So tall ... so handsome ... so *debonair.* ..."

I felt oddly cheered by all this nonsense, however, and as I stripped off my borrowed academic regalia and ambled in mufti among the People I forgot about the half-finished concrete structures, the mud, the faculty blockheads, the manifest twerps and incompetents in the administration, and began to experience a sense of community. Were there not good people too at Simon Fraser? People like Jerry Zaslove, Michael Bawtree, Murray Schafer? And would we not build a *proper* university together? It would be a genuine alternative to the bland but pompous institutions spread across the country. Such as the University of British Columbia some twenty miles away which was filled with punctuation fetishists and obsessed by grades, prerequisites, and educative rituals. Surely we had enough

68

people of brains, energy, creativity, and imagination to build a new, experimental, community of scholars and artists unique in North America. And it would be a genuine monument: not to Social Credit, not to Gordon Shrum, not to the fuglemen, publicity agents, and planners who had made the physical plant possible, but somehow to the Human Spirit.

This afflatus began to die the next day though some of it lingered with me for another year and some remnant of that nostalgia to be part of a "community" lingers with me still, as it does with us all. But I am a pessimist by nature, though, I hope, a cheerful one, and I have grave doubts as to the possibility of such a community ever existing in the Kingdom of this World. And when I consider whether or not the modern universities can provide the right soil for a community to grow my doubts become even stronger. For what the idealist or planner has to reckon with here is not just Fallen Man but Fallen *Academic* Man and it is to this problem I would now like to turn.

II. The Face of Academic Man

The stereotype of the academic as an absent-minded, horn-rimmed, shabbily-dressed, unworldly but rather loveable buffoon became out of date in the late forties and fifties when the young entry began to run the universities as a business. It was in those days one first heard men speak of models, scenarios, budgets, inputs, modules, unit-cost, production-line techniques, first, second, and third line officers, print-outs, operatives, and "all-systems-go." One could not, by the time the early sixties came around, easily distinguish the new button-down, skin-headed, dacron-suited, white shirt and bow-tie hotshot of a professor from IBM executives, *Britannica* salesmen, and FBI agents. Bloodless automata from M.I.T. even took over the White House and so university professors began to acquire a certain weird glamour. It is not hard to see why. In control of a new and baffling computer technology, completely at home in the burgeoning and jargon-laden science of business management, they seemed totally unaffected by the moral ambivalences considered by most of us to be part of the human condition. They wielded the sort of authority the sighted man is said to enjoy in the country of the blind. Rather pathetically, men and women in the humanities began to imitate them. Literary critics started to speak of "scholarly apparatus" and "research tools" when they meant footnotes and libraries. Even our first president, an experienced and subtle Canadian civil servant, was fond of giving lectures to the public on the "value" of university education based on the difference supposed to exist between the life-earnings of graduates as opposed to non-graduates.

When I arrived at Simon Fraser in the summer of 1965, it was still possible, for those who enjoy such polarities, to divide academics up into the "old guard" on the one hand, and the "skin-headed" on the other. Skin-heads were publication and administration conscious — they spoke of the Ph.D. being the absolutely minimum requirement for the job, of "résumés," of "curriculum vitae." They believed, very strongly, in publish-or-perish and in hiring-and-firing. The old guard saw them as a dreadful threat, for your old-style teacher is essentially on Oblomovic niche man, half in love with easeful mediocrity, whose need to intimidate students is topped only by his inability to impress those students with his scholarship. I felt rather sorry for these outdated Anglophiles since their chief fantasy was that they taught at Oxbridge and that they were basically gentlemen of leisure dedicating bottles of port to one another and standing for Values and the Mind. Harmless stuff and yet, suddenly, into their imaginary cloisters and hallowed courtyards strut these shiny-suited, nylon-shirted Aliens with their plots, caucuses, points-of-order, and mysterious in-group mutterings about bibliographies and learned journals. They were the Enemy. They were *Americans*!

The rivalry that developed between these two groups dwindled by the Fall of 1966 and, by the new year, had changed into an alliance. Two other breeds of academic had arrived and both of them were inimical to the older traditions. The first, relatively harmless, consisted of the beautiful young people whose clothes were inspired by Quant and Carnaby Street, the Beatles, and the psychedelic revolution. The second breed emerged from the generation of antinomian graduate students brought up on James Dean and politicized by the Berkeley Free Speech and Civil Rights movements. These were the militants. They dressed in combat boots and camouflage pants; wore earrings and Black Panther hairdos. They said "Right on!" and "Up Against the Wall" and they made poor McFog's life a misery. They believed in confronting administrations with impossible demands and, when these were rejected, in occupying the buildings. Government by quiet, low-toned, gentleman's agreement between senior tenured faculty in secret sessions was replaced, as it were overnight, by the daily proliferation of *ad hoc* committees, clenched-fist signs, cries of "lackey" and "fascist pig," demonstrations, and strikes.

70

Encountering three models of a university in as many months was too much for most people. First we had to think of a university as a somnolent establishment den, then as a branch of the National Aeronautics and Space Agency, then finally as an emerging Third World Nation. It was certainly too much for me. I had supported, by and large, the so-called "radicals" but grew bored with their hysteria, dogmatism, lack of humanity, and self-righteousness. They were ineffective, even as revolutionaries — Lenin would've booted them out of his office within five minutes. Most of them were members of the PSA Department (Political Science, Sociology, and Anthropology) and were squeezed out of it by an outrageous series of administrative manoeuvres. The *coup de grace* was delivered by McFog's successor, Kenneth Strand, who abrogated the dismissal procedures he himself had helped to inaugurate by firing the group who had "gone on strike" a couple of years before. The university sat back in some suspense. Would Strand survive a vote of censure? He did, by a large majority of faculty — much to my own disgust and that of about twenty others. The censure of the university by the Canadian Association of University Teachers followed, is still in force, has meant nothing, and has this year been resurrected as an issue confronting the new president.

III.   The Academic Soul

The reader will observe that in our age, when verbal communication is unfashionable, men and women have had to invent other means of signalling to one another. Personally I was brought up within the British Class Structure in which these signals were projected by accent and intonation. *What* was said was totally unimportant, but *how* it was said precipitated either comfortable feelings in the audience or sheer hostility depending upon whether the speaker was considered to be "one of *us*" or "one of *them*." Mouths are opened nowadays only for the purpose of uttering slogans and since we live in a classless society "class" has to be measured otherwise than by accent. *Clothing* is used as a signal nowadays and this is why I have concentrated on the *appearance* of academics. A bearded, jeaned, combat-booted, Afro-headed fellow grunting some political bromide at you is actually saying "I consider myself, *pace* Herbert Marcuse, as a member of the young, intellectual élite with a radical life-style. Furthermore, I am a leader of the revolution." The tweedy Don with pipe and dog and stick is saying "I want you to know that I am busy Affirming Human Values against all this chaos." Fair enough. You can take it or leave it alone. We are also in the age of melodrama, of stereotyping, and never, as far as I know, have human beings so fervently wished to be identified as members of groups. Yet beneath these very different styles, these forms of communication, there remains to be identified the common factor—the academic soul.

The reader may well ask "what soul?" Is it a metaphysical entity? A set of behaviour tendencies and reaction patterns dignified with a metaphor drawn from doctrine? Many commentators hold that this soul consists of a hankering for status. Others believe that academics are chiefly motivated by a need for financial security. A third school of thought, neo-Transcendentalist in tendency, maintains that what a professor wants above all is to divorce himself from Real Life. It is worth examining each of these positions in turn.

It is true that a man who can introduce himself as Doctor or Professor at cocktail parties enjoys a certain deference among the uneducated or the easily intimidated. Joe Blow is mortal clay but Professor Joseph Blow is defined—he has space, time, and position; he has a beginning, a middle, and an end. He is an Aristotelian *thing*. But among the more sophisticated the word "Academic" has become a term of opprobrium—synonymous with "fink" or "turd." About the only status fringe benefit we enjoy these days is the dubious privilege of signing passport applications for students who wish to drop out of the system and seek the best hash in Katmandu. In cultured circles even a book reviewer receives greater respect.

Again, a man seeking financial security would do better to become a plumber, narcotics squad operative, or alderman. We have tenure, of course, but what does this mean? It means I can be fired *only* by the department Chairman, the Dean, the Academic Vice-President, the President, the Board of Governors, by the legislature through an Order-in-Council, or by anybody else not covered in the above list. I can be fired only for cause (sic), which means moral turpitude, buggery, drunkenness, double parking, or anything else depending on the nature and fancy of whoever calls the shot. Or somebody can declare me redundant. The humblest choker-man in a logging camp enjoys greater security precisely because he has a union to fight his battles for him and most academics have not. In fact the very word "union" is anathema to most academics since it seems to them to imply a lowering of professional status and in any case most of the ones I know, including myself, would be hard put to organize so

72

much as a shower for one of the girls in the typing pool.

We need here concern ourselves only with the third proposition—that the academic is a man reluctant to grapple with Real Life. I have heard the unlikeliest people affirm this—ad men, lawyers, key-punch operators, automobile mechanics, and so on, and the implication is that *they* are in touch with Reality and that the academic is not. They have all of them, or so you would think to listen to them, succeeded in getting down to what they call the "nitty gritty," A mere glance at such a claim from such people shows how ludicrous it is. What does an advertising copy writer have to do with Reality? What does a lawyer? The latter *thrives* on fantasy—the fantasy that his client is innocent and that his accusers are guilty. He is paid, as Swift pointed out in the eighteenth century, to say that black is white. As for automobile mechanics, though they may be proud of their oily hands and can claim, with some show of validity, that they are up to their armpits in this "nitty gritty," what can one say about a man who, confronted with a broken spark plug, asserts and *must* assert for the sake of his livelihood, that your car needs a new engine. How "real" is an automobile anyway? A badly assembled structure of scrap metal which the manufacturer hopes, and *must* hope, for *his* livelihood, will revert to junk within the year. No. In our modern age it is impossible not to be sceptical about a man's claim to be in touch with Reality.

Though status, insecurity, and escape from "reality" are not in themselves sufficient to distinguish the soul of a professor from that of an insurance salesman, I think most people recognize that there *is* a difference. What characterizes the academic man? The short answer, I believe, is fear. Your average professor is a man shaken to his very roots by a special sort of terror—the terror of being *contradicted.* Disagree with him about the interpretation of a poem, a movie, an event in history and he blenches. Persist and you'll find his defences beginning to operate and he becomes enraged. Stay cool, be persistent in your contradiction, and he will begin to liquefy, collapsing wetly on the carpet, his anger detumesced. If you take matters beyond this point, you do so at the risk of being counted cruel and uncharitable, for the poor fellow will be driven by your dissent into a ward in a mental institution. Though other men and women fear contradiction strongly, only professors, I maintain, are utterly transfigured by it. From sane, reasonable, smiling people maintaining some sort of grip on life they become, at the merest hint of disagreement, gibbering, slavering, blood-engorged lunatics, shrieking imprecations at you and lurking in wait for you along corridors with an axe.

73

For seven years our department meetings have been nightmare battlefields of clashing egos, trumpeted warcries, oaths, flying tape-recorders, hurled slogans, denunciations, injunctions, and the like, and though there seems to be some sort of truce at the moment, I sense no permanent improvement.[1] In fact, to quote Céline, if the world were to turn into a radio-active heap of ashes you would still find, in some cave or other, a group of survivors — haggard lunatics — wandering around in circles violating, imprisoning, torturing, one another. And these would be the last academics. Frankly, I always make a point of agreeing with the last speaker and find myself saying, at the end of our meetings, such things as "Mr. Chairman, I just want to point out that I agree with everything that's been said here this afternoon." Charity demands nothing less, though there is also the duty of self-preservation.

At this point I ought to make it quite clear that these somewhat scornful descriptions of my colleagues could be applied *ad hominem* to myself. I too have experienced the joyous surge of rage directed at someone in the department who has either just struck me as a cretin or whose bland facade has been stripped aside to reveal the horns, tail, and cloven hoof. I cannot claim to be a stranger to the sudden flow of adrenalin, the inflamed eyeball, the rapid pulse, the soaring cholesterol count, the mounting blood pressure, the engorged spleen. On the other hand I feel somewhat more detached about intellectual and academic matters than most people in the profession partly because in their terms I am an imposter. I do not have the same stake as they have in the university system and in most of the issues they confront with such emotional energy strike me as paper dragons. Thus, I feel objective enough to cite as the distinguishing characteristic of academics — whether Oxbridgeophile, skin-head, fop, or Afro-headed freak blurting jargon — the horror of dissension. This theory explains, at least to my satisfaction, their repressed violence, their hostility towards students — particularly those of independent mind — their inability to form part of an assembly, or to address their remarks to the chair, or to speak to the measure and not the man; it explains their tenacity with which they pursue feuds and their love of intrigue; the tendency to venality, alcoholism, seduction of female students with higher grades as bait, and the poisonous contempt in which they hold one another.

Though I am speaking very generally and with a natural tendency to exaggerate I nevertheless keep my door firmly bolted on the inside.

IV. Yo-Yos and Conkers

I see that these random notes, begun in a spirit of generalization, have taken on the quality of a mild denunciation. If I have concentrated on my colleagues, it is because they swim most persistently into my consciousness. Obviously, though, a university community consists of other elements — students, administrators, and general staff. Of the latter I am not qualified to speak and I can add little to the current literature on administrators beyond agreeing that they are dispensable, fissiparous, and prolific. I know a little more about students. They tend to work through, generation by generation, the same fashions of behaviour manifested by faculty — fashions which remind me very much of my own schooldays when suddenly a rash of yo-yos would be seen in the playground. I would, with the rest of my "peer-group" (as the vile jargon has it), rush out to buy yo-yos. Then, without a word being said by anybody, these pleasant toys would be retired. The yo-yo toting child would be sniggered at and scorned. There would be a loaded pause. Then, cataclysmically, the conker season would start! I'd wander through the woods looking for horse chestnut trees — identified by the ripe, spiky, green globes littered at their feet. Inside each globe is a lining of white, evil-tasting flesh but, as this is peeled away, the conker is revealed! It is a brown, shiny nut delicately patterned — glowing like a French-polished piece of Brancusi sculpture. The shine wears off after an hour and the conker becomes mundane. A hole is meat-skewered through the centre and the conker is suspended on a knotted string. Now it is ready for action. One challenges one's peers (that word again) to combat and the conkers are swung against each other until one is shattered. Tough, resilient conkers that could survive half a dozen matches were greatly prized, nurtured, and conditioned. One school of thought held that conkers should be soaked in water to increase their performance while others believed they should be very lightly baked. But conkers, like yo-yos, would suddenly vanish and woe unto the child disconsolately walking across the playground, conker dangling from his pocket. Other games, Bung-the-Barrel, for example, or mutual masturbation would have taken over.

So it has been at Simon Fraser. The first generation of students, before the revolution, were cowed High School graduates brought up to respect the System and to call one "sir." They brought in old high school habits to the place almost as though they thought they were dealing with UBC or the University of Toronto. Thus, they organized rivalries between Arts and Science and between themselves and other universities. There was even an attempt at a panty-raid though, to the best of my knowledge, nobody swallowed a goldfish. On the whole a tractable lot and the first student government assented rather too eagerly to the plans of the administration. The key issue, in those days, was a notoriously shady deal made between the Board of Governors and the Shell Oil Company—a deal I do not wish to document without legal advice. The student government supported it while faculty slept and McFog was able to claim that the student president was even present at "the sod-turning ceremony" marking the construction of a very controversial gas-station.

But in 1966 the student picture had changed. Navajo hats, head-bands, Che Guevara kits, Ho Chi Minh beards—the paraphernalia of dissent—made their appearance. Students now tended to treat faculty as natural enemies, as spineless servants of the "military-industrial-complex." Such influential essays as Jerry Farber's "Student as Nigger" convinced these middle-class kids that they were an oppressed group and many of their actions, it seemed to me, were directed towards precipitating retaliation of the sort to confirm them in their world-view. Now and again a student would stand up in class and demand to know the relevance of the professor's course.

SELF: (*Pedantically*) What do you mean by relevance?
STUDENT: What has *The Faerie Queene* got to do with the exploitation of the masses? With the war in Vietnam? With great historical figures such as Che, Castro, and Mao? With the Pentagon? With the dictatorship of the proletariat?
SELF: Nothing.
STUDENT: What relevance has Spenser to the problems of our time? If he has no relevance why are you teaching this crap? Why are we here?

Those are good questions of course but they cannot be answered on the terms by which they are posed. The "correct" answer is "well, it's relevant to *me*" and, beyond hoping that one's classes will contain people who either share one's enthusiasm or at least maintain an open mind, that is about all one can do. As the sixties ended, however, the radicals began to vanish from the campus and a man began to smell, almost everywhere, the sickly, aromatic fumes of marijuana. Gentle addicts began showing up whenever, as they put it, they could "get their heads together" in my seminars where they would sit smiling benignly except on those occasions when a sudden "bad trip" would start one of them chewing the carpet. Nobody criticized, nobody asked aggressive questions. I began to feel uneasy. S.F.U.'s suicide rate began to climb as young men and women sailed off the tops of walls in the belief that they could fly or that they were evacuating the Titanic.

Lately, High Seriousness seems to have become once again fashionable. Most of the students I come across seem to have switched over from drugs to wine, a substance that does not blow the mind and in fact leaves it on the whole unimpaired for the next day's activity. Acid seems to have disappeared and, at least in Vancouver, marijuana is mostly cornered, ringed, and traded among the younger generation still at Junior High School. Admittedly the university still contains many students insecure enough to seek out membership in some gang or other. For example, there is a group of occultists presently on campus. I get the odd one or two drifting into my courses but they are by no means obnoxious. About the only remnant of the drug culture is the phrase "hey, *man*," used in the vocative. A student opens my door and says "Hey, *man*, are you inta myth?" I assure him that I'm not and send him down the corridor to Professor Acmon. Another announces "Hey, *man*, I'm a nature poet, who do I go to see?" I send him to Professor Mopsus in revenge for the ghastly Buddhist that Mopsus sent to *me*. "Hey, *man*," another mumbles, swinging open my door. "I'm really into the poetry of Bob Dylan . . . ." Calmly I send him to Professor Dote. On the whole my door remains open to students but closed to most of my colleagues and, as I've already explained, firmly bolted on the inside.

V. The Idea of a University

The first Chairman of S.F.U.'s English Department and its Academic Planner was fond of telling all who would listen that "this is a University, not a model democracy." To which we could only reply — true, but then it's not a model oligarchy, tyranny, or benevolent despotism either. It is not, as the businessmen on the first Board of Governors insisted, a kind of skill and knowledge factory serving capitalism with the student as product, nor is it the kind of factory envisaged by the Board's class enemies in the left-wing of the PSA Department wherein the professor is an assembly line worker-cum-shop-steward whose rights include the withdrawal of his labour in strike action so as to punish and intimidate recalcitrant administrations by halting production. Its purpose is not to maintain standards and traditions, grading systems and intellectual élites on the one hand, nor is it to act as a spearhead of social change on the other. In fact, if one wishes to define the idea of a university all models break down and one is forced to apply Nicholas of Cusa's Doctrine of Ignorance — that is, one can describe the Idea only through negative predications.

This was not clear to me at the time I was hired nor was it clear to the people that hired me, most of whom were high on that euphoria experienced by human beings when challenged to complete a gigantic project against time. No two people would have either agreed or disagreed on the nature of what was being created, only on the need to meet deadlines, so that my naïve and vague notion of a university as a "community of scholars and artists" not only went unchallenged but was greeted by benign smiles, and it took a year or so for this and similar bromides to be denounced publicly and vitriolically for the poppycock they undoubtedly are. Thus we missed the chance to debate these issues under conditions of good-will. During the late sixties, a curiously bad time for rational discussion, the ideas in people's heads froze into outward postures and attitudes in ways I have been trying to describe. Partly this was the result of fashion and conformity, partly because of the inner dislocations of human beings generally and academics in particular. These factors were exacerbated at S.F.U. by the speed of the construction and the incompetence of the first administration. Yet even this is not all. There is something about the air on that mountain, some enclosed quality that inheres in its concrete walkways and plazas, that produces an atmosphere of latent violence. For example, the issue of "Canadianism" is being raised in our department. It is an important issue, but it has degenerated into a mindless debate on "what is a Canadian?" during which I was amused to discover that, though I have been in this country longer than most of my students and though I paid five dollars and swore an oath of a egiance to "Queen Elizabeth the Second and all her heirs and successors" as long ago as 1958, I do not count. That's O.K. with me. Yet I am bothered by the fervour of our chauvinists — I worry about their pop-eyed anger and their racing pulses and above all I am disturbed when, as I creep back to the safety of my office, they pass me in the corridors. I catch from them the faint but unmistakable whiff of jack-boot leather.

Yet as I walked away from last September's festival I was conscious of a warm, rather smug, glow. This is not just the natural self-congratulation of a survivor. It persists in spite of the banners and manifestos distributed around the campus urging the reinstatement of the "PSA Seven." Though this serious issue may yet become encrusted with melodrama, I sense that the melodramatists are getting tired and it is possible that this time we may actually be able to debate the problem without the departmental purgings, the anonymous, threatening phone calls, the tamperings with car brakes, and the bouts of pugilism. There is still no sense of "community" and there never will be, anywhere, either, until after the mushroom-cloud has appeared in our skies, but I have cause, on a more practical level, to feel a certain warmth towards S.F.U. No other Canadian university has been so hospitable to writers, film-makers, theatre people, musicians, and painters. Many campuses retain a pet writer who, in return for his stipend, sidles in once a week to run a seminar or pick up his mail; but our English Department alone shelters six poets, one novelist, two playwrights, and one director, all of them active, all of them incorporated, despite occasional attempts to polarize them out, into the academic structure. I have literary friends who regard this incorporation as a "bad thing." I don't think it has harmed any one of us and in some cases, namely my own, it has done positive good.

1975

Note

[1] And they are worse in other departments. Interested readers may obtain, on application to the author, xeroxed copies of certain public memos which have fallen into his hands. I do not include them in the text out of pity, probably misguided, for their originators.

Part II
Adventures in the Counter-Culture

Enter FOLLY, shaking his bauble, capering about, and playing on an instrument:

FOL. Masters, Christ save every one!

—John Skelton, *Magnificence*

Preface

One evening in the middle sixties I found myself in a cavernous room, part of an old warehouse, in the company of the poet Milton Acorn, a Berkeley activist named Stan Persky, a colleague of mine called Leonard Minsky (a New Yorker in the habit of buttonholing everybody who would listen with the news that he "had the key" to *Piers Plowman*), a man dressed in cap and bells who proclaimed himself Vancouver's Town Fool, two or three dope dealers euphoric but incoherent on mescalin, a defrocked minister of the United Church who had been caught substituting guitar ensemble work and light shows (does the reader remember "light shows"?) for services of a more orthodox nature, and a couple of poets thinned out on macrobiotic diets looking for handouts and sympathetic audiences. There was also present a thin, blond, gangling youth of faintly adenoidal cast as to mouth and nose whom I had met at the University of British Columbia while studying mathematics and who had turned from functions of a complex variable to Black Mountain poetry — his name was Dan MacLeod. We had all of us come to discuss the necessity of setting up an underground newspaper as a corrective to the establishment press, and as a means of protesting the joylessness of Vancouver life.

Thus was born the *Georgia Straight*, one of Canada's first alternative newspapers and one which, I am happy to tell you, still survives—though it has changed its name to *Vancouver Free Press*. Milton Acorn dropped out after a month or so on the grounds that we weren't Marxist enough and started a rival newspaper called the *Georgia Grape* which lasted a couple of years until torn apart, as is sometimes the case with leftist enterprises, by factionalism. Minsky was kicked out of Simon Fraser but became academic planner for a new university or junior college in Terrace, in the northern part of B.C., which became known as "Minsky Tech." Persky, a man of great talent, intelligence, and energy, became the Tech's Dean of Arts and later the author of a deservedly popular book about Bill Bennett, B.C.'s premier, entitled *Son of Socred*. The hippies, the minister, the poets, all vanished back to the Void from which they had so briefly emerged and it was left to Dan MacLeod to run the newspaper. I decided that my gifts for administration were limited and that I would prefer to write a column. This I did, with great pleasure, for a couple of years until my own publishing house—the Pendejo Press—began to absorb my energies. In any case, the newspaper had by that time become markedly less anarchistic in tone and content and had begun to proselytise for drug reform and pop-music in which subjects my own interests were (and they remain) peripheral to say the least. I wrote a few more articles for the paper in the seventies by which time respectability had set in and it was able to command such talents as Ben Metcalf and George Woodcock. But once again I ran out of energy. Only Dan MacLeod, there at the paper's inception, survived and over some very difficult years, constantly under attack, constantly the victim of persecution—by the mayor, the attorney general, the city licensing inspector, fire marshals, etc.—all the rag-tag-and-bobtail of officialdom. The profits, and they were fairly substantial, were all of them used to pay not only the fines, legal debts, and bail monies accrued by the newspaper's staff but also by any young person off the street of approved antinomian disposition who happened to find himself victimized by the Law.

When I first arrived in Vancouver in 1961 there was no Sunday entertainment, no restaurant outside Chinatown, no bar or night-club where you did not have to take your own liquor hidden under the table in a brown paper bag, no place to go in the evening unless you were an afficionado of laundromats. The city was run by a council composed of real estate crooks and insurance agents dedicated to the proposition that streets must be cleared by nine p.m., that the purpose of such streets was to allow traffic to move quickly and smoothly to its destination and that no one must "obstruct the sidewalk"—a crime almost as severe as that of dealing heroin. Thus, for several years, the jails were filled with "vagrants"—a term applicable to anyone at the discretion of the police. The town was dominated by Puritans—a breed, to quote Mencken, haunted by the terrible, sneaking fear that someone, somewhere, is having a good time, and in this respect Vancouver seemed even drearier than Toronto or Montreal, from which my wife and I had escaped, though it did not suffer their revolting climate. Whatever the pretensions of the so-called "counter-culture," of which the *Straight* was a House Organ, it helped civilize Vancouver; it made, for example, the event described in my essay "The Donkey and the Law" a rarity in the seventies and it is difficult to see how it could be repeated at all in 1980. Shortly after the column appeared, two plain-clothes bogies rapped peremptorily on my door very early one morning to question my allegiances and to inform me that the attorney general's office in Victoria was contemplating busting me for "criminal libel." Their manner softened appreciably when they discovered that I worked for a living (insofar as teaching at a university could be described as "work"), and that I owned my own house and hence paid their salaries with my property taxes. I heard no more, but Dan MacLeod, who had awarded in the same issue the *Straight*'s "Pontius Pilate Award for Justice" to a different snapping turtle was not so lucky. He was found guilty and fined a thousand dollars—but by then he was used to it.

I have selected three of the pieces I wrote for "The Georgia Straight" and include them here for their period flavour, as I remarked in the Foreword to this book, and for any historic interest they may have.

DEW-Line Days

In the course of emptying a cupboard full of papers I encountered a half-forgotten document rolled up, like a college diploma, and housed in a cardboard cartridge. I stretched it out and examined it. There was a badly executed drawing of a radar station, white against a blue background, with white heaps like flocks of cotton wool done in the foreground to suggest snow. Across the picture stretched these words,

TO JOHN MILLS FOR HIS PART IN THE DEFENCE OF NORTH AMERICA IN THE NORTHERNMOST BOUNDARIES OF THE CONTINENT.

There followed an illegible signature.

I gawked at this preposterous certificate for well over an hour while my mind, never, even at the best of times, full of very much, became glazed in with what Wordsworth called "vacant musings." A decade slipped away....

In 1956 some friends of mine and I heard that a line of radar stations was to be built along the 55th parallel and that fairly large sums of money were changing hands. We spent a couple of days in the library and swotted up enough basic electronics to pass a test and applied to the company which had landed the contract. We were in and, almost before we could draw breath, were on a plane for Knob

85

Lake, now called Shefferville, in Northern Quebec.

It turned out to be a good place to work. The job involved helicoptering out of Knob Lake to a construction site, shoving in the electronic equipment, tuning it up, and moving on to the next.

A group of us spent about three weeks at Knob Lake waiting for the next series of sites to open up, lying in our bunks most of the day and gossiping. We'd get up at meal times, dress up in our heavy outdoor clothing, and stagger over to the mess, about five hundred yards away. I remember bitching about the fact that this distance was too great, and that arrangements should be made to feed us more or less where we slept. Since my companions were all of them malingerers, buggout artists, skivers, and goldbricks, the conversation in our hut was good and memorable. One by one, however, we were dragged off, bitching noisily, to various sites and forced to actually earn, in some sense, our $650 a month and all found.

Life was harder at the sites. For one thing we were housed in oil-stove heated tents in constant fear of being burnt alive while we slept. The more neurotic among us turned the stove off at night so that we'd wake in the morning with a faceful of ice. Worse than this was the fact that the latrines were unheated and so constipation became one of our occupational hazards. I remember someone trying to solve this problem by planning to excrete within the hut itself on a sheet of newspaper, wrapping up the turd, then throwing it outside for the wolves. The plan misfired, however, for what this strategist had failed to bargain with was the fact that it is almost impossible (except perhaps to a Yogi) to release the sphincter muscles without releasing the muscles that control the bladder. But we solved the simpler problem of urination after two attempts. The first involved a spare piece of copper tubing poked through a hole in the wall and fitted, at the hut end of the tube, with a funnel. This was no good since the piss would freeze in the tube and back up into the funnel. We substituted rubber for copper, however, gave the pipe an occasional good flexing and found the device satisfactory.

The worst time came when most of the equipment was installed and one technician remained on his own to finish up while the others moved on. I remember being left alone at a site for three weeks in this way while awaiting the arrival of something called "A hybrid and combining amplifier." The site was weathered in, no helicopter could get to me, there was no mail and no reading matter. My companions were two French Canadians from some horrible rural backwater who spoke no language known to man or beast. Every day I'd get on the radio to Knob Lake and the following conversation would take place.

Knob Lake, this is site such and such.

Go ahead, site such and such.

When the hell are you going to send me that mother-effing amplifier?

Just as soon as we can fly it to you, such and such, and don't use that kind of language over the air.

One day they radioed me that the DC3 was bringing me the amplifier and three weeks mail. They'd drop it off at the lakehead, they explained. Eagerly I put on my Arctic clothing and a pair of snowshoes. I'd meet the plane at the lakehead, five miles away, I thought, and drag the amplifier back on a sledge. It was a long, misty, three hour slog through the woods and dark by the time I got there. The guys that ran the Lakehead terminus had put flares down on the ice and were waiting for the plane. Finally we heard it overhead and the pilot radioed in:

I see your effing flare pots, he said, you've got them North to South.

Right, I said.

Well, the wind's from the west . . . turn 'em around East-West, he said, and for Christ's sake hurry up or I'll miss the movie back at Knob.

The stunned labourers at the lakehead had put the flare pots down in the wrong line. We slithered out onto the ice and moved them all, two half-mile long lines of them, rotating them through ninety degrees. It took us over ten minutes of frantic labour and by the time we'd finished it was weathered in again and the plane was twenty miles away.

But it worked out all right in the end. Two days later the sky cleared, the wind dropped, the helicopter brought the amplifier to my front door, I bolted it in its rack, twiddled a couple of dials, and ten minutes later was on my way back to Knob.

When the contract ended and I was back in Montreal spending my savings as fast as I could get rid of them, I discovered that I could no more go back to a conventional job than an alderman could turn into an honest man. I knew that a line of radar stations was in the process of construction some thousand miles north of Knob Lake and that the money was even better than one could get from Marconi. I applied at the Montreal Office of Federal Electric and filled in an elaborate set of forms. One of them was a personality test — I flunked it miserably. The personnel manager called me back for an interview.

Question Four, he said, "which do you prefer, your mother or your father?" Do you remember what your reply was?

I did indeed. I'd written than I'd hate to have to make the choice since neither could accurately be described as a human being of any kind and that a man's desire to escape his parents was the historical secret of Westward expansion. It wasn't, under normal circumstances, a satisfactory answer, but they were desperate for staff and allowed me to lie my way out of it. I was on—$850 a month and all found.

It seemed a lot to me at the time. That was in 1957 when money was more valuable and in any case there was nothing to spend it on up in the Arctic. The technicians who were being recruited in the States got $200 a month more. This was not the fault of the Americans but of the Canadian government who felt, as far as I can make out, that high salaries were bad for our moral fibre . . . they would give us delusions of grandeur and we would be hard to control once we got back to civilization again. But the figure of $850 (about $10,000 a year) was, according to the Wilkes-Anderson study done in 1957, just about the sum the average cop, or city councillor, picks up each year in graft. Maybe there's some connection.

In any case the DEW Line was, in its heyday, a chain of radar stations roughly along the line of the 69th parallel which brought it, for the most part, into somewhat inclement regions as any reader can discover for himself by consulting a globe. Together with the Mid-Canada and Pine Tree Lines it formed part of the North American Air Defence (NORAD) system by means of which Governor Wallace, Police Chief Bull Connor, and Richard Nixon were to be saved from the demon Communism. Along each coast there were clusters of steel towers legged into the sea bed called Texas Towers. You may remember that one of them made news a few years back by giving up its ghost and collapsing into the cold green element thus drowning its unfortunate operators, one and all. And as though this was not enough, radar planes, constantly in the air, winged up and down each coast while SAC squadrons, also on constant alert, flew moodily back and forth across the Arctic ready and anxious to strike a blow for Americanism by reducing Russian cities to charred flesh and radio-active dust.

Notice that I am using the past tense. Though many of its stations still exist the DEW Line was defunct even while it was being completed since plans were made, almost simultaneously, for a ballistic missile early warning system centred in Greenland. The DEW Line's purpose was the already obsolete one of detecting high and low flying "enemy" aircraft and could do so at a top range of 160 miles. Such detection would presumably give a couple of hours warning to the richer sections of the American public during which they could grab their shot-guns and head for their A-bomb shelters.

The DEW Line was a sad business. The wild, anarchic, definitely pleasurable days of construction (such as we'd experienced on the Mid-Canada Line) had ended when I got there and the Arctic was gradually being taken over (as everything is, from business to universities) by professional administrators—what George Orwell called "the little men with beetle brows." The project had become structured—"Lines of Communication" had been established; there was a "Chain of Command"; "Channels" had been laid down. Messages travelled up from headquarters discouraging long hair and unkempt appearance, insisting on standardized wording for written reports. Most of these were signed by Admiral Cruzen, the man in charge, who turned out to be, believe it or not, a little man (five feet four) with beetle eyebrows. After a while the instructions began to take on the almost incredible inanity of these interdepartmental memos you find at IBM or General Electric. I still have one of them:

> To all personnel: It came to my attention, during my last inspection tour, that field personnel have in many instances taken to affecting beards. Apart from the unsanitary aspects of this procedure, beard-growing is a sign of immaturity and personality deficiencies. It is in all our interests that this practice cease forthwith.

And again:

> To all clerical staff: It has come to my attention that not all movements of trucking and cartage are receiving the documentation provided for under section 5-36 of the Procedures Manual. Wastage disposal will henceforth be accounted for on the new form D-81.

This message referred to the flushed out contents of the heads which were stored in a huge tank, emptied, when necessary, into trucks and driven off to a distant pit (ordinary sewage lines, of course, are impossible in the Arctic). The new form that arrived required details of the volume of excrement carted and the number of man-hours employed per month in its removal.

89

On the Mid-Canada Line I noticed that each man seemed to be an individual—usually worthy of respect—and the amiable relationships existing among us included even the supervisors. But on the highly structured DEW Line we soon ceased to regard each other as sovereign states peacefully coexisting but began to think in terms of stereotypes. Ordinary citizens of good will turned (as they do in the army, or any other organization) into lickspittlers, Eichmanns, number one artists, narks, power-jockeys, establishment toadies, hatchet men, and miscellaneous finks. It was best to keep out of it and in any case the work was boring. Many of us slept fourteen or fifteen hours a day and used to bitch bitterly when woken up to go on shift. And, as is the case elsewhere, a man's degree of finkdom was inversely proportional to his competence at his ostensible job.

The food was excellent, the living conditions comparatively civilized, there was a bland assortment of books in the library; a paternalistic authority down at headquarters in charge of entertainment sent us Doris Day movies three times a week or so (anything other than Mom and Americanism was presumed to be too hard on boys away from home); we were allowed a ration of six cans of beer a week. Materially we were well-off—but it was like living under Social Credit.

Each month a bunch of generals and civilian observers did an inspection. We responded to this in accordance with a regulation entitled "Visiting Dignitaries, Reception of," spit and polished the site and kicked the lower echelon workers out of their rooms and into tents for the duration of the visit. The generals were little men of uniformly low intelligence; the civilians were usually physicists and engineers who tried to keep out of everybody's way. The worst affected were the USAF officers, many of whom, when all the smoke had cleared away, were members of the human race. They had to shave closely and put on their best blues. At every main station on the Canadian sectors, there was an RCAF officer whose job, believe it or not, was to "preserve Canadian Sovereignty." These men stayed out of it as much as possible.

The DEW Line, obsolete though it was, gave the Democracies a breathing space. This is what everybody tells me. In which case I am truly sorry for having been involved in it. Perhaps it was the presence of the DEW Line that enabled John F. Kennedy to attempt to invade Cuba; perhaps it gave him the security to precipitate a crisis in Berlin and encouraged him, a year or so later, to express his animosity against Cuba in the form of the famous "quarantine." Soon after I had

90

left the DEW Line and began to read the papers again I noticed that a left-wing government in Guatemala had been toppled by the CIA, Negroes were being clobbered in the Southern States, and American "advisors" were on their way to Viet Nam. If it were not for the DEW Line, perhaps, some of these things could've been prevented or at least would have been reduced in scale. My excuse for playing my tiny role in American "defence" is that at the time I thought I needed the money. (I was wrong, of course; I spent it within a year.) I was not a political animal, or at least, that's how it seemed to me.

If it were not for me and people like me, the DEW Line could never have existed.

Mea Culpa!

1967

•

The Great Centennial Rebuke

Since I've been loafing in the bush these last few months I've "missed" this summer's two major events — the Arab-Israeli war, and the Great Centennial Rebuke administered by Lester Pearson to Charles de Gaulle. About the first I have mixed feelings for I admire in the Jews their ability to preserve their tiny nation and on the other hand I admire in the Arabs their inability to fight. But the Rebuke gave me unalloyed pleasure.

It is the first time that Pearson, probably the world's least memorable man, has made me laugh.

Let me put it this way. Anybody who goes in for politics can only be redeemed, in my opinion, by his capacity to keep his long-suffering fellow countrymen in a state of hilarity. Churchill was good at this. Blood-letter though he was, he managed to keep the British entertained from the days of the Boer War to his death a few years ago. He had style — he was eccentric in his life, pungent in his speech, comic in the excesses of his toryism. He often came out with some very good things — for example, some admiral approached him once complaining that such and such a course of action was contrary to the traditions of the Royal Navy, to which Churchill replied, "the traditions of the Royal Navy, sir, are rum, buggery, and the lash!"

The late John F. Kennedy tended to play it more straight but he made at least one remark of an idiocy so intense, so sublime in its utter brainlessness, that one's mouth had no choice but to gape, wordlessly, in astonishment and admiration . . . . *"Ich bin Berliner"* he once told an audience of Germans! Kennedy, as I say, seemed often serious but generally it is true that, from the drunken, peculative U. S. Grant, through the dead-pan Calvin Coolidge with his Buster Keaton style, right up to the gloriously inane Dwight Eisenhower, the Americans have been fortunate in their public men.

Even here, in a somewhat humourless Canada, we've enjoyed the presence of one or two good politicians who were often good for a laugh. John A. Macdonald, for example, one of the three Great Lushes of his time, would send out in the middle of a speech for a glass of water and an accomplice would bring him a tumbler of neat gin. And there was Louis St. Laurent, one of the very few prime ministers whose face could be said to actually *express* something, and who would come on over television with a sort of nibbling unction, like that of a neutered rabbit. And of course we've had John Diefenbaker, a truly *great* clown — one of the finest in this or in any other country. In fact, and this brings me closer to the point, if you cube Diefenbaker's pomposity, square his self-importance, and multiply his brains, ability, and imagination by a factor of three or four hundred, you get Charles De Gaulle.

I have absolutely no wish to white-wash De Gaulle. He is probably as corrupt and treacherous as any other political figure. But he has a streak of High Seriousness in him that has enabled him to get certain things done that badly needed doing — he extricated his country from Algeria; he recognized Red China; he has disentangled France from NATO, and he's kicked out the Americans. This last, in particular, became a noble and dangerous course of action for any statesman to take ever since that day in history, whenever it was, when the Marines began to outnumber human beings. He invented a Ministry of Culture and used a first class mind, André Malraux, to run it. Imagine *Pearson* setting up such a ministry! Who'd be in charge, do you suppose? Pierre Berton? John Robert Colombo? Jesus! . . . it's enough to freeze your blood!

Let's face it; with all his pomposity, his sense of greatness, his hunger for power (and these are the qualities that make De Gaulle in part a comic figure) he is to Lester Pearson what a pachyderm is to a cheese-mite.

It is a moot point, of course, whether or not Pearson could be said to exist at all. What has he *done*? Other, that is, than to increase his country's dependence on the U.S.? Consider, for example, his attitude towards the war in Vietnam—the policy of "quiet diplomacy." Pearson thinks that by uttering mild and vaguely phrased "protest" into the ear of some flunkey at an Embassy cocktail party he stands a chance of influencing the course of events. But say what you like about L. B. Johnson, the one thing in his favour is that he could no more even *hear* the whisperings from Canada of this poor, ineffective little twerp than he would hear the gentle farting of a half-frozen gnat in some remote and vacant attic of the White House.

(Is Lyndon Johnson a clown? It is a difficult question and an interesting one. I haven't the time to go into it here. But at least I can offer you the "parameters" of the problem. On one level this beagle-breeding, barbecuing, red-necked ignoramous has some of the hallmarks of one of the greatest unconscious comedians in American history. But is he actually *funny*? Lizzie Borden, for example, was not funny when she Raskolnikoved open her father's head . . . . It was only *aferwards* that comic songs were written about her. Mussolini strikes us in retrospect as hilarious but did he amuse us when he walked into Abyssinia with his armoured cars and poison gas? Perhaps it will only be in the years to come, if we ever *have* any years to come, that Johnson's true clownishness will receive its due.)

It is at this point that the comic aspects of the Great Rebuke begin to emerge. For one thing, it was delivered by a pathetic nonentity to a man of style, intelligence, ability, and courage. For another it was a resentful and xenophobic expression of English Canadian culture (which is not a culture but a collection of fifth-rate attitudes such as servility, Presbyterianism, cultivated anonymity, politeness, and the celebration of the two deadly virtues of wealth and mediocrity) directed against a man who, for all his pomposity, has the guts to see life in heroic terms and who has succeeded in bettering his own country. It is a tribute to the civilizing effect that France has had on the world that we say "every man has two homes, his own and France" but what can we say about Canada, in this Centennial Year? Only that it has not yet contributed one iota to the sum total of the world's culture and that it is unlikely ever to do so while its establishment is composed of men like Lester Pearson.

The cheap image-building job the Liberal party was able to improvise for Pearson at the expense of a superior individual tends to obscure both the contrast between these two men and the contrast between our own, coca-colonized country and independent France. The Rebuke was funny, but we should not be too smug about it.

1967

Afterword

In a polemic of this sort, the writer is never trying to be fair, reasonable, or judicious. His aim is to entertain those who agree with him and to goad into a frenzy those who don't. I want to state my present conviction, however, that history has so far been unfair to Lyndon Johnson — not *very* unfair, but nevertheless unfair. The "counter-culture" chant,

> LBJ
> LBJ
> How many kids have you killed today?

was not only cruel but undeserved. Johnson, like most politicians who reach the top of their dubious profession, was a victim of his circumstances. To jeer at him for not extricating his country from its Viet Nam adventure is to demand of him guts and imagination far beyond the competence of the chanting hippie that puts him down. On the other hand, Johnson *could* have made history and his own heroic reputation by stopping the war. He blew it, but so, I think, would most of us.

About the unspeakable Lester Pearson, of course, I retract nothing.

The Donkey and the Law

Last week I was called in as a witness in the defence of a young lad charged with "publishing an obscene item, to wit: the words 'fuck you.'" He was run in while walking the streets of the town wearing a denim jacket with the phrase in question printed on its waist-band. The defence lawyer phoned the *Georgia Straight* who referred him to me.

Since I know a little about contemporary culture, and since I am a man in whose conversation the word "fuck" occurs with the frequency to be expected of anybody with experience in the army or at Simon Fraser University, I considered myself qualified to give evidence in this matter. I talked to the lawyer who arranged a defence and eagerly I awaited the dawn (10 a.m.) when the case was due to be heard.

The lad was to appear before a magistrate named Mulligan who seems to enjoy a reputation (whether deserved or not I do not know) for broad-mindedness, a reputation which seemed to have reached the ears of those responsible for the prosecution since the latter arranged for the hearing to be shifted to another courtroom presided over (according to the defence lawyer, hissing with anger and frustration in my ear) by a hanging judge. The lawyer's brave attempt to get the case transferred back to Mulligan failed and we sat waiting for His (Hanging) Honour to appear.

Enter the magistrate. He was a white-haired, rheum-eyed, ancient little man with a brown complexion and dirty moustache which looked as though it belonged to a snuff-addict of untidy habits. He had the manner and appearance of a snapping turtle. It occurred to me that this man was unlikely to be sympathetic to the word "fuck" on two counts: (1) he looked too puritanic to enjoy using the word as it is normally used (as a kind of oral exclamation mark) and (2) he was far too long in the tooth for the word to retain in his mind any of its pleasant, sexual, denotation. Indeed, he was in that stage of senility when the thought of what one (let us hope) has done in one's youth strikes the mind with horror and rage.

For Christ's sake, I said to myself. *Don't lose your cool.*

The prisoner was brought in. He was manacled. He'd been in jug since the beginning of June awaiting trial. He'd been offered bail but, new to Vancouver, knew no one who could put up the fifty dollars and was broke himself. He did not seem to have been roughed up at all but I was not sufficiently close to him to be more definite than that. He pleaded not guilty. A court officer struck off his manacles.

They kicked me out of the court while the bogey who had arrested the youth gave evidence and I was brought back in and offered a Bible to hold.

My witness, the defence lawyer said, is an expert on language and literature and will testify as to the obscenity of this word.

SNAPPING TURTLE: I'm willing to accept him as an expert on language and literature, but it's the court who decides whether the word's obscene.

LAWYER: Mr. Mills, could you give us a history of this word?

SELF: Well, it's an antique word which . . . .

SNAPPING TURTLE: Yes-yes-yes, we know all that.

LAWYER: Are there people who do not find this word offensive?

SELF: Certainly, and what's more . . . .

SNAPPING TURTLE: Yes-yes-yes, some find it offensive and some do not. We don't need *you* to tell us *that.*

SELF: What I'm trying to say is that we have to distinguish between a word's denotation and its connotations. This word *denotes* a sexual function . . . .

SNAPPING TURTLE: We don't need you to tell us that, either.

SELF: I'm trying to point out that in its denotation the

word can only be thought obscene by those who think that sex itself is obscene. And such people, even in British Columbia, are becoming fewer and fewer....

SNAPPING TURTLE: Or more and more ... or more and more.

SELF: I'm trying to say that when it's used denotatively it could even be construed, as D. H. Lawrence construed it, as beautiful....

SNAPPING TURTLE: (Snorting with disgust): Hrr! Beautiful, indeed!

At this point it became obvious, even to me, that I was dealing with what I consider a very British Columbia phenomenon. It exists elsewhere, of course, but nowhere have I encountered it with the frequency I've encountered it here. The phenomenon is this: suppose man X makes a statement; man Y, horrified (since the statement touches some deep prejudice) refuses to consider it, discuss it, or even try to refute it. He interrupts X with such words as "nonsense," "rubbish," or even (if he is a fairly emancipated British Columbian), "bullshit." He gets up from this chair and leaves the room. It is not always that he is stupid; he is merely terrified that he might be made to change his mind. I've never known any effective, polite way to deal with man Y. Perhaps a punch in the mouth is the only possible retort.

On this occasion it seemed equally obvious to me that I was saying things the snapping turtle did not want to hear (whether they were worth saying or not is a different matter — a matter which man Y is never willing to debate) and that I was, therefore, not doing the prisoner any lasting good.

When at last I was allowed an uninterrupted flow I tried to make the following argument. That the word is rarely used to describe the sex act — it is used instead as an intensifier, a means of giving emphasis to one's remarks — in which case it has no definite meaning. That when it is used in this meaningless way it is absurd to talk about obscenity.

What, finally, is obscenity? That which conjures up in the mind images provocative of disgust and nausea. Does sex conjure up nausea? I can only feel sorry for those thus afflicted. What kind of thing produces this nausea? Surely this is an individual matter. To anybody of my generation the sight of young motor-cyclists dressed in leather jackets decorated with swastikas is nauseating. Swastika is a dirty word to me. But do I ask of the law that it remove such a spectacle from my sight? I do not. Which is the most obscene, the word "fuck" or the word "napalm"? Which, in other words, produces in you the most disgust and nausea? The point is why should either of these words be censored? Or rather, if you censor the one, why not the other?

No, you cannot talk about the obscenity of the word "fuck." What you *can* talk about is its function as a taboo word. Taboo words change from generation to generation and what was tabooed in the early part of the century is not necessarily tabooed now. An example is the word "bloody," tabooed in Shaw's day when he used it in *Pygmalion*. Few people would regard it as a taboo word nowadays. Similarly the word "fuck" is rapidly losing its strength as a taboo word. Almost everybody (I claimed) uses it in normal conversation. It appears in books, in movies, even on posters. I cited as an example the famous FUCK COMMUNISM poster which expresses a sentiment an establishment might find impeccable in language it might decide is taboo. The movie *Ulysses* employs this word (to the best of my knowledge) and was passed by the B.C. Board of Censors.

What does it mean to say that such and such a word is taboo? It means there are certain circles where I can use the word only at the risk of being thought not quite a gentleman. A Lady's Golf Club, let us say. If I were to use the word in front of such a group it would imply that I knew the word was taboo as far as they were concerned and that my intention was to shock them. But to shock a particular group I would have to know their taboos. If I wanted to shock a group of Jews, for example, I would start praising the institution of concentration camps. And so on. So that young chap, walking around with "fuck you" written on his jacket is innocent of everything but childishness and a probable streak of Puritanism in his own nature. He cannot be accused of shocking people since he cannot know who, out of all the people that see the jacket, would be shocked and who would not. His gesture is random and meaningless.

This, basically, was what I said in court. It did not emerge in quite this form, of course, but the argument (if you can thus dignify what I said) was developed by cross-examination by the defence and prosecution.

The defence's position was to ask the court if the words "fuck you" in the present context led readers down the paths of moral corruption and depravity. But the snapping turtle refused to answer this particular question. Instead, he ruled, without any further discussion, that the phrase was obscene. The prosecutor helped him by pointing out that the movie *Ulysses* was restricted in audience and was advertised only with the caveat that the dialogue might be offensive to some people to which His Honour riposted that he personally never went to see such movies anyway.

So the prisoner was found guilty of "publishing an obscene item" and given an extra five days in the clink in addition to the time he'd already served. About the only person who understood the distinction I was trying to draw between the obscene and the taboo was the defence lawyer for it was not in the prosecuting attorney's interests to admit there *is* a distinction, and it was beyond the capabilities of the snapping turtle to understand any cultural event that has taken place since the death of Her Late Majesty Queen Victoria.

And the point of this article is not just simply to express horror at the notion of "justice" lying in the hands of an impertinent and bigoted old man, or at the thought of a young man, no more than twenty or so, started out with a police record for a cause as trivial as this, but to ask, what can be done? How the hell do you deal with man Y generally? I suggested earlier that the only viable response might be a punch in the mouth but there are other, more constructive, alternatives.

There is a novel by Ignazio Silone called *Fontamara* which is about the Fascist take-over of a small Italian town. One of the Fascists, a man named Innocenzo, hangs a notice on the wall of the local pub. The notice reads "All argument is forbidden, by Order." One of the local drinkers pretends to agree. "Good idea," he says:

My principle has always been: never argue with the bosses. Arguing and discussing are at the bottom of all the peasant's misfortunes. The peasant is a donkey, a donkey that argues. That's why we're far worse off than real donkeys, who never argue, or at least pretend not to. Your real donkey will carry fifty, seventy, a hundred pounds, not more; but he doesn't argue. Your donkey will travel at a certain speed and no faster, he doesn't argue . . . no argument will convince him and no speech will move him . . . the peasant on the other hand will argue. You can persuade him to work beyond the limits of his strength. You can persuade him to go without his meals. You can persuade him to die for his master. You can persuade him to go to war. You can even make him believe there's such a place as hell. Look at the consequences . . . just imagine what would happen if the six thousand peasants who cultivate the Fucino, instead of being donkeys who argue, in other words donkeys you can tame, talk around, bully with carabinieri and priests and judges—just suppose they were real donkeys who couldn't argue at all...

For example, what has prevented us from murdering *you*? What stops us is that, not being donkeys, we argue and know the consequences of murder. But you wrote on that notice board in your own hand, Innocenzo, that from this day onwards all arguing is forbidden... you've cut your own throat.

At the centre of liberalism lies the belief that men are possessed of good will and are willing to be convinced by rational argument. Along with this is the belief that there is such a thing as common sense. But the failure of liberalism seems to be due to the fact that the exponent of the common-sense position is forced to argue with man Y who will brook no discussion. And very often man Y does not *have* to argue since power lies in his hands. The common-sense position here might be that the prisoner has as much right to express his form of Puritanism as Prime Minister Bennett has to express *his*. I do not expect anyone, least of all a snapping turtle, to reach this conclusion or to agree with me. But I expect him (or at least *used* to expect him) to retain an open mind and to discuss the matter... to meet my arguments and to try to convince me.

This case is a symptomatic one, it seems to me. All over the Western world people are wondering why there are riots at places like the Sorbonne, or Columbia, or why there is such a thing as a Black Power movement. It is because young people generally have become donkeys. They have stopped arguing and they have stopped precisely because of man Y.

As far as I'm concerned the man Y in this case has dignified an unimportant gesture by punishing it. There *was* no point in wearing the words "fuck you" on one's jacket but perhaps *now* there is. It is a way of not arguing. Personally if I start to wear such a jacket I shall preface the phrase with the kind of caveat used by the B.C. Board of Censors:

WARNING: THE FOLLOWING PHRASE MAY DISGUST AND OFFEND YOU.

That should make it all right.

1968

Part III
Two Revaluations

A Book for the Shelter

Let's suppose you're late for an appointment. You need a clean pair of socks — perhaps it's that kind of appointment. You keep these socks in the top right hand drawer of a chest. You pull at the handle and of course the drawer sticks. You wrestle with the drawer, fighting it, catch-as-catch-can, yanking on one side of it then the other. Diabolically, it resists you with an energy it has never shown before. It is as though it knows you are late and is determined to make your life troublesome and wretched. You curse and swear, one eye on the clock. You kick the chest and, because your feet are bare, immediately wish you hadn't. You've acquired instant metatarsalgia destined to make you hobble for weeks. You howl with pain and rage and attack the drawer in earnest — with a kind of systematic frenzy. The chest is lucky you don't have a hammer in the bedroom. It knows that, of course, and sneers at you. Just as you've decided to go downstairs and get it, the drawer gives way and slides free, giving you a smile whose oiliness is combined with the lordly air of one who says "See? everything comes to he who waits. I have chosen, out of my magnanimity, to accede to your wishes." Snarling in humiliation you select your socks, which the drawer has by some dark magic turned into different colours and patterns, and limp away, late and evil tempered, to your assignation.

Everybody is familiar with this kind of thing. It is an example of the well-documented hostility of material objects to human kind. *Things*, as the humorist Paul Jennings wrote, *Are Against Man*. This is the central thesis of his philosophy of *Resistentialism* (*Res* is Latin for *thing*) derived in part from the experiment conducted by Professor Clark-Trimble in 1935 in which four hundred pieces of carpet were arranged in ascending order of worth from coarse matting to priceless Chinese silk and pieces of toast and marmalade, graded, weighed, and measured, dropped on each piece of carpet and the marmalade-downward incidence statistically analyzed. The toast fell right side up every time on the cheaper carpet except when the cheap carpets were screened from the rest (in which case the toast didn't know that Clark-Trimble had other and better carpets) and it fell marmalade-downwards every time on the Chinese silk.

The knowledge that things are against us really needs no such experimental verification, for it is one I think we must be born with. One of my first memories is of trying to squeeze an orange down a drain outside Morgan's Crucible Works in Battersea, London, at the age of three. I remember to this day the grinning smugness of the grating, the round unsquashability of the unripe orange, my own pantings and heavings as I tried to marshall my small strength for this encounter, the paternalistic mockery of adult passers-by who knew, from bitter experience of the world, that one can never manipulate objects the way one wants. Later I began, like the rest of us, to take the hostility of material objects as a constant in the human condition.

Clearly there are two ways by which we learn to adjust to the situation. The first is coldly rational: a man, tending his garden, learns to place the rake tine-side down. It will still try to trip him up with that part of it raised above the ground but, unless he is extremely self-destructive, it won't actually put an end to his life — as a rake did to that of the unfortunate Clark-Trimble. He learns that the drawer he keeps his socks in will stick only if he has allowed insufficient time to get dressed, for under normal conditions the drawer thinks it not worth its while. A car, a breed of object with a malignancy all of its own, will torment him only if he is stupid enough to rely on it; a house will burn itself down only if he has allowed the insurance to lapse. This, as I see it, is one method of dealing with the physical world. You need, however, to be the sort of person who runs his life efficiently, who looks before he leaps, who does not spit against the wind, who never steps out of his house without a doctor on his left and a lawyer on his right. Honesty is always the best policy with a man like this; he is neither a borrower nor a lender and he can always keep his head when all about him are losing theirs and blaming it on him. A glum, button-down, shiny-suited, matched socks kind of an individual who scrapes from birth to death with a minimum of risk and inconvenience but also, I must insist, with a minimum of adventure. It was not in such a cautious, bourgeois, penny-pinching spirit that Columbus discovered the New World, that Einstein published his paper on relativity, that Dalton, or whoever it was, risked drowning and pneumonia by taking a bell jar out onto a swamp and collecting marsh gas by either upward or downward displacement, who knows which, and that the giant step for mankind was taken by that anonymous fellow on the moon.

No, the more swashbuckling alternative is to fight back against the tyranny of things by transmuting matter in your imagination into the stuff of which adventures are made. That drawer you wrestle with becomes a monster out of epic poetry — you are Beowulf, for example, tearing at Grendel's arm. It resists you, of course it resists you, who wants his arm torn off? But you know you will win, for you have become a hero and victory is written in your script. You can beat your automobile similarly by pretending that it is Satan (surely not such a wide leap of the imagination) come to tempt you in the guise of a beautiful woman — Helen of Troy — and that you resist her subtle blandishments by turning your back and adopting the monastic but ultimately invigorating abstinence of Public Transport — thus not only saving money but preventing the Trojan War. An hour pacing the asphalt near a bus transfer point is surely better than breaking down on the highway and you can always imagine you're a Victorian soldier trapped in Mafeking, or Ladysmith, or some other desert outpost and that the bus when it arrives is Kitchener, perhaps, or General Roberts. In this way an inconvenience, as G. K. Chesterton once said, is nothing more than an adventure considered in the wrong spirit and, conversely, an adventure is an inconvenience considered the right way. Looking backwards, my struggle with drain and orange becomes an archetypal encounter, symbolizing life generally, between the free human spirit and the imprisoning world of things.

Obviously there are limitations to this point of view. A war, for example, whether Kitchener features in it or not, is neither adventurous nor inconvenient, but an evil. But even during a war, if you are very young, there are occasions when the imagination can turn a minor inconvenience into an adventure. The London blitz occurred when I was ten years old; my parents were concerned about it as, of course, I would have been had I the benefit of their years and deeper knowledge of the hostility of objects. For instance, a piece of shrapnel, to them so lethal, was to me a magic talisman of the sort I could collect. Four pieces of shrapnel "of a certain length" could be exchanged for a nose cone. Two nose cones equalled half a tail fin. Thus shrapnel would be traded, cornered, and marked up as though my peers and I were ironmongers and philatelists combined. The whole bomb, of course, was dealt with in unexploded form by special squads and was not a unit of exchange. In exploded form it was merely something I wished fervently would hit my school. The terrors of school were far more real to me than those of the bombing raids *they* merely formed an adventurous excuse to troop down away from the hated classrooms to the air-raid shelters and it was here, in the shelters, that I first came across that poet of inconvenience, that chronicler of thing-hostility, that exponent of the resistential banana-skin, Jerome K. Jerome.

Let me start with Jerome's account of the can of pineapple.

When George drew out a tin of pineapple from the bottom of the hamper, and rolled it in to the middle of the boat, we felt that life was worth living after all.

We were very fond of pineapple, all three of us. We looked at the picture on the tin; we thought of the juice. We smiled at one another, and Harris got a spoon ready.

Then we looked for the knife to open the tin with. We turned out everything in the hamper. We turned out the bags. We pulled up the boards at the bottom of the boat. We took everything out on to the bank and shook it. There was no tin-opener to be found.

Then Harris tried to open the tin with a pocket knife, and broke the knife and cut himself badly; and George tried a pair of scissors, and the scissors flew up, and nearly put his eye out. While they were dressing their wounds, I tried to make a hole in the thing with the spiky end of the hitcher, and the hitcher slipped and jerked me out between the boat and the bank into two feet of muddy water, and the tin rolled over, uninjured, and broke a tea-cup.

Then we all got mad. We took that tin out on the bank, and Harris went up into a field and got a big sharp stone, and I went back into the boat and brought out the mast, and George held the tin and Harris held the sharp end of his stone against the top of it, and I took the mast and poised it high up in the air, and gathered up all my strength and brought it down.

It was George's straw hat that saved his life that day. He keeps that hat now (what is left of it), and, of a winter's evening, when the pipes are lit and the boys are telling stretchers about the dangers they have passed through, George brings it down and shows it round, and the stirring tale is told anew, with fresh exaggerations every time.

Harris got off with merely a flesh wound.

After that I took the tin myself, and hammered at it with the mast till I was worn out and sick at heart, whereupon Harris took it in hand.

We bent it out flat; we beat it back square; we battered it into every form known to geometry — but we could not make a hole in it. Then George went at it, and knocked it into a shape, so strange, so weird, so unearthly in its wild hideousness that he got frightened and threw away the mast. Then we all three sat round it on the grass and looked at it.

There was one great dent across the top that had the appearance of a mocking grin, and it drove us furious, so that Harris rushed at the thing, and caught it up, and flung it far into the middle of the river, and as it sank we hurled our curses at it, and we got into the boat and rowed away from the spot and never paused till we reached Maidenhead.

There are several things I want to say about this passage. When I first read it, back in 1940, in that air-raid shelter which stank of mildew and dirty socks, it struck me as hilariously funny. The lead up to the central statement — "It was George's straw hat that saved his life" — with its progression of "and" clauses, seemed perfect. They used to read us bits of the Bible at that school and I recognized faint echoes — "worn out and sick at heart" is another example — of the sort of language a man would find in the Old Testament describing ancient battles against Midian and Philistine, so that the effect is to turn this minor inconvenience of a lost tin-opener into an epic struggle. Secondly, a lesser writer would have rendered the tin as a passive object mauled about by three angry men. But this tin has a life and malevolent energy of its own. It rolls about and breaks a tea-cup. It assumes diabolic shapes. It grins triumphantly. The almost ritualistic deep-sixing of the can smacks of exorcism and the men row away from the spot as though it were accursed. And it is not merely the can: scissors are said to "fly up," in search of an eye to gouge; the hitcher jerks the narrator into muddy water in an attempt to drown him. I had never up till then lost a tin-opener but the texture of the experience, to an old orange-squeezer like myself, was instantly recognizable. There are many anecdotes of the sort scattered throughout the book and I have selected my favourite, though fellow resistentialists might choose others equally deserving of quotation—the tow-rope, for example, which prefers to think of itself as a badly woven door-mat; or the technique by which you get a kettle to boil; or the yachting expedition which ends happily only because the boat assumes the beginner yachtsmen are out for a day's suicide and is resolved to frustrate them. The book delighted me because it confirmed my limited knowledge of the more trivial aspects of existence and made them adventurous, heroic, and above all, funny. Secondly, the prose is alive; pungent and colloquial and entirely modern. In its day it was thought to be vulgar, slangy, infected by American writing. The art-for-art's sakers who were Jerome's contemporaries put him down, as they put down the so-called New Humorists generally, as a crass popularizer. Tastes have changed and how much better does Jerome read today than Harland, Le Galliene, or Maurice Hewlett.

Three Men in a Boat is an account written in the first-person mode of a summer trip up the Thames in a double-sculling skiff from Kingston as far as Oxford and back about half-way until, as happens so often in England, rain intervenes and the journey is abandoned. I had, of course, never made such a trip—furthermore I never will and neither will anybody else. The Thames and the people and places along its banks have changed dramatically since Jerome's day. George, for example, one of the three men of the title, offended the ears of those around him by learning to play the banjo. Tape decks and stereos have taken over from George whose nuisance value was confined to a meagre range of fifty yards; odd things floated in the river—a dead dog on one occasion; the drowned body of a woman on another—but the water was free of scum, phosphates, and its present day thin film of oil and you could even drink it, if you were thirsty enough and didn't mind taking a chance. Nowadays it is better not to even put your hand in it. George, J., and Harris could abandon their boat for the evening and wander around charming Thameside villages undesecrated by parking lot or concrete supermarket and unpolluted by petrol fumes or the racket of motorcycles and transistor radios. They could spend evenings listening to old men telling lies about the fish they never caught in pubs not yet given over to the juke boxes, chemical beer, and pin-ball machines. In 1940 I knew, of course, that Jerome's world had gone — vanished, my father often used to tell me, in 1914. I knew that the straw hat had gone out with wasp-waisted dresses and the colour and gaiety of the locks and tow-paths had disappeared to make way for something more drab, long before the Second World War. The Alhambra, to which the trio resort at the end of the book, was razed to make way for Leicester Square and, in fact, music hall itself had become a victim of radio and the cinema and survived only on radio variety shows as a sequence of turns — Arthur Askey, Anne Ziegler and Webster Booth, Flanagan and Allen. Otherwise, as a live entertainment, it was as dead as King George V whose jubilee I dimly remember celebrating at about the age of five. There are occasions, in Jerome's book, where people gather together around a piano and sing; this survives only in debased form as a Saturday night ritual when the veterans at the Legion have reached the maudlin stage and are ready to choke out, beneath their sobs, choruses of *There'll Be Bluebirds Over the White Cliffs of Dover* or *We'll Meet Again*. But Jerome's world was close enough in time for me to believe in it as a sort of substitute childhood — a country of the past where inconveniences, such as that adamantine tin of pineapple, are the only source of conflict.

But apart from its comedy, *Three Men in a Boat* is, recognizably even to a young child, a very *innocent* book. Disease is treated only as an illusion of hypochondriacs, politics are entirely absent, sex — very much on my own mind, not as an actual problem, but as a future reality, looming up — is present either in heavily diluted homo-erotic form or as the subject of exasperated jokes about courting couples. Women in the book are either decorative, or silly, or both, in accordance with Victorian male conventions, and women already seemed to me more complex than Jerome gives them credit for. The other obvious omission is the problem of work. At the age of ten I knew that work was one of modern civilization's worst afflictions. Daily we were warned by our teachers and our depression-obsessed parents of the results of idleness at school; we were threatened with the dole, with lines at labour exchanges, with becoming like those grey-faced men one saw when the Jarrow shipyards closed who hung around on street corners going to pieces as human beings. The alternative, punching clocks, crawling to a boss or a shop-steward, commuting to the city every day in a bowler hat and furled umbrella, seemed even less desirable. Nobody works in *Three Men in a Boat*; admittedly George has some sort of a sinecure in a bank where he sleeps on Saturdays until noon, at which time they kick him out, but work does not play that central and sinister role in people's lives of

110

which I was very much aware and this in itself makes the world of 1888 enviable but unreal—innocent, in fact. In this world there are minor inconveniences, treated as adventures, but no urban jungle, no Land of Jobs, no cops, truncheons, jack-boots, or gas chambers. No bombing planes overhead and no adults trying with great heroism to hide their terror from their children.

Thus the book looks back to a vanished world in many ways even harsher than our own, had I known the truth about it then, but rendered with great verve and immediacy as idyllic. So immediate, in fact, that from the dank cellar of that shelter in which we hid from the men overhead trying to kill us I felt I could reach out and touch it—a kind of security blanket, as we now say. That land you never knew is nevertheless part of you as an Eden—an innocent, stressless playground and the book goes some way towards fulfilling that mysterious, ultimately unsatisfiable yearning to recapture it. But, if *Three Men in a Boat* suggests a past towards which we feel nostalgic, it also suggests a future—a sense of an ending—for one of the most powerful effects of Jerome's work is contained in the last pages when George, Harris, and J. abandon their boat in the drizzling rain, return by train to London, and make their visit to the Alhambra. Afterwards they retire to a restaurant where, the narrator boasts, "you can get one of the best-cooked and cheapest little French dinners or suppers that I know of, with an excellent bottle of Beaune for three and six; and which I am not going to be idiot enough to advertise."

I must confess to enjoying that supper. For about ten days we seemed to have been living, more or less, on nothing but cold meat, cake, and bread and jam. It had been a simple, a nutritious diet; but there had been nothing exciting about it, and the odour of Burgundy, and the smell of French sauces, and the sight of clean napkins and long loaves, knocked as a very welcome visitor at the door of our inner man.

We pegged and quaffed away in silence for a while, until the time came when, instead of sitting bolt upright, and grasping the knife and fork firmly, we leaned back in our chairs and worked slowly and carelessly—when we stretched out our legs beneath the table, let our napkins fall, unheeded, to the floor, and found time to more critically examine the smoky ceiling than we had hitherto been able to do—when we rested our glasses at arm's length upon the table and felt good, and thoughtful, and forgiving.

111

Then Harris, who was sitting next to the window, drew aside the curtain and looked out upon the street.

It glistened darkly in the wet, the dim lamps flickered with each gust, the rain splashed steadily into the puddles and trickled down the water-spouts into the running gutters. A few soaked wayfarers hurried past, crouching beneath their dripping umbrellas, the women holding up their skirts.

"Well," said Harris, reaching out for his glass, "we have had a pleasant trip, and my hearty thanks to Old Father Thames — but I think we did well to chuck it when we did. Here's to Three Men well out of a Boat!"

And with this the book comes to an end. Even apart from the details of the long skirts and the gas-lamps, it is a very Victorian conception — akin to Chesterton's vision of an inn at the end of the world — plentiful food, freedom from danger and hardship, women kept at a distance on the outside. As a glimpse of paradise, it is hardly adequate and I prefer that offered by the Koran which visualizes hordes of nubile concubines, sherbert, and reclining chairs. "They shall be arrayed," the Koran says of the righteous, "in garments of fine green silk and rich brocade, and adorned with bracelets of silver. Their Lord will give them a pure beverage to drink." But Jerome's will do for a start: 'twill serve, for it hints at the satisfaction of our greatest need — a refuge from the storm and terrors of the dark, a safe harbour, and good companionship forever, and forever.

1979

The Horse's Mouth and Stanley Spencer

Much of what Joyce Cary had to say about art appears in *Art and Reality*[1] and it can be paraphrased as follows: the artist always starts with a discovery he makes regarding the essential nature of experience —the sort of discovery a child makes constantly about the actual world. He perceives, perhaps quite suddenly, the "real" quality of an object, a person, or a relationship and the "sudden glory" that arises from this perception prompts him to fix it within an art form. I use the Hobbesian phrase deliberately despite my feeling that Cary would have rejected its original context while accepting it as a good description of a sense of joy—the fundamental basis of art. Certainly he would have accepted the Platonic implications of "real" since to him the major problem an artist faces is the translation of his intuitions into colours, patterns, and designs that will convey their magic quality.

Clearly this description of the creative process is something like Stephen Dedalus' in *A Portrait of the Artist as a Young Man.* In both cases the artist apprehends epiphanies—the showings forth of the inmost nature of things. In Cary's view this epiphany is usually a showing forth of something rooted in the physical world and in fact it is difficult to imagine any serious writer or artist claiming he had set out one morning to imitate, or show forth, an abstract principle—not even Gulley Jimson's Blake, discovering that "energy is eternal delight," felt that *that* was what he had to get down on paper or canvas. An example of an epiphany is Conrad's observation, in an Eastern port, of a young officer emerging from a trial in which he'd been found guilty of cowardice in deserting his ship and its passengers after a collision. The officer had lost his honour and, as Cary says, Conrad must have realized instantly what this meant to him and wrote *Lord Jim* to fix and communicate this discovery in its full force. Another example, though probably unknown to Cary, is the case of Faulkner who claimed he got the idea for *The Sound and the Fury* from observing a young girl with muddy drawers playing in the boughs of a tree. This experience, banal though it may appear, prompted him to invent a history and a future for this girl and to ask such questions as "who is she?"; "what's in store for her?"; "why is she in the tree?"; "why is she alone?"; etc. and in answer to these questions the novel emerged.

Such epiphanies or, as Cary called them, intuitions are evanescent and the artist in trying to fix them must do battle with all the forces — tradition, training, the refractory nature of his materials and tools — that Jimson calls Old Mother Necessity together with the fixed patterns in his own temperament which tend to substitute a conception of the finished work for the original intuition. *Art and Reality* describes this struggle between intuition and conception experienced by any artist trying to preserve the truth and freshness of his discoveries against the very forces he must draw upon to communicate them. One might speculate as to what sort of discoveries or intuitions lie behind one of Cary's own novels such as *The Horse's Mouth*. What means does Cary use to translate such experiences into a work of art? How does he wage his particular war between intuition and conception? What sort of difficulties does he encounter, what choices does he make, and how does the waging of this particular war modify the original choice of subject? These are obviously questions of first importance to both writers and critics and Cary's *Art and Reality* is an extremely interesting attempt to grapple with it. It is worth examining the sources of *The Horse's Mouth* since the novel is not only expressly about this question, but also, in one aspect, a dramatized rendering of Cary's own ideas. Its central character is an artist based on "real-life" models and it is therefore possible to assess how Cary translated reality to fiction and, more importantly, what precisely it was that he translated.

Cary claimed that Gulley Jimson was based on a conflation of Augustus John and Stanley Spencer. The paintings of neither artist resemble very closely what we can infer of Jimson's work though Spencer, a painter of allegorical, religious tendency, probably comes closest. He was obviously an impressive figure — three parts mad, sex-crazed, a painter of genius — single minded in pursuit of art and totally original; an attractive figure for Cary who, in general, liked "pilgrims" — men and women whose own fingers stopped their ears against the calls of normal life. John was the more obvious bohemian — basically classless, striking in appearance, extroverted and, despite his "irregular" sex-life, accepted in society. Spencer, on the other hand, was furtive, grubby and, until the end of his life, an outcast. His habits and personality remained persistently lower-middle class and indeed he looked less like a painter than a solicitor's clerk out of Dickens. His sexuality, weird though it was, lacked the exuberance of John's and even now, in this permissive, tolerant age, it seems sleazy and, though John's excesses caused amused gossip among the intelligentsia and aristocracy, Spencer's were indefatigably *News of the World* material. Certainly there is a component of Gulley's personality modelled on John's, but the metaphysics, the endless rantings, the sexual attitudes, above all the self-perpetuated image of the undersized artist dwarfed, manipulated, and bullied by the two large women with whom he is locked in a quasi-bigamous relationship is entirely Spencerian.

Further evidence that Cary modelled Jimson on Spencer is cited by Malcolm Foster in the latter's biography:

> Sir Stanley, in particular, famous for his huge paintings of resurrection scenes... his distortion of the human figure for the sake of the design of his works, and his flow of quotations from the Bible and William Blake, was a strong influence in the creation of Gulley Jimson.[2]

I would like, therefore, to turn to a discussion of certain aspects of the artist's life.

Information regarding Spencer's personality is best obtained through the painter's own private writings which were gargantuanly voluminous, hardly intelligible, often obscene, and jotted down over a period of many years on hundreds of cheap notepads and, a favourite medium, yards of toilet roll. All of it was off-loaded by Spencer's executors onto Maurice Collis, the painter's biographer, who used it guardedly. The portrait of Spencer that began to emerge from that careful book[3] was confirmed and enlarged by Lady Spencer (the

Fig. 1. *The Apple Gatherers*

former Patricia Preece) in an account of her marriage.[4] This appeared posthumously and was ghost written by Louise Collis. Both writers were neighbours of Spencer and knew him even before his "Sage of Cookham" days when he'd become respectable but even they were unprepared for the revelations provided by the Spencer Scrolls.

These new villagers were charmed by the famous man they found scuttling in and out of the shops with paint on his hands, dressed in suits bought at boys' outfitters in Maidenhead. He was so frank and friendly, never putting on the airs of success, although he had risen from undistinguised beginnings. He was ready to settle down in anybody's room and talk the hours away, rambling from one subject to another of his own choosing, and generally preserving the gay and genial manner of one who floats like a cork over the undeserved misfortunes which beset an artist in this life. He seemed without pride or guile, wrapped up in his

Fig. 2. *The Resurrection, Cookham*

own imagination, unaware of snares laid by designing people, in particular by his second wife, Patricia. Many of his hearers had a firm impression that he was a saint.[5]

It was an impression that was belied by Lady Spencer's recollections but ought to have been belied, and probably was to many people, long before by the nature of Spencer's work.

Probably the most Jimsonesque of Spencer's pictures is *The Apple Gatherers* (Fig. 1) finished in 1912 when Spencer was twenty-two. It is his first major work and the influence of Gauguin is obvious in the deliberately primitive rendering of the human figures, the bucolic subject matter, and the gestures of the central couple. They seem frozen in the middle of a mystical experience and Spencer himself said of them that they have just been possessed by the God of Love who has enthralled them in that apparently crucial instant "between breathing in and breathing out," though later he amended this slightly by explaining that God Himself had just appeared to them and had spoken to them of sex. The mysterious, enraptured expression on the faces appears again and again in Spencer's work almost like a trade mark and the sexual interpretation of his own work, and of this characteristic, is one that intrigued him more and more. He sees *The Resurrection, Cookham* (Fig. 2), for example, as erotic in nature since the figures bursting out of their graves are rising from a death-in-life to a realization that they are living in paradise — a paradise of sexual love

117

Fig. 3. *The Meeting*

which, in turn, he equated with what he called universal and heavenly love. The God and Christ figures under the church porch are sympathetic and encouraging onlookers while the figure on the extreme right is turning away from this scene towards the more explicitly erotic pictures to come.

The Resurrection, Cookham, was first exhibited in 1927 and it was painted during a particularly happy time for Spencer, for he had been married only two years to his first wife Hilda Carline with whom, evidently, he experienced sex for the first time. "It roused a side of his nature which was more violent than he had supposed . . . he was to discover that sex was the strongest of all his wants [and it] was to be the main source of his inspiration."[6] At any rate Spencer's life at this period was blamelessly domestic, even uxorious, for Hilda's lethargy, lack of sympathy for his painting, fits of rage, and growing fanaticism with regard to her Christian Science had not yet begun to irritate him and he spent much of his time working on household tasks — cutting wood, bathing infants, scrubbing floors, and washing dishes — a humble male servitor, he might have thought, to the Female Principle represented by his wife. Clearly one woman is insufficient, given her obvious imperfections and frailty, to carry such an archetypal load and by 1929 Spencer had begun his affair with the unfortunate Patricia Preece — an event celebrated in *The Meeting* (Fig. 3). The scene is Spencer's garden at Cookham and Patricia is represented in back view wearing an enormous fur jacket while Stanley gently touches her hands, his eyes expressing that same rapt fascination so much a feature of *The Apple Gatherers*. Patricia was Spencer's neighbour at Cookham and knew his family mostly through its more obviously eccentric members such as Spencer's sister Annie, hopelessly lost in melancholia, his brother Horace, a music-hall conjurer turned dipsomaniac who stripped the household of furniture and clothing for quick sale to support his habit, and Spencer's doddering father who, through Horace's depradations, was left with nothing to wear but a dressing gown, slippers, and a bowler hat:

> Thus arrayed, he would wander down the street to the churchyard, weather permitting. The tombstones seemed to comfort him. He could be seen picking an unsteady way between them. Sometimes he stooped to read inscriptions he must have known by heart. Sometimes he stood and stared about him, just as he does in so many of Stanley's later pictures, wearing his dressing gown and slippers, though not the bowler hat, daftly impersonating God, the disciples and saints.[7]

Something of this eccentric quality was obvious in Spencer's behaviour right from the start. On the one hand he was a vital, lively, chattering little man exercising a kind of "magnetism," as she put it, over her, but on the other there were sinister aspects to his personality which caused her at several points in their courtship to have second thoughts about him. There was this equation of sex and love for one thing, an unfashionable concept just then, but this was not too serious taken on its own. But what about the growing interest in polygamy? In vile smells? Excrement? Ugliness and the grotesque? And, above all, the clothes fetishism with which he made her life a misery?

Mad with excitement, he would take me to shops in Maidenhead and London and insist on trying on everything in the place. Seeing how I wearied of the performance, the mannequin belonging to the shop would sometimes offer to show the dresses. But he would have none of it. I must put them on. I must parade up and down before him while he stared with gleaming eyes and a peculiar enjoyment, pouring out a string of incoherent compliments. . . . Then he would hurry me into a shoe-shop. If I demurred he was likely to make a scene in the street, shouting abuse and waving his fists. Here it was the same all over again, though not quite as exhausting as dressing and undressing. I would only have to totter up and down in innumerable pairs of bright and beastly shoes with enormously high heels as he stared at my feet and legs with fascination.[8]

Granted that Patricia Preece was no Germaine Greer or Kate Millett, one is still puzzled as to why she agreed to continue her relationship with Spencer. Her explanation is that he cast a spell over her and in any case the gossip about her in Cookham was making life there difficult. Spencer, at least ostensibly, regarded his marriage with Hilda as finished and had little difficulty getting Patricia to agree to marry him as soon as he obtained a divorce. With some misgivings Patricia readied a cottage they'd rented in Cornwall for their honeymoon but a few days after the marriage actually took place Spencer presented his new wife with his proposition:

The third day was nice and fine, so we decided to walk along the beach and look for shells to complete a mirror frame I was making. As we were returning he suddenly said that he had slept with Hilda while she was at Lindworth . . . for he was no ordinary man, he said ardently. For artistic reasons, absolute sexual freedom was necessary to him. All that stuff about divorce and remarriage was mere lawyer's jargon. It had nothing to do with the real facts. He was above the law. It must be so because he was a genius. He would sleep with Hilda whenever he felt like it.

Never in my life have I been so angry and upset as I was then. . . . He too became angry, shouting and waving his arms in a furious manner on the sand, against the background of Atlantic surf. Two wives were the very least he could do with . . . .[9]

Fig. 4. *Beatitudes of Love: VIII Worship*

Despite Spencer's incredible loquacity, his habit of regaling friends and acquaintances with the most intimate details regarding himself and the two women who were, according to him, oppressing and manipulating him, this bigamous plan, so Patricia claims, came as a complete surprise to her. It ended their sexual relationship and on their return to Cookham they took up separate establishments. Spencer had no intention of retracting his proposal; the situation seemed to suit him perfectly. He had also failed to enlist Hilda in his scheme so that except in fantasy he was without any wife at all. Sexual expression became for him a matter of writing things down. He was a

121

Fig. 5. *Love on the Moor*

frequent visitor at Moor Thatch, Patricia's house, with his exercise book in which it was his habit to write out longhand intensely boring accounts of his dreams and ideas — both religious and sexual — not only in the form of a journal, but as letters to Hilda. At the same time he was busy explaining, to his friends, even to complete strangers, that Patricia was refusing to live with him for mysterious and cruel reasons. He cast himself in the role of a little, innocent, unassertive genius overwhelmed by gigantic and rapacious women whom, at the same time, he worshipped.

The obvious psychic gains from such a self-assessment are

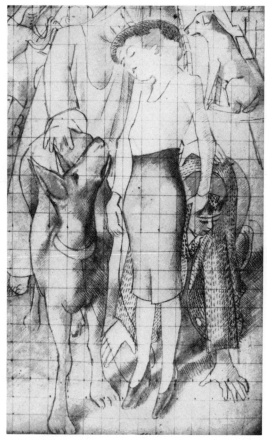

Fig. 6. Detail of *Patricia and I*

apparent in the *Beatitudes of Love* series. In *Beatitudes of Love: VIII Worship* (Fig. 4), for instance, Patricia is represented as the right-hand figure wearing one of the dresses Stanley had bought for her while another representation of her fondles the left-hand partner while miniaturized Spencer figures kneel on the floor in attitudes of awe-struck worship. The money on the floor, the facial expressions, and the scent-spray provide appropriate sexual symbolism. Spencer linked one aspect of his sexual obsessions with his earlier resurrection theme by bringing his re-vivified parishioners out of the earth into a sexual paradise presided over by Hilda as Venus (*Love on the Moor*, Fig. 5).

123

Fig. 7. *Dogs*

She stands on a plinth decorated with her underclothes while a tiny, nude Stanley embraces her legs. Some of the resurrected point ecstatically at the underclothes while others try on or remove garments of their own.

Patricia and I (Fig. 6) illustrates that component of Spencer's sexual personality aroused by being dominated. Here he equates himself with the dog gazing adoringly on Patricia's right while the deity, fondling the buttocks of both animals, gives approval. Dogs, indeed, occupied a special place in Spencer's sexual iconography:

Dogs were sex. Through them he was able to express his lavatory fixations. Their excretions roused him to passion. He liked to dwell on them, to play with them and smell them. The habits of dogs are the literal translations of such desires . . . moreover they are privileged creatures. They go about doing things he longed to do and no-one objects.[10]

Dogs (Fig. 7) is an apotheosis of this fantasy. The prone Spencer is among dogs, almost a dog himself. His father, or God, is present in this as in so many of Spencer's pictures while two tough, athletic women in control of the dogs, or sources of pleasure — whether this pleasure be odours, excrement, or untrammelled sex — allow him to fondle the animals.

Spencer's fame grew, along with his oddities. Patricia became more of a recluse at Moor Thatch until her death. Spencer carried on an elaborate and one-sided correspondence with Hilda during the latter's confinement in a mental institution and the letters continued after her death. Spencer became Sir Stanley Spencer and a member of the Royal Academy which had rejected his *Dustmen* and *St. Francis and the Birds* so many years before.

It is possible that Cary knew the truth of the situation between Spencer and his wives — he knew people too well to be taken in by Spencer's own propaganda. Even if he did not he could hardly have failed to have seen the *Beatitudes of Love* series for it was completed in 1937 and condemned by public opinion almost instantly.

The public's reaction to *The Beatitudes* cannot be better put than in Spencer's own account of how he took Eddie Marsh to see them at Tooth's. "I shall never forget Eddie Marsh confronted with them. It fogged his monocle; he had to keep wiping it off and having another go. 'Oh, Stanley, are people really like that?' I said: 'What's the matter with them? They're all right, aren't they?' 'Terrible, terrible, Stanley!' Poor Eddie."[11]

It is not likely that Cary missed the evident masochism of these pictures or the fetishism of such paintings as *Dustmen, Love Among the Nations, Sunflower and Dog Worship, Village in Heaven*, etc., all of which were exhibited before *The Horse's Mouth* appeared in 1944. Yet Spencer's personality and obsessions are not Gulley Jimson's — at least, not directly. It is as though Cary deliberately ignored the story that was staring him in the face or, having embarked on it, recoiled from the material at his disposal. One can imagine, paraphrasing E. M. Forster, what a French novelist would have done with it — he would have drawn a febrile picture of festering emotions and incestuous passions in a small village, namely Cookham, in which all his characters are driven to madness by their sexuality. A German or New Englander, on the other hand, would have started the novel with a panoramic survey of Spencer's grandparents on both sides, their love affairs, their business dealings, their children, their gradual decline as a family into eccentricity, depravity, and, again, madness. Cary, an Englishman (by taste if not by birth) chose a heartier, more expansive genre beloved of cheerful Englishmen — the cheese and tavern picaresque.

If we assume that Spencer *is* the chief model for Gulley Jimson, then the problem, as I see it, is to keep the story hearty and therefore clean. Spencer's life, for a writer of Cary's temper, does not bear too much close imitation and even the artist's ideas about creativity had to be filtered away from his epiphenomenal view of sex. In the process, these same ideas become abstract, or at least this is the risk that Cary took, and thus dramatically etiolated. (Few novels successfully dramatize ideas or intellectual debate — Peacock and to a certain extent Huxley are exceptions — though this is because the "ideas" are rendered as lunatic humours; a "straight" dialogue, for example, Robert Boyle's *The Skeptical Chemist*, is usually hardly readable.) Cary had the talent needed to write a novel of ideas in this vein but, instead, he tackled the problem of dramatizing Spencer, of involving him in action. This strategy enabled him to take Jimson's ideas seriously — they are, of course, his own — and what is more compel the reader into accepting them. He intensified them by referring them to Blake's Prophetic Books and could transfer to Gulley an autobiographical essay taken from *Art and Reality* on the problems of outworn style.

Secondly, either Cary remained unaware of Spencer's sexual oddities or he did not wish to deal with them. In either case, his choice of first-person narration encumbered with editorial comment presents the simplest way out. He could, for example, have printed passages from a fictitious diary "written" by Jimson and obtained a third-person narratorial detachment, with or without commentary. The author could then have made it clear, explicitly or implicitly, where Jimson was telling the truth, or where he was lying or concealing information. Some objectivity of this order was obtained by Cary through the use of the novel as part of a trilogy, but the relationship

126

between the three books is complex since they involve presentation of those aspects of the lives of the trio of central characters which do not intersect. The trilogy, in other words, is not Rashomonesque. The "confessional" mode which Cary chose for *The Horse's Mouth* always involves the novelist in certain elisions and evasions. The narrator is either totally honest, selectively honest, or totally dishonest and there is no moral authority expressed or implied within the technique except the fallible (or unreliable) narrator. Thus, such incidents as the treatment of Old Hickson, or the "little push" with which Jimson sends Sara into "some dark hole" depend for their moral effect entirely upon the predilections of the reader. This, of course, enriches the novel for those readers attuned to ambivalence but the main point is that Jimson tells us only what he chooses to tell us so that whole dimensions of his life, notably the sexual, are almost entirely missing from his account. There are no Spenceresque musings about sex and love — on the whole they are replaced with sublimated visions of Woman first as Muse, then as Ball and Chain; Sara and Rozzie are seen only in so far as they help Jimson to create works of art — by providing him with material, models, food, clothing, and motherly comfort.

A further problem of elision is presented by the picaresque form itself which depends upon a complex or "busy" narrative. By this I mean that the character has to be engaged in a series of *agons*, or must/cannot situations, and these in turn are subsumed under one overriding must/cannot situation. In *The Horse's Mouth* the central situation is that Jimson must get the physical means to paint, but he cannot. The emphasis of the plot is thus diverted from psychological to economic problems and only secondarily can Cary deal with the theme of "creativity" and hardly at all with his subject's sexual life except, as we have seen, in a rather perfunctory way. Moreover, the writer of a picaresque novel usually feels that his central character must be plunged into a series of quite sharply dramatic episodes and that the hero himself must be given a slightly villainous caste. If this were not so, the writer cannot have the hero thrown in jail, brought out again, on the run, committing minor crimes, exploring different social milieus, etc. The "good bore-Joyce" as Jimson calls him is not, presumably, quite so subject to the wild swings of Fortune's Wheel — an oscillation the picaresque form is expressly designed to imitate. The author must take care, obviously, not to risk alienating the reader's sympathy by making his hero too villainous (Céline's *Voyage au Bout de la Nuit* runs this risk) so the hero must be villainous in the service of

127

a morality higher than the bourgeois one. In Jimson's case, Art. So the *agon* between Jimson and his economic environment is rendered in terms of a war between the Artist and the philistine non-artist of every social class—Hickson, Mrs. Coker, Pepper Pot, the Seal, City Council, Mrs. Barbon, etc. They win in the end, of course, but so does Jimson, which probably produces the faint tragic overtone of this novel. (Defeat seen as victory seems to me the essential description of tragedy.)

As parts of the *cannot* component of Jimson's situation, the author presents us with Rozzie and Sara or, if we assume that Spencer's own life suggested some of the themes for Cary, Hilda and Patricia. But Rozzie is dead and Sara and Jimson are old. Sara becomes obsessed with age, death, and burial, while Jimson can reminisce antiseptically about his relationships with both women. Women in the book are normally dealt what bridge players call a "yarborough"—a hand without high cards. Coker is an example. Or they are supine objects like Lollie, the model, or Rozzie. Or, like Sara, they are romanticized through Jimson's incredible loquacity into Eve/Muse/Bitch figures. There is, partly through Cary's inability to deal with the theme, very little sexuality in this novel and Jimson's method of evading sex is to deliver abstract, conceptualizing, philosophical essays on the subject. Yet there is a very definite link between Spencer's notions of sex and Jimson's:

Girl going past clinging to a young man's arm. Putting up her face like a duck to the moon. Drinking joy. Green in her eyes. Spinal curvature. No chin, mouth like a frog. Young man like a pug. Gazing down at his sweetie with the face of a saint reading the works of God. Hold on, maiden, you've got him. He's your boy. Look out, Puggy, that isn't a maiden you see before you, it's a work of imagination. Nail him, girlie. Nail him to the contract. Fly laddie, fly off with your darling vision before she turns into a frow, who spends all her life thinking of what the neighbours think. . . .
And I thought how I used to powder . . . [Sara] after her bath. I wonder she didn't kill me, the old Aphrodisiac. Fancy how once I was mad for that ancient hair-trunk. I ran after her skirts like a little dog, when she wouldn't have me. I wanted to cut my throat—or I thought so. And even when I got her at last, how I hung upon her. How I washed and dressed for her, and let her trot me about like a puggy upon a ribbon. . . .

> ...Materiality, that is, Sara, the old female nature, having attempted to button up the prophetic spirit, that is to say, Gulley Jimson, in her placket-hole, got a bonk on the conk, and was reduced to her proper status, as spiritual fodder.[12]

This image of Jimson being groomed like a poodle and led about on the end of a ribbon may be accidental or it may be a sly reference to what Cary knew, from Spencer's paintings, if from no other source, about the artist's tastes. To Spencer it seems that all varieties of sexuality — coprophilia, clothes fetishism, sado-masochism, etc., as well as "normal" intercourse, were equally delightful and equally holy. They were signs that God was in his heaven and all was right with the world. The female was in charge of the distribution side of God's cornucopia of favours. Thus, she was to be both adored and feared. Her role was to dominate men and to grant them or hold back from them sexual pleasure at her own whim and whatever she did was evidently all right with Spencer. If she chose to grant, then he had cause to be even more grateful and worshipping; if she held them back, then this too would give him sexual pleasure, though of a "refined" sort and in addition he could, through her lack of grace, enjoy the role of victim.

Jimson's attitude is a rarefied version of this. To him, woman is a sort of Blakean emanation. She is both matter and spirit. In the latter aspect she exalts the artist and in the former, once he is sexually satisfied, she oppresses him. She becomes "Mother Necessity." She is therefore to be adored and feared. And resented, in Jimson's case, quite actively. The "bonk on the conk" that reduces her back to spiritual fodder becomes, towards the end of the novel, less playful. It is the tap that sends Sara to her death. But, in any case, it is clear that his concept of the role of women in his life is an intellectualized, "fancied-up," version of Spencer's.

To conclude: there may have been some deliberate resemblance intended between Jimson and Spencer — indeed, Cary himself stated that his fictional artist is partly based on Spencer and, even if he had not, the resemblance between the circumstances of their lives and sexual natures is too close to be coincidental — but the effort to cope with form and expression change the subject of the book. The exigencies of the picaresque form force Cary to present his hero's relationships with others as basically material and economic. The intricacies of Spencer's sex-life are not forgotten but they have to be played down since the first-person narrator in search of sympathy expressing himself to a public audience would be naturally reticent about the less orthodox side of his behaviour. Thus, the sexual theme is made more external and Spencer himself is given an outwardly adventurous life. The choice before Cary was a simple one: either a comic novel in the picaresque mode or an intense psychological study. The reasons why Cary chose the former and neglected the possibilities of the latter are not clear to me though they probably have something to do with his heartiness, his "once born" optimism, and his sense, evident throughout this novel and the rest of his work, that sex is a kind of "side-issue."

Notes

1 Joyce Cary, *Art and Reality*, Clark Lectures (New York: Cambridge Univ. Press, 1958).
2 Malcolm Foster, *Joyce Cary: A Biography* (Boston: Joseph, 1968), p. 375.
3 Maurice Collis, *Stanley Spencer: A Biography* (London: Collins, 1962).
4 Louise Collis, *A Private View of Stanley Spencer* (London: Heinemann, 1972).
5 Louise Collis, p. 5.
6 Maurice Collis, p. 88.
7 Louise Collis, p. 29.
8 Louise Collis, p. 72.
9 Louise Collis, p. 93.
10 Louise Collis, p. 110.
11 Maurice Collis, p. 144.
12 Joyce Cary, *The Horse's Mouth* (London: Penguin, 1958), pp. 56-58.

1978

Part IV
Contemporaries

Preface

When I first arrived in this country and asked what I should read I was appalled at the low quality of the recommended fiction. The Hugh MacLennans, Sinclair Rosses, Ernest Bucklers, Morley Callaghans, etc., struck me as devoid of imagination, of narrative skill, of sensitivity to language, of descriptive power, of metaphor and image, and above all of that joyful spirit of play by which anything worth reading gets written in the first place. Instead, all of them seemed to write out of some weird Puritan work-ethic—as though they figured that if they failed to write 1,000 at least of their inept words a day they would burn in pits of everlasting fire. The sad fact is that nobody without a vested interest in this country's culture would waste more than five minutes on any one of them. Furthermore, they were aided and abetted in their mediocrity by reviewers and critics whom I never found to be anything other than timid and placatory.

In the last twenty years or so the situation has improved somewhat. Though the best Canadian novel remains the one written by an alcoholic, English remittance man concerning going to pieces in Mexico, two, at least, world-class novels have appeared: Mordecai Richler's *St. Urbain's Horseman*, a very *sane* book, and Leonard Cohen's delightful *Beautiful Losers*. Both of these, since written by expatriate Jews, are atypical but there are several other novelists relatively new on the scene whose work has interested and excited me—for example, Hugh Hood, John Metcalf, Michael Ondaatje, and Margaret Atwood. Other people may claim literary importance, even greatness, for Alice Munro, Rudy Wiebe, Sheila Watson, and Margaret Laurence and I will agree that what little I have been able to tolerate of these doubtless worthy people seems a notch or two above the abysses established by the Old Guard.

The rest of this volume, then, consists of selected essays in literary criticism or a collection of book reviews (and which term you prefer will depend almost entirely upon whether you approve of them or not) chiefly about CanLit. Personally, I make little distinction between the two forms: I might feel less inclined to express such emotions as contempt or displeasure in a piece to be regarded as "pure" criticism but, in practice, restraining them tends to make me come out in spots. Thus, unlike most of my academic colleagues, I would not normally attempt writing a critical article on somebody unless I wholeheartedly enjoyed his work. As a reviewer, on the other hand, I find it challenging to write about whatever the editor sends me, good, bad, or indifferent—though I must admit I enjoy getting a positively bad book through the mail; it is much *easier* to write about Evil than it is to say something interesting about Good, as Milton himself discovered. The reader will encounter in the following pages essays that attempt to bridge whatever gaps there are between criticism and reviews; many of them deal with poor and sometimes totally incompetent work—much of it, perforce, Canadian.

The Bloody Horse

Callaghan, Morley. *Close to the Sun Again.* Toronto: Macmillan, 1977.

Moore, Brian. *The Doctor's Wife.* Toronto: McClelland and Stewart, 1976.

Hood, Hugh. *A New Athens.* Ottawa: Oberon, 1977.

If *Close to the Sun Again* were a first novel by a young writer, I would say of it that it shows some awareness of the technique of plot construction, that, though the dialogue is inept and the prose generally abysmal, there are signs in the last two chapters that the author is beginning to slough the deleterious effects of high school training on his writing habits, and that he might also move on to themes of greater interest and importance if he could only empty his head of jejeune notions of psychological realism picked up God-knows-where. The writer is Morley Callaghan, however, who has been around a long time and is unlikely to improve; nor would he, on the evidence of what is written about him on the dust-jacket, particularly want to. Nor is it my first encounter with him, for I have read the first few pages of several of his novels and once, for the purposes of an examination, I even penetrated two-thirds of *The Loved and the Lost* before the weather improved that spring enough to make me decide I would sooner risk failing the exam and the consequent consignment to the urban jungle once again than finish one of the most lackluster novels ever written in this country — in itself rather a large statement.

Hemingway is invoked twice on the dust-jacket. Callaghan worked with him on the *Toronto Star*, then lived on the periphery of his circle in Paris where, presumably, he joined the Master's declared war against rhetoric in general and the adjective in particular, while remaining well-insulated against that peculiar electricity that used to flow through Hemingway's early writing. We are also told that Edmund Wilson called Callaghan "the most unjustly neglected novelist in the English-speaking world," and that, despite this neglect, his last novel sold more than half a million copies in the Soviet Union. We are not told directly whether or not Callaghan succeeded in squeezing his royalties out from behind the Iron Curtain, but there is on the dust-jacket a photograph of the author laughing uproariously as though on the way to the bank — a rouble millionaire. It is in any case good to know that sixty years after the Revolution petit-bourgeois notions of what constitutes a novel are still alive and well in Mother Russia. Apart from that I don't know why Callaghan succeeds in foreign countries. Perhaps he translates well and there is some internal evidence to suggest that *Close to the Sun Again* was translated from manuscript into, let us say, Lithuanian then back into English for Macmillan by some well-intentioned, polygot, but tone-deaf and maladroit Pole.

A passage like "The scratching little hollow ping was like the beating of a heart, only not muffled like a heart: it came throbbing in the vastness of cathedral space . . ." makes a man clutch and fumble at his chest to ascertain whether his pacemaker's working properly. My own heart, and I am speaking now as a hypochondriac, does *not* make these scratching little pinging sounds, muffled or otherwise, and in any case there is, in my opinion, a contradiction between the ideas of *scratching* and *throbbing*. It is a clumsy, sloppy metaphor but at least it represents a step, or rather stagger, in the direction of colourful prose. In contrast to such sodden, dispiriting stuff as

She went on to say that her father had taken her to Europe, and in Paris they had gone to one of those small clubs that had fight cards. Her father had been impressed by a good-looking boy named Robert Riopelle, a middleweight, a lonely-looking boy, a kid, with all the great natural talents. The French boy had a strangely moving, noble character. The kid took a shine to her father, too. . . .

it shines "like a good deed in a naughty world." So this French boy "had a strangely moving, noble character," had he? Apart from the stylist poverty of using an auxiliary verb instead of a proper one, the sentence with its vagueness and pomposity breaks every rule in the book of narrative art (including the Jamesian ukase that the reader must be *shown*, not *told*), while creating no new rule of its own. Perhaps this is what the dust-jacket writer means when he says, perhaps a little too glibly, that "the novel is told in Morley Callaghan's distinctive style — so easy and flowing that it seems to be no style at all." But the style is *there* — and it is abominable.

The content of this novel concerns an impeccably efficient managerial person named Ira Groome who finishes a successful career in Brazil to take up a post as police commissioner of a Canadian city. He is tough, unapproachable, and authoritarian, so everybody calls him "The Commander," only partly because this was his rank in the navy during the war. His wife has died of alcoholism and his son is estranged from him as indeed is the rest of the human race with the exception of another navy veteran who acts as his factotum. In the Canadian city he begins to go to pieces, becoming progressively more drunken until an accident, which turns out to be fatal, lands him in hospital where he recalls his past life — in particular a wartime experience we are asked to believe he has repressed all those years. It transpires that during the war Groome was a lieutenant aboard a corvette doing convoy duty in the North Atlantic. The corvette picks up a boatload of survivors from a merchantman sunk by a U-boat and these survivors include a mysterious young couple — a girl, called Gina Bixby, and a man who rejoices in the name of Jethroe Chone. There is something a little squalid about this pair, for one of them is supposed to have raped the other who, in turn, appears to have endured the experience with not much more than purely formal misgivings for, when the corvette in turn is sunk and everybody is on a raft, some for the second time, and when Chone, mortally wounded in the battle, does a sort of nautical Captain Oates over the side, Gina, the rapee, then follows him into the cold green element with a cry of "Come back, you bastard." A love-hate relationship, you must understand.

Groome is in love with this — on the face of it — unlikely girl and does not want to remember anything connected with the corvette's action-packed voyage. He makes a decision to forget it, there and then, and to devote his life to "a high purpose." The reader may choose, I suppose, whether to reject this nonsense (that a human being can make a conscious decision as to what he stores in his unconscious) utterly, or to accept it as what poor Kenneth Burke used to go around calling "symbolic action." If this is the case, however, the novel still fails since action of a "symbolic" or allegorical kind must arise from a narrative that is credible at the literal level. *Close to the Sun Again* is not credible on the literal level partly because its characters are stuffed with sawdust and partly because of Callaghan's stylistic inability to describe adequately the natural world.

Bad as this novel is I have no wish to attack Morley Callaghan. For what would be the point? He threatens no one and gives pleasure to many, particularly, it would appear, to our Slavic brethren. In any case he is one of those good, grey figures of the post-Hemingway generation — the MacLennans, the Bucklers, the Sinclair Ross's, the Hugh Garners — who occupy on Canadian-literature course lists that penumbral zone between, say, Frederick Philip Grove at the top and Margaret Laurence at the bottom. There are two things to be said about them. On the negative side I could not do better than to quote Roy Campbell's famous lines:

> You praise the firm restraint with which they write —
> I'm with you there, of course.
> They use the snaffle and the curb all right;
> But where's the bloody horse?

But on the positive side they kept the stable of CanLit warm for that same horse when it began to make its presence felt in the late fifties and early sixties — among the Richlers, Cohens, Hoods and even, to stretch a point, the Brian Moores.

Brian Moore is an Ulsterman who took out Canadian citizenship and who now lives in Malibu, California. Therefore, colour him "Mid-Atlantic Man." Whoever claims him for Canadian Letters ought to take this personal history into consideration and to remember also that Moore is not in the Canadian thematic tradition as defined by our more fashionable critics: he does not, in other words, write about stones in snowballs, or Indians, or losers surviving away in ghastly hick towns on the Prairies. What he shares with most Canadian writers is what strikes me as an unreasonable obsession with representationalism and thus his work, like theirs, always risks drifting into mirror-up-to-life banality. His earlier books did not interest me very much and I would probably not have read *The Doctor's Wife* unprompted by the review editor. I am glad I did so, however, for within the narrow limits of its genre it is immensely readable and very nearly first rate.

The doctor's wife of the title is a still presentable woman in her late thirties who, on the way to the south of France where she is supposed to meet her husband for a "second honeymoon," encounters in Paris a friend of some friends and, tentatively at first, embarks on a passionate affair with him. Almost immediately, however, she begins to experience a number of pressures — from her husband, who wants her to return home, from her rather nasty son who does not want to lose his egg-cook-and-bottle-washer, from her brother who reminds her that nervous breakdowns run in the family, from her friends, the go-betweens in Paris who keep asserting that she is too old for her lover and that she should not take a casual one-night stand so seriously, and from the lover himself who wants her to go to America and marry him. No one in the novel, then, is inclined to take seriously her own perspective — that this sexual relationship is the most ecstatic thing that has ever happened to her and it is its own justification: "It was as though wrong were right. Her former life, her marriage, all that had gone before, now seemed to be her sin. These few days with Tom were her state of grace. She turned, went back to bed, and lay down beside him, holding him in her arms, pressing against his warm body. She closed her eyes. I am in grace. In my state of grace."

I think Brian Moore is tackling two modern attitudes of increasing popularity. The first is the belief that sex can or ought to be a substitute for religion — an élitist philosophy since it eliminates as celebrants the very young, the very old, the crippled, the sick, the sexually undesirable; and the second is the notion that "it's cool to be cool," best expressed in the words of the late Fritz Perls in *Gestalt Therapy Verbatim*:

> I do my thing, and you do your thing.
> I am not in this world to live up to your expectations.
> And you are not in this world to live up to mine.
> You are you and I am I,
> And if by chance we find each other, it's beautiful.
> If not, it can't be helped.

This is certainly the attitude towards life of Tom, the doctor's wife's young lover, yet at the same time he makes, implicitly and later explicitly, demands on her she finds impossible to fulfill. Moore's descriptions of her physical ecstasies are written with such skill and panache that I am certain they will excite most readers, and what is equally skilful is his rendition of her desperation when she begins to recognize that each new action, including those same ecstasies, involves a new network of relationships and responsibilities and that wanting to cop out of them *à la mode de* Fritz Perls is like wanting to cop out of the human condition. There is plenty of human condition around — Moore plays this affair out against a backdrop of the street-fighting and bombings of Belfast, the protagonist's home, creating thereby the most sinister effects. The woman does in fact toy with the notion of suicide and even visits a priest who quotes Camus at her and what she does finally is drop out of her world altogether and find a job in a laundry in London — thus committing a kind of "mind suicide."

Moore writes carefully with the snaffle and the curb — he never sends the reader to the dictionary to look up an unusual word and his sentences are short enough to suit the attention span of the sort of reader he is aiming at. His themes are familiar — in fact they suggest the moral dilemmas of soap opera; but then, of course, so do those of *Anna Karenina*. The novel errs, in my opinion, only in the direction of melodramatic extravagance — the doctor and his child are made so revolting that the reader's respect for the woman, who has over the years allowed herself to become their doormat, is endangered. But the bloody horse is there — in the powerful characterizations, the juxta-positions, the sympathy evoked for the central character and, above all, in the narrative drive.

The other horseman under consideration here is Hugh Hood whose book *A New Athens* contains at least one rather obscure reference to Anthony Powell. Such playfulness suggests that Hood feels some affinity with Powell but in fact all they possess in common is a desire to creat a *roman fleuve* occupying twelve volumes. Powell's work, despite the use of some of Proust's technical machinery, is traditional in that it is rooted in the English comedy of manners and conventional in the sense that Powell is not much interested in progressing beyond social realism. Social realism is the least of Hood's concerns despite the dust-jacket's claim that the "twelve novels [deal] with the experience of living in Canada in the middle of the twentieth century." Secondly, each volume of Powell's series is shaped and structured into a fairly conventional novel, whereas *A New Athens*, like its predecessor, *The Swing in the Garden*, cannot with profit be described as a "novel," in the usual sense of that word connoting narrative, plot, conflict, characterization, etc., at all. I might use the expression "prose poems" to describe them if this in turn did not carry misleading, indeed disreputable, associations. Let us settle for the moment on the term "fictions."

Despite the lack of narrative, things "happen" in *A New Athens*. The narrator, Matt Goderich, goes on a hike, meditates about the landscape of his region, its flora, the architecture of its buildings, the railroad that once ran through it, the last train along that railroad, the girls on the last train, the girl he married, his courtship, an epiphany regarding a "ghost ship" locked under the ice, his wife's mother, her Danteesque paintings, and the house on the river front turned into a memorial museum for visionary art, and much more. The book's "argument" is encapsulated in the presentation of Matt's mother-in-law, an artist named May-Beth Codrington who paints, on panels of masonite, subjects with titles like "His Worship, John Baker Lawson, Sometime Mayor of Stoverville, Robed as Herod." At her death a huge triptych is discovered which depicts the population of Stoverville, Ontario, entering the New Jerusalem and Hood says of it that it captures "much of the heavenly and eternal rising from the things of this world which is the recurring given in the works of Stanley Spencer." Hood means, of course, the visionary Spencer, the God-intoxicated man whose motto might have been Suger's *mens hebes ad verum per materalia surgit*, the painter of *The Resurrection, Cookham, St Francis and the Birds*, and the *Christ in the Wilderness* series. He does not mean that same Stanley Spencer who, in kinkier, fetishistic, polymorphous, and coprophilous mode did paintings like *The Beatitudes of Love, Dustmen, Love on the Moor, Dogs*, in pursuit, delightfully, of less orthodox truths. I found, when reading *The Swing in the Garden*, that such elisions, such apparent refusals to regard human experience and behaviour with anything other than the blandest-seeming optimism, caused irritation. I am inclined to think that this is because Hood had not, in that fiction, acquired complete control over his method and because *A New Athens*, with its references to visionary art, incorporates clues as to how these fictions should be read—as celebrations of God's creation from a sort of Dantean perspective, whereby contradictions are ultimately resolved, human propensity for error and corruption is seen as trivial, and "everything," as Matt says in the earlier volume, "can be atoned for." Thus for the narrative of the conventional novel Hood substitutes a sequence of emblems, *topoi* for meditation, in which nothing is dramatic, although almost everything is rendered vividly and in which the characters, though unbelievable in their serenity, are intensely alive. These fictions are therefore without conflict, but it is as though Hood wishes to ignore conflict altogether and instead to catch these characters between speeches and gestures in some mystical and eternal moment, to quote Stanley Spencer, "between breathing in and breathing out," when "the God has descended and spoken to them." Thus in many of these emblems there exists that same rapt intensity you would find in such Spencer paintings as *The Apple Gatherers* and *The Meeting*. For example, at the end of the first section Matthew returns home at night from his walking tour to discover his wife working at a draughting board on the deck of their cottage:

> She was sitting there, head glittering under the green shade of the lamp. I stole up onto the deck and stood looking at her and silence fell completely, total. She turned and looked at me seriously, switching off the lamp. The whites of her eyes shone in the dark. I took her in my arms as she rose to meet me.
> I said, "I saw you today, Edie. For the first time."

Later in the book the "ghost ship" glitters under the green river ice in a similar fashion and in fact part of Hood's structural principle in *A New Athens* is making one event or object stand as metaphor for another and then another until the visible world in all its multiplicity is caught up in one great metaphysical knot and rendered as an aspect of the Divine. May-Beth Codrington tells Matt that "depiction of the great religious subjects is the core of human art" and later that art is a form of Pentecostal fire. Though one might quarrel with the phraseology, it is not easy to disagree with the sentiment it expresses, and it seems to me that in *A New Athens* Hood succeeds in the elevated task he has set himself and has produced a work of visionary art which makes most ordinary novels, no matter how well crafted, seem like what Gulley Jimson, another fictional version of Stanley Spencer, called "farting *Annie Laurie* through a keyhole."

1978

Afterword

The Editor of *Queen's Quarterly*, where this review first appeared, received some hate mail obviously intended for me. I quote it verbatim:

Sir,

John Mills will no doubt enjoy the attention that his review of Morley Callaghan's *Close to the Sun Again* is bound to attract. Iconoclasm is always a popular spectator sport, and when an unknown like John Mills starts to prance around shrieking up insults at someone like Morley Callaghan, crowds of literary curiousity [sic] seekers will certainly gather around. Perhaps this pleasing prospect was not far from John Mills' mind when he began to write his review.

And yet, what are we to make of a supposedly serious critic who cheerfully confesses that he has never been able to finish any of Morley Callaghan's novels? I would suggest that this fact casts doubt on John Mills' qualifications to review anything more serious than a Harlequin Romance. Worse, it raises questions about the morality of his accepting an assignment to review a new book by Morley Callaghan; unless, of course, Mr. Mills saw the assignment as an opportunity to seize the limelight, there to pose as brave little John Mills squeaking defiance against the thunder of the critics here and abroad who have recognized Callaghan's greatness.

I suspect that your readers—aware that critics like George Woodcock and William French, respectively, have found this book to be "Callaghan's best book in 40 years," and "the best Canadian novel of 1977"—will treat Mr. Mills' review with a great deal of caution, and will soon decide that this particular public spectacle is an embarrassing one which people ought not to watch. Let us hope that somebody will be kind enough to lead Mr. Mills home before he makes an even bigger fool of himself.

This letter was signed by a senior editor for Macmillan. And just when I was thinking of laying a manuscript on him, too! I make it a principle never to let hate mail go unanswered, and pointed out that I thought it a noble thing for a publisher to spring to the defence of one of his authors, but that he had not, in fact, replied to the substance of my critical comment that, whatever else Callaghan was writing, it was not English prose. Also that I, as a novelist and critic, relied heavily on my editors to correct grammar, remove solecisms, question syntax, structure, vocabulary and, in general, to tidy up any sloppiness. An editor is like a good valet, careful to make sure that his "gentleman" does not appear in public with a fly unzipped or dressed in unsuitable attire. He would die rather than let his master be seen, as Wodehouse probably said, in a bowler hat during Goodwood Week. I asked him how he could sleep at night with the knowledge that he had allowed sentences like those which I had quoted in the review to go to press. I added that the B.C. writer Jack Hodgins had spoken highly of this editor's talents—why was it he had let one of his old established writers down so badly?

The correspondence ended with the editor's reply to the effect that one of Jack Hodgins' greatest admirers was none other than Morley Callaghan. I may let a couple of years go by then lay that manuscript on Macmillan after all.

Sexual Paranoia

Metcalf, John. *Girl in Gingham*. Ottawa: Oberon, 1978.

One of Sigmund Freud's better known fantasies postulates that little girls are in general afflicted with a state of mind called "penis envy." Experience demonstrates, however, that little girls are afflicted with nothing of the sort: that penis envy, in one form or another, is a male phenomenon and is extremely wide-spread. It creates in most of us a lingering anxiety with regard to sexual performance which no amount of successful cockmanship can quite eradicate and which can lead, in its extreme form, to inhibition, sexual poltroonery, Stendhalian *fiasco*, melancholy, and, as is popularly supposed in the case of poor Malcolm Lowry, to drunkenness, frenzy, and what Chaucer called "wanhope"—"that is despeir of the mercy of God, that comth somtyme of to muche outrageous sorwe... thurgh which despeir or drede he abaundoneth al his herte to every maner synne, as seith Seint Augustin." That sexual paranoia is conjoint with despair was confirmed to me by a herbalist in Mexico City whose wares were displayed on the sidewalk outside the main post office. Over one small heap of what looked like wilted alfalfa was a sign which, translated, read: "For sadness and impotence." *Exactly*. And the same herb will do for both. On the subject of residual penis envy each one of us can tell his tale. Once, for example, I needed a medical check-up and the

144

doctor I visited was a woman, rather attractive, quite chatty. We talked of this and that, and then, just at the point when she began examining me for hernia, she asked, quite conversationally, "And what does your wife do?" It was on the tip of my tongue to reply, hotly, "As you obviously suspect, madam, she resorts to a variety of mechanical aids," when it occurred to me, just in time, that this was my own paranoia at work.

John Metcalf's narrator in *Private Parts: A Memoir,* one of the two novellas in this new book, looks back on an experience, primal in its way, involving a village idiot who worked on his uncle's farm in the north of England during the war:

> I am staring at Bobby's thing. It hangs down from a bush of black hair and it reaches nearly to his knee. It is as fat as my arm.

Clearly this is a false epiphany, and what the gods have afforded him a glimpse of is the Platonic ideal of a penis to which the human varieties are but shadows. Thus, a delusion is created which is reinforced by writers like John Cleland —

> ...it might have answered very well the making a show of it; its enormous head seemed, in hue and size, not unlike a common sheep's heart; you might have troll'd dice securely along the broad back of the body of it; the length of it too was prodigious...

and which no amount of poring over quasi-scientific treatises on the male organ as it actually occurs in nature by Sir Richard Burton, Robert Dickinson, and Masters and Johnson will dispell. The narrator has seen Bobby and he *knows what he knows.*

Private Parts, then, deals at one level with childhood sexuality — with the routine business of masturbation, of fumblings with the other sex, of the bright fantasies of adolescence, of finally losing one's virginity. As such it invites comparison with *Portnoy's Complaint,* but it is better than Roth's slick, chic, opportunistic, and shallow book by a long way; and its comedy is in part created by a spare, understated, classical style beyond Roth. Here, for example, the narrator contemplates an early fantasy in which he tells a girl he is a painter:

> She would be overcome. She admits she's always wanted to be drawn by a real artist. I offer to sketch her. She says she lives

145

near and her Dad's at work and her Mum's out shopping. We are in her bedroom. She is rather shy at first.

In our century subject matter like this has only just been released for imaginative literature from the clutches of psychologists and pox doctors in whose hands, so to speak, it resided from the death of Havelock Ellis to the advent of Lenny Bruce. Thus it is still fresh enough to be entertaining in its own right, and most of us can, from a plain description of someone else's experience, enjoy the *frisson* of recognizing our own. But the novella doesn't stop there. The narrator's father is a self-effacing Methodist minister whose eccentricity is only revealed to the son much later in life and after the former's death. Parental authority goes by default to a fanatical, perhaps diabolical, mother. It is she who teaches the narrator that life is joyless or, if it is not, that it then should be and that flesh is "sinful." Her Manichaeism extends beyond this simple body-spirit dichotomy to include, in its polarities, regions of the body. Thus, when she bathes her son she leaves his genitals out but hands him a sponge and orders him to "Wash yourself" thereby setting up in the boy's mind a moral inferiority residing in the private parts of the title. There is no forgiveness in the narrator for this kind of thing. "My mother was mad," he says:

Her mind festered. It was a pit of unimaginable filth — a contagion I did not escape. I hated her. I am happy she is dead.

As he grows past puberty, however, he engages this woman in battle. He disobeys her; he introduces taboo subjects, like the derivation of the word "bugger," at dinner table. When he takes her on, he is conscious that he is also doing battle with the entire Puritan, life-denying, ethical tradition which he inherits and which he also associates with dark north-of-England towns and bleak moorlands:

I vowed that my life would be filled with laughter, beautiful women, warm flesh; my life would be lived in the sun.

In one of the story's most brilliant and harrowing scenes, his mother discovers a copy of a nudist magazine from which he is in the habit of culling masturbation images and makes him kneel with her in prayer, dragging him to the floor, wallowing in a sadistic orgy of religiosity sexual in its intensity until he is reduced to "shuddering, tear-wracked hysteria":

> I cried until I could cry no more. I felt empty, exhausted, sick. I
> turned my pillow to the dry side. I hated myself. I looked with
> loathing through *Health and Efficiency* which had been left on
> the bed in accusation.
>
> I stared at the roses on the wallpaper grouping them into
> different patterns.
>
> Mournfully, I wanked myself to sleep.

Thus the scene is detached from sentimentality and self-pity. The last
sentence produces the complex sort of comic effect which intensifies
the seriousness of what precedes it by knitting together the suffering
child, his triumphant sexuality, the *comfort* inherent in the act of
"wanking" together with that same act's flagelliferous quality suggested in the term *self-abuse*.

How, in conventional morality, ought this boy to be punished?
He is clearly not, in accordance with Baden-Powell's *Scouting for
Boys*, one of those "decent, clean-living chaps who will have nothing
to do with this beastliness." Will he go blind? Catch tuberculosis?
Rachitis? ("Will I be OK if I just do it in strong sunlight?") The
modern, liberated adult, of course, rightly laughs at such myths. He
will tend to replace them with canting nonsense of his own. He might
say that the child stands in danger of preferring fantasy to reality. (So
what?) Or he might say, as Norman Mailer says somewhere, that he
will pay for masturbation by sluggishness of sexual response in later
life. By and large, however, it is *all right* to masturbate. But what
about hating his Mum? About not forgiving her? Will he not pay for
that? The liberal permitter might argue that the boy will eventually
grow to tolerate his mother, to love her even, as he begins to
understand her and to recognize the nature of her problems. On the
other hand, of course, why should he learn to love that which is
hateful, to tolerate the intolerable? A Christian would say that the
narrator should love his mother whilst hating what she does, but this
would require him to be a saint. Metcalf has to deal with this issue,
obviously, since his narrator is writing about his childhood from the
perspective of a married adult. What, then, given this background,
happens to him in later life?

It is here that Metcalf's narrative darkens. In the final section of
the book the narrator, whose name, we discover, is written up in his
university catalogue as T. D. Moore: Modern British Poetry (1003)

and Contemporary Fiction (2001), is observed washing dishes after a party. It is early morning and he can't sleep. A hangover partly explains his gloom. On the other hand, there is much to be gloomy about: he teaches at a university, some would say a form of purgatory in itself, to support his art. His art consists of writing "finely tuned" stories in a minor key about "loneliness and self-discovery." A partitioned-off section of the basement between furnace and washing machine serves him as a study. So much for the life that "would be lived in the sun." The "laughter," the "beautiful women, warm flesh" all have been reduced to this stale domesticity, his sex-life withered to a Saturday morning fumble while the children are pre-occupied with a television program. His wife, in any case, is not as attractive to him as she used to be.

At first sight it looks as though Metcalf is punishing Moore for his sexual fantasies and hatred of his mother by plunging him into boredom and alienation. In fact, however, Moore knows exactly what has happened to him:

> It's as if I exhausted all my passion by the age of sixteen: nothing since has compared with the drama of that battle of wills, a titanic struggle fought against the backdrop of Hell.

It is against this backdrop that his sense of being was at its most intense. The backdrop is removed. He wins his various battles. But without the melodrama of conflict his sense of being begins to wane. Boredom and alienation are the penalties for "winning through" to a lack of belief. He is also aware that to his children he is almost a Bronze-Age figure who pre-existed TV and the Age of Permission. Is he depriving his children of this strong experience of selfhood by refusing to provide them with a melodramatic household like the one provided for him by his mother? What alternative is there to living blandly and producing bland and spineless children whose demands are no sooner stated than they are met?

Moore is honest enough to admit that in some moods he wishes on his children his own history. This, of course, is the false, seductive glitter of Manichaeism: let's put conflict *back*, let's give our kids some *edge*. On the other hand, it is clear that artificial conflict is not conflict at all and one might just as well suggest a man seek spiritual regeneration by taking up tennis.

Metcalf ends *Private Parts* by having Moore finding a second-hand store in an "unfamiliar" part of Montreal. On some obscure

148

impulse he walks in and buys a sextant. He smuggles it into the house and hides it from his wife. When he is alone, he takes it out to admire its mirrors, lenses, and adjusting screws. He enjoys the feel of it but, he says, "I'm not quite sure how it's supposed to work." But work it does. I suppose one could argue that Metcalf is using this sextant as a rebus — a punning device. On the other hand, an allegorist might say that the point of a sextant is that one focuses part of it on the sun, an image of transcendence, and another on the horizon, an image of the earth, the material. A Jungian would probably want to know what seas the narrator hopes to navigate towards the goal of totality. But the true meaning of the sextant is Metcalf's secret and I hope he keeps it to himself. All I know is that it ends perfectly, one of the most profound and delightful works of fiction I have read in a long time.

The subject matter of *Girl in Gingham* is more secular than that of *Private Parts* and thus its power and interest are consequently diminished. It is a third-person narrative concerning a divorcee who — lonely, bored, and depressed — finds himself acquiescing in a friend's hoax whereby his name is placed on a computer dating list. The computer presents him with a list of women some of whom he is able to disqualify by phone, another he actually encounters in the highly neurotic flesh. These episodes are hilarious. It is one of Metcalf's great strengths as a writer that he is able to reinforce the comedy with which he treats his material with the fundamental seriousness of the protagonists' situations. In *Girl in Gingham* the hero, between his attempts at romance, tries to live his day-to-day life but cannot adjust to the absence of his wife. In desperation he phones the last number on his list and subsequently meets his ideal — the girl of the title. But Metcalf does not allow him to enjoy her, and, in fact, the narrative takes a strange, even grotesque, twist which does not seem to me to be anything other than gratuitous. It is as though Metcalf *really*, in this story, wants to punish his protagonist but for reasons he doesn't make clear to the reader. Or perhaps he wishes to create a romantic mood in his reader then castigate him for it! It is not possible to discuss this story in any detail without giving away the ending and I shall say no more.

1978

Sexual Liberator

Berger, John. *G*. New York: Viking, 1972.

I have just finished reading John Berger's extended essay *A Fortunate Man* first published in 1967. It is a beautifully written, often moving, account of a general practitioner working in a remote part of England. It begins by presenting this particular doctor in terms of his daily work, his relationship with his patients, and his position within the culturally deprived society in which he lives but, almost imperceptibly, the essay moves from documentary to philosophical speculation about the nature of "universal" man, freedom, and happiness, and concludes with an attempt to assess its subject. Sassall, Berger's doctor, began his career consciously comparing himself to those Master Mariners one finds in Conrad who deny the expression of their imagination but project it onto the sea which then becomes both their enemy and their personal justification. Later he discovers that this somewhat apocalyptic attitude is too simple, that the imagination must be lived with on every level, and he begins a rigorous self-exploration in order to discover what this imagination, what his motivations, amount to. Berger calls him a fortunate man because, unlike most people in society, he is doing what he believes in and is able to enmesh his total personality with his work and daily life. He seems to be the opposite of the "alienated" man—alienated in both the Existential and Marxist

150

senses of the word—yet Berger believes, and I am inclined to agree with him, that this is not enough. How does one finally evaluate a man like Sassall?

> ... unaccustomed to choosing, unaccustomed to witnessing the choices of others, we find ourselves without a scale of values for judging or assessing one another. The only standard which remains is that of personal liking—or its commercial variant, which is Personality.
> Many will say that this is our good fortune. I doubt it. Our exemption from having to make choices has been so far at the price of the constant deferment of problems—basically economic ones—which vitally affect our future....

Berger is here speaking of national or social crises which "test all who live through them" such as, let us say, the American Revolution, or the Fall of France in 1940. And I think it is true that the main life and death issues, and Berger cites such examples as racialism, class exploitation, the struggle for personal freedom, are experienced by Western intellectuals who care about such things at one remove. They choose, perhaps through no fault of their own, opinions and sides rather than actions—like soccer fans. That this spectatorism has a debilitating effect upon society cannot be doubted. One only has to look upon the pathetic, masturbatorial, attempts to foster a sense of what has been called a "Canadian Identity" to become aware that nationalism cannot exist unless the emergent "nation" has passed through some great, defining action. Unlike the U.S., Canada has never experienced a revolution—the rebellions, led by Riel, Papineau, and William Lyon McKenzie, were based for the most part on paper issues. Against the banality of this choiceless society how can one assess what a human life is worth?

> There can be no final or personal answer—unless you are prepared to accept the medieval religious one, surviving from the past. The question is social. An individual cannot answer it *for himself*. The answer resides within the totality of relations which can exist within a certain social structure at a certain time.... All I do know is that our present society wastes and, by slow draining process of enforced hypocrisy, empties most of the lives which it does not destroy: and that within its own terms a doctor who has surpassed the stage of selling cures, either directly to the

patient or through the agency of a state service, is unassessable.

A Fortunate Man is a deeply serious book—alive with all the intelligence, originality, and lucidity that Berger has brought to the field of art criticism—a branch of belles-lettres which attracts so much obscurantism, one-upmanship, and logorrhea. The questions that Berger explores here are presented less clearly, far more ambivalently, in his novel *G.*

Berger himself seems in two minds as to whether it should be described as a novel: it might be better to call it an essay, a treatise, or, as he puts it, " a description of a dream." It contains elements of each but its core is fictional. The protagonist is the son of an Italian merchant and a rich American woman. He is brought up by two cousins on a farm in England and is eventually seduced at the age of fifteen by one of them named, ironically enough, Beatrice. The author leaves him for eight years or so then reintroduces him, a young adult, with the initial G. instead of a name. This enables Berger to link him, quite deliberately, with at least two historical figures—the revolutionary hero Garibaldi and Geo Chavez, the first pilot to fly the Alps. There are more tenuous, perhaps accidental, links with the bourgeois politician Giolitti, who is quoted as saying, in 1911, "Karl Marx has been relegated to the Attic," and to Gabriele D'Annunzio, the "self-elected poet of Italian Nationalism," clown, charlatan, and proto-fascist, but the major association is with the name Giovanni, or, in Spanish, Don Juan. The anonymity of the protagonist signals Berger's intention to use him as a literary chess-piece: we know nothing about him except the uses to which he is put and even these are sketched in with a series of episodes: G. seducing a hotel servant while Chavez penetrates the sequestered passes of the Alps (the metaphor implied here is Berger's, not mine); G. seducing the wife of an industrialist and getting shot by her husband; plotting a campaign of fornication here, setting up an adultery there; being mistaken for an Austrian spy in Trieste where he meets his nemesis in the form of a watery grave. Cut back and forth between these episodes are descriptions of an abortive revolution in Milan, a day on Auvers Ridge during the First World War, Chavez' flight, and so on together with philosophical essays on human sexuality.

G. is intended as an early modern version of Don Juan. He is gat toothed, like the Wife of Bath, running to fat, faintly but apparently not obnoxiously diabolical. He leers like a villain from melodrama. The male reader may well ask "what's he got that I haven't got" and the answer is that G., like Garibaldi, is a liberator — he is compelled to present himself to the woman he desires "as he is" such that she can respond with the discovery that "he has come for me." This, at any rate, is how Berger tries to explain him though the sources of G.'s personality and obsessions remain mysterious. (Berger includes a curious, phantasmagoric incident involving the death of three horses which helps to create G.'s individuality but the meaning of the incident is unclear, probably even to the author.)

Other factors distinguish G. from his fellow men; sexual adventurism forms the ground of his being; he enjoys independent means and is thus dissociated from the history being made around him and, in an early episode, he is even shielded from "history" (the workers' struggle in Milan) by a young girl. He is uninterested in "love." His actions following a sexual encounter seem callous or cruel. For example he mounts a quasi-militaristic campaign to conquer the wife of a rich industrialist, wins, spends an idyllic afternoon with her, gets shot and wounded by her husband, and promises her he'll become her constant lover once the entire entourage is back in Paris. But at Chavez' funeral,

> ... he made his plans quickly. He would go to Paris, visit the Hennequins, make a point of ignoring Camille, reassure the husband and would quickly begin an obvious, public affair with Mathilde le Diraison. In this way he would avenge himself on Hennequin by making the whole shooting incident appear ridiculous ... and he would disabuse Camille of her fond illusion that passion can be regulated and that a lover can be something different from a second husband.

The stock response, in the world-view of the bourgeois sentimentalist, would be that G. is clearly acting like a bastard. The *good* man does not beseige the chastity of a married woman and even if he did it would be a question of *love* connected with a willingness to assume some sort of responsibility for her afterwards. Readers of Berger's book are not likely to make judgements of this kind though they may evince the stock response at the next level of sophistication — that of the Liberated Swinger. Here, G.'s message to his women folk seems fairly simple: sexual passion is, despite the frequency with which one may experience it, always unique, and can thus be neither regulated nor commoditized and it is the medium through which women may slough the accidents of circumstance — the quotidian, the bourgeois

153

husband, the status as possession, and so on and make contact, if only briefly, with their true selves. It is through sex, according to this view, that human beings achieve their full potential: the Liberated Swinger might thoroughly approve of G.'s action with regard to Camille. On the other hand this view strikes me as the most rampant form of male chauvinism and it would, were G. genuinely the hero of the book, render Berger's dedication "For Anya and her sisters in Women's Liberation" both insulting and insensitive. But Berger's elaborate, metaphorical structuring suggests that G. is not "the hero." Instead the protagonist seeks individual fulfilment — his function as a sexual Garibaldi, "liberating" his paramours, is, when it occurs, only a by-product. He ignores history and it is history, at the end of the book, that rears up and bites him in the ankle. In any case "happiness" is not quite enough — it is, at the present stage of social evolution, a bourgeois ideal, and Berger makes this quite explicit:

> Yet Garibaldi was effectively constrained by his alliance with the existing ruling classes. His gestures defied them: the political consequences confirmed them. The national genius was used to create the pre-conditions for a bourgeois state.

In Dr. Sassall's case the question of evaluation, of moral judgement, hovers only on the fringes of even the most critical mind. There is no separation between what Sassall wishes to become and what he is. He is "fortunate" because our culture approves of his actions and he is able to have it both ways. G. appears to be fortunate because his total being is engaged in enacting many of our own fantasies: he is, or he seems to be, a free agent and he is the cause of a certain kind of liberation in others. In a society whose highest value is the pursuit of individual fulfilment he has the makings of a culture hero. But at the end of the novel Berger shows him drifting, floating in a moral vacuum, caught up without his volition in a crowd of Italian patriots, aware that the example of his own life has provided him with no bearings with which to grapple with the future. The word "liberation" is meaningless until it is subordinated to the principle of *caritas*, though Berger would probably prefer the word "humanity."

This, I believe, is what Berger is saying in this very remarkable novel, though other possibilities are suggested and perhaps I am treating it as a literary Rorschach test, projecting onto a work of art my own values. The book is flawed, in my opinion, by a kind of tight-lipped moral earnestness — you would not think, from reading Berger,

154

that sex contained any element of ecstasy, any hint of Dionysus —
nevertheless it is far more than an interesting experiment in the fusion
of literary modes. I predict that it will not only survive for a generation
but that it will, God help it, be "taught" in the academies.

1973

Promethean Buffoonery

Burgess, Anthony. *The Napoleon Symphony*. London: Cape; Toronto: Clarke, Irwin, 1974.

It is said that the inhabitants of the Cornish town of Mevagissey mistook a monkey washed ashore from a shipwreck for a Bonapartist spy and hanged it — an action which comments either on the insularity of Cornishmen or, more satirically, on Cornish opinion of the French Threat. Meanwhile, at the other end of England, the minstrels of Kent were singing:

> If Bonaparte
> Shud zummon d'eart
> To land on Pevensey Level,
> There are three men
> In Horsemonden
> Will blarst un to the devil.

It is perhaps difficult for those who fought against him and won to feel any more about Napoleon than that he was a bloody nuisance distracting his betters — peace-loving and ordinary citizens — from their pursuit of happiness, beer, and skittles. The Great Man is an irrelevant mountebank as far as Tolstoy was concerned, while to the

English he is possibly even now the comic ogre evoked by mothers grappling with recalcitrant children—"Impotence," as Plato said of comic characters generally, "masquerading as Fate." In a rhymed epistle to the reader, Anthony Burgess appears to share this view:

> My Ogre, though heroic, is grotesque,
> A sort of essay in the picaresque,
> Who robs and rapes and lies and kills in fun
> And does no lasting harm to anyone.

Except, he ought to have added, to the Tyrant's victims.

Structurally the novel follows the movements of Beethoven's *Eroica* symphony and thus starts, as John N. Burk puts it, in his *Life and Works of Beethoven*, with "an insignificant figure on the common chord." Nothing could be more appropriate. Napoleon is at the very start of his career; insignificant despite the whiff of grapeshot that saved the Convention, and as common as dirt. Almost immediately, however, Burgess plunges you into the *allegro con brio*, announcing themes and sub-themes on a vast range of instruments with such enormous zest and energy it is as though, to quote Burk again, "the pencil [can] hardly keep pace with the outpouring thoughts." A member of the Directory's ruling clique discards a mistress and marries her off to this Corsican up-start who thereupon kicks the Austrians out of Italy, drags the Enlightenment, kicking, bleeding, and dying of thirst and dysentery, into Egypt, then strands it there to turn his ambitions on the Directory itself, thus fulfilling the prophecy of another Burke (Edmund) who pointed out that "in the weakness of authority . . . some popular general shall draw the eyes of all men upon himself." Against a backdrop of effete wits and drab intellectuals, N.'s brisk speech, coarse humour, and sheer luck, coupled with a spurious decisiveness, make him outstanding enough to draw any eye, yet, at the same time, he remains a vulgar little fellow comically obsessed by the delectable Josephine though afflicted with premature ejaculation and also, as a perfectly natural consequence, with cuckoldry. This movement cuts back and forth boisterously from the salons of Paris to the locus of its peripatetic central figure in a rich variety of narrative modes such as doggerel, Joycean free-association, heroic couplets, authorial intrusion, etc., and it ends triumphantly with N.'s consecration and enthronement—"the most glorious and noble and august Napoleon, Emperor of the French." Part II, in slower tempo, begins with a dirge and finishes with Napoleon, chin cupped in hand, a detached and amused spectator at his own funeral and it includes such set pieces as the meeting in the pavilion on the Nieman between N. and Alexander I where Europe is shared out, and the campaign in Russia — one of the Three Great Balls-Ups of that tormented century — seen for the most part from the perspective of the unknown, but brutal, not to say licentious, soldiery.

At some stage in the composition of the *Eroica* symphony Beethoven evidently grew disenchanted with Napoleon and introduced into the last movement a theme he had already used for his ballet music *Prometheus*, as though to suggest that the essence of heroism is not to be found in historic figures and men of destiny — human and therefore self-vaunting and corrupt — but in the archetype of whom Napoleon is a faint shadow. Prometheus is heroic not only because he disobeys the gods and brings men fire from heaven but, at least in the ballet, because he brings men to Apollo and thus civilizes them through the ministry of science and the arts. So in his *scherzo* Burgess introduces a play about Prometheus which Napoleon watches with some suspicion, sniffing satire, while the author slyly converts him to a new character, Promethapoleon, who winds up chained to St. Helena, his rock, while the forces of hepatitis, cancer, and sheer displeasure eagle out his liver.

Something of a *pyrophoros* in his own right, Burgess is not a didactic writer. His philosophy, as expounded by about twenty novels, amounts to a version of Manichaeism and hinges on the by now well-known dialogue between St. Augustine and Pelagius, but he has never allowed it to elbow aside his true subject matter, which is language itself. This new book is therefore not an exploration in depth of its freakish central character, nor is it an analysis of history; instead, it is a script empty, thank God, of Message but crammed with a host of minor figures, all of them slightly mad — gourmets, con-men, courtesans, marshals, diplomats, queens, Napoleon himself — all of them driven by their bright, particular humours and seen from the outside and slightly above as though by a cameraman or film director (the book is dedicated to Stanley Kubrick) and given robust, idiosyncratic lines to speak while Burgess hops exuberantly across a linguistic gamut ranging from soldier's demotic to a gratuitous, extended, and very funny parody of Henry James to present his true hero — the shaping spirit of the artist.

There are more profound writers than Burgess in the canon, but I can think of few who are so literate and no one who is as marvellously entertaining. *Napoleon Symphony* is, in my opinion, the best novel so far in his extraordinary career.

1975

158

Of Dukes and Schmucks

Jones, James. *Whistle*. New York: Delacorte, 1978.
Heller, Joseph. *Good as Gold*. New York: Simon and Schuster, 1979.
Updike, John. *The Coup*. New York: Knopf, 1978.

My first encounter with American troops took place during the war when I was a child. They seemed amiable and lethargic young men from whom it was easy to beg chewing-gum. Later, when I was in the British Army and stationed in Germany, I counted this same generosity as a strike against them: they *gave away* stuff like coffee, cigarettes, and gasoline that we were trying to *sell*. We depended upon the black market for a living wage and here were these pampered Yanks ruining the free enterprise system by dispensing chocolate bars, soap, bully-beef, hospital morphine, contraceptives — the inexhaustible wealth of a mighty nation — for nothing in return but popularity. Furthermore, they were not only paid enough to get somebody else to press their uniforms for them, but also to take skiing holidays in the Austrian Alps. Once I ate at a neighbouring American mess-hall and was offered a choice of steak or chicken — food we might be issued at Christmas if we were lucky so that apart from administering an unofficial Marshall Aid these soldiers themselves inhabited what to us looked like a gigantic Butlin's Holiday Camp but with better food and an unlimited supply of drabs, camp-followers, and *viviandières*. Thus, when I first encountered

James Jones's army novel *From Here to Eternity* I thought it a most paranoid and black-a-vised story—as though, dead and newly promoted to angel, a man might start bitching about harpists' working conditions.

Nevertheless, the book is still impressive, even after thirty years. It ought to be read, not as it usually is—as a highly touted example of literary Realism—but as an Auschwitzian fantasy in which the evil and insane apparatus of Fascism is embodied for symbolic purposes by the U.S. Army. Admittedly the fantasy is vitiated somewhat by the fact that the victims are, in the days of uneasy peace immediately before Pearl Harbour, volunteers, but the alternatives confronting them are very little better. Once released into civilian life they discover the jaws of the depression gaping wide for them—a Hobson's choice between unemployment or some vile labouring job in Gimbel's basement. It is part of Jones's vision that life is no better on the outside, so that in Schofield Barracks the problems of civilians are merely intensified and that in the army civilian life is carried on by other means. Human beings cast themselves automatically into those roles they would probably adopt in the concentration camps: there are the victims like Prewitt and Maggio, sadistic Kapos entrusted with administering the Terror (the Stockade is this novel's central image), survivors like Malloy, and men like Sergeant Warden who, indispensable to the system they support, nevertheless try, though vainly, to humanize it. Jones's attitude towards his characters is in general compassionate: his contempt is reserved for the bitchers and whiners, and his praise for the tough, the *macho*, the preservers of grace under stress. The latter resemble one another so closely in style and language it seems as though the same man appears over and over again in the different parts of the army hierarchy: as though Jones's had cast the late John Wayne first as a loser, then as a top-sergeant, as a miner from Harlan, Kentucky, as an ex-Wobbly (not, on the whole, a part Wayne would've been seen dead in), as a pre-selected victim, as an executioner. This is not exactly "Realism" nor is the following passage:

> ". . . and how come most evry non-com in 'your compny' is one of Holmes' punchies? Don't give me that crap."
> The whites of Warden's eyes turned slowly red. "You don't know the half of it yet, kid," he grinned.

The dialogue is authentic Wayne but what about this matter of the eyes? Does Warden make them turn red at will? If so, it's a trick I wish I could master, if only the better to deal with students seeking a change of grade. But I doubt if even the Duke himself could do it — even in his prime.

Jones planned a trilogy dealing with these characters, following their fortunes throughout the war in the Pacific until their repatriation. A combination of technical requirements and the masochism inherent in his world-view forced him to kill Prewitt off at the end of *From Here to Eternity*. He discovered, however, that Prewitt was needed for *The Thin Red Line* — a conundrum he solved by invoking the resurrection principle and renaming the character Witt. In *Whistle*, the not-quite completed third volume of the trilogy, Witt becomes Prell and, by means of similar mutations, Warden becomes Winch and Mess-Sgt. Stark becomes John Strange. By 1945 the tough and durable bodies of these he-men have done the States some service but in the course of it have become broken by war and anxiety. Prell has caught a burst of machine-gun fire across his thighs and is confined to his wheel-chair; mortar-shrapnel has done for Strange's hand; and Winch suffers from congestive heart failure, the same disease that carried Jones off at fifty-five in 1977, brought on by drinking, smoking, and the tensions of command. Much of the action is located in army hospitals and in the apartments and hotels of hospital towns. The book is dominated by two themes — the first is of sickness and approaching death, as though Jones is asking the question: what sustains human beings when the body, and the sensations it lives by, begin to fail? What becomes of the Code after the arteries have hardened, the testicles dried out, the lungs filled with mucous, and doctors have forbidden drink, sex, and cigarettes? Loyalty to old comrades of one's lusty youth is Winch's tentative solution and it is a pity that these comrades disgust him — a contradiction that eventually drives him mad. Others choose versions of the Hemingway route — Prell picks fights in bars until a drunken soldier obligingly kills him with a billiard cue; a character named Landers steps under a car; and Strange HartCranes it over the side of a ship. Had Jones not been dying himself he might have ended his army novels on a more cheerful note — have Winch, for instance, surviving into the seventies as a refrigerator salesman and Kiwani dressing up in his legionnaire's forage cap on Friday nights to sing "The Boogie-Woogie Bugle Boy of Company B" around the piano, but the exit from life that he documents is perhaps more dignified and certainly far less inconsistent with the grain of his characters.

The second theme is much odder. Jones seems both fascinated and repelled by human sexuality, particularly as it is expressed in oral stimulation, and much of the dialogue is taken up by these wounded and tattered men musing on the aesthetics, ethics, ontology, and epistemology of cunnilingus. Some revel in it for the sake of the sensations it gives them, others for the delight it gives women, others again are appalled by it as though it threatens their masculinity and offer to punch out any woman who suggests it to them. None feel neutral. Women, in this novel, are sexually insatiable, treacherous towards those who do not satisfy them, fickle and impatient when the money runs out, and automatically adulterous when married. The point of a man's life, one of the male characters thinks, is to serve women and give them sexual satisfaction, mostly in oral form, and the point of a woman's life, presumably, is to receive this satisfaction from her lover of the moment and move on to the next when, for whatever reason, it stops. The reader might find this a limited, if rather charming, view of human nature. Oral sex, to Jones's characters, is an act which combines worship and humiliation—a domination of the masculine spirit by the female. Jones seems to be working with the ancient paradox, that sex emasculates the male, to be found in Ovid or in those Renaissance representations of Venus and Mars in which the warrior's armour is strewn on the ground and used by cherubs as playthings; Mars is post-coitally somnolent, his eyes closed and mouth agape; and Venus is sitting up, wide awake, a knowing little smile on her lips. Venus herself is Death ("just another whore," as Hemingway once put it) an equation neatly represented by the destiny of Landers who, throwing himself under a car, seeks out the perfect weapon:

> As he stepped out, he realized he would not have done it if she had been a man, driving a jeep or a GI truck. But she really was so beautiful. Her coat was thrown back open in the heat of the car, and in the sweater under it her breasts swelled out thrusting their weight against the lapels deliciously. So delicious. And her hair fell to the collar of the coat with an equally delicious feminine grace.

Thus the masochism of Jones's novels reaches that ultimate point where it also becomes revenge.

Whistle is a fascinating and extremely readable book which, like its predecessors, is less a field of study for those who admire Realism as it is a playground for critics of the psycho-analytic school. Jones's

162

civilian novels are feeble by comparison and *Whistle* makes clear the reason—in the army, and masculine enterprise within it, he had discovered a complex network of symbols that transcend the merely political and thus achieved a profundity which eluded him whenever he dealt with other themes.

From Here to Eternity appeared just at that point in time when the "cult of experience" in American writing was beginning to die out but when raw energy, great blocks of physical description, representations of working-class speech, etc. could still break through the best-seller barrier into the fat pastures of critical esteem. Joseph Heller's *Catch-22*, on the other hand, though it also deals with the stupidities and cruelties of the military, is in style, content, and attitude towards life and art a totally different kind of writing. If Jones admires fortitude, Heller admires the survival instinct; Jones is sombre in tone, almost elegiac, and frequently sentimental, but Heller's vision is comic and thus capable of a terrifying and grotesque imagery beyond the reach of Jones; Jones tried to keep his fantasies pinned down to a concrete world, while Heller gives his free reign often, in fact, too free; honour, truth, and loyalty mean something to Jones; to Heller they are so much claptrap. *Eternity* and *Whistle* are conventional with regard to narrative technique, while *Catch-22* spirals around its epiphanies which slowly intensify in horror. If the Renaissance obsession with the story of Mars's seduction by Venus can be seen as a key to Jones's work, then one can also look back to Tudor novelists for parallels to Heller's way of seeing the world:

> Though all men be made of one metal, yet they be not cast all in one mold; there is framed of the self-same clay as well the tile to keep water out as the pot to contain liquor; the sun doth harden the dirt and melt the wax; fire maketh the gold to shine and the straw to smother; perfume doth refresh the dove and kill the beetle . . . .

This is a typical passage from Lyly's *Euphues* in which the universe is seen as various, dazzling, contradictory, inaccessible, and best communicated in a series of oxymorons or antithetical statements that cancel one another out. It is not such a far cry from:

> There was only one catch and that was Catch-22, which specified that a concern for one's safety in the face of dangers that were real and immediate was the process of a rational mind. Orr could

163

be grounded. All he had to do was ask; and as soon as he did, he would no longer be crazy and would have to fly more missions. Orr would be crazy to fly more missions and sane if he didn't, but if he was sane he had to fly them. If he flew them he was crazy and didn't have to; and if he didn't want to he was sane and had to. Yossarian was moved very deeply by the absolute simplicity of this clause of Catch-22 and let out a respectful whistle.

"That's some catch, that Catch-22," he observed.

"It's the best there is," Doc Daneeka agreed.

Like Lyly, Heller sees the raising of a respectful whistle at the brilliance and absurdity of the universe as part of his job and, like Lyly, he is one of the founders of an entire school of fiction.

In *Good as Gold*, Heller's new novel, the technique survives and logical, oxymoronic idiocies are written into the speeches of government bureaucrats where, unfortunately for the novel, one would expect them. In this respect Heller is entertaining the already converted, for nowadays few would look for truth, sensitivity, and intelligence in Washington, Ottawa, or London, or in any other institution or hierarchy — Heller and his fellow absurdists have done their earlier work too well. Yet, the treacherous, slithery logic of official utterances still baffles and outrages Gold, the protagonist of the novel, who is a middle-aged academic who doesn't teach, whose father won't go to Florida, and who isn't offered a lucrative job in the nation's capital only on condition that no job exists. "It's high time you got what you deserved," Gold's non-benefactor tells him, "although it may be too soon." Gold himself is rather a flat character, more of a comic-strip figure to whom things happen, who is also trying to write a book about the Jewish experience in America despite his father's sneer that he wasn't even born in Europe and who only comes alive when infuriated by the sly goading of his brother and when he contemplates the career of Henry Kissinger.

The novel is at its best when Heller focuses on Henry Kissinger (*zol er oysgemekt vern* — may his name be erased). If the eviscerated Snowden, dying in the back of a bombing plane, is Heller's image for the forties, then the spectacle of Richard Nixon begging Henry Kissinger to kneel and pray with him at the height of the Watergate crisis will do for the seventies. What better synechdoche, when you come to think of it, for these last post-flower-child, cynical, narcissistic, come-and-get-it ten years than this revealed con-artist who lied and cheated his way into the presidency grovelling on the

White House mat with a man who once said of the Christmas bombing of North Viet Nam "we bombed them into letting us accept their terms," who then invaded Cambodia and was rewarded both for his sentiments and his actions with the Nobel Peace Prize. With these two religious caterpillars around, who needs fiction at all? All Heller had to do was collect news-clippings and quotations and lists of Kissinger's jobs, appointments, sinecures, moonlightings, sponsorships, and cony-catchings — all matters of public record. Many of them are displayed in the novel together with Gold's running commentary couched in a mixture of English and Yiddish — the latter language, indeed, might have been designed for verbal aggression generally and for the encapsulation of Kissinger in particular. The invective is delightful — the twentieth century's answer to Metternich would, it seems, only be impressive to a *goy*; to a Jew he is not only a *schmuck*, a *putz*, a *schnorrer* but, less familiarly to me, a *grubba naar*, a *schmendrick*, a *trombenik*, a *klutz*, etc. and is thus attacked with such a battery of brisk and ugly syllables, which do not really need translation, that I tremble for the solidity of Heller's defence in any forthcoming libel suit. I suppose he can always say it is not him but Gold.

The second structural device of the book concerns Gold's relationship with his family. They are both proud and ashamed of his success in the world but he seems to occupy in their minds the sort of place Kissinger occupies in his. His brother baits him with snippets of misinformation, his father rants at him, his mad step-mother feigns politeness towards him only the better to set him up for an insult. He is afflicted with one revolting daughter and his marriage has gone dead. The talk around the dinner table, the interactions of these highly idiosyncratic but not very sane people, is beautifully done and very funny, but the Kissinger analogy is not sufficient to sustain it as essential to the novel. The third motif, Gold's attempt to find work in Washington, though mildly comic, seems to spin out of control altogether and is entirely unbelievable even on the level of good fantasy. Thus *Good as Gold* oscillates rather uneasily between social comedy, Skeltonic satire, and Strangelovean burlesque and would have been a much more powerful work had Heller blue-pencilled the latter.

John Updike has published much more than either Heller or Jones but despite his wit, intelligence, and sensitivity at least equalling theirs he has failed, in my opinion, to write a major novel. Even *Rabbit Redux*, probably his best and least mandarin book, smacks more of the inkhorn than it does of the genuine involvement with the

165

predicaments it describes. So it is with *The Coup*, a novel in the form of the memoirs of one Colonel Rakin Felix Ellelou, ex-president of a fictional African state called Kush which, if my memory of British Army Arabic is correct, is an obscene word for the female genitals. Ellelou has been deposed by a subordinate just as he himself deposed, then later decapitated, the former king—an aging sinner whose imprisonment prior to his execution turns him to the consolations of Islam. Kush is practically a desert at the best of times but now, as a result of a long drought, it has become like its non-fictional sub-Saharan counterparts, a wasteland where what little vegetation there is appears wanly along roads where car radiators have leaked a few drops of water. Over this unpromising realm Ellelou has tried to impose a dictatorship combining theocracy and Marxism, but his inability to create even a minimum prosperity helps to bring about his downfall.

The memoir, written from the security of exile in the south of France, describes varieties of search; in space, across the stricken landscape of Kush as he investigates, sometimes in disguise like Haroun al Raschid, at others *en grande tenue* as absolute ruler, the state of the nation and the truth of rumours concerning American and Russian duplicity; in time, as he explores the his past sometimes in the first-person voice as "the I who experiences," sometimes in the third person as the "I who acts," his education during the fifties at a small American university, his first encounters with each of his wives, his acquisition of power, and his fears for his waning sexual potency and humanity. The Americans, he fears, are attempting to destroy the morality of his people by dumping vast quantities of breakfast cereal on his borders—worse, there are rumours that a pair of mysterious golden arches have been spotted in the middle of the desert. The Russians have levanted with the old king's head, turning it by means of miniaturised electronic components into a combination of magic talisman and speaking oracle. From the communist world and from the materialistic West come tourists, oil experts, engineers, and PR men to threaten the noble visions of Islam and to strew its austere ground with popsicle wrappers, Fritos, Coke bottles, and dropped popcorn. There is even an American oil town parked in the middle of the desert complete with drug-stores where you can buy a lime-phosphate, suburbs with ranch-style bungalows and lawn sprinklers, and bubble-gum snapping teeny-boppers. Updike is extremely good at describing these horrors—in fact his great strength as a novelist lies partly in his Nabokovian eye for the minutiae of everyday life and in his ability to render these things, ghastly or not, with such vividness they become mandalas expressive of an entire culture. Considered as an exercise in style, then, *The Coup* is dazzling and, surely to anybody trying to write good prose, enviable. But there is not, as far as I can see, anything very weighty behind it. One can forgive Jones and Heller their infelicities, their self-indulgencies, their occasional lapses into pure silliness, because each possesses a coherent vision of the world and because their novels urgently communicate it. They have, to put it very simply, *something to say*. In novel after novel Updike has proved himself, like Nabokov, a brilliant mimic, a gifted observer of manners and trends — experimenter, ironist, poet, and polymath — but, unlike Nabokov, he has not yet found, for his vast talents, an underlying theme.

1979

Munchers and More

Kosinski, Jerzy. *Cockpit.* Boston: Houghton Mifflin, 1975.

Kosinski's first novel, *The Painted Bird*, concerns a young boy inadvertently abandoned by his parents in Eastern Europe during the Nazi occupation and is structured as a series of vignettes linked together by the consciousness of the boy as he seeks refuge in first one village or farm then the next. The novel is a sort of narrative equivalent of Goya's Disasters of War series — one atrocious, diabolical event follows another, each described with that Goyaesque reined-in moral horror and in a manner suggesting that, however grotesque, however ferocious and sub-human these events may seem, they did, in fact, take place. Kosinski's vignettes are utterly nightmarish, yet so believable they form hard, evil little gobbets of reality in the reader's imagination so that though it is some years since I read the novel I can recall without effort the incident of the disembodied eyeballs squashed flat between stone floor and boot-heel, the incident of the flayed hare, the murder of the half-witted girl, the manic rape of the village by the cavalry brigade. I wish I could not recall these things and it is a tribute to Kosinski's narrative power that these horrors remain alive. The tone is cool and objective and each sequence is preceded by a closely observed description of an analogous event in the animal world as though Kosinski saw himself in the role of scientist studying the

168

parallels between animal and human patterns of aggression — as though he were Konrad Lorenz, let us say. On one level the novel works as an assault on whatever idealism the reader may retain concerning "human nature" and one cannot say of Kosinski what Orwell said of Swift: the latter accuses human beings of being "worse than they are." The Second World War takes care of that objection. At the same time built into the novel is an almost cynical challenge to the reader to persist until the end without throwing the book aside in disgust at his own queasy but sadistic fascination. Implied throughout, despite the objectivity, is a moral outrage that human beings are like this and that they can perpetrate these revolting things on one another.

The moral outrage fades in Kosinski's next book, *Steps*, and begins to turn into a moral gloat. The boy victim of *The Painted Bird* has become an adult and it is time for him to get his own back. The vignette form is preserved though the reader senses no clear personage behind that of the narrator. The episodes deal mostly with sexual relationships and encounters in which the participants enjoy tormenting one another. The boy has learned his lesson and is now prepared to teach it to others. The novel, if one can describe it thus, might possibly appeal to those readers who enjoy the notion that humanity is composed of two-parts Hobbes and three-parts de Sade.

I suppose the end-point of this process is reached when a man can say, along with Nashe's character Cutwolfe, that "the farther we wade in revenge, the nearer we come to the throne of the Almighty. To His sceptre it is properly ascribed; His sceptre He lends unto man when He lets one man scourge another." Tarden, the hero, if that is what he is, of *Cockpit* is such an avenger. He escapes from a police state somewhere in Eastern Europe and arrives in America where he becomes a spy for the secret service and later, retiring from his occupation, a millionaire with the means and contacts to indulge his whims. These whims concern the working out of a variety of adolescent fantasies such as vengeance, the enslavement of women, and the achievement of poetic justice — the punishment of the pretentious, for example, or the castigation of a bully, together with the intrusion into the lives of perfect strangers in order to play destiny. Once again the novel is a string of episodes, but these come over as accounts of pranks, many of them sadistic, such as the murder of a rebellious female slave by exposing her to high-energy radar beams, others merely puerile such as the one involving the use of a wooden Indian to frighten a group of children. Tarden shares with adolescents the love of expensive and complicated gadgetry but above all he enjoys elaborate plots and intrigues often perpetrated in a spirit of random competitiveness. For example he spends weeks practising skiing down a slope in order to land with a flourish and a dead halt on a narrow wooden balcony and the purpose of this is to lure the resort's ski-studs and hot-shots into emulation so that the countryside may resound with the snapping of bones and the cracking of skulls. Here and there the book is oddly reminiscent of Terry Southern's *The Magic Christian* though it lacks the latter's comedy and rather attractive silliness. Tarden's silliness is depraved, humourless, and malevolent and there is no reason to suppose that the author does not wholeheartedly approve of it.

Kosinski may eventually redeem himself by exploiting a new vein of unconscious humour. There is a pleasant passage concerning a freak known as The Snapper. This fellow hangs around porn houses and cons old men into booths by offering them what amounts to a new and unusual fellatiocinative experience:

[The Snapper] would take the man's flesh in his mouth, easing it gently into his throat, then suddenly bite down. With one bite the victim's organ was severed. The Snapper would push through the booth and run down the centre aisle, his mouth full of blood and scraps of flesh.... With blood oozing through his pants, the victim would clutch his groin and beg the peepshow manager not to summon the police.

How's that for a fantasy? Frankly, I would not care to encounter this snapping cock-muncher, as Nashe might have called him, and would encourage the reader to avoid him too. Indeed, I would advise the reader to toss this rubbishy book along with its Snapper into the nearest garbage-can where they belong were I not afraid that Kosinski, who undoubtedly changes into Tarden at nightfall, has something rather nasty worked out for hostile reviewers.

1977

A Plinth for L. B. J.

Layton, Irving. *The Shattered Plinths*. Toronto: McClelland and
Stewart, 1967.

I hesitate to review *The Shattered Plinths* for I do not want to share
the luckless destiny the poet once predicted for the critic from
Dayton —

> Who censured a poem by Layton.
> To expiate this
> In Hades he'll kiss
> The clotted black arsehole of Satan.

Nevertheless I intend to risk it.

Irving Layton is one of the very few genuine poets this rather
prosaic country has yet produced and has secured this reputation with
a considerable body of work, some of it magnificent, some of it
indifferent, and some of it incredibly bad. Since he seems to regard
every poem he writes with equal affection it is sometimes difficult for
the reader to separate the genuine poet from the poseur forced to
defend obviously fifth-rate doggerel under the illusion that everything
he touches turns to gold. What, for example, are we to make of the
following lines?

Instead of being jolly
The poets voice their melancholy,
Repetitious as a polly
Trained by human folly.

Straight out of McGonnegal, you might say, and totally vacuous; but
what makes me uneasy is this sense I have of the writer smiling over
the lines with warm approval. "It's camp," I can hear him saying.
"Don't you recognize deliberate camp when you see it? How stupid
can you be, not to understand that this parodies the style of precisely
those poets I wish to attack?" To which the reader can only mutter the
phrase "Fallacy of Imitative Form" and slink off to his book shelves to
check his impression that no one of literary importance writes like a
Georgian poet anymore. There is much, in fact, about Layton's targets
to suggest two-dimensional cut-out men dressed in spats, boaters, and
parti-coloured shoes. Consider the following sentence from the book's
preface:

> The more sophisticated reader who believes with the new
> academics that the last word in modern poetry has been said by
> Messrs. Yeats, Pound, Eliot, Frost, Graves and Auden may also
> not find this volume to his taste: he will probably shut it with a
> bang before he has finished reading a single poem.

When a man comes across a statement like this he feels like asking
"Where have you *been*, Layton? Where are you *at*, for Christ's sake?
Do you really think that people are still reading Eliot? Or that
anybody considers Frost 'the last word'?" No one I know, "new
academic" or otherwise, would regard Auden as any longer a modern
poet nor would he read Graves for anything other than the latter's
splendid prose denunciations of his fellow poets. As for Pound, he
long ago slipped from the grasp of those who would bracket him with
others as a modern and has come back into fashion as one of the
progenitors, along with Whitman, of a "new American" poetry which
Layton mentions not at all. A man who wants to attack fashions had
better attack the current ones. But to read parts of this preface is to be
in a time machine with the button pressed at "1939." Having presented
us with these over-riddled targets Layton then goes on to say:

> For my part I must confess that the poems of these gentlemen
> strike me today as only a little less quaint than the sight of a

172

horse-and-buggy at a frantic intersection in Montreal and Toronto.

Does he really expect us to respond to such a statement with anything other than a bored nod?

The answer, I regret to say, is "yes."

Let us admit that while he is addressing his compatriots (the bulk of whom have only, where they care about poetry at all, recently become adjusted to the promotion of Sir Charles G. D. Roberts to the Canadian pantheon and to whom the phrase "avant-garde" conjures up the threatening image of Edgar A. Guest—see a magazine called *Canadian Poetry* if you think I exaggerate) Layton stands a good chance of succeeding in his self-appointed task of causing bourgeois hackles to rise. But a rising hackle *there*, it seems to me, cannot compensate for a drooping eyelid *here* and Layton's habit of calling attention to owls pre-stuffed and already long ago denounced by the very audience to which such a book as *The Shattered Plinths* is directed—i.e., serious readers of modern poetry—often brings him toppling on the edge of bathos.

In dedicating his book to Lyndon B. Johnson, the poet falls over this edge and into something far more serious.

When I first encountered the dedication (with the help of a double take) my immediate reaction was to ask: why Johnson? Why not Kaltenbrunner? Or Hangman Heydrich? Or Lavrenti Beria? Or, in fact, any other murderous thug? Obviously, I thought, Layton cannot be serious and the dedication reflects no more than a laudable wish to tweak the noses of liberal intellectuals most of whom, as far as I can see, are solidly opposed to Johnson's policy (insofar as a president can be said to have a policy of his own) in Viet Nam. Layton has always believed, along with Kierkegaard, that a majority opinion must necessarily be a wrong opinion. Yet there is plenty of evidence in the book itself to lead the reader to suppose that Layton, who normally has such a sharp and ironic eye for political and idealistic cant (see such squibs as "Proper Reading Light," "The Larger Issue," "For the Cause," etc.) has not only been suckered in by one of the greatest cant-mongers the Western world has yet produced, but has lent himself to that kind of gloating over violence in defence of shabby idealism more appropriate to the adolescent fans of Steve Canyon and Bonnie and Clyde. For example, the poem "The New Sensibility":

Never mind
beating out your exile, Ez:
that's literary hogwash,
vintage quaintsville

A more efficacious
epigram
for stopping the mouths
of tormentors
is a bullet in the head:
it opens a hole
and closes the matter for ever ...

... Do you hear me, Old Man?
a dead shot
sending the bullet
winging like a finished stanza
straight between the eyes

That's the new poetry
minted June 1967
in Tel Aviv and Sinai

I thought
I should let you know.

And again, from "For My Two Sons, Max and David":

The wandering Jew: the suffering Jew
The despoiled Jew: the beaten Jew
The Jew to burn: the Jew to gas
The Jew to humiliate ...

... Be none of these, my sons
My sons, be none of these
Be gunners in the Israeli Air Force.

Though I like and admire both these poems and can sympathize with
the "new" Jewish self-image expressed in them, I find that they are, as
contributions to an understanding of the human condition, somewhat
secondary to the draft-resister's awareness that a man's only real

enemy is the smooth son-of-a-bitch who places a rifle in his hands and orders him forth to do some fighting for the Cause.

In a book of poems many of which denounce genocide I find no poem denouncing American foreign policy; within a body of work that sneers at generals and dictators (provided of course, that they are not Israeli generals and dictators), I find no unflattering references to such people as Ky or General Westmoreland who, you would think, would be very suitable targets for satire. But there is a symmetry, however, of a strangely negative kind. For every poem which attacks violence and the man who lives by violence there is a poem approving violence (such as "The New Sensibility" quoted above) provided it can be justified with whatever holy word the author finds acceptable. The dedication, in the light of this, is clearly intended seriously.

None of this would matter if the author were not claiming in his preface

> ... the right to enter imaginatively into the seminal tensions and dilemmas of our age.... I've become aware of the extent to which the 'political fact' governs our lives. I suppose what I chiefly have against the older poets and, for that matter, some of the contemporary ones as well, is their astonishing ignorance of the social sciences, an ignorance matched only by their political naïveté.

It is precisely this charge of political naïveté that I would bring against Layton's own, highly partisan book.

It may seem churlish to dismiss in a few words the *good* things about *The Shattered Plinths*, but the fact is that what has always been said about Layton remains true. What emerges from his work is a joyousness, an infectious zest for life, love, and contention. His prose is probably the liveliest ever written in this country and his poetry, the best of it, has that indefinable grace of the best poetry anywhere which can only be talked about in metaphors — of, for example, the wing of a jet-plane flashing in the sun.

1968

By God, We Are Alive

Carrier, Roch. *La Guerre, Yes Sir!*. Toronto: House of Anansi, 1970.

The central event in this novel is the delivery to a primitive French Canadian village of the corpse of one of its inhabitants who had gone off to the Second World War. Seven English soldiers stand guard over the coffin while it is parked in the victim's home which becomes the scene of a combination wake, orgy, prayer-meeting, and Bacchanalian revel. The novel opens brilliantly with a villager chopping off his hand to avoid military service; the hand becomes a puck for an ice-hockey game until it is retrieved by the malingerer's wife and thrown to the dogs. Carrier interrupts this sequence with a short *fabliau* comedy in which a deserter shares his wife with a draft-dodger she had arranged to hide while her husband was overseas, then switches to the arrival and delivery of the coffin. He uses the celebration to build up the tensions betwen the villagers and the *Anglais* then resolves them by having the draft-dodger shoot one of the soldiers. He is then able to end the book neatly with a new corpse to replace the one just buried in the frozen ground.

It is not hard to see why this book has appeared so prominently on the so-called best-seller list this summer. It has many popular ingredients. For the low-brow reader Carrier presents the *Clochemerle* sexual morality of the villagers. The women are well-endowed and

176

sexually aggressive. Breasts are heavy; bellies burn. Sometimes these breasts are "as firm as hot rolls"; at other times they "spill out of brassieres" where they do not swell under necklines of dresses or pop out of night-robes. All very delightful and a little romanticized, although Carrier tries to cerebral-up his frequent sex-scenes by giving them a metaphysical heaviness:

> Bérubé rolled onto Molly. It was death that they stabbed at violently.

For the WASP reader there is plenty of opportunity to indulge that exquisite and masochistic pleasure I have had occasion to describe in the pages of this magazine on previous occasions of finding himself inferior to his counterpart in a minority race. (It is not numerically true, of course, that the Anglo is in the "majority" in Eastern Canada. But up until fairly recently he has *acted* as though he were "in the majority"—which comes to the same thing.) This WASP reader will have the pleasure of identifying with the tight-lipped, disapproving, repressed soldiery who think only of their duty and of the Frenchman's essential vulgarity. The WASP will enjoy rejecting the implicit rationalization: "How right we were to oppress them!" The middle-class French Canadian will have a similar masochistic reaction but based on a slightly different phobia. He will regret having sold his beautiful, primitive, pastoral soul to become trivialized as an electronics engineer, oil salesman, or computer programmer in Montreal. The peasant *Canadien*, holed up in isolation in his priest-dominated village, will not read the book at all—in fact it's probably on the index already—while the Anglo middle-class drop-out *may* have time to read it between bouts of work on the commune and if he *does* it will confirm him in all his prejudices.

Best-seller or not, it is an excellent book, and this despite it being riddled with what I think I shall start calling "The Zorba Fallacy" which can be stated as follows: "We are crass, vulgar, violent, blood-thirsty, and primitive, but by God we are Alive!" I have no objection to the sentiment: but whenever I hear the word "we," I reach for my revolver. Carrier's book seems to me a version in prose of what Krieghoff attempted in painting; grotesquely comic and, in places, terrifying. And those readers who encounter in this novel for the first time the *Canadien* version of blasphemy will find an entire, new, and delightful world opening up to them.

1970

177

Sonnenkinder, Weltschmerz, Sturm, und Drang

Keneally, Thomas. *A Victim of the Aurora.* London: Collins, 1977.
Greene, Graham. *The Human Factor.* London: Bodley Head; Toronto: Clarke, Irwin, 1978.
Le Carré, John. *The Honourable Schoolboy.* London: Hodder and Stoughton; Toronto: Musson, 1977.

In Martin Green's estimable but long-winded literary study of the twenties and thirties, *Children of the Sun*, there is a page of three photographs, one of King George V, one of Lord Beaverbrook, and the third of Winston Churchill out on the town with David Lloyd George. The period is clearly World War I. George is tightly uniformed, his eyes are heavily pouched, his mouth is in the open position to deliver a royal pronouncement. One of the Empire's leading flackmen, Rudyard Kipling, is obsequiously in attendance. Beaverbrook smiles at the camera with that mixture of bonhomie, ruthlessness, and mendacity perhaps characteristic of him while Churchill and the Welsh Wizard are dressed to kill, the latter sporting a buttonhole, as though they were arriving at, or just leaving, the house of a fashionable courtesan. Churchill's slack-jawed leer certainly suggests aroused sexual appetite while the Welshman's smirk seems more to indicate that the visit has been satisfactorily concluded. Kipling's expression is neutral, as is proper to one enduring the conversation of his monarch, and he is dressed conservatively in top hat, frock coat, and collar *à la garotte*. This picture Green subtitles "the fathers, against whom the sons rebelled." The other two depict "three of the uncles who sponsored the rogues among the sons." The rogue sons, the *Sonnenkinder* of the book's title, are Harold Acton, Brian Howard, the Sitwells, and Evelyn Waugh as far as the arts are concerned, and Randolph Churchill, Mosely, Burgess, MacLean, and Kim Philby in the world of politics. Green includes photographs of these people too and what is common to them all, fathers, uncles, rogue sons, is that they are all of them utterly infuriating. In no other country, even France, is the Establishment, whether in its straight or rebellious manifestations, quite so irritating as it is in Britain. It irritated Orwell and Leavis, also included, and it irritated the so-called Angry Young Men such as the highly irritating Kingsley Amis, shown here clutching a small child against a backdrop of country cottage as though to assert his domesticity, his sexual normality, his decent chapedness against those upper-class artists and writers who supported filthy, *continental* cads like Cocteau and Diaghilev. Thus a Kipling infuriated, for example, a Christopher Isherwood and Isherwood in his turn so maddened George Orwell, who denounced Christopher and his Kind as "the pansy left," that he was led into a reluctant defence of Kipling and to the assertion, often repeated throughout his work but most notably presented in *Coming Up for Air*, that Edwardian England was a good, stable, world where it seemed to be "summer all the year round," whose Kiplingesque values of work, duty, thrift, honesty, heterosexuality (if at all), and High Seriousness vanished in 1914 to be replaced by cynicism, frivolity, totalitarian politics, androgyny, and the Century of the Common Man.

It is some of these assumptions and Edwardian England generally, hateful to some, idyllic to others, that are subjected to scrutiny in Thomas Keneally's novel *A Victim of the Aurora*. The narrator, a nonagenarian artist called Anthony Piers, looks back to his youth as a member of an Antarctic expedition led by a charismatic adventurer of the Scott and Shackleton tradition named Sir Eugene Stewart. It is 1910, before the perfection of photographic techniques, and Sir Eugene is impressed enough by Piers's artistic work to offer him a job as the expedition's official artist. "I want paintings which will stand prominently on the stairwells of this nation," he says innocently, and this remark alone will give some indication of Keneally's quality. Sir Eugene also includes an acerbic but fashionable journalist named Victor Henneker to act as historian, and the rest of

179

his followers are chosen from the "three thousand members of the Edwardian middle classes [who] lined up to apply for positions on Sir Eugene's staff." A selection is made carefully—men are chosen for their qualities of endurance and obedience as well as for their clubbability. The "other ranks" are chosen less carefully, but they are considered automatically reliable—obedience and endurance, it is thought, have been ground into them.

Once it is on the shores of McMurdo Sound the expedition begins to fall apart. Henneker is discovered frozen stiff outside one of the huts with his head bashed in by, it is established later, a frozen skua gull, and with the marks of strangulation around his throat. Sir Eugene gathers together a small group, which includes Piers, who was involved in finding the corpse, and gives it the task of investigating the murder. It is, at first sight, unthinkable that a member of this carefully selected league of gentlemen would first cosh then choke another to death: Piers doesn't say it, but a chap would almost sooner risk being seen in the Royal Enclosure at Ascot wearing a bowler hat than being suspected of murder. Fortunately there exists an alternative hypothesis—that Henneker was done to death by an outsider named "Forbes-Chalmers." Forbes-Chalmers is mentioned first as "an illusion, a trick of the light which had caused members of the expedition to report having sighted a man high up on glaciers or far out on the ice of the sound." The name itself is a conflation of those of two men who disappeared on a previous expedition some years before and it is unlikely, to say the least, that either would have survived as a maroon living off the land and sea and abandoned store huts. Thus Sir Eugene is at first reluctant to ascribe real existence to this wraithlike entity let alone making it responsible for Henneker's death, but as the novel progresses the evidence for the Forbes-Chalmers alternative grows more convincing and at last a sub-expedition is mounted to seek him out. Meanwhile, however, the evidence grows in favour of the murderer being within the expedition itself: Henneker's journal is discovered—a collection of scurrilous and potentially blackmailing documents pertaining to his colleagues, such that almost any one of them would feel motivated to put him out of the way. He is also, and this places him completely beyond the pale of an official culture still reeling from the Oscar Wilde scandal, a homosexual.

Keneally underplays this potentially melodramatic plot with great skill. For one thing, he has chosen to tell the story in a plain and unobtrusive style, though at one point he allows himself the luxury of including a paragraph of very good parody of Bernard Shaw. For

180

another, the accuracy of his presentation of the minutiae of life in frozen wastelands may mislead the reader into supposing that this is an adventure story. But it is as an analysis of the motives, confusions, hidden lusts, the *mauvaise foi* of a whole epoch, the epoch of "the fathers against whom the sons rebelled," that the novel succeeds. Forbes-Chalmers, when they get to him, is a perfect symbol for a society whose king, as Piers discovers later, dies shortly after the expedition's launching. The outcast is literally a survivor — he is wildly bearded and his teeth have fallen out; his arm dangles paralyzed at his side, the result of an accident with an overturning sled; his breath stinks like a newly opened grave; he has committed an offence for which, though there is an excuse, he feels there can be no forgiveness — *he has eaten his comrade.* Thus he is either Forbes or Chalmers — they have become indistinguishable, and here Keneally risks a grim joke to the effect that "you are what you eat."

The novel ends with the discovery of the murderer and his execution. The expedition, from which Sir Eugene and four others do not return, can then go about its business, whatever that is. But as far as Piers is concerned the investigation has revealed too much about his fellow Edwardians and their secret lives for him to be anything other than sceptical about the effort and aspiration that went into such undertakings as the "New British South Polar Expedition." It is as though he has discovered that men tried to get the Pole in exactly the same spirit as they climbed mountains — not "because it is there" but because there is nothing *else* there. Their own culture was antagonistic to the notion of self-examination just as it opposed, even, the idea of an "unconscious." Thus their boredom, their spiritual malaise, created the inspiration for these meaningless, though artificially heroic, adventures while the inspiration itself was hidden from them under such murky labels as "high endeavor." After 1918 self-deception of this sort was harder to maintain, though many regretted they were no longer allowed it: "There never was such a break-up," Viscount Esher, friend and adviser to King Edward VII wrote, concerning the king's funeral. "All the old buoys which have marked the channel of our lives seem to have been swept away." Keneally's narrator, Anthony Piers, puts it like this: "As for me, the crime and execution were the act which rendered the condition of the century terminal. Nothing ever since has surprised me."

Keneally is an excellent and undervalued novelist. *A Victim of the Aurora* traces its theme of decadence with great skill and subtlety. As an Australian Keneally is able to analyze British ruling-class idiocy with less animus, even, than Graham Greene who tends to present his establishment figures as caricatures. In *The Human Factor*, for example, the ruling-class is represented by senior members of the British secret service. They are faintly comic country gentlemen, perfectly clubbable, judges of wine, tormentors of trout, assassins of pheasants, and slayers of grouse. They know their port and are prudent with cheese. They spend their mornings hanging around the haberdashers, tobacconists, and stationers of Jermyn Street and their afternoons at White's or the Reform. One might have supposed that such men died long before Wodehouse himself and that the lives they lead, with their flats in Mayfair, Albany, St. James, only possible nowadays to football players, pop singers, and Arabian oil magnates. But in Greene's world they still exist — as nonchalantly incapable of running the nation as they ever were. How right, one can't help thinking, Sir Thomas Hoby was in translating, for English consumption, Castiglione's fine word *sprezzatura*, meant to describe one of the chief characteristics of a gentleman, as "recklessness," and what better word is there to describe the chilling mixture of casualness, brutality, and lack of evidence with which they eliminate one of their underlings. *Sprezzatura* also describes perfectly the well-bred insouciance with which they enter a sinister operation against African guerrillas in combination with the secret services of America and South Africa, thus supporting and helping to perpetuate the apartheid regime. The operation is ironically code-named "Uncle Remus."

In furtive opposition to them is Greene's central character, one hesitates to call him a "hero," an aging employee of the British secret service who passes information of the minor sort with which he has to deal onto the Russians. Unlike most double agents in literature, he lives a life singularly devoid of external incident as a resident of the outlying town of Berkhamstead (where Greene himself spent his childhood playing Russian Roulette), commutes to London daily, and is in no way distinguishable from the legion of clerks, accountants, and sales assistants who hit the suburban stations each weekday morning with the regularity of a planet turning on its axis. Maurice Castle is, technically speaking, a "traitor," not because he is a *Sonnenkind* irritated, as well he might be, by his Establishment colleagues, nor even a communist, but because he wishes to pay a debt he owes to the people who helped him and the black woman he later married to escape from South Africa. The novel's action begins with the discovery of a leakage of information and its attribution to Castle's fellow agent. Though not under immediate suspicion himself, the investigation endangers Castle who nevertheless feels he must file one last report to the Soviets concerning "Uncle Remus." His situation, which necessitates his cooperation with his former prosecutor from BOSS, becomes increasingly untenable and the novel ends with him being Philbyed out of the West to Moscow where the gates of Purgatory open up for him.

As the complex plot unravels, the reader's sympathies are entirely engaged by this man Castle who loves his wife, her child by a former lover, and the security of his domesticity. He is one of Greene's melancholy, world-weary characters, like Wormold of *Our Man in Havana*, whom the fates victimize for their qualities of wit, imagination, and compassion. In fact the novel is similar in tone to those more playful works Greene has labelled "Entertainments" to distinguish them from fictions he considers weightier. There is a similar use of melodrama and some of the conventional paraphernalia of the spy novel but, above all, *The Human Factor* is fundamentally comic — some parts of it, such as the wedding scene filled with beautiful people and porcelain owls, and the encounters between "C," the head of the service, and the casually villainous doctor who knows how to induce instant but undetectable liver failure, are very funny indeed. The novel's seriousness, of course, is in no way invalidated by its humour. In fact Greene's view of cold-war politics is fundamentally a weary one, perhaps predictably so. His moral position with regard to Castle, his double-agent, has already been stated in a 1968 essay defending *Sonnenkind* Kim Philby, with whom he worked during the war and whom he liked as a man. "Who among us," he wrote in that essay, "has not committed treason to something or someone more important than a country? In Philby's own eyes he was working for the shape of things to come from which his country would benefit." One feels that things are more complicated than that, and in any case Philby was undoubtedly motivated by deeper personal forces than some abstract vision of the future. But there is little of Philby in Maurice Castle except the persistent habit of deception carried on for years. *The Human Factor* is never didactic, however, and it is written with great *sprezzatura* in the original, and perhaps ungentlemanly, meaning of the word. Greene, one of my favourite novelists, has seemed to me to be off form in the last decade; but he has seldom written better than this.

The secret service also forms the background for John Le Carré's *The Honourable Schoolboy*. But where Greene leaves the nuts and bolts of espionage deliberately vague, Le Carré seems to revel in them, and an earlier novel, to which this is a sequel, consisted of very little else. But the nuts and bolts he likes are of a particular kind—the amusing hardware, the funny pistols, death-rays, see-backroscopes, etc., that made Fleming's spy stories such charming and innocent curiosities are not for Le Carré. Instead he seems to delight in the committee meetings, the betrayals over Ministry of Works teacups, the filing systems and paper empires of a bureaucracy. There is more blood-and-thunder in this novel than in its predecessor, but the red-tape entanglements seem to be Le Carré's favoured theme. He writes of them with a zest rather hard to understand and makes his spies seem more like members of an unusually nasty university department plotting coups against the head—and perhaps he is right to do so.

As the novel opens the department known as the "Circus" is in ruins following the defection of a Philby-like figure to the Russians. It has, therefore, lost its honour, its credibility, and its funding and it devolves upon George Smiley, a scholarly and rather immobile spymaster, to restore them. The resemblance to a campus is reinforced not only by Smiley's hobby, a study of arcane German poets of monolithic dullness, but by his cohorts, a huge and boisterous woman from Oxford, good with the five-by-three cards, a lounge lizard with gigolo moustache and "Mississippi dandy's smile," a quiet but deadly hatchet man named Fawn. Surely a representative group—one can see it plotting in the corners of faculty clubs anywhere in the Western world. Much of Smiley's work consists of research. His effort is directed to studying the files left by his traitorous predecessor in the hope of discovering evasions, elisions, and contradictions and, after many man-hours, a line of attack presents itself. They locate a "gold-seam" or flow of money from Moscow to Southeast Asia which has been used to bankroll subversive operations centred on the figure of Drake Ko, a Hong Kong millionaire whose brother, Nelson, lives in Peking—probably as a Russian "mole" or secret agent. Smiley intends to disrupt this operation and he sends as his instrument Jerry Westerby, the honourable schoolboy of the title, to the Far East. Westerby goes on an anabasis in search of Ko which takes him to Bangkok, Vientiane, Phnom Penh—all of which are rendered vividly. This aspect of the novel is very well done—Le Carré handles the *Sturm und Drang* of the spy thriller with great panache thickened into "seriousness" by the inclusion of a huge cast of characters each brought to life, perhaps speciously so, by the Dickensian trick of the single eccentricity or mode of speech. Westerby starts out as a sort of big and affable clown who addresses people as "sport." He falls in love, however, with Ko's girlfriend and grows in dignity until, at the novel's end, he is torn apart by the familiar contradictions between political duty and private emotions.

Thus the novel alternates between the London schemers and the Eastern men of action and it is the London part of it that proves most disappointing. Smiley comes over as a bloodless cipher despite Le Carré's attempts to invest him with personality. The Smiley of the earlier books, particularly *A Murder of Quality*, operated in a shadowy world fundamentally evil in nature and he was capable of experiencing horror at the tasks duty impelled him to perform, and this horror was communicated to the reader. He spends much of his time in this book being congratulated by his colleagues who spend the rest of their time congratulating themselves. The Circus itself has ceased to matter and Le Carré fails to make its existence urgent for us. A peculiar lack of intensity hangs over the novel, a debilitating *prankishness* as though these spies were doing nothing more important than putting pieces of calcium carbide in ink-wells or the school milk. To Greene, a figure like Philby or the men and women opposed to him are, rebels or not, part of a relatively stable value system threatened by individual action. What his characters do *matters*. But *The Human Factor*, excellent though it is, is an oddly dated novel. English culture is rapidly growing towards a bland, mid-Atlantic classlessness in which a Labour cabinet minister is just as likely to be an ex-Etonian as a graduate of the trade union movement. Thus the English novel, whose grand traditional theme has been class and generational conflict, begins to lose its empire without finding another role. Le Carré seems to be one of the poets of this deracination which, though possibly socially desirable, robs English fiction of much of its edge.

1978

Quick! Quick! Phone for the Pound!

Engel, Marian. *Bear*. Toronto: McClelland and Stewart, 1976.
Atwood, Margaret. *Lady Oracle*. Toronto: McClelland and Stewart, 1976.
Williams, David. *The Burning Wood*. Toronto: House of Anansi, 1975.
Richards, David Adams. *Blood Ties*. Ottawa: Oberon, 1976.

Everybody involved in the teaching of literature racket knows the distinction one makes between books that are teachable and books that are not and that these categories do not necessarily refer to literary quality. I remember a discussion with a colleague regarding Arthur Miller's *Death of a Salesman* during which I remarked that I thought it a bad play. Yes, he said, it *is* rather a bad play—*but it teaches well.* He was right—*Salesman* is eminently teachable and conversely there are good plays and especially novels, like those of Evelyn Waugh, that I wouldn't be able to teach at all. Fortunately for the pedagogue's sanity there are books that are both good and teachable—such as Conrad's *The Secret Agent*. *Do cannibalism imagery* (so run my last semester's lecture notes); *do irony; time shifts; point of view. C. thinks it's "Winnie Verloc's story." Is he right? No. Then what? Do conscious vs. unconscious intention, etc.* And there are other novels, both good and bad, that we as teachers turn into allegories as though we were patristic theologians producing Christian documents out of the Old Testament.

All this is relevant when we come to Marian Engel's *Bear*. It is rather a silly novel but, particularly within the context of CanLit, it would teach well. The heroine is an archivist who spends her days in the basement of a historical institute and her lonely nights in a nearby apartment connected to the institute by a sort of tunnel of outside air she gets through as quickly as she can. Her sex-life is correspondingly bleak, for it consists of a weekly roll on the institute's desk with the director amid yellowing maps and papers during which both of them pretend they are shocking the government — a fantasy presumably vital to their achievement of a climax. She is given the opportunity, however, to investigate the literary contents of a house in Northern Ontario left to the Institute by the scion of a pioneering British family. So she journeys north in her car, into the fresh air and a land "hectic with new green." No hard-core student of CanLit need read any further, unless compelled by the Dark and Chauvinistic Gods within him, for he will know as surely as God made little hectic-green apples that the fresh air will revitalize her, that the contact with the land will fortify her for her return to the urban jungle, and that she will not only resolve her identity crises such as they are but will somehow "come to terms with her sexuality." If the reader *does* proceed then he will be soothed by the soft thuds the clichés make falling into place. What may make him uneasy is what Engel does with the animal kingdom.

It turns out there is, along with this house, a large male bear chained up in the yard and part of the heroine's job is to feed and look after it and, as is only to be expected, there lives in the neighbourhood an old, wise, Indian woman whose relationship with the bear and indeed with the land and lakes, plus denizens around the house, is quasi-mystical; and not only that but she speaks that curious brand of substandard English our novelists seem to think suitable for non-Aryan Canadians. For example: "New lady. New lady. Good bear. Good bear." Thus begins a relationship between the natural phenomenon and the city dweller which, at its beginning, puzzles the latter and provokes her into speech: "Bear," she whispered to it, "who and what are you?" This must surely be one of the *dottiest* lines in our entire canon. It is delivered without the hint of a crack of a smile on either the heroine's face or on that of the narrator. Bear's reaction, however, seems to me to be more human: "Bear did not reply, but turned its head towards her with a look of infinite weariness, and closed its eyes."

By this time I was experiencing problems with the weight of my own eyelids, but there was enough residual interest in this bear as a character for me to persist. She lets it into the house to lie by the open fire and what with her own boredom, what with there being nothing on television, and what with there being no television set in the house anyway, and what with the absence of light reading matter other than anecdotes both taxonomic and mythological concerning bears which Engel quotes to stuporous effect — what with one thing and another, then, she starts to masturbate. The bear, interested in what she's doing, this strange New Lady, joins in and begins to lick her and she trains it to concentrate on her vagina where "like no human being she had ever known it persevered in her pleasure." This is actually quite a good scene and it held my interest. Later in the novel she actually tries to mount the bear but, despite the bone in its penis,[1] she is unable to arouse it sufficiently. Then one day both she and the bear are surprised by the latter's majestic erection but, as she crouches eagerly before it, the bear rakes her back with its claws — an incident symbolizing the disjunction between the human and animal worlds; an epiphany at last. "You have to go to your place and I to mine," she pidgins to the bear and thus, reintegrated into the great scheme of things, she drives back to the south with the window open and overhead "the Great Bear and his thirty-seven thousand virgins kept her company."

At first glance the novel didn't seem to me to be teachable at all since at no traditional level of meaning — allegorical, tropological, anagogical — beyond the literal does it cohere. It struck me as a failure even within its own terms for the change in the heroine's consciousness towards which the book strives is either totally unrealized or trivial beyond belief. The major insight, if you can so dignify the climactic episode, reduces to the statement "humans cannot successfully mate with beasts" which, as any soldier in the Black Watch Regiment could've told Engel, isn't even true. On the other hand I'd heard they think a lot of this book "back East" so perhaps it was either pornography or what passes in Toronto for Liberation Literature. Is it, in fact, pornography? Well, it is certainly solemn enough but I was not personally aroused by it. I would much sooner have sneaked off into some quiet corner with my volumes of *Stag*, *Dude*, *Leather*, *Playgirl*, *Playboy*, and *Discipline*. It then occurred to me that its erotic power was faint because I am a male (a human and thus boneless male, but male nevertheless) and that I should check out its arousal power on some women friends of mine since I knew that the fantasy of loveless but passionate sex with some huge, hairy, and uncaring beast is fairly widespread among the Gentle Sex. But they all denied that the novel held any sexual interest and asked me to go away and leave them in peace with a copy of *Story of O.*

Honest pornography, then, it is not and I turned in desperation to the dust-jacket to find out what the establishment had made of it: "The theme of *Bear* is one of the most significant and pressing in Canada in our time—the necessity for us who are newcomers to the country, with hardly four hundred years of acquaintance with it, to ally ourselves with the spirit of one of the most ancient lands in the world." In this passage Robertson Davies, an otherwise worthy and respectable writer (he did the one about the stone in the snowball—good—quite teachable) has reached with one short, effortless trope (done, apparently, with the left hand) that far-off, most arcane plateau—home of the purest drivel—towards which slog for a lifetime but with little hope of achievement my hardest-working colleagues.[2] He has thus brought off a considerable coup. So the novel is irritating not because of its theme, style, or author—who is presumably an energetic lady merely trying to make a dollar and a literary reputation—but because it provokes powerful literary figures such as Davies into making wildly extravagant (if meaningless) claims for it based on some vague and extra-literary nationalistic feeling.

Let me quote two more heavies from the McClelland and Stewart stables and I am done with *Bear*. First, Margaret Laurence: ". . . an outstanding novel, both earthy and mythical, which leads into the human self and also outward to suggest and celebrate the mystery of life itself." Life is a mystery, certainly, but the reader will not find it celebrated here. The human self into which the story leads is a self at the most primitive level of development while the mythical is not organically related to the narrative but is thrown in as a padding the cost of which, as they say in the advertising business, is "passed on to the consumer." Now Margaret Atwood: "*Bear* is a strange and wonderful book, plausible as kitchens, but shapely as a folk tale, and with the same disturbing resonance." Atwood knows about this mysterious and disturbing "resonance" because she caught it in *Surfacing*, a very good novel, just at the point where it was growing into the Canadian consciousness and before it became kitsch. Notice, though, she is just as reluctant as the other two to say what the book is actually *about*—the non-resonant sex-play between a woman and a bear. But at least she and the others enable me to teach this novel if it ever comes to the crunch: Bear—*do imitation versus originality; do literary nationalism and compare/contrast Spenser, Shakespeare, Dante. Throw in some Reich . . . but, above all, use Nabokov's book*

189

on *Gogol for the essay on "poshlost"* — an invaluable word that describes perfectly the novel and the three puffs on its dust-jacket.

Canada badly needs a Gogol of its own. Atwood, like the rest of us, falls short of those exalted heights but there is something faintly Chichikhovian about the heroine of *Lady Oracle*. The novel opens with her attempt to establish herself in a small Italian town after faking her own death by water in Lake Ontario. She puts pen to paper, for no very clear fictional "reason," to tell the story of her life, the central image for which seems to be the emergence of the exotic butterfly from the unattractive and mundane grub. Thus she starts out as a fat, though jolly, child and, under the twin stimuli of a legacy conditional on her losing weight and a dose of blood-poisoning, she succeeds in breaking out from her cocoon of lard to become like a "lush Rossetti portrait, radiating intensity." Attached to this rather intimidating figure and trying to float free are two even more rarified personae; a writer of Gothic novels named Louisa K. Delacourt and a poet, Joan Foster, who seeks inspiration by means of a planchette. The men to whom she is attracted are, like her, walking panoplies of mask and anti-mask — a bogus Polish count who writes doctor and nurse stories under the name of Mavis Quilp, a young conformist tuned into radical politics, a flamboyant non-artist whose real name is Chuck — each trying desperately to escape from his basic ordinariness. The narrative, which also involves blackmailers, mediums, flashers, Girl Guide mistresses with names like Miss Flegg, eccentric parents, etc., is complex and presented with much wit and *brio*. In fact, the spirit of play dominates this novel entirely and perhaps I should quote a typical passage. Here the heroine fights with her mother:

> I shouldn't have given away my plans. She looked at me with an expression of rage, which changed quickly to fear, and said, "God will not forgive you! God will never forgive you!" Then she took a paring knife from the kitchen counter — I had been using it to spread cottage cheese on my RyKrisp — and stuck it into my arm, above the elbow. It went through my sweater, pricked the flesh, then bounced out and fell to the floor. Neither of us could believe she had done this. We both stared, then I picked up the paring knife, put it down on the kitchen table, and placed my left hand casually over the wound in my sweater, as if I myself had inflicted it and was trying to conceal it. "I think I'll make myself a cup of tea," I said conversationally. "Would you like one, Mother?"

"That would be nice," she said. "A cup of tea picks you up." She sat down unsteadily on one of the kitchen chairs. "I'm going shopping on Friday," she said as I filled the kettle. "I don't suppose you'd like to come."

"That would be nice," I said.

Gogolian "poshlost" lurks here like a trace-element in the deliberate crossing of the realm of high tragedy (the mother's rage, her calling upon God, the stabbing) with that of the everyday (RyKrisp, cottage cheese, nice cups of tea) in such a way that the latter trivializes the former into a sort of low-rent *schwärmerei*. It is perhaps too crude for Gogol and more in the style of *Beyond the Fringe*, but it is unified perfectly with the central issues of the novel. These have to do with Atwood's concept of the "human self" (see above) which, at least as far as *Lady Oracle* is concerned, is bound up with that of theatre. Each stage personage acts out a series of emotions against a backdrop of trivia while the actor beneath the role stands back mentally trying to puzzle out (a) who he really is and (b) would it matter if he knew the answer. Thus the narrator treats stabbings, love, marriage, success as though they were towels, sweaters, doughnuts, underpants, RyKrisp (she is very good with brand-names) — all of them are equally bewildering. Life and the Gothic novel get interwoven in her mind because the life she leads *is* a Gothic novel. I am aware that I am making *Lady Oracle* sound more ponderous with theme, image, comic device — with *teachability*, in other words — than it actually is. It is an unpretentious, comic novel designed, very successfully, to entertain and the reader, parched by the *longueurs* of *Bear*, will come upon what amounts to a far more serious work of art with delight.

Now we come to two sub-Faulknerian regionalists, one of whom writes about the Saskatchewan prairies, the other about northern New Brunswick. David Williams' *The Burning Wood* deals with the cultural disjunction between the Plains Indians and the Fundamentalist White farmers. Its protagonist, named Joshua, is brought up by the latter but feels himself inexorably drawn towards the former. The odd thing about Joshua is that even as a young boy he is bald and this affliction is regarded, by his family, as a natural and Divine result of his great-grandfather's sexual adventures on the Indian reserve, a place of iniquity which, the family hopes, will one day be swept clean, specifically by Joshua himself and his Christian Fundamentalist faith. The Indians, on the other hand, see Joshua's baldness as a magical sign of Divine favour and thus admit him, though tentatively at first, into their society where he becomes renamed "Scalp-by-Manitou." Delighted with his new identity he leads his new comrades on a buffalo hunt but, hampered by the shortage in this part of the country of the traditional buffalo, they are forced to make do with the neighbour's cattle and stolen, lumbering, Clydesdale horses. What begins as a farce ends tragically with the death by goring of Joshua's Indian friend. This episode is the climax of the book after which the narrative seems to me to become rather incoherent. The next section deals with a strong and tensely written conflict between Joshua's father and a next-door neighbour which seems unrelated to what has preceded it, as though it had been written as a separate piece. Then follows a reconciliation scene between Joshua and his grandfather wherein the latter delivers himself of a death-bed revelation, though what the revelation is I do not know. Perhaps, through no fault of Williams, my attention was beginning to wander.

There are several excellent things about this book. The Indians and their culture are not presented sentimentally; there is nothing about their way of life held necessarily superior to anything that Western European civilization has to offer. Similarly the rigid and authoritarian Fundamentalists, villains of so many legends concerning the evils of the Protestant Work Ethic, are depicted as also honest, industrious, and solicitous about the spiritual development of themselves and other people. Thus Williams is to be congratulated on rejecting the fashionable, melodramatic attitude: Indian man, good; White man, bad. Both groups are portrayed sympathetically and the virtues and vices of each presented with considerable detachment. I enjoyed very much the hell-fire sermon in which the Indian reservation is likened to the City of Jericho. I did not much care for the biblical language carried over into the rest of the novel, nor the long, sidewinding, Faulknerian sentences in those places where Williams attempts epic. But it is an interesting and very talented first novel.

I do not feel particularly competent to say a great deal about David Adams Richards' second novel, *Blood Ties*. Regionalism has never attracted me very much and naturalism, in all its aridity, even less. Thus I was able to read the novel only with the greatest difficulty and it has left no residue whatsoever. Perhaps it is the author's intention to minimize the distinctions between one of his characters and the next by means of pronoun confusion, to leave the reader vague as to whom he is talking about, and to stop me cold with passages like the following:

192

She sighed. Irene said nothing. The old one's head seemed weighted. They turned her left and began to walk just as slowly, ever so slowly so that it was tiring for her just to move, through to the small hallway and then into the washroom. Irene shut the door. The pink tile of the bathroom walls, because Maufat last winter spent two months doing it over, because Irene had said:

"Don't you think it needs to be done, perhaps Lorne can help you do it." He did it alone because Lorne said he couldn't help — though he came over once or twice in the nights when Betty came with Irene. So he uprooted the floor and redid the walls. Sometimes Cathy came over and watched him work when he was working alone with the sound of *her* upstairs.

Intensive textual analysis establishes precisely and beyond doubt that the "she" of the first sentence refers either to (a) the old one, (b) Irene (c) a girl called Cathy mentioned in the preceding paragraph, or (*d*) anybody else. What does the reader make of the quasi-Faulknerian "because" in the sentence beginning "The pink tile"? Is this Stream-of-Consciousness? In which case why is the third-person narrator coming on like Benjy in *The Sound and the Fury*? Who are all these people — Lorne, Maufat, Betty, etc.? The novel's been on for thirteen pages and I still don't know. Why should I care about this pink-tiled bathroom? Is there some line-by-line significance escaping my sensitivities coarsened, as they are, by many years of reading for enjoyment? Why is Richards making me *work* so hard? What's in it for me? Etc.

I admit that I have a tin ear for this sort of thing — its cadences are either non-existent or too subtle for me to grasp. Therefore, I deliver this novel over to the reader. If he can make sense of the passage I've just quoted, if he *likes* it, then I wish him, in all sincerity, the joy of it.

Notes

[1] It'll show you how out of touch I am with Basic Reality when I confess I did not know that bears were thus endowed. But I know about other animals. Eskimos near to us used to carve phallic bones belonging, I believe, to narwhales into rod-shaped sculptures called "ooziacs." This explains the nickname, Dewziac, for the aircraft bringing to the various DEW-Line sites the visiting dignitaries from parent companies in the United States.

[2] The reader may think this a hyperbole in which case let me ask him whom does Davies mean by "us"? Who's been here 400 years? (Personally I

arrived in 1953.) Why do "we" need to "ally(?) ourselves" with the "spirit" (paraclete? Great Spirit?) of the land? And what is the significance of "ancient" here? Geological? Anthropological? His remarks are rubbish however you look at them.

1977

The Novel in Lesbos — and Beyond

Rule, Jane. *Against the Season*. New York: McCall Publishing House, 1971.

Grossvogel, David I. *Limits of the Novel*. Ithaca, N.Y.: Cornell Univ. Press, 1968.

Jane Rule's novel is set in a small, decaying port somewhere in the western United States. Her central character is a crippled, elderly lady of independent means named Amelia whose sister, Beatrice, dies shortly before the novel's action begins. Beatrice, however, figures in the narrative through her diaries which, according to her last instructions, are supposed to be burned. A mild suspense plays over Amelia's reading of these diaries but we discover little of interest about the sisters' relationship except that it is based on mutual need tempered, in Beatrice's case, by a sort of waspish irony; "some of us can be grateful," she writes, "there are cripples who need us." The passions (such as they are) of the two women are repressed by and sacrificed to the necessity of maintaining a facade of social grace and virtue and their usefulness to their society takes the somewhat ambivalent form of providing jobs as maidservants for a long string of pregnant but unmarried girls.

Unpromising material for a modern novel, the reader thinks as he lets *Against the Season* slip from his nerveless fingers while he reaches, somewhat lethargically, for his Mrs. Gaskell, but the book is enriched by a variety of minor figures such as a thirty-six-year-old spinsterish librarian attempting an asexual relationship with a backgroundless bank manager of mysterious tastes; a female furniture renovator of Greek parentage whose wish to marry well in accordance with the traditions of her race is complicated by her indulgence towards the various women attracted to her; a young male cousin of Amelia's who wafts rather feebly between homo- and heterosexuality; another old spinster inured, this one, to solitude, whose peace is disturbed by an ancient widower who wishes to cope with his own loneliness by marrying her but who drops dead of a heart attack before he has a chance to do so. The cast is rounded out by a sprinkling of unwed mothers and the Lesbian social worker responsible for them.

Since there is very little narrative interest the reader is thrown back on Rule's resources as a psychologist — on her evocations of the emotions her characters experience towards one another and on the subtlety with which she follows the labyrinthine thwartings, denials, and expressions of these emotions. The trouble is, however, that Rule fails to make me give much of a damn about any of them. The feelings are plausible enough and I do not deny the author's insight but they are embodied in characters too feebly presented to carry them. It is not that Rule's characters are "flat" — they are convincing enough as "real" people but "real" people thinned down and etiolated. Perhaps the most dynamic character in the book, for example, is the one called Agate, last of Amelia's pregnant housemaids. We are told (not by the narrator — Rule is too cautious for that) by other characters in the book that she is rebellious and difficult. Yet in spite of a certain amount of flippant talking back to her social worker there is no evidence, when Agate appears, that she is any more than an honest and energetic young woman whose basic respect for her elders takes the very acceptable form of affectionate mockery. This, I think, is supposed to be her attitude at the *end* of the novel where the author wants Agate to "come to terms" with her life.

Part of the problem is that Rule wants not only to "imitate" the love lives of a group of characters in a small town, but she wishes, through this imitation, to communicate a sense of human "seasons." Consequently she shows us, a little too systematically, old, middle-aged, and young people with the dead and unborn present and intermingling but off-stage. Agate, for example, is made to carry, along with her child, a symbolic weight. She makes Amelia burn the diaries and she steers Amelia's young cousin into non-masturbatory sex. Both these acts are represented as life-affirming though *why* they are so remains unclear. The point is that she is over-constructed within the novel as a kind of recusant and irrepressible life-force — over-constructed to the point where one is distracted by the faint but persistent squeak of machinery.

What Rule is attempting to do in this book is not only worth doing but, in my opinion, extremely difficult to do. She has to get me assenting to the reality of her small world before I'll assent to the reality of her pagan life-cycle. She has chosen to work within "the novel of plausibility," a form whose energy has been sapped by formal psychology and the rise of the social sciences. Her best bet, I think, would've been to have entered the novel herself as a narrator or as one of the characters and to have created a distinctive voice. She could have beguiled me with some interesting prose (or maybe not — I spotted only one attempt where she tries to break out of the flat, impersonal style; one of the characters, we are told, has "jade and jaded eyes" and, if this is a sample of interesting prose, Rule is quite right to avoid it). She could have chosen to work with characters who are not repressed and devitalized and would have thus avoided risking a rather lifeless book.

While I'm on the subject of lifeless books I want to take the opportunity of saying a few belated words about Professor Grossvogel's *Limits of the Novel* which, though published in 1968, has only just recently been received. It interests me because it purports to be an account of the "evolutions of a form from Chaucer to Robbe-Grillet" and I turned to the Chaucer section first since that, as we say in the academic racket, is my field. It is not, manifestly, Professor Grossvogel's:

> For [Andreas Capellanus], love . . . is the supreme good whose efficacy engenders other goods: it gives a man the kind of character that renders his bodily defects insignificant; it confers a nobility of the soul that transcends class distinctions; it commands the virtues of generosity, obedience, humility, and discretion in the lover.

Had Grossvogel read further into Capellanus he would have found this:

> If you wish to practise the system, you will obtain, as a careful reading of this little book will show you, all the delights of the

flesh in fullest measure; but the grace of God, the companionship of the good, and the friendship of praiseworthy men you will with good reason be deprived of, and you will do great harm to your good name, and it will be difficult for you to obtain the honours of this world.

Capellanus may or may not be serious about the first two sections of his work where he codifies the behaviour of lovers, but there is no doubt of the seriousness with which he retracts his position in the third section and delivers a fanatic if conventional diatribe against women. Thus Grossvogel's statement that "Criseyde is the ideal object of Capellanus" takes on an ambiguity that Grossvogel himself seems unaware of but which is certainly built into the poem. In fact, Grossvogel seems totally unable to account for one of the most striking features of Chaucer's work — its generally Christian and specifically Boethian substructure. It is completely untrue, for example, that "Troilus is one of the great figures in literature that are brought down through virtue in love: he loses the object of his affection because of too great submission to it." Troilus loses Criseyde largely because of the political situation of Troy, a situation over which he has no control, but the point is not that he loses Criseyde but that he loses his "pleyn felicitee" — his full happiness — by attaching it to one of the "goods of Fortune." This is not a subjective matter: it is the chief, explicit, philosophical point of the poem. Similarly Grossvogel ignores another of the poem's major themes — the distinction that Chaucer makes between Courtly Love in its sex-in-the-head aspect and sexual love. It is the former that creates a comic character out of Troilus in the first half of the poem and the latter which "matures" him and gives him a tragic dimension in the second half. Troilus, it is true, is so paralysed by his expected confrontation with Criseyde that he prays for help to a whole pantheon of deities including, comically enough, the Goddess of Chastity, and eventually he is literally thrown into bed by Pandarus. Once there, recovered, he ceases to be a Courtly Clown and becomes a lover:

> This Troilus in armes gan hire streyne,
> And seyde, "O swete as evere mot I gon,
> Now be ye kaught, now is ther but we tweyne!
> Now yeldeth yow, for other bote is non!"

What, then, is the statement that "Troilus . . . [has] the twin visages of the ideal hero of courtly romance, who is meek in the bedroom but masterful on the battlefield" supposed to mean? If it is intended as a generalization about such heroes it is a highly inaccurate and misleading one; if we are asked to believe that "Troilus is meek in the bedroom" we would have to twist the poem out of its shape in order to do so.

Since Grossvogel's handling of this Chaucer material places his ability to interpret a text in a somewhat lurid light, I approached the rest of his book with a good deal of scepticism. Unfortunately, Grossvogel's prose is not designed, at least when dealing with abstract matters, to either communicate or clarify. "The artifact is a metaphor ... and is therefore, ultimately, a thing, though its objective tangibility varies according to its ontological mode" is a fair example of his pretentious, obscurantist, tautological style. If the reader will permit me a metaphor (ultimately a Thing), I found it difficult to scoop from under the dross of the author's verbiage the refined metal of a definite argument. The following, however, is what I think he wants to say: the artist generally begins with a powerful urge to communicate a truth, an urge that transcends minor impulses such as the spirit of play, desire to decorate, etc. The first writers (of antiquity) begin as storytellers able to relate their work to mass audience with which they share a collective social vision. As individualistic concerns become uppermost, however, simple mimesis through straight narrative loses its power to command the reader's assent. The story no longer imitates that reader's world. Writers must, therefore, develop other strategies with which to inveigle their increasingly sophisticated reader/critics. One such strategy is the comparative subordination of the narrative to the lyric—an appeal to the reader's moods, yearnings, or perceptions —rather than to his recognition of outer surfaces and events. This fails when the reader and the hero of the narrative no longer share a common ground and when the reader develops a new interest in the pattern or form of the writing rather than in its lyric effect. The writer then tries to engage the reader on the level of his intelligence as a critic and presents him with, among other things, allegory. The novel proper begins when the writer tries to create characters with which the critical reader can partly identify and place them within a pattern of sufficient scope to keep that reader engaged. Grossvogel attempts to trace the growing sophistication with which novelists fight their duels with their increasingly critical readers culminating in the recent experiments of such writers as Robbe-Grillet, who, by attempting to remove the narrative altogether, hope to turn the novel into an absolute

199

phenomenological statement providing the reader with a "pure phenomenological object."

Grossvogel's handling of some of these authors, particularly Kafka and Robbe-Grillet, is neither incompetent nor totally uninteresting. He demonstrates the self-defeating aims of those writers who, in order to command the reader's assent to their "truths," hope to create a completely alienated reader and this discussion of the so-called avant-garde is probably the most valuable part of his book—the historical material, and Grossvogel implicitly acknowledges it, is heavily dependent on Arnold Kettle whose *Introduction to the English Novel* covers the same ground and has the advantage of being written in a recognizable modern language.

As one who writes novels myself I would agree with much of the argument I've just laid, by default, on Grossvogel. It seems very likely that most novelists, certainly nowadays, are aware as they begin a novel that they are embarking on a duel with a potential reader. I think it is going too far to assert, as Grossvogel does, that the complexities of the form have developed out of the writer's sense of urgency regarding the acceptance of his "truth." The spirit of play which Grossvogel denigrates, is, in my opinion, the chief motivation for writing a novel in the first place. Even those writers of the Cinque Ports School of High Seriousness, Earnest James and Lugubrious Conrad, were, whether they knew it or not, dominated at least as far as technique goes, by the urge to play. It would've been hard for them, as well as for their followers, to admit this since to the Puritan consciousness art must *teach* as well as delight. Yet both James and Conrad chose the essentially playful form of the non-mimetic novel over more didactic forms of writing, and their "truth," if it is a truth, is that Aristotelian mimesis is impossible since nobody really knows what's going on. At this point I hear over my shoulder the ghost of Cocteau (was it Cocteau?) whose injunction to the artist was "Astonish us!" The serious novelist, in my opinion, wishes to astonish people far more than he wishes to communicate a truth. (Why this is so is anybody's guess—perhaps a lack of progressive toilet-training when young.) The novelist arranges little schizophrenic slivers of his personality, projections of his *agons*, nightmares, baked or half-baked moral judgements, into a prose pattern he hopes will astonish and delight if only himself. It is not, I think, possible to astonish the reader with accuracy of representation of reality any more. Why repeat, even if one possessed his enormous talent, the work of Emile Zola? Hence the post-Cinque Ports concern with angle of narration, point of view, reliability and unreliability of storyteller, and so on. And this is why a talented writer like Jane Rule is, I believe, wasting her time writing a plausible novel like *Against the Season*. There's no longer any point in it. It is too static and psychological to win a mass audience and too formless to attract the critical reader, the answers to whose questions (who tells it? how does she know? why choose *this* event over *that* possibility? etc.) the author fails to build into the structure of her work.

1971

A New Model from Detroit—
Good Vacuum: Slow Brakes

Oates, Joyce Carol. *Do with Me What You Will.* New York:
Vanguard; Toronto: Copp Clark, 1973.

Do with Me What You Will opens very promisingly with a
progression of brilliant and powerful scenes. In the first a seedy,
middle-aged man abducts a small girl from the playground of her
school—a madman, the reader thinks, pederast, perhaps, or flasher—
but he turns out to be the girl's father come to claim illegal custody of
his child. He takes her on a wild anabasis across the States to
California, periodically taunting the girl's mother, his ex-wife, with
insane letters. In San Francisco his mind goes completely and he
vanishes, perhaps to commit suicide, leaving this helpless infant to be
discovered by neighbours and the police who deliver her back to her
mother. This woman is strongly orientated towards success and sets
herself and her daughter up by promising marriage to a rich and
doting businessman whose money she runs off with. The action
switches to a curiously grisly and well-conceived murder at a luxurious
house in Detroit but at this point the reader has to put the book aside.
He does so regretfully, but he has the lawn to mow, a shower to take,
and there is honey, still, for tea. In any case he ought to be preparing a
lecture, or at least reading the assigned text so as to keep one step
ahead of his students. At this stage in the novel, though, Joyce Carol

Oates is a step or two ahead of *him*. The situations she has created excite and intrigue him and her narrative has been driven along by a taut and agile prose. He tries to concentrate on other tasks, but the novel lures him and he finds that he is hooked. His copy of *The Faerie Queene* drops from his nerveless fingers. He yields.

During his absence from it, however, something seems to have come over this novel. As he tries to gather its themes and characters together in his head he experiences an odd muzziness, as though he were wearing a shirt with a 14½ inch collar. The abducted girl, whose name is Elena—"the year's most transfixing heroine" as the dust-jacket says—does not seem to be human in any sense he has learned to recognize. She has grown up to be a very beautiful woman but she seems stupid and vacuous in a way that causes his eyes to glaze. Her ambitious mother has succeeded in marrying her off to a powerful lawyer—*omnipotent lawyer*—whose hair greys at the temples. He enters the novel with a proud, conquering smile as though delighted with his recent, lucky escape from the pages of a Harlequin Romance. He defends the Detroit murderer and gets him acquitted, thus attracting to himself mixed feelings of love and hate from the murderer's son. The latter becomes a lawyer in his own right. He specializes in defending blacks, radicals, and otherwise innocent young people busted for possession. He runs into Elena and they begin a love affair . . . .

But what *is* all this? Why is this book turning into soap-opera? Or into one of those mid-cult novels like *The View from Pompey's Head*? What's Ms. Oates up to? The prose, which seemed so alive, no longer compels the reader since it seems directed to no purpose. Instead it has become, taken in bulk, inexorable—tight-lipped and unrhetorical—*anal*, in fact. The reader's attention starts to wander so that he even tries to keep focused on the page by running his finger-tip along each line. *The finger-tip keeps grinding to a halt.* Wordsworthian "vacant musings" enter his mind and take it over. Baffled, the reader returns to the dust-jacket to find out what this novel is all about. "Romantic love," Oates tells him, "is one of our Western religions and must be respected as such . . . . But the West is also a culture of Law: American society will never be transformed by stray acts of violence . . . it will be transformed only through the courts. And they, in turn, will not be transformed until the men who run them are changed, individual by individual."

That's O.K. then. The book is about the Conflict Between the Law and Romantic Love. But the reader is only moderately soothed by this bromide. What she means, he thinks, is that it's a *thesis novel.* This expression doesn't look too good. He goes to his dictionary to check the spelling of *roman à thèse.* He nods wisely to himself, however, if only to conceal the fact that he doesn't really know what she's talking about. While she's been explaining her views to the reader her characters, in their middle-class fashion, have begun a kind of adulterer's quadrille behind her back. It is true that they are all of them connected with law and crime; equally true that they are given to stopping what they're doing to deliver abstract and banal utterances concerning the law. But the talk doesn't seem to have much to do with their various predicaments. And of these predicaments there is a serious one they share in common — they are all of them bores. Marvin is a smooth bore; Jack is a loud-mouthed, ill-tempered bore; and his wife, Rachel, is boring in her shrewishness. Elena is the sign and symbol, essence and existence, of boredom. It takes a better novelist than Oates to carry this kind of thing off.

The novel improves somewhat as the author introduces a young American guru in the process of being martyred and driven crazy by the forces of Law and Order. She is in fact at her best when presenting madness, obsession, and the grotesque. The guru, the murderer, Elena's parents, are certainly the best things the book has to offer. But in general the whole enterprise falls apart, undermined by two major flaws. The first is the chalk-and-blackboard fallacy — that is, that you can start with a theme or proposition and successfully illustrate it and flesh it out by means of fiction. The second flaw is its grimly humourless manner. At one point in the novel one of the characters says: "The only people who make jokes are serious people. You need intelligence, moral intelligence, to make jokes. You wouldn't understand that." Neither, on the evidence of this novel, does Oates. Even without its structural faults *Do with Me What You Will* is far too solemn to be taken seriously.

1974

After You, Jack London

Garner, Hugh. *One Damn Thing After Another.* Toronto: McGraw-Hill Ryerson, 1973.

Some writers attempt to advance the limits of the medium in which they work; others are content to remain within the conventions inherited from their predecessors. These are the two main streams in modern fiction; neither is in my opinion inherently superior or more serious than the other, and, to quote Fluellen, there are salmons in both. Hugh Garner places himself, fairly accurately, I gather, in the ranks of those hard-working, professional writers whose self-imposed task is to entertain their readers without troubling them with unnecessary adjectives, experiments in technique, or heterodox opinions; the ranks, in other words, of John P. Marquand and John O'Hara. Fidelity to real-life (sic) is their aim and straightforwardness their manner. Such fiction is usually harmless, kitchen-sinkish, and often best-selling. I read, many years ago, some of Garner's short stories and can remember about them only that they were flat, bland, technically uninteresting, and by a man called Garner just then floating belly upwards into the stagnant waters of CanLit. I haven't read his novels but his autobiography makes me feel that, given a month's leave-of-absence, they might be worth a cold eye.

One Damn Thing After Another is not a bland book by any

means. For one thing it is an example of the "unreliable narrator" mode of discourse and, God help us all, could be taught as such in any freshman literature course. This is not to say that Garner tells us lies: I'm quite sure the factual information he gives us—that he was brought up in Toronto's "Cabbagetown" slum quarter, that he went on an extended walk-about during the depression, that he fought in the Spanish Civil War and later, as a seaman, in World War II, that he is intermittently a lush ("has an alcohol problem" as we say nowadays in our mealy-mouthed enlightened fashion), that he has in his time been a prodigious boozer, whoremaster, brawler, and braggart, that he has buckled his swash in every province in Canada and in every state in the Union—is true and verifiable. No, what I mean is that the things he asserts about himself—that he is antinomian, rambunctious, and rebarbative (I use such words solely because Garner himself would never use them in a piece of writing though he undoubtedly knows them—are reasserted so many times the reader wonders what he has to hide. For example he tells us so emphatically that he is a loner, confident of his talent, that any reader capable of racking up a score of half-a-dozen on an I.Q. test just *knows* that Garner is a sensitive, other-directed man anxious to receive the signs and signals of approval, and what clinches this knowledge is the repetitive listings of contests won, monies accrued, and contracts made together with such loving descriptions of what the Governor-General's wife said to Garner on the occasion of his receiving the award for fiction and what Garner turned round and said to *her*. The burly, rough, tough, Prole mask that Garner adopts wouldn't even deceive a Nixon supporter, and I feel like paraphrasing Max Eastman's remark "come out from behind that hair on your chest, Hemingway, we know you!" So I think we have to forgive Garner his hard-hat Bunkerisms and beer-parlor, loud-mouthed crudities, strained though our charity may be by the repeated attacks on "bearded wierdos," radicals, intellectuals, spinsters, "women's libbers," homosexuals, "string-haired broads," and so on. (He never, give him credit, refers to women as "slits" but one feels that "slits" lurks always on the periphery of his vocabulary.) An integral part of the mask, of course, is his sentimentality about World War II, which brings to mind those Saturday nights when the boys get together to warble lachrymose renderings of "We'll Meet Again" down in the Legion beer-halls, coupled with a mindless love of winding up anecdotes with phrases like "so I told him to perform an impossible sexual act" or "I told him to stuff it where the monkey stuffs his nuts." What few pictures he gives us of his family life read like a parody of Ring Lardner's "Golden Honeymoon":

During the nineteen-sixties we took longer and longer trips across Canada, to Mexico City by car during which we drove fifteen hundred miles through Mexico, to Florida several times, New Orleans, to Nassau on a cruise ship from Miami, and finally a trip to Europe, which was the first one for my wife. My final driving project was to drive through every state in the continental United States except Alaska, and this we did over a few summers. We went everywhere . . . from Fort Kent, Maine to San Isidro, California, and from Blaine, Washington to Key West, Florida . . . .

Despite Garner's self-acclaimed professionalism his book is sloppy, repetitive, unrevealing, and, with certain exceptions, feeble. Slabs of previously published magazine work are juxtaposed with tedious details concerning their first appearance. There is, for example, a piece on landladies and another on Toronto Island. Both read like defanged and castrated Mencken. The point of view is . . . shee-ut! I've had it with this! I'm goddamn tired of coming on like one a them faggoty academics. So you know what I'm gonna do now? I'm gonna sit right down and write that ornery ole son-of-a-bitch a letter:

Dear Hugh,
Just a line to let you know I kinda liked your book even though I been saying some bad things about it. But a reviewer's *gotta* say a few bad things about a book because if he don't ain't nobody gonna believe him when he praises it. But, shit, I don't have to tell you how it is in this racket — everybody's gotta turn a trick the best way they can, though what Fred Candelaria pays for a review wouldn't keep either of us in gin for more than about three-quarters of an hour. Anyway, what I liked about your autobiography is that once in a while I found myself identifying with its hero. I wasn't brought up in no Cabbagetown, but I spent my boyhood in a place called Battersea — that part of London which lies between Price's Candle Factory and Morgan's Crucible Works where we used to play tennis with hammers. Then again I was too young for the war but I remember the Blitz all right — particularly that day a goddamn Messerschmidt come down our street about four hundred miles an hour. I was outside at the time so I ducked into the nearest doorway which happened to belong to F. W. Woolworth and

Company—it was about the only time I've been glad to get into a Woolworth's but I learnt this about myself—if ever I were to hear another shot fired in anger I'd get my arse into the nearest five-and-dime—in a flurry of green shit and yellow feathers. I was too young, once again, for the Spanish Civil War, though I remember the Basque children coming to London, but I respect you for having gone over there. You weren't conscripted; there were no social pressures on you; shit, you weren't even a goddamn communist. Ain't nobody gonna take that away from you, Hugh. And you wanna know something else? That part of your book that's about Spain is the best thing in it. By a long way. It's almost literature. And from a literary point of view you can stuff the rest of your book up your Khyber.

I was in the army, though, after the war and that experience is a good thing to have behind you—like Dachau. Your "glasshouse" reminiscences were right on! I got a few of my own so those bits really made me feel as though we should get together in a beer parlour one a these days and mebbe have a coupla beers. But I got worried, as I read the book, about the way you kept saying if there were two types of man you couldn't get inside the skin of, one was a psychotic and the other a homosexual. Why did you *keep* saying that, Hugh? Made me feel I perhaps ought to keep away from that beer parlour after all. I don't think you *are* those things, but if one day you find yourself drifting that way my advice to you is—relax. Enjoy it. Close your eyes and think of Canada. Who *gives* a shit anyway?

You got this little joke about how you might be a candidate for the Nobel prize on the grounds that most of the prizewinners are drunks. Maybe that's why you found it so hard to stay off the sauce. But what with one thing and another, Hugh, I don't really see you as a Nobel prize-winner—not on present showing. You're a good professional writer, though, even if you kid yourself a little. Here are two things you kid yourself over which you ought to think about. First, you ain't that independent of mind. No writer is, professional or otherwise, because of the nature of the activity itself: i.e., reaching out for and holding an audience. Second, you ain't classless. No writer is that either. I ain't gonna put you in a class, Hugh, but you might think about it.

Well, Hugh, must close now. It's good to know you ain't no goddamn faggot, though I never said you was. Keep writing, hey? And I hope this finds you as it leaves me ... in the pink, ha! ha!

1974

The Soft Underbelly

Mitchell, Ken. *Everybody Gets Something Here.* Toronto: Macmillan, 1977.

Just recently in Hawaii I experienced an epiphany concerning what could be termed the "soft underbelly" of Canadian culture. On three consecutive nights there my sleep was disturbed by a party of whooping and screaming people in the next room — a party which, on investigation, turned out to be the Canadian contingent of some group tour. They were very hospitable, inviting me to join them, but I declined on the grounds that not since my early days in Canada as an encyclopaedia salesman had I got stoned in a hotel room. It struck me as odd behaviour, particularly for tourists who, almost by definition, are people on the move, and I wondered whether this very *sedentary* form of tourism is a Canadian characteristic—perhaps an aspect of the famous Fortress Mentality. One cannot, for example, imagine an *American* tourist locking himself in his room to get drunk — he would be out in the town investigating the bars and so, a step or two behind him and in the hope of copping a free drink, would his English counterpart be. I was curious enough to discuss the matter with a colleague, one of our department's token Canadians, and he was very surprised that I had not noticed the phenomenon before. *The Grey Cup Syndrome* was what he called it.

209

Of course! The Grey Cup! The hotel room party is naturally appropriate to a country whose liquor laws are even now illiberal by most civilized standards and whose climate is usually too bastorial to allow the investigation of down-town bars. One can see how the habit's become engrained. On the other hand "The Grey Cup" is a good portmanteau phrase quintessentializing the Soft Underbelly of our culture and indicative of the fact that it is unconnected with social class, education, or income bracket: doctors, lawyers, politicians, bus drivers, nickel smelters, construction workers—the Soft Underbelly encompasses them all. Nor has it much to do with the old hostility between the "hip" and the Philistine: the Soft Underbelly bears no malice, nor is it hostile to things it doesn't understand and for the most part is totally unaware of the existence of the "hip." It is idle for you, reader of magazines like *The Fiddlehead*, to feel superior towards it. In fact, though most elements of the Soft Underbelly have to move their lips while reading the sports section of their local papers, though the phrase "classical music" means, perhaps, Julie Andrews singing "My Favourite Things," though the name "Margaret Atwood" might suggest to them some nineteen-forties skating queen and "Northrop Frye" a Winnipeg Blue Bomber, though their idea of entertainment might be to re-enact, on the island graveyard of Captain Cook and King Kamehameha, the heady pleasures of the Grey Cup week, it is more than idle for you to despise them: for one thing they represent all but about 25 percent of the population; for another they are, in general, people of amiable and hospitable impulses; and for a third, and this is what my epiphany amounted to, they have, but seldom exercise, every right to feel superior towards *you*—at least they don't have to read books like *As for Me and My House*.

What they *could* perhaps read, if it were thrust at them, is a collection of stories like Ken Mitchell's *Everybody Gets Something Here*. Even though the title promises too much and the book would do little for George Steiner or even Northrop Frye, the stories seem aimed at a much wider audience than one would expect from a writer based, as Mitchell is, at a Canadian university—aimed, in fact, at the Soft Underbelly and with particular, though somewhat broad, emphasis on its blue-collar component. All but two of the stories are written in the first person, and Mitchell has devised for this narrator a sort of toneless dialect one could call "Soft Underbelly Demonic":

... Milt and me ran into this Koffman guy. We pull into town just beat. It's later than hell, and it's been raining on and off all day.

Strict accuracy might demand *into* be replaced by *inna* and *later than hell* by *later'n hell*, but some compromise with legibility must be made. The stories themselves are amusing anecdotes involving roustabouts, farm workers, lushes, itinerants, etc., anecdotes which do not stay in the mind, but which generate a vague feeling of good cheer—the kind of feeling of good cheer one experiences, for example, in a Winnipeg beverage room after holding up five fingers for the beer waiter who loads, and makes groan, the table with these glasses of urine-coloured, permanganate tasting liquid, purportedly draught beer, into which, one observes, a neighbour begins to trickle tomato juice.

As anecdotes they mostly hinge on gimmicks and one, hilariously though perhaps shamelessly, on the punch line to a shaggy dog story—as though the author had decided to write a story that could plausibly end with the words "the koala tea of mercy is not strained." This is not Mitchell's phrase, but there is one rather like it. In another story, amateur electricians tap the power lines to feed the radios of a tenement full of depression-struck paupers; another focuses on a group of losers holed up in Miami—most, though, use a Prairie locale and seventies time setting. They are all of them mildly entertaining, but the beer parlour bonhommie grows wearisome when taken in large doses, and the uncritical presentation of these brainless narrators going about their brainless occasions seems to be to be empty of context.

1978

Dust-Bowl Stock and Ontario Farmers

Ryga, George. *The Hungry Hills*. Vancouver: Talonbooks, 1974.
Cohen, Matt. *Wooden Hunters*. Toronto: McClelland and Stewart, 1974.

Ryga's reputation rests mainly on one major play, *The Ecstasy of Rita Joe*, and a minor one, *Captives of the Faceless Drummer*, which achieved the rare distinction of being rejected by the Vancouver Playhouse Company on political grounds — or so it is alleged by local theatre people. The truth is that though neither is a particularly good play (*Ecstasy* has a slight edge, as far as literary quality is concerned), both are topical and both deliver their messages with a certain amount of raw power.

The same can be said by anybody willing to stretch a point about *The Hungry Hills*. The protagonist is a young man returning to his home country, a God-forsaken spot up in what Mencken would've called the hookworm-and-Bible-belt of Alberta, after three or four years of forced absence. He spends part of this in a welfare home to which he is taken by the government agency on receipt of a petition got up by the neighbours who wish to punish his family for its atheism. He breaks out of the orphanage, however, and works as a garage mechanic for a loser named Pete. When Pete's business folds the young man (among whose considerable burdens in life is his name—

Snit Mandolin) is endowed with three hundred dollars and it is with this sum, sizeable for the fifties, that he returns to make something of the farm now run, since the death of his parents, by his Aunt Matilda. This is all told in flashback form and Ryga establishes a vivid though familiar picture of this hill country which is not only hungry but a dust-bowl filled with stock characters from the thirties depression novels. Thus the cast includes a hell-fire preacher, his sycophants — particularly a corrupt grocery store proprietor who plays a key role in the narrative, durable and feisty old women like Aunt Matilda, and a host of monosyllabic and cretinous dirt-farmers. There is some Dark Mystery about Snit's parents hinted at — as though Ryga thought that the sinister, sidewinding touch of Faulkner might help to ginger the book's banal and naturalistic landscape. Snit gets himself involved with a moonshiner named Johnny Swift and the plot, such as it is, develops around this relationship as Snit tries to extricate himself from it while Johnny — even more of a psychotic than the other characters in the book, intensifies it like a well-applied hammerlock. The Mystery is cleared up, the reader will be glad to hear, but except for establishing some rationale for Snit's role as a scapegoat, it is thematically and dramatically gratuitous.

Technically, the novel is clumsy and ineffective. It could be used in university creative writing courses as a compendium of what not to do. The dialogue is feeble, the characterization, with the remarkable exception of Snit's pathetic father, is minimal, and characters switch from manic aggression to depressive cringing within the space of one sentence without any accompanying psychological validation. The credibility of the novel is undermined from the start since Ryga walks straight into the trap a just and righteous God sets for naturalistic novels about barely literate people. The action is observed through the consciousness of Snit himself and the book is written in the first person in taut, grammatical, sometimes lyrical sentences. Since Snit is supposed to be one of these hill people, where did he acquire this ability? When he represents his own and the speech of others, the prose in quotes suddenly fills with "yas, yores, aws, g'wans, ain'tchas" and the like together with dropped final g's and tortuous, Okie-like grammatical constructions. So Snit is the sort of bastard, is he, that has one language for his reader and another for his mates and peers? . . . a well-educated observer posing as a hill-billy. The duplicity, however, is not Snit's; it is due to the clumsiness of the novelist himself whose job is to get me to assent to his fictional reality by eliminating this sort of objection before it even arises and before he does anything else. As it stands, the reader can trust neither the narrator's sensibility nor his perceptions.

Henry James might well have affirmed (though, of course, hesitantly, without, on the one hand, pointing the matter too fine, nor, let it indubitably be said, alternatively, postulating a welter of qualifications on, in fact, the other) that novels are written primarily to afford both novelist and reader aesthetic pleasure. In other words, both parties wish to enjoy the spirit (cf. Nietzsche) of serious play. There is little enough of that in Ryga's novel. So what is the point of *The Hungry Hills*, and why was it written? The short and simple answer, of course, is "money" but Ryga is not a commercial writer (though I think he would like to be) and his book is empty of such popular elements as sex, sadism, soap opera, etc. — there is not even a young lady of Snit's own age to leaven the solemnity — and from this point of view he was lucky, given the early sixties when the novel first appeared, to get it published at all. Its interest, then, like that of so many Canadian novels, is extra-literary. It is a novel with a message and the reader does not have to dig very far to mine it out. Towards the end of the book Aunt Matilda tells Snit about her earlier life in the farming country of northern Saskatchewan with her Ukranian neighbours:

> ... those of us who didn't speak their language called them dumb bohunks — the silent ones. They worked hard, stayed outa trouble and lived on next to nothing. Then one day we heard that twenty young men among them — chosen to speak for everybody, themselves and us — had left on foot to go to Regina and ask the Government for better prices on grain and livestock, or else gives us relief.
>
> ... a lot happened — but I didn't understand it then. For one thing, the whole community started to work and think together — not like here, where one neighbour don't know another, an' every family is afraid of itself. They really got through — used to come together into the schoolyard on Sundays, and everybody would talk and argue about how we needed better roads, an' fertilizer for the fields, weed-killers, and all that sort of thing ....

Aunt Matilda, you'll notice, has very nearly forgotten to speak the dialect she's been given up to this point so it is clear that the paragraph contains the book's gist which might be paraphrased as follows: the penalty for rejecting co-operative living and group action is a downward slide on a spiral leading through alienation, isolation, and mutual hostility culminating in brutalization and madness. Ryga's characters are illustrations of this thesis since they are represented as lost, tormented souls forced to live out their miserable lives on these parched and sterile foothills—a kind of secular hell. It is a message, *qua* message, with which I happen to agree and even if I did not I would still respect the sense of urgency with which Ryga delivers it. But the novel as a *literary* structure is, in my opinion, almost worthless, part of its author's juvenilia, and it is difficult to see how its resurrection by Talonbooks could enhance his reputation.

After two quite lively, but slender and trendy warm-up novels Matt Cohen produced *The Disinherited*, an ambitious work centred on a dynasty of Ontario farmers. This novel is highly successful in its adroit manipulation of time shifts, its inventiveness, its sustained sombre and elegiac tone. Many of the episodes are moving, some horrifying, and the novel generally established Cohen as the most interesting of the Anansi writers. The book, though dynastic, avoids cliché—and this alone, given the genre, was a considerable achievement.

I do not thing the same could be said of *Wooden Hunters*. The sombre style, so effective in *The Disinherited*, here becomes merely portentous as the themes and characters struggle in vain to deserve it. The prose takes on a frozen, static quality, as though Cohen had composed each sentence with pencil and eraser, honing, pruning, winnowing—a poet in search of the perfect, filigree phrase:

> He blew out the lamp. In the candlelight the walls disappeared altogether, were replaced by irregular shadows swaying and jumping with the draft. The kettle was beginning to come to a boil. He brought the pot over to the counter and then took a piece out of the top of the stove, so that the kettle was exposed directly to the flame. When he poured the water the steam puffed out of the pot in large balloons of liquid smoke, hissed about his head like a motorized blanket.

I would personally have blotted the "motorized blanket" simile but the irregular shadows are good and the passage on the whole is quite typical. Cohen is clearly trying to capture everyday experience precisely and minutely and somehow turn it into poetry. The problem is that the "he" of the paragraph is not very interesting. Most readers, I am convinced, would be bored by "his" adventures with this stove and so the care taken with the style becomes gratuitous. One would not question such a passage in *The Disinherited* — and the latter is full of them.

The novel's action is located on an island somewhere off the coast of B.C. There are four main characters: Johnny Tulip, an Indian with lung disease; two young drop-outs, Laurel and Calvin; and a hotel owner named C. W. who intends to log what's left of the island forest. The island is described with great care and I have seldom seen the peculiar dripping, luxuriant, melancholy landscape of this part of the world rendered so effectively — overcast skies, thin layers of wet snow, webs of logging roads scarring through the bush, the odd *untidyness* of everything. As far as physical description is concerned, the four characters are presented very vividly. All of them are maimed in some way — Laurel falls over a cliff and injures her spine, Calvin endures violent, crippling pains in his guts, Johnny a savage, blood-spitting cough. Johnny's family could have come out of Beckett's *Watt* for his mother is blind (though she "has the sight"), his sister Victoria is a cancer victim who commits suicide before the novel's action begins, while another sister, Mary-Gail, who doubles as C. W.'s mistress, has what amounts to a permanently high temperature. Cohen is extremely good with these complaints: he can do you a fine osteophyte such that you can almost feel it noduling away beneath your fingertips; he can describe, in loving and minute detail, what it is like to lie half-paralysed, or to force the diaphragm to plunge deep within the body in search of that ultimate, existential, gobbet of phlegm and to have that same diaphragm find it and bring it triumphantly to the surface like a diver with a pearl. You can *feel* the bitter stomach cramps suffered by the neurasthentic Calvin. C. W. seems in relatively good shape but his soul is corrupt — he is an evil capitalist bent on ripping off the land. He is, of course, an *American* — a man brought up to believe that all the world is contained in the plains of Montana.

The characters tremble always on the verge of cliché. So much so that the reader finds himself creating alternative characters for the sake of symmetry. A predatory and insensitive *Canadian* business man, for example, and Cohen, during his sojourn in B.C., would surely not have had far to seek for models. Or an American victim. Drop-outs who aren't also losers and drug addicts. Teetotal Indians, pillars of their community, who are neither diseased nor afflicted with blind mothers with second sight. The plot, too, treads, though warily, a worn path for it is a muted version of the homesteader versus cattle-baron melodrama to which the movies have inured us. Johnny and the drop-outs sabotage C. W.'s new tractor (recalling, for some reason, *The Trail of the Lonesome Pine*) though their activity seems mindless and unmotivated — as though they were a group of teenagers, who, smoking marijuana on the beach, had casually decided that dynamiting a heap of expensive machinery might be a far-out thing to do. The motive for Johnny's hatred of C. W. at least becomes clear. His sister is ill-treated by the would-be logger who also threatens the Indian family's ancestral burial ground. But it is not so clear why Laurel and Calvin should find themselves in alliance with him. Perhaps out of boredom, for boredom in all its varieties seems to lie at the heart of this novel. There is no reason why the drop-outs should assist the Indians; there is equally no reason why they should not. Their lives, like the lives of the other characters, are totally joyless and mundane and there seems no expectation of any future happiness so that Cohen might just as well have had them lie supine on a bank within the rain forest, festooned with creepers and lianas, covered by slowly rotting cedar logs, growing between their ribs and shoulder-blades the huge ferns and poisonous fungi peculiar to the region. Such, at any rate, is the atmosphere of the book.

Cohen's main strength lies primarily in his competence as a prose poet. He is skillful with narrative and can leap convincingly from one point of view to the next as he gets within the skin of each of his main characters. This technique served him beautifully in *The Disinherited* because he was interested enough in his creations to provide them with background and density. *Wooden Hunters* retains these skills but the vacuity of plot and character turns them into self-indulgent mannerisms.

1975

Oral, So to Speak

Watmough, David. *Pictures from a Dying Landscape*. Kanata, 1972.

Over the last couple of decades the Victorian custom of the public performance of literature seems to have been revived. Poets become declaimers and Thespians devote energy to the reading of poetry— even the wealthier hams such as Richard Burton will attempt to keep their names sweet in cultured circles by occasionally turning a trick with a recording of some version of Dylan Thomas. In the fifties a young bard of moderate talents could recite his commonplace lines to quiet jazz and in later years to guitar and song like Leonard Cohen or Rod McKuen. Nowadays the fledgeling on the make in this country has "The League of Canadian Poets" to arrange his readings for him so that what started as a plastic culture rite now winds its way into a business. By these means the poet stands a chance of at least becoming a celebrity, "one who is famous for being known," and may even cut a disc. A rather treacly High Seriousness began to spread around the poetry scene so that a man has only to stand up on a platform with a sheaf of manuscripts to be proclaimed a genius. This is the Age of the Charlatan and also the Age of the Benefit of the Doubt.

I am sceptical about the value of these performances partly because they usually involve poetry, a field wherein for every genuine practitioner there gambols a hundred mountebanks and half a dozen critics unable and unwilling to denounce them, and partly because most good poetry requires elucidation. Once you get past iambic pentameter, the rhythms and verbal patterns of modern poetry are too subtle to be communicated readily to the ear and the meaning of a poem does not fully exist until it is mulled over in the recipient's mind in privacy and peace. This includes poetry of the Black Mountain School which, though it has been highly touted by its exponents as "oral" and "bardic," needs several careful and sympathetic readings until its meaning is yielded up and even then one has to be very lucky. Audiences plunged into the cold medium of listening to verse tend to drift off, their minds wander into fugues, sensibilities become dissociated such that a fly buzzing on the window-pane offers more than the *vates* on the platform, and a man slips with relief into catatonia as into the womb. Probably the only type of non-élitist poetry that can hold an audience composed of "average people," by which I mean plumber's mates, ad men, English teachers, coal heavers, and so on, is narrative poetry of the block-and-tackle sort and how much of that has there been since E. J. Pratt laid down his lyre? Another reason for scepticism has to do with the sheer incompetence of this ambitious member of The League of Canadian Poets to read aloud. From anything, let alone his own etiolated verse. Ask him to declaim a stretch of Tennyson, an oral poet if ever there was one, and he will make it sound like a Brandon, Manitoba, prayer meeting or a solo rendition of "Lead Kindly Light" delivered by an autistic child with a speech impediment. It is not necessary for a reader to be one of the great geniuses of the spoken word such as Dylan Thomas who was able to entrance vast audiences while communicating very little content, but it seems to me essential that before a poet is allowed out in public he be given a short course in method acting, elocution, voice projection, etc. If we *have* to be confronted with culture, at least make it enjoyable.

The proof, though, that there is such a thing as oral literature and that it can be communicated in public effectively and valuably exists in the work of David Watmough. He has two things going for him; the first is that he writes in prose, a medium eschewed by most writers since it is harder to write and easier to judge than verse, and the second is that he is an actor and mimic of considerable skill. Watmough is a Cornishman embarking on his forties who has made his home, or perhaps his centre, in Vancouver for more than a decade during which he served time, in the Dartmoor sense of the expression, as theatre critic. His increasing reputation focuses nowadays on these mono-

219

dramas, an art form whose roots lie in the theatre and whose effect is produced by a chemical interraction of voice, gesture, and narrative catalyzed by the presence of an audience. Watmough's monodramas are basically original short stories written in simple but lively prose and structured along a strong narrative line. I have been present at one of his performances and found myself recalling these stories long afterwards, remembering their protagonists, and even passages of dialogue. I have not seen them in cold print (they are about to be published by Talonbooks) and I fancy that they might be *too* simple, too unrhetorical, for that medium. As Watmough delivers them from the stage they are extremely impressive. Each is narrated in the first-person singular and deals with some imaginatively recreated experience in the author's life. In the first the narrator and his brother, young children, arrange an exchange of goods with a hobo who welshes on the deal. The traded items are trivial — a discarded dress on the one hand, a white rat on the other — but the principle of betrayal is not and neither is the interplay of character between the brothers one of whom is trusting, genuinely childlike, while the other evinces the beginnings of adult cynicism and "catastrophic expectations." The title of the second story, "First Job," refers both to the narrator's introduction to the world of work and to his first sexual experience. The latter theme is not too well integrated with the first, in my opinion, but the newspaper office material is related with a Dickensian gusto and relish for eccentricity. The best of these monodramas is "Ashes for Easter." Here the narrator visits his old home in Cornwall and promises his mother to dispose of his father's ashes resting in an urn in the living-room, but finds it no small task. It is a beautifully understated story, nostalgic without sentimentality, and through it runs a sly, mocking, thread of the grotesque, brilliantly controlled. Functioning almost as a human protagonist in these stories is the "Dying Landscape" of their joint title — an un-English landscape of barren moors punctuated by steep, narrow valleys of astonishing fertility, of dark cliffs and impossible-looking harbours, of granite towns, slate chapels, and abandoned farms, and those white slag heaps near the chinaclay pits — all this is evoked accurately and lovingly.

The prose content, the short-story aspect, of these monodramas solve without apparent effort one of the chief problems the prose writer encounters — that of context. It is as though the writer and the reader are engaged in a silent, continuous dialogue wherein the latter asks such questions as "why is he telling me all this" and the former builds the tacit reply into the structure of his fiction. The novelist has time, by virtue of his genre's conventions to create this context, but the short-story writer does not. The context is created immediately or not at all and the story fails. Watmough's stories establish their context immediately and it is reinforced by his anecdotal, conversational manner so that the listener is drawn, by his voice and mimicry alone, instantly into the world he creates. Some of this original effect is lost in the recording and there is a slight but somewhat irritating breathiness in some sections, but this recording should provide sufficient proof to the sceptical, such as myself, that, given acting skill and talent, there *is* such a thing as a worthwhile oral presentation of literature.

1973

Games of Hide and Seek

Bely, Andrei. *Petersburg.* Trans., annot., and introd. Robert A. Maguire and John E. Malmstad. Bloomington: Univ. of Indiana Press; Toronto: Fitzhenry & Whiteside, 1978.

Hyde, G. M. *Vladimir Nabokov: America's Russian Novelist.* London: Boyars; Toronto: Burns and MacEachern, 1977.

When I was young and easy under the gates of the Notre-Dame-des-Neiges cemetery I used to know a wealthy, Middle European lady who liked what she called culture, collected poets, was kind to novelists and dumb animals, and would pose, to all she met, her basic question: "Vot," she would say, "Vot is ze meaning of life?" At a party I took her to, she even approached Irving Layton with it. "The meaning of life, Madame?" he answered. "It is to read my poems." A facile though perhaps overly Draconian reply.

Certainly the generation of Russian poets, intellectuals, and novelists writing between about 1900 and the Revolution would have sympathized with the urgency of the lady's quest, but they might not have agreed that her encounter with Irving Layton ended it. To many of them, and particularly the group which labelled themselves Symbolists, poetry, together with other branches of artistic activity, constituted an attempt to establish a world-view, a system of metaphysics. Unlike their French confrères (Mallarmé, for instance, or

222

Verlaine) who sought primarily for new modes of poetic expression, the Russian Symbolists selected from a welter of psychological, philosophical, and biblical traditions a network of symbols they hoped would reconcile polarities, fuse inner and outer experiences, eliminate distinctions between form and content and, in general, tie together all areas of human knowledge into a complex syncretic knot — not for the sake of art, but for the sake of first formulating, then resolving, ultimate questions. When that had been done, they thought, the New Man would slouch through the ruins of corrupted and tenth-rate civilizations to be born.

Art was, thus, as far as they were concerned, not only a branch of epistemology but also theurgical in tendency. It is not surprising that Russian intellectuals began hankering for esoteric doctrines and for individuals amongst them to identify themselves as initiates in a body of secret knowledge derived from the Theosophy of Madame Blavatsky and from Rudolph Steiner's rather more respectable system called Anthroposophy (of which Saul Bellow has recently become a devotee). Nor should the post-Marxist reader, who has been taught that a man's consciousness is determined by his class circumstances, be amazed at the presence, in such writers as Andrei Bely and Aleksandr Blok, of images taken from Apocalyptic sources: Whores of Babylon, Lions, Antichrists, Women Clothed with the Sun, Seven-Headed Beasts, and so on — the whole somewhat lurid paraphernalia of Revelation seems singularly appropriate to an upper-class intelligentsia threatened, even before Dostoevsky's time, with annihilation. After the Revolution, of course, Symbolism was replaced in Russia by even drearier aesthetic theories — Acmeism, for example, then Futurism, then Socialist Realism (perhaps the dreariest of the lot). The Symbolists were first denounced, then almost totally neglected. But this earlier, esoteric tradition wafted, after 1917, across the chernozem plains to the salons of western Europe and North America on the wings of such men as P. D. Ouspensky and the astonishing George Gurdjieff, where it ceased to have much to do with art and became instead a substitute religion among disaffected elements of the bourgeoisie. I regret that I have been endangering the reader's immortal soul by confronting him with the heresy of Gnosticism — for this, with its claptrap of secret books, Hermetic knowledge, devils, fiery eyes, and death-dealing swords, is what mystical Russian Symbolism amounted to — but unfortunately Bely's *Petersburg* is riddled through and through with the latter and, without some preliminary sketch of its intellectual — for want of a better word —

backgrounds, the novel is unintelligible.

The real name of Andrei Bely (or Biely, or Belyj, as it is variously spelled) was Boris Bugaev. He changed it to Bely, the Russian word for "white," apparently to identify himself with the colour of one of the four horsemen of the Apocalypse or, alternatively, to link his Ego talismanically to the white stone mentioned in Revelation: "He that hath an ear, let him hear what the Spirit saith unto the churches; To him that overcometh will I give to eat of the hidden manna, and will give him a white stone and in the stone a new name written which no man knoweth saving he that receiveth it." (This is quoted by Samuel D. Cioran in *The Apocalyptic Symbolism of Andrej Belyj* [Mouton: The Hague, 1973] to which I am indebted.) This overcomer, this denizen of a Higher Realm of Being, was born in Moscow in 1880 from upper-class, but not aristocratic, stock. He appears to have plunged himself quite frenetically into the explosive literary controversies of his day and, by 1913, had produced an extensive body of writing which included books and articles on literary theory, studies of classical authors such as Gogol, Dostoevsky, and Tolstoy, together with novels and stories. Much of this work was polemical, some of it violently so. Just before the war he travelled to Switzerland to join the Rudolf Steiner colony at Dornach (also frequented by Mondrian and Paul Klee), but left in 1916 to return, adventurously and Leninwise, to Russia where he died in 1934.

Petersburg is said to be his masterpiece. It was first published in 1916 and a revised version in 1922. Both were pronounced "decadent" and therefore deleterious by the new culture czars who allowed the Symbolists—with some exceptions, Blok, for instance—to sink gently into oblivion. Outside the country, however, there was some sporadic interest. A German translation of *Petersburg* appeared in 1919, an Italian in 1961, a French in 1967, an English in 1959. But for a novel so ambitious, so well-reputed, so complex, there has been remarkably little criticism in English. It is as though the Royal Graduate School Artillery, the Block-and-Tackle Textualist Gang, has sheered completely away from Bely, perhaps to engage less rebarbative targets. Thus this new edition of the novel, with its fine introduction and elaborate notes, is something of a pioneering work.

The translation alone must have presented enormous difficulties. Bely, along with other Russian Symbolists, considered language as a mystical Logos reverberating with meanings of various kinds, many of them occult. The name Apollon Apollonovitch Ableukhov, for example, one of *Petersburg*'s central characters, is intended to suggest

"Apollonius," the Antichrist in a popular short story by Bely's fellow Symbolist, Solovyov. It also refers to Apollyon, the corrupter in Revelation, and to one element of the Nietzschean dichotomy celebrated in *The Birth of Tragedy*. And, as though this were not sufficient bone for the reader to pick, the last letters of the surname, *ukhov*, spell the Russian word for "ear," a portion of anatomy with which this character is well-endowed. But we are only at the beginning of things. Consider the following line of dialogue, spoken by Sophia, with whom Nikolai Ableukhov, son of Apollon, is in love: "Ooo, you...monster, ooo, you...frog...ooo, you red buff*oo*n." The editor comments as follows: "*Ooo*: This is not a long *o* but the *oo* of buff*oo*n, and the *u* of Ableukhov. It also occurs in the Russian for 'monster' (*urod*), 'frog' (*lyagushka*), 'buffoon' (*shut*) and 'doll' (*kukla*). Bely often builds whole paragraphs around it, but a translation can, of course, only hint at this. Throughout the novel it is associated with revolution (and occurs in the word itself: *revolyutsiya*)."

The novel's plot is comparatively simple. A young student, Nikolai Ableukhov, gets mixed up with a revolutionary organization at a meeting in which he expresses willingness to assassinate his own father, Apollon Apollonovitch, a high-ranking government official. He does not, at the time, declare his intention of marrying his mother, though Bely later builds into his structure elements of the Oedipus cycle compounded with anthroposophical symbolism. Nikolai's promise is part student talk and part idle boast, but the committee takes him up on it, hands him a time bomb, due to explode in twenty-four hours, to be planted in his father's room. He is thus confronted with a moral and metaphysical problem of considerable dimensions. But Bely's main purpose seems to be the presentation as a symbol of Petersburg itself: a pseudo-Western city carved out of the fly-blown swamps and creeks on the Finnish border by Peter the Great as an act of the will; a city of "prospects," wide avenues, malarial canals, slums, and gaunt public buildings all swarming with bureaucrats, agents, double-agents, revolutionaries—one tenth of the male population in uniform of some sort, even including students and schoolchildren; a city teeming with Gogolian homunculi which seem to loom out of its streets, lampposts, and statuary—a demented horde. Bely's rendering of this incredible scene is as powerful in its own way as Dostoevsky's in *Crime and Punishment* and well within the tradition of Russian literature. Ever since the place was hacked out of the wilderness its symbolic possibilities have been exploited by generations of writers some of whom, Pushkin in particular, are involved in the book's texture. Bely himself sees St. Petersburg as the result of a hubristic attempt to impose Western order and rationality on Eastern chaos; his devil-obsessed revolutionary, Dudkin, from the security of his hovel on Vasilievsky Island, imagines that an evil genius hovers over the city across the water: ". . . there buildings blazed out of a wave of clouds. There, it seemed, hovered something spiteful, cold. From over there, out of the howling chaos someone stared with stony gaze, skull and ears protruding into the fog." The spectral and foggy avenues leading back into the swamp also look out onto the Void: "Beyond Petersburg," says Bely, "there is nothing."

Nikolai Ableukhov's struggle with patricide takes place during the first week of October 1905. The fogs, sleet, the icy drizzles, and sharp winds from the southwest all correspond, apparently, to the weather reports in the Petersburg daily newspapers concerning that period. Many of the political intrigues of the time and some of the personages involved in them are also included and, in general, Bely has attempted to capture the combination of dread and tension of the times prompted by sporadic outbursts of pre-revolutionary terrorism and fear occasioned by the lost war with Japan. This, in turn, gave rise in many people's heads to nightmare visions of swarming yellow hordes. But because Bely clearly wishes to ignore the claims of mere representationalism he uses deliberate anachronisms and fantastic events — Pushkin's bronze horseman prances through the streets, the Antichrist hovers, Nikolai spends much of his time dressed in a red domino partly in order both to fascinate and terrorize his stupid and doll-like inamorata. The dreams and paranoid fantasies of the characters occupy a vital place in the novel's structure and provide it with much of its anthroposophical and apocalyptic underpinnings. A good example is Nikolai's dream which casts his father as Saturn or Chronos, the archetype of despotism, while Apollon Apollonovitch correspondingly dreams of his son as an agent of chaos and destruction, as the archetype of Mongolian Horde.

What is one to make of all this? It is useless to judge the novel by the conventional critical yardsticks of plot, character, and portrayal of psychological motivation. The plot is absurd, the characters gro-tesque, and nobody in the book's fictional world behaves as though he possessed a brain, let alone a psychology. The puns, verbal play, and tonal effects remain largely inaccessible, though the translators have obviously done their best. In English, these manipulations of language are either irritating or trivial beyond belief. The sensibility behind *Petersburg* seems to me both ridiculous and outmoded, though I predict a mild vogue for the novel among those readers finally bored with the inane profundities of, let's say, Hermann Hesse. On the other hand *Petersburg* is worthy of considerable respect — not only as the final flowering of a now dead but once very much alive artistic credo, but for its influence on greater novelists such as Nabokov, for its status as an attempt to expand the boundaries of fiction, and above all for the spirit of play that dominates it.

Nabokov himself, in fine, coat-trailing fettle, says this: "I have been perplexed and amused by fabricated notions about so-called 'great Books.' That, for instance, Mann's asinine *Death in Venice* or Pasternak's melodramatic and vilely written *Zhivago* or Faulkner's corncobby chronicles can be considered 'masterpieces' . . . is to me an absurd delusion, as when a hypnotized person makes love to a chair. *My* greatest masterpieces of twentieth century prose are, in this order: Joyce's *Ulysses*, Kafka's *Transformation*, Biely's *Petersburg*; and the first half of Proust's fairy tale *In Search of Lost Time*." Three-quarters of the last sentence would be acceptable to most readers of literature. There can be no doubt in anybody's mind regarding Joyce, Kafka, and Proust. But Biely? Biely *who*? Maguire and Malmstad's fine edition of *Petersburg* ought to be sufficient answer to these questions for many years to come.

There has been no dearth of literary criticism concerning Nabokov himself, whose Bely-like obsession with word games, puzzles, parody, mirrors, levels of reality, doubles, and so on has attracted the busy labour of exegetes whose ingenuity often rivals his own. A glance at the bibliography of G. M. Hyde's book, which includes such titles as *Crystal Land: Artifice in Nabokov's English Novels*, *The Literature of Exhaustion*, and *Escape into Aesthetics*, might suggest that most critics feel Nabokov's "erection of verbal citadels" is related to the predicament of the writer in the modern world, that he creates his shimmering illusions from a spirit of despair, that he is a sort of existential cop-out like Roquentin in Sartre's *Nausea*. This kind of approach, like the purely exegetical one, has always struck me as fundamentally wrong. First, some analysis of Nabokovian comedy, though comedy is never precisely the effect of any given work, with special emphasis on the influence of Bergson's theories is long overdue. Second, Nabokov, as Hyde points out, has assimilated more completely than his critics the Modernist devices which afford them such pleasure, many of which are anticipated by classic Russian literature. Thus Nabokov's work ought properly to be seen in the context of his predecessors such as Pushkin, Bely, and above all Gogol, on whom Nabokov wrote a joyous, eccentric, and penetrating monograph.

Much of this commentary is provided by Hyde in *Vladimir Nabokov: America's Russian Novelist* and Hyde is particularly good on the author's debt to Gogol. Some of his critical apparatus is derived from the Formalists, especially where he discusses that phenomenon known in Russian as *skaz*. *Skaz*, evidently, is cognate with the word *skazka* (folk-tale) and originally referred to a narrative told by a fictitious narrator, rather than by the author directly. But James, Turgenev, Gide, and so on all wrote first-person narratives some of which call attention to the narrator's "reliability" in true Modernist fashion, but they are to be distinguished from the *skaz* form by their polished, highly literary language. The true *skaz* is to be found in what may be called oral monologues, in which the story is told so as to imitate phonetic, grammatical, and lexical patterns of actual speech, thus producing the effect of oral narration. One ought, therefore, to imagine the narrator as a kind of showman/raconteur manipulating a highly appreciative audience; he switches abruptly from farce to pathos, makes jocular asides, plunges into irrelevancies, imitates the accents of his characters, weaves fantasies about their names and appearance, gesticulates wildly, and acts out bits of drama in an extended, extempore performance. A far cry from James and Gide! But not from Sterne, regarded by the Formalists as the "archetypal novelist," not from Céline, nor Bely, and certainly not from Gogol.

In *skaz* the actual centre of the narrative is skewed away from the plot-line towards verbal intricacies and to the personality of the narrator whose inventiveness is the real subject of the performance. Nabokov's book on Gogol may be taken as a classic example of the genre. Nominally a scholarly essay, *Nikolai Gogol* begins with a long and very funny analysis of *poshlost*, a word defined unsatisfactorily by Prince Mirsky as "self-righteous mediocrity." It continues with a chapter on the author's horrifying death—a victim of paranoid delusions and incompetent doctors who covered his nose with leeches, a fate that strikes Nabokov as singularly appropriate to an author obsessed with noses throughout his life. Hyde quotes from *Nikolai Gogol* a lovely passage which is quintessential *skaz*: "In Switzerland, [Gogol] had quite a field day knocking the life out of the lizards all along the sunny mountain paths. The cane he used for this purpose may be seen in a daguerreotype of him taken in Rome in 1845. It is a very elegant affair."

One of the effects achieved by *skaz* is a distortion often by parody of literary conventions. The conscious or unconscious aim of this is to produce, using another Formalist expression, "defamiliarization" whereby the surface strangeness and ingenuity makes us "see what is really there" — a moral purpose to art which Nabokov himself pretended quite vehemently to reject. Nevertheless, Hyde makes good use of his critical approach. He is able to combine very neatly the idea of defamiliarization with Bergson's Vitalist theory of laughter and to apply the result with great success to the earlier novels such as *The Gift* and *Pnin*, less satisfactorily to the later novels, particularly *Ada* for which he apparently shares my distaste. After *Pale Fire*, his masterpiece, and the translation of *Eugene Onegin*, Nabokov seems to have grown tired, perhaps, Hyde speculates, because the methods of parody and pastiche depend too much on an accepted set of values they travesty. The later work, he says, has situated itself nowhere and by doing so has tried to make a virtue out of solipsism. Which, of course, is where we came in.

1979

Games with the Publish-or-Perish Set

Dembo, L. S., ed. *Nabokov: The Man and His Works*. Madison: Univ. of Wisconsin Press, 1967.

I have a recurrent dream in which Joseph Conrad, Henry James, and Ford Madox Ford sit sipping tea together some time around the turn of the century discussing their novels-in-progress. "Right here," Conrad says, "is where I baffle them with a switch in point of view. And at *this* point I propose confounding them with my *progression d'effet*." There is a genteel chuckle from the other two and the soft sounds of teeth nibbling into thin watercress sandwiches. And this is how, in my dream, *Nostromo* came to be written. Seldom has such dynamic material, possibly the most dynamic ever assembled for a serious novel, been so systematically diluted by aesthetics, so gelded by "angle of narration," so etiolated by "significant form." The reader who succeeds in penetrating the formal gymnastics of such a novel is only too liable to find (according to E. M. Forster, calling the kettle black) a thin whisp of vapour.

There is no such vapour at the centre of Vladimir Nabokov's oddly similar work. There is, instead, a boxing glove attached to the end of a sprung pair of lazy tongs. Like Conrad, however, he sees the art of fiction as primarily a matter of "construction" and he shares Conrad's fascination with doubles, mirror images, melodrama, and the grotesque. Like Conrad he sees human beings as Bergsonian encrustations of the mechanical and, unlike Conrad, is honest enough to admit it. Conrad's most successful works (*The Secret Agent, Heart of Darkness*) were written when its author could no longer resist the tug of that mode of expression (the grotesque) which came most naturally to him and from which he so often shied away; Nabokov, happy to work within his limitation (if it *is* a limitation), has achieved success with almost every novel.

About Nabokov's intelligence and cleverness there can be little doubt. His prose style is one of the most pungent, most coruscating that has ever appeared and one would have to go back as far as Swift or Thomas Nashe even to rival it. Yet at the end of even his most brilliant performances (*The Real Life of Sebastian Knight, Lolita, Pale Fire*) there is a question lingering in the reader's mind best phrased by the simple words "so what?"

It's a question we don't ask about Conrad. The mist, the vapour, prevents us from asking it. We can never be certain, of course, but we vaguely *suspect* that a Conrad novel is *about* something—that the author has something to say. What Nabokov has to say, in this sense, is even more enigmatic, yet his surface meanings are only too clear. His view of the world consists of a bad-tempered, almost Muggeridgean, reaction to modern civilization from which he singles out special targets such as, most consistently, Sigmund Freud. It is not surprising, then, that Nabokov criticism has, in general, evaded the difficult question of assessment and has preferred to take him on his own terms as a contriver of puzzles, anagrams, and acrostics; as a layer of "clues," and a setter of "traps." *Nabokov: The Man and His Work* is a collection of such criticism and it begins with an intensely amusing interview conducted by Alfred Appel, an ex-student of Nabokov's and a young critic obviously anxious to corner the Nabokov market. (He appears later on in the book not, as I had hoped, as "Pedral Flape," but as a full-fledged, wigged, and robed commentator on *Lolita*.)

I wish I had the space to fully analyze this interview—it is so obviously the best thing in the collection, mostly, I suppose, because nearly half its prose is contributed by Nabokov himself. It is literally as good as a play—an *agon* between a pedantic, pseudo-profound, but by no means stupid critic whose questions are set speeches aimed at the Publish-or-Perish crowd, and Nabokov at his most Chichikhovian —mocking, elusive, bubbling with a mad energy. I must, at least, try to give you some sense of this interview's quality.

After a warming-up exercise or two Appel asks about American writers and Nabokov replies:

> My feelings towards James are rather complicated. I really
> dislike him intensely but now and then the figure in the phrase,
> the turn of an epithet, the screw of an absurd adverb, cause me
> an electric tingle, as if some current of his was also passing
> through my own blood. Hawthorne is a splendid writer.
> Emerson's poetry is delightful.

Appel cautiously refrains from treading on any of these trailed coats
and replies by sending a whiff of chalk-dust across Nabokov's bows:

> **Q:** Would you care to comment on how the *Doppelganger* motif
> has been both used and abused from Poe, Hoffman, Andersen,
> Dostoevski, Gogol, Stevenson, and Melville, down to Conrad
> and Mann? Which *Doppelganger* fictions would you single out
> for praise?
> **A:** The *Doppelganger* subject is a frightful bore.

Appel retreats for the time-being and slyly sets Nabokov up with a
question concerning Dostoevsky, a writer who is often the butt of
Nabokov's most hilarious and corrosive jibes, but the Grand Master
refuses the gambit and, after a rather side-winding middle game,
finally scotches Appel's reintroduced *Doppelgänger* threat by taking
his pawn *en passant*:

> Those murky matters have no importance to me as a writer.
> Philosophically, I am an indivisible monist.

But Nabokov doesn't have it all his own way. In the penultimate move
Appel launches a massive attack on Nabokov's Queen by cracking a
joke so leaden, so pedagogical, that it tumbles upon the chess-board
like a chunk of anti-matter, or like the gothic novelist's cast-iron
helmet falling from the sky:

> **Q:** And as a closing question, sir, may I return to *Pale Fire*:
> where, please, are the crown jewels hidden?

It foxes Nabokov almost completely and he can only reply by
parodying his opponent's tone. The Game is his, all right, but only by
a hair.

The book is worth buying if only for this interview. The other contributions are far more predictable and not nearly so interesting but they are useful in demonstrating to the reader unused to Nabokov how incredibly complex this writer is. Gleb Struve plot-summarizes some of Nabokov's early work and Andrew Field, who has written a rather ponderous full-length study, contributes an essay entitled "The Artist as Failure in Nabokov's Early Prose" in which he asserts the commonplace that the novels are about "artists and artistic problems." Another commonplace, Nabokov's fascination with doubles, is taken up by Claire Rosenfield in a discussion of *Despair*, and Charles Nicol contributes a pleasant, impressionistic page or two on *Sebastian Knight* — a Borgesian novel that surely merits fuller treatment. Equally skimpy is the discussion of *Pale Fire* by John O. Lyons and the space that could well have been occupied by somebody or other's illuminating article on this work is wasted on Ambrose Gordon's unsuccessful attempt to defend *Pnin*. Appel comes Quilty-ing in at this point with a florid essay on *Lolita* sub-titled "The Springboard of Parody" which makes, convincingly enough, the points which *have* to be made about Nabokov's work before a serious consideration of the implications of this writer's methods can begin. The following is a typical statement:

> Parody is in *Lolita* the major means by which Nabokov breaks the circuit of reader-character identification one associates with the conventional novel. In his other novels this is accomplished by a complicated sequence of interacting devices which, by constantly reminding the reader of the novelist's presence in and above his book as a puppeteer in charge of everything, establishes the fiction as total artifice.

Despite the tautology constituted by the last four words it is true enough that Nabokov, even more than Bertolt Brecht, is concerned with producing the so-called "alienation effect." But why? There is, of course, a philosophical "high seriousness" suggested by Nabokov's technique and Patricia Merivale, in a rather belle-lettristic article, attempts to define it by linking Nabokov and Jorges Luis Borges, the difference being that:

> ... Nabokov usually dismisses his actors "into thin air" and returns us to the real world, Borges takes the argument to its conclusion, and perpetually reminds us that both author and

reader "are such stuff/As dreams are made on."

The problem is stated, as in Appel, but once more evaded.

There are essays on Nabokov's plays and on his translations and the book is rounded off with a checklist of criticism in English which, as they say, "is nice to have."

The book serves, then, as an excellent introduction to Nabokov. It does not probe very deeply nor does it answer the question about Nabokov's stature but, on second thoughts, it matters little whether Nabokov is a great writer or not—he is so much *better* than most great writers that the question is hardly worth asking.

1970

A Tame Beast

Yates, J. Michael. *The Abstract Beast.* Queen Charlotte Islands: Sono Nis, 1972.

Back in the heyday of the Beatles and the Stones when the young were young I would occasionally switch on a pop radio station not always from some patronizing urge to plug into the Youth Sub-Culture but to allow an oddly enjoyable form of musak to flow through the house. This musak was punctuated by hebephrenic disc-jockeys anxious to impart advice on where to buy the latest threads, gear, and cuts, and it was during one of these commercial intervals that I first heard of J. Michael Yates. I was told to read Yates's poetry because it would blow my mind; because it would freak me out; because it was . . . it was . . . like *poetry*, man, the real thing. The amiable young huckster then went on to push some new boutique a visit to which, he assured his listeners, would Expand the Consciousness. There was something vaguely disturbing about the idea that an artist could, and perhaps would, allow himself to be sold over the air between hit tunes like dry-cleaning establishments, take-out restaurants, and candidates for political office and I wondered what sort of a poet would be either stupid enough or brass-necked enough to allow himself to be commoditized in this way. Then it occurred to me that I had the wrong angle—I was being too "linear"—I was "hung up"—I hadn't got "into" it. We're into a new era, I reminded myself, and we all of us have to use the media to hustle our own egos. And why not? Didn't Alexander Pope use all the contemporary media in *his* day to establish his own reputation? And where would English 200 be if Pope had been either too modest or too ironic about his talent? Perhaps this Yates is rather a swinger, I thought, a *Jerry Rubin* of a poet mocking outdated establishment values concerning art as High Seriousness and eager to treat poetry the way it should be treated — as a joyous lark. I looked forward to reading the work of J. Michael Yates with some interest.

Shortly afterwards I ran across a book of stories called *The Man in the Glass Octopus*. There was a blurb on the cover written by a man named Bob Hunter who creates daily for the *Vancouver Sun* what is undoubtedly the *silliest* newspaper column in the so-called free world. Yates's book, Hunter warned, was a "mind blower." It was also, he explained, "about entropy . . . that ultimate subject." Uneasy about all this psychedelically entropic detritus of blown minds, zapped skulls, freaked heads, and stoned brains that appeared to surround the figure of Yates, I opened the book in much the same spirit as an Israeli ambassador opens a parcel postmarked *Araby*.

It was singularly unexplosive. It is a disappointingly bland book of short prose pieces; carefully pruned and worked-over exercises in a fashionable Surrealism tinged with sentimentality but without much narrative interest. It was not that they were *bad* within their own genre — which could be described as milk-and-Kafka — it was that there was a disjunction between the quality of this book and the "swinging" image of its author as poet/culture hero which Yates and his followers, by this time a considerable number by West Coast standards, were trying to project. This image-making has its positive aspect; Yates worked for a while in U.B.C.'s Creative Writing Department where he has stimulated and encouraged writers of genuine talent such as George McWhirter, and he was a founder of the "Sono Nis Press" which gives his protégés a much needed outlet and which is notable for its beautifully produced books. It is perhaps a pity that Yates's reputation, such as it is, is not frequently associated with his actual *work* but with his efforts at self-advertisement, at polarizing the West Coast "literary scene," at denouncing other poets, and at heckling during their readings — activities for which serious writers should have little time. There is a smoke screen over the work itself created by Yates's self-fostered reputation but his poetry, when you come across it, is on the whole quite good — again by West Coast standards — and one of the Sono Nis stories, about an "incredible

236

shrinking disc jockey" still hovers, though rather faintly, on the fringes of my mind.

The Abstract Beast is a self-published collection of plays and short prose pieces beautifully printed and lavishly bound. The plays were broadcasted by the CBC and by various European radio stations and they are, without exception, abysmally bad. Here and there are the germs of interesting ideas, such as in the first "play," *Night Freight* which inverts the relationship between a would-be mugger and his victims, but what is lacking is any sense of drama — of construction, narrative, *agon*, and dialogue. It could be argued that these are radio plays and thus need voices before their quality emerges and, in fact, the reader can observe a creaking attempt to enliven the monotonous stichomythia with auditory effects:

Woman: Isn't this a dangerous way?
Man: It's the only way, after all, isn't it?
Woman: I suppose it is right on our way.
Man: The only way.
Woman: If you say so.
Man: The only responsible way.
Woman: I don't like the dark.
Man: How about the mist?
Woman: *Awful*

and so on. If this drivel works only on the air, and I can't believe that it does, then why go to the bother of printing it? There *are* radio plays, such as those of Giles Cooper, which lie quiescent on the page but produce electrifying effects when performed, but it is very difficult to believe that *Night Freight* is one of them. In *Theatre of War* even the ideas fail and we are presented with a string of clichés marshmallowed with an appallingly heavy-handed irony which produce a total effect of mind-boggling callowness. It is more pleasant to consider the short prose pieces which punctuate this arid waste of non-drama.

These are much more successful. They are extended metaphors about the so-called human condition and take the form of phenomenological musings.

I like particularly the one entitled *De Fabrica* and about the first half of *Pile* — before, that is, Yates's inability to write effective dialogue mars it. But, at their best, these meditations have the hard-edged, faintly disturbing quality of the best of Yates's poetry.

There is one other feature of this book which may delight

connoisseurs of dust-jacket horseshit. In listing his achievements, Yates writes of himself as follows:

He is listed in *Contemporary Authors, Contemporary Poets of the English Language, The 200 Men of Achievement, Outstanding Young Men of America* and several other honorary journals.

I have been too busy to check with my friendly librarian as to whether or not these hilarious journals actually exist. I might almost be inclined to credit Yates with a sense of humour for inventing and listing them were it not for the solemnity of the book's contents.

Finally, *The Abstract Beast* will set the reader back a full $9.95 plus sales tax where applicable so that Yates's adulators will have to pay dearly for their kick.

1973

Hail to Thee, Dense Spirit

Lessing, Doris. *The Story of a Non-Marrying Man.* London: Cape, 1972.

Today, ladies and gentlemen, we do some Fem. Lit., namely this book of short stories by Doris Lessing, the heaviest author in the movement, which has lain around the *West Coast Review* office for two years because there wasn't one of us eager to take it on. This is not because we think Lessing mediocre, far from it; it is because the reviewer fears he will have to take into account those massive, monumental, prose edifices that occupy the horizons of her career like skyscrapers in a modern city amongst which pedestrians of fragile ego feel dwarfed to insignificance. She is everything conveyed by Matthew Arnold's phrase "High Seriousness" which is not only a critical yardstick but an entire genre. Her novels seem to me, varying the metaphor, long expanses of arid Realism across which her heroines inch their way, "developing" and "reacting," testing their world-views, synthesizing out of their experiences sets of attitudes, and the parched reader totters after her like one of those prospectors in the cartoons crawling off on all fours with swollen tongue. Nothing is left out; nothing left unrealized; nothing left to the imagination of the reader and not one glimmer of comedy. That same exhausted, dehydrated, reader is forced to examine the surface and underside of every stone on his journey—an inch and a quarter, precisely, from his eyes—until he arrives at the Message: all women are losers, men bastards, socialism doomed, apocalypse certain unless human beings develop extra-sensory perception. Pessimism applied with a bludgeon is one thing; being dragged by the scruff of the neck over Lessing's stony surfaces quite another and it is this I find intimidating and insulting. Her best fiction, in my opinion, is *Briefing for a Descent into Hell*—an imaginative and symbolic novel of great beauty, brevity, and intelligence—but this is regarded by her admirers as very minor Lessing.

This present volume of short stories contains perhaps three pieces worth reading interspersed with filler-fragments of diaries and autobiographical essays of a desultory, coyly-written sort. The first is about a nondescript, middle-aged diamond cutter who presents a perfect pearl to the daughter of a rich Alexandrian merchant and then returns to his obscurity in Johannesburg. He meets her again in Italy when their social positions have been reversed—he is a soldier in the occupying army and she a destitute war-widow. The story is framed by a discussion among a group of air-line passengers concerning the virtues of the Roman fountain which bestows good luck when activated by tossed coins—a process ironically inverted during the course of the story. It is written with a light, playful touch and it reads like a fable. The second is one of Lessing's African tales concerning a bigamous vagrant whose wanderings alternate with periods of domestication until he settles down as a villager in a kraal—perhaps one of the last free men. Finally, there is "The Temptation of Jack Orkney" in which Lessing condenses to 30,000 words or so material a less experienced writer would pounce on for a fully-fledged novel. Its protagonist is a middle-aged socialist dedicated to political journalism and a variety of libertarian causes whose man-of-action routine, and so on, is thrown out of kilter by the death of his father. He experiences a series of disturbing dreams, many of them involving anima figures composite of his wife and daughters which appear to wish to guide him towards new modes of consciousness—modes in which, during his waking hours, he sees his colleagues in a strange and different light:

> Walter's face, usually a fist of intention and power, was beaming, expansive: they all looked as though they were at a picnic, Jack thought. Smug, too.... Yet now, looking at Walter's handsome face, so well known to everyone from newspaper and television, it had over it a mask of vanity... a film had come over his eyes,

distorting the faces of everyone he looked at. He was looking at masks of vanity, complacency, stupidity or, in the case of Walter's Norah, a foolish admiration.

He finds himself joining his daughters in a procession carrying banners that say "JESUS CARES ABOUT BANGLADESH" and is caught by his "old guard" — all of them middle-class atheists. Lessing derives a rich but low-profile comedy from this situation. The "old guard" is sympathetic, it tries to reason with him, tries to establish "where he stands." But the genuine selves of these friends, selves of which they are unaware, nauseate him, for they are compounded of power-hunger, self-approval, and superficiality:

> ... he wanted to howl out, in a protest of agonized laughter, that if the skies fell (as they might very well do), if the seas rolled in, if all the water became undrinkable and the air poisoned and the food so short everyone was scratching for it in the dust like animals, Walter, Bill, Mona, himself, and all those like him, would be organizing Committees, conferences, Sit-downs, Fasts, Marches, Protests, and Petitions, and writing to the authorities about the undemocratic behaviour of the police.

Things have gone too far and too wrong. Action based on the spirit of Victorian liberalism is no longer relevant — it is to fart against thunder. Doubly depressing for Jack is the spectacle of his radical activist son despising the squaredom of the old guard but repeating its mistakes and unconsciously copying its attachment to self-aggrandizing "protests," "struggles," and "blows for freedom." He sees human beings trapped in the patterns of history unable, because of their blindness and inability to learn, to break out. At the end of the story, however, Jack's vision begins to fade and, much to the relief of his friends and family, returns to "normal."

These are some of the themes, as I understand them, of *Briefing for a Descent into Hell* whose central character experiences visions of the true nature of Man's physical and spiritual condition and is thus described by people who do not share it as mad. Both the professor in that novel and Jack Orkney are brought back to the "real" thus insane world accepting that their glimpses of the grim truth are temptations — or temporary aberrations. Friends tell me that this concept of the human being as an animal doomed to self-destruction unless there is an inner and radical change in human nature is also the mainspring of

The Children of Violence sequence — an array of massive novels I have been unable, though very willing, to read for reasons expressed above. If true, then I can recommend "The Temptation of Jack Orkney" as a finely structured, enjoyable novella to those readers who would like to know what Lessing has to say but who are repelled by her densely Realistic manner.

1974

Le Merdeur

Ostrovsky, Erica. *Céline and His Vision.* New York: New York Univ. Press, 1967.

There are certain writers who seem to have been neglected and despised because their works represent opinions which are "unpopular" in every sense of the word. T. E. Hulme sneered at democracy, Wyndham Lewis admired Hitler, Roy Campbell supported the "wrong" side in the Spanish Civil War, Malaparte was a Fascist, and Bernard Shaw himself has only barely got away with his flirtations with Stalin and Mussolini because, as far as the public was concerned, he came on as a clown. To many people Louis-Ferdinand Céline's Anti-Semitism is enough to damn him into a deserved oblivion even though, and memories tend to be short when this subject is discussed, the sentiments expressed in such works as *Bagatelles pour un massacre* were no more than the conventional "wisdom" of the time. Céline wrote these fifth-rate diatribes during the period when Hitler was regarded as a "respectable" politician "good for Germany," and when such professional Anti-Semites as Sir Oswald Moseley were receiving the tacit support of the Conservative Party of Great Britain.

But hypocrisy is not the only reason for this strange neglect of a man who is certainly the greatest writer of the century thus far. For one thing he was a kind of impressario—a grotesque P. T. Barnum of man's depravity. He saw life as a seething panorama of venality, betrayal, paranoia, masturbation, chronic disease, suffering, deformity, stench, vomit, bestiality, cowardice, and physical and moral corruption. In the words of some critic, "as a mudcaked and bloody nightmare of meaninglessness." He saw the human being as a walking corpse, carrion — "a bag of worms . . . stuffed with maggots . . . enclosures of lukewarm and unhealthy, rotting guts . . . a travesty of agitated and banal molecules" or, simply, as "meat." His Anti-Semitism is no more central to his work than reactionary politics is to Dostoevsky's — it is merely one aspect of his savage disgust for mankind in general. He turns no more ire against the Jews than he does upon himself whom he sees as a weak, cowardly, but vicious and cornered animal — *le maudit* — and as a murderous and self-befouling moral leper. He saw human societies as rotting, disintegrating structures built for the perpetuation of vice and insanity, and he saw the world, symbolized by the Germany of 1945, as a bomb-ruined and devastated landscape over which groups of demented human beings drift in agony, flailing and twitching, torturing and destroying one another. And over all, particularly in the early novels, *Voyage au bout de la nuit* and *Mort à crédit*, there plays Céline's sinister and gigantic humour: he has written, as Wylie Sypher says, "the incredible, the depraved, comedy of our concentration camps, the atrocious pains of inquisitions, the squalor of labour camps, and the efficiency of big lies." There is only one writer like him, Swift: and he makes Swift look like a Rotarian.

Apart from Trotsky's famous *Atlantic Monthly* article and Milton Hindus' *The Crippled Giant* there has been little work done on Céline in English. Erika Ostrovsky's book is thus the first, full-scale book of criticism to appear. She begins with a brief, and therefore unsatisfactory account of the author's life and attempts to trace the influence of his style and manner on such writers as Henry Miller, Jack Kerouac, Allen Ginsberg, and William Burroughs. This entire first section is marred by a curious kind of dissertationese:

> . . . (the critic's task) must be to explain, or at least to probe, analyze, dissect in order to reconstitute the work of art.

And this in the very first paragraph! On page sixteen Ostrovsky's at it again:

> Thus, one must examine Céline's work both as with a magnifying

glass and through a telescope: dissect and synthesize, note the minute detail and the enormous edifice.

It is almost as though she were about to break out into a discussion of "scholarly tools" and "critical apparatus." What she actually does, however, is drop the jargon of pseudo-science and determine, from the almost overwhelming mass of material in front of her, what Céline was actually trying to say. She describes him as a humanist *à rebours* whose appalling vision is accompanied by an excruciating nostalgia for a state of perfection wherein, as he says, "all of youth reaches the glorious beach, at the edge of the waters, there where women seem finally free and are so beautiful that they no longer even need the lie of our dreams," and which is utterly unattainable. She links Céline with more traditional modes of literature by considering him as a tragedian who forces us to witness "the fall rather than the ascension, the befouling rather than the purification through suffering," as the artist of the deluge embarking on an "apocalyptic crusade." Céline's vision, she points out, finds its correspondence in the paintings of Bosch and Breughel and she compares *Mort à crédit* with Breughel's *Children's Games*: "what is central, though, is the common concern of the two artists with capturing the moment which precedes destruction."

All this is not only good, but true. Ostrovsky finishes with a truly masterful account of the author's preoccupation with myth and epic and his kinship with the bardic tradition, with the *aède* and perpetuators of legend. "I'm first of all a Célt-day-dreamer bard," Céline wrote to Hindus, "I can turn out legends like taking a leak . . . legends are my music."

Ostrovsky's book, after its uneasy start, is filled with insight. Above all, it is honest. Critics of Swift, for example, often fail to look their author squarely in the eye: they tend to claim that the real Swift was the Swift of *A Journal to Stella*. Céline had his tender moments too, as in *Ballets, sans musique, sans personne, sans rien*. But Ostrovsky resists the temptation to say "the thing which is not" about Céline. Her book remains an excellent introduction, and an essential work for serious students.

1967

Return of *Le Merdeur*

Ostrovsky, Erica. *Voyeur Voyant*. New York: Random, 1971.

> ... the stories we tell are a bore ... our plays, more yawns! and
> the movies and TV ... disaster! what the people want and the
> elite too is Circuses! the gory kill! ... honest-to-God death
> rattles, tortures, guts all over the arena! ... no more silk-and-
> something stockings, false tits, sighs, and moustaches, Romeos,
> Camellias, Cuckolds ... hell no! ... Stalingrads! ... tumbrils full
> of lopped off heads! heroes with their cocks in their mouths ...
> you come home with your wheelbarrow full of eyes, like the
> Romans ... What a novel that would be! I'll start right
> in ... evening dress required? hell no! "The vivisection of the
> wounded"! ... That's it! so much art, centuries of so-called
> masterpieces, all for nothing! swindles! crimes!

This passage, from *North*, with its manic, colloquial, phantasmagoric
prose, the assumption that man's achievements are nothing in contrast
to man's depravity, and the writer's self-abasing eagerness to act as
pander to this depravity are quintessential Céline whose reputation, in
Anglo-Saxonia, rests mainly on *Journey to the End of the Night* and
Death on the Installment Plan, both published before the war in bad

246

translations. I discovered these books for myself in the early fifties at a time when I had graduated to the status of encyclopaedia salesman from that of day-labourer so that it was only too easy for me to identify with Céline's central characters—outcasts, losers, shills, lepers, derelicts, Jonahs, wastrels, malingerers, Schwiks, dead-beats, masturbators, and paranoiacs to a man. Like most people I had been brought up on the polite literature of an official culture maintained by the upper and middle classes of society, and it was not until I read Céline that I found a spokesman for the unofficial culture that anybody who ventures outside the salons and academies knows exists. It is this aspect of Céline's work that enabled Trotsky, in a well-known and very good article, to begin considering him as a proletarian novelist, but there is, of course, much more to Céline than that. For one thing he wished to be, and to a great extent he was, a poet of the Apocalypse—the twentieth-century Apocalypse of slums, poverty, racism, political lunacy, B-29's, H-bombs, and economic and environmental collapse. As a writer of epic he is, to the conventional novelist whose subject is manners, or sexual triangles, or minute changes of moral awareness in middle-class men and women, what Eisenstein was to the conventional cinema, or Artaud to the theatre. But, finally, Céline is, in my opinion, a great *comic* writer—probably the greatest in French literature after Rabelais to whom Céline is most akin. I have given up trying to explain why a book like *Death on the Installment Plan* is funny. It has something to do with Céline's stance as a pornographer of excoriation; something to do with the "humour," in the Renaissance sense of the word, of his narrators whose "bad-faith" model of the universe becomes mechanical and, therefore, comic. But it is better to just read the passage I have quoted at the head of this review. Either it strikes you as comic, in which case it needs no explanation, or it doesn't, in which case no explanation is possible.

There has not been much work done in English on Céline. *Death on the Installment Plan* has been retranslated and translations of *North* and *Castle to Castle* are now available. All these are the work of Ralph Manheim and they are excellent. There is Erika Ostrovsky's somewhat rickety full-length study of the novels which has now been followed by her even more eccentric biography—*Voyeur Voyant*. Irritating as this latter work is, I do not feel quite as hostile towards it as other reviewers. Ostrovsky has resisted, perhaps too well, the factual approach—the day-by-day, blow-by-blow enumeration of mundane events—whose *reductio ad absurdum* is the scholarly and ineffably boring life of Hemingway by Carlos Baker which has all the literary impact of a *PMLA* bibliography. Yet the end of her book sprouts scholarly apparatus — footnotes, letters, interviews, and sources, though, oddly, no index. The interviews themselves must have been of considerable interest since they represent encounters with such people as Arletty, Marcel Ayme, the critic Robert Poulet, Céline's wife, and old mistresses such as Erika Landry. One would liked to have known more about these people — what it meant to be Céline's friend, how these friends reacted to Céline's collaboration with the Germans, his Anti-Semitism, his imprisonment. It would have made a different, far more exciting book, though any biographer contemplating such an approach may be forgiven for being intimidated by *The Quest for Corvo.*

The chief problem with Ostrovsky's book is not its juggling with time, its linking of passages in Céline's life thematically instead of chronologically, but its style. It is impossible, I think, not to be influenced by Céline in one way or the other — either by his treatment of language, his view of human beings, or his paranoia. Ostrovsky is chiefly influenced by Céline's staccato sentence fragments linked by the famous "three dots." Unluckily she lacks Céline's ear:

> The story of a life (distant from his, yet so strangely similar) was taking life within him. Feeding upon his body. Flesh of his flesh. It clamoured for birth. With threat of anomaly or destruction; promise of delivery and joy. Child of his pain. Slowly forming within male entrails. Fruit of parthenogenesis which swelled a womb made fecund by its own powers — mingling male and female in creation. Hidden hermaphroditic joining in the night.
> (p. 46)

I would suggest that before Ostrovsky publishes another book she read any passages like this she may be tempted to write aloud to an audience of strangers in a brightly lit room. Admittedly, *Voyeur Voyant* does not always attain this high level of sheer drivel, but there is enough of it to delight the most jaded connoisseur. At the back of the volume, however, there is a straightforward chronology, in table form, of the bare facts of Céline's life — extraordinary enough to stand alone without Ostrovsky's stylistic cosmetics and her "thought balloons" by which she attempts to get inside Céline's head and provide him with motivations. These motivations are so enfarded with arty metaphor, so pore-clogged with fine writing, that it is very difficult indeed to make head or tail of them. It is still unclear why

248

Céline left his first wife, why he left Montmartre for Germany in 1944, why he wrote those racist pamphlets, and what he was actually doing in Siegmaringen. I cannot tell, from Ostrovsky's account, whether the gold that Céline had stashed away in Denmark actually existed *qua* gold or whether she uses it as some sort of cheap poeticism—the temptation devised by the trolls so to speak, Luring Mortals to their Own Destruction. Ostrovsky has thus acquired, though in diluted form, another of Céline's literary characteristics—she is an "unreliable narrator." The events of Céline's life are concealed in the novels since all of them are autobiographical, but the novels are spin-offs from these events—fantasies, reveries, nightmares, and, above all, legends. "I can turn out legends like taking a leak," Céline once said. What Ostrovsky does is to seize on one of those legends and make it over into myth. Thus Céline becomes the Scapegoat Figure—the man who is driven out of the tribe, carrying the sins of that tribe on his shoulders, as part of a ritual of purification. This is, if I understand Ostrovsky correctly, how Céline begins to see himself—his own jest turning to earnest. His activities become self-fulfilling prophecies— they become more and more outrageous as he seeks out and finds ways of making himself hated and despised. He sees potential enemies—Jews, Negroes, the Chinese, the "Narbonnoids"—and cannot rest until he has made them into real enemies by denouncing them. Later he makes no distinction between the Nazis, who persecute the Jews, and those Resistance fighters who persecute women caught sleeping with Germans and who would have torn Céline limb from limb if they'd got the chance. And perhaps there *is* little distinction. It is not difficult to imagine Céline rejoicing, had he lived to see it (and if rejoicing is quite the right word) over the mutual assassination and tarring and feathering now going on between rival gangs of Christians in Northern Ireland; nor to imagine how he would have gloated over the racism of the Black Panthers. One cannot, I think, explain Céline's attitudes in terms of literary myths, or by using the resources of abnormal psychology. The final thing to be said about Céline, and Ostrovsky is too caught up in her own sensationalism to say it, is that behind the grotesque façade, behind the "black comedy" (as though there were *any* comedy that is not, to some extent "black") there lies a rare sanity.

1972

Le *Merdeur* Strikes Back

McCarthy, Patrick. *Céline: A Biography.* New York: Viking, 1975.

Years ago when I first started to write I wished to record on paper a depressing and unpleasant experience of my own. I showed the result to a friend. Look, he said, you can't *do* this to me—why don't you write about a *rose*? This rather limited though perfectly understandable response is, with far more justification, of course, what Céline had to put up with all his life and it is what his supporters have had to grapple with since his death. Literary critics, gentle people for the most part, brought up as they are on Beauty, Truth, and Goodness, can't handle Céline—there is not a single rose in his entire opus—though many of them recognize his greatness. Robert Poulet, for example, once said that "in the history of contemporary letters, Louis-Ferdinand Céline is a true phenomenon. We must not explain him; we must simply note his existence as we would St. Elmo's fire or the Messina earthquake." This is typically evasive: it is true that many people experience a Céline novel as a cataclysmic event and that others feel they are being subjected to that oriental torture whereby a prisoner is locked in a cell with a homicidal maniac who never sleeps but who waits for the inevitable droop of his victim's exhausted eyelids then leaps at his throat. Most people, however, ignore Céline altogether. The novels seem to offer nothing positive to the reader, nothing that will lull him with sweet dreams into the dark. No rose, in fact. As far as Céline's narrators are concerned life is not only a useless passion, it is an ague with no good hours lived out on a corrupted planet among fellow humans infected with evil right from the start. Céline is the purveyor of a pessimism so black and unrelieved that most people brought up to believe that literature affirms the Great Human Verities cannot read him at all: he is the great prophet of evil in twentieth-century literature and thus his influence has been minimal. Henry Miller read Céline and so did Jack Kerouac and the Beats but they imitated something of his manner without sharing his vision of human life and against him, they are, as Patrick McCarthy says, like children. Perhaps the best thing written about Céline's style appears in Kurt Vonnegut's introduction to *Rigadoon*:

> He did not seem to understand that aristocratic restraints and sensibilities, whether inherited or learned, accounted for much of the splendour of literature. In my opinion, he discovered a higher and more awful order of literary truth by ignoring the crippled vocabulary of ladies and gentlemen and by using, instead, the more comprehensive language of shrewd and tormented gutter-snipes.
>
> Every writer is in his debt, and so is anyone else interested in discussing lives in their entirety. By being so impolite, he demonstrated that perhaps half of experience, the animal half, had been concealed by good manners. No honest writer or speaker will ever want to be polite again.

Impoliteness and pessimism are two of the reasons why Céline is neglected, but there is, of course, another. Céline collaborated with the Nazis, wrote Anti-Semitic pamphlets of great virulence, then fled, when the Allies landed in Normandy, to Germany to throw himself upon the mercy of his masters. His escape route from Siegmaringen across Northern Germany to Denmark in the company of his wife, an actor named Robert Le Vigan, and his cat, Bébert, was an epic one and the subject of the last three novels, or rather, nightmares-in-prose. The Danes tossed him into jail to appease the French who denounced, victimized, and finally tried him in 1950 when he was sentenced (Liberationist passions having cooled somewhat by then) to a year in prison, "national unworthiness," and the confiscation of half his property. Céline did his own share of denouncing: "Where was your famous Resistance," he screamed at them, "in 1940?" A good, profound, and highly embarrassing question. He was pardoned a year later and returned to France, resuming his practice as a doctor in the Parisian suburb of Meudon and his career as a novelist, though *D'un château l'autre*, *Nord*, and *Rigadoon*, extraordinary as they are, do not in my opinion capture as perfectly the amalgam of fantasy, epic, hallucination, and stark naturalism of his best work done in the thirties. Nevertheless, by the time of his death in 1961, he could be acclaimed, and *was* acclaimed by a remarkably large number of people, as not only the greatest French writer of the century but as one of the world's leading novelists — of any place and any time.

McCarthy's book is the second biography of Céline I have read. The first was by Erica Ostrovsky — a wildly eccentric book written with little visible system and in an attempt to capture, in Evelyn Waugh's phrase, "rather more than is known" of Céline's vision through a thin and somewhat risible imitation of his style. McCarthy is more scholarly: he attempts to deal not only with Céline's life but to come to grips with his insane politics (which, even more so than in the case of Pound, cannot be ignored), to discuss each of the works sensitively, to tie Céline's method and world-view not only to a tradition — Rabelais, Rimbaud, Baudelaire — but to contemporary writers such as Samuel Beckett and John Hawkes. He tries, I think successfully, to avoid the trap into which so many of Céline's less evasive critics fall of making the novelist into something that he is not — a socialist, a fascist, a simple-minded racist or, as in Ostrovsky's book, a demented, self-elected *pharmakos*.

Céline was born in 1894 in Courbevoie, a suburb of Paris, of petit bourgeois stock. His mother kept a lace shop on the Passage Choiseul while his father worked as a minor functionary in an insurance firm. Céline was sent to Germany and England to learn languages then left school to embark on a series of errand boy jobs, none of which he kept very long, until he joined the cavalry in 1912. These are the bare bones of his childhood and early adolescence, the source material for *Mort à crédit*. The narrator of that work is the adult Céline, or rather a projection into fullness of one aspect of Céline, who looks back upon his childhood as a nightmare dominated by demented parents, self-lacerating, hateful people verging on the brink of complete breakdown and given to delivering great torrents of invective at one another while both victimize and castigate their son, Ferdinand, the *merdeur*, masturbator, outcast, and villain. The truth about the "actual" Céline is a lot blander. His parents seem to have been jovial, honest people who lived quite happily together and who doted on their son. "Seem" is the correct word here for, as McCarthy says, information about Céline's life is highly unreliable. Yet the author's diaries of that period support the notion that Céline's childhood was relatively normal, despite "a stamp of melancholy" in which Céline claimed he "lived and moved like a bird in the air," for he says that his time in the army was "the first really painful [period] I have endured." This melancholy he mentions is not to be explained by the "facts" on which *Mort à crédit* is based—it is not, in other words, created by his childhood. Instead, it seems a given of his temperament, as though inflicted upon him like a curse. On the other hand, one of his army friends said that Céline was "...a likeable companion, the first thing one noticed was his attitude of modesty and polite reserve, he was a quiet observer, sometimes a rather mocking look about him, a subtle smile." This is not surprising for Céline is, among many other things, a great *comic* writer and his comedy is not at all at odds with this melancholy, this despair, but instead is a function of it—the "melmothian" laughter, satanic in origin, which Baudelaire describes in his *Mirror of Art*.

Two months after the start of World War I, Céline found himself volunteering to carry despatches under heavy fire. He was wounded, awarded the military medal, and was written up lavishly by *L'Illustré national* as a war hero praised, in the citation for his medal, by General Joffre himself. The famous head wound, which, in later life, he claimed caused violent headaches and loud, continuous buzzings in his ears to drown out the noise of which he was forced to write at full tilt, was a self-created myth. He was invalidated out of the army and sent to work in the French passport office—a sober desk job, as McCarthy describes it, which bore little resemblance to the adventures described in *Guignol's Band*. Back in France he obtained a series of odd jobs, one of which sent him to the Cameroons wherein he caught a "head-full of tam-tams and tropical jungles" and a dose of chronic enteritis. When the war ended he conned the Rockefeller Institute into giving him a job as a propagandist—part of a team that travelled Brittany lecturing the inhabitants on how to fight T.B. by improving their standards of hygiene. McCarthy tells a good anecdote about those days, with Céline in Quilpish humour:

> In the evenings [Céline] showed magic-lantern slides of microbes to a horrified audience, which had never suspected that such creatures existed.... He screamed at the villagers to boil their milk and water before drinking. He frightened everyone so much that the parish priest came up. He asked whether his well might

not be infected since it stood next to the cemetery. He brought some of his water to be analysed. "What you're drinking isn't water, Father, it's concentrated meat juice," bellowed the delighted Céline.

He appears to have become a doctor by using his Rockefeller contacts wisely and by marrying the daughter of one of the medical faculty at Rennes. By 1923 he had become a general practitioner and near bourgeois. He was remembered by a fellow student as "a very attractive spirit, happy, mocking, interested in everything with original ideas on all problems." The ideal graduate student, one might almost say. Yet his thesis, on the pioneer hygienist Semmelweis, reveals the darker side, if one can call it that, of Céline's personality, for it is negative and bitter in tone and takes for its subject a very Célinesque hero—a man persecuted by society and by the medical establishment of his time, who was driven by his own scientific passion to madness:

His end is worthy of *Voyage*: demented, he rushed into a dissection theatre, cut up a corpse, infected himself and died in agony.

It is in this thesis that some of Céline's major themes begin to assert themselves. The basic truth about any human being is that he must die and the moment in which the patient faces that truth is the moment the doctor sees—when "happiness, that absurd, arrogant, trust in life gives way to truth." The patient, of course, fails to accept it at first. He wishes to be restored to the illusion of happiness and responds with "ingratitude and insolence." The doctor must expect to be hated though this should never undermine his sense of pity. At any rate the overwhelming, determining fact about life is that it ends, usually under painful circumstances, and it is this realization that lies at the heart of Céline's melancholy, of his sense of evil.

After this thesis and a few years of practice in Rennes, he was ready to begin his own career. He deserted his wife, practice, and Rennes, got a wanderer's job with the League of Nations and wrote the play *L'Eglise*. He studied, on behalf of the League, the links between disease and poverty, one of the subjects which obsessed him and which was to be part of the thematic structure of *Voyage*, to such an extent that Trotsky, in his famous *Atlantic Monthly* article, was misled into believing that Céline was a proletarian novelist. McCarthy makes the point that it was during the Geneva years that Céline's Anti-Semitism began to develop for he chose to see in the Jew an incarnation of all that was wrong with modern life — its deracination, materialism, and political and economic confusion — an attitude that began to spread throughout Europe more and more quickly as one of the by-products of the Stavisky affair. There is, however, little Anti-Semitism in the actual novels: *Voyage* is informed much more by a horror of industrialization Céline acquired as another result of his work for the League, for it was during this period he was sent to the United States to study the health conditions of the Ford workers and his hallucinated account of life in Detroit makes me wish that I could have shown Céline a copy of Tolkien's *Lord of the Rings*:

> Mordor was a dying land, but it was not yet dead. And here things still grew, harsh, twisted, bitter, struggling for life . . . . There was a bitter tang in the air of Mordor that dried the mouth . . . . The wind of the world blew now from the West, and the great clouds were lifted high, floating away eastward; but still only a grey light came to the dreary fields of Gorgoroth. There smokes trailed on the ground and lurked in hollows, and fumes leaked from fissures in the earth.

Céline never knew about Mordor but he would have recognized this description as the shape of things to come for France.

McCarthy deals with all this material thoroughly and provides an equally adequate account of Céline's adventures as a pamphleteer, as an Anti-Semite whose aberration became, in 1940, the official doctrine, as a refugee fom the Allies and the "Resistance," and as a prisoner then highly unwelcome resident of Denmark haunted by disease and poverty. He makes little attempt to confront the "why" of Céline's racism, perhaps because such derangements have been explored so thoroughly by, among others, Sartre, whose *Portrait d'un Anti-Semite* McCarthy directly and indirectly quotes. He is at his best, in my opinion, on the relationship between the man and his work and in his discussion of the novels. *Voyage* he understands as a vision of the world totally dominated by triumphant evil in which human beings, nearly all of whom are despicable, drag out their lives as puppets controlled by an invisible hand. He sees Céline's treatment of sex as almost entirely negative: men and women destroy one another in what should be their most intimate moments. Bardamu, the novel's narrator, is like Ferdinand of *Mort à crédit* engaged upon a sort of anti-quest — an attempt to "discover the worst" as he moves from one

255

blasted landscape with its driven and maniacal inhabitants to the next. Céline establishes his subject matter in *Voyage* and, in subsequent novels, plays variations on it.

All this is true and McCarthy states it well. He seems reluctant to draw the obvious theological conclusion that Céline is a sort of Manichean, while wishing that he were not, who does not totally believe in the principle of light. McCarthy tries to demonstrate that this latter principle is asserted by Céline's recurrent image of the dancer but the argument is not convincing. Thus the unrelenting focus that Céline maintains upon the negative side of human experience could easily be criticized as a sort of reverse sentimentality. Surely it is perverse to visualize creation in such black terms, to create a series of narrators whose lives are so totally desperate and joyless. To such a criticism two replies are possible: first, nobody in "real life" who feels the way Bardamu feels about the human condition would bother to put pen to paper to start with. Madness, suicide, and silence would, I think, be his destiny. The second is that just as, for example, Joseph Conrad's solemnity of content is denied by his playfulness of manner, so Céline's pessimism is to a large extent invalidated by his role as a creative artist. The zest, passion, and wit which accompanies the joyous flow of language no matter what that language explores constitutes "the rose" I spoke of earlier in this review. McCarthy finds in this language "a monument to the human greatness [Céline] so strenuously denied. These two things account for his importance as a writer: his vision of catastrophe and his style. All else is secondary . . . . From the depths of the night he returns with the gift of tongues."

1977